To Sister
Margret
psalm 91v11
For he shall give his
Angels charge over thee
to Keep thee in all thy
ways

Enjoy

Rashida Denise Ali
Myers
-04-

There's A Tear In Angel's Eye

{A 'Mama's Drama'}

By Rashida Denise Myers

ISBN 0-7414-1952-1

Published by:

INFINITY
PUBLISHING.COM

1094 New De Haven Street
Suite 100
West Conshohocken, PA 19428-2713
Info@buybooksontheweb.com
www.buybooksontheweb.com
Toll-free (877) BUY BOOK
Local Phone (610) 941-9999
Fax (610) 941-9959

Printed in the United States of America

Printed on Recycled Paper

Published May 2004

CONTENTS

DEDICATION

To my Angels: Thanks for all of your help and guidance, protection and messages.

To God the Father and Creator of Me: I pray I have done well! To you I give the glory! Thank you for saving my life. Without my existence my precious grandbabies would not be born.

To my father David Myers May God bless your Sprit.

This book is dedicated to the person who wants to die; 'All' those who has succeeded in suicide, May God bless their sprits, and may God comfort their family.
To those who welcome death and those who have been abused, cheated on and to anyone who lives with depression.
To those who have lived in pain and loneliness or have been neglected or abandoned and scream in silence daily.
To those who have loved ones in painful situations and who feel powerless and don't know what to say or do I pray you find some answers in this story!

Our suicide rate is the highest in history, especially among our children. Our children see us and ask, "Why care about anything or anyone? No one cares about anything and no one cares about me!"
We pass our attitudes down. They say they didn't ask to be here, and the dead are just dead. Just maybe dead is not dead but worse than life in a miserable waiting process to be judged.

No one really knows what to say to a suicidal person. What can you say to a person who has no value for their life much less for others? It is easier to pick up a gun or drugs and destroy us then it is to pick up a holy book and love and forgive others and ourselves and tolerate life.

Our generation has proven there is little to no fear of God. Some of us believe we have been too bad or are unworthy to pray; too unclean to be heard or loved, so we don't go to God on a deep level, if at all. Some live like there is no judgment or believe we will be excused because we have been wronged so others deserved to be wronged too!

Some believe God will accept our lifestyle because of the times we live in so we take matters into our own hands and do things our way. But there is guidance so I wrote this book for them.

Some just believe, "Death must be better than Life."

Most people don't believe Angels exist and assist us and it's even harder to believe that there is life in death.
Most people I spoke to believe death is just a deep sleep. Some believe that to be absent from the body is to be present with their Lord.

Whatever your belief this book is not trying to change that; it just gives another view.

This book is for the spiritually thirsty, and to those whom the enemy attacks viciously.

This book is dedicated to drug users and the abusers and to "all" of their victims whom no one hears their cries and they suffer in silence.

This book is dedicated to those who want to live with peace through acceptance and forgiveness!

This book is dedicated to the Ali Family for all of their struggles, pains.
This book is dedicated to the death of the old me!

This Story May Change Someone's Decisions and Sprit and Hopefully There Choices in Life! Most importantly understanding the importance of Forgiveness in order to LIVE and DIE in PEACE!

AUTHORS NOTE

This very emotional story is a work of fiction exacerbated from some true similarity of the author's life experiences and beliefs.

This book is not intended to place fear or to impose pain or to impose religious beliefs in anyone.

This book was written in pain and tears to help someone in pain and tears to hopefully find some answers and strength within there self.
If I can help one person consider life over death, or if one person is more interested in God and Angels, or if one person understands the importance of not allowing a person to become their whole universe…

…Or if one person learns how to focus on themselves and began a search for their talent and live life more fulfilling, or if one person stops using drugs or selling them, or if it encourages one person to think and consider the consequences before shooting off a gun or if it helps one woman deal with love…
Then all the painful words were worth writing and all the suffering was not in vain.

This novel is sad and depressing because it deals with suicide and depression but it's also mind cleansing, heart-healing, motivating, thought-provoking and honesty at a level we all need to deal with.

A smile, a nod, a "hello," a "peace," a "how are you," anything would have been nice after being confined to my house for three months and sitting in Love Park for two hours alone, totally ignored.
Someone's smile would have given me confirmation of my existence.
Smile or say "hi" to a stranger today. It could help save their life.

PLEASE excuse the profanity but I had to "keep it real!"
It was very important to me to choose my cover, title and not be told what I can't say so I did it Print-on-Demand way.
I Pray: "God, Please Bless Someone with these stories!"

ACKNOWLEDGEMENTS

I would like to thank my Father God Almighty and the word of God Jesus my friend, and my Angels for saving my life to help save others.

I thank my cover designer, Cat; my editor, Caryn; Infinity Publishing; and all the bookstores and companies for helping me reach the community with this beautiful heartfelt novel.

I am very thankful for my six children's opinion, approval, permission and encouragement to write and finish this book. When I was too depressed or unsure of my ability to write it, they said, "It is needed on the bookshelves.
Rashida, Fahtima, Omega, Tamara, Nubia, Rahmeil
Thank God for all of you, I love you all and please never die by your own hands.

Thanks so much to my mother-in-law Ruth A. for her love, prayers and support.
To Rasheem: Thank you for the learning experience, Thanks for the beautiful children and being the best father you can be; you always gave us all you had; you stayed when most men would run away, thank you!
To Kasim Ali: I believe in you; you are a great man and will do great things, believe in yourself. I will always love you.

I thank my mother Shirley and my two sisters for excusing my isolation and giving me love through my resentment and anger towards them. I love them with all my heart. I want them to know that through this book I was able to forgive them and myself.
Now I pray my children will forgive me!

I would like to acknowledge Mr. Malcolm Poindextor from KYW-3, who wrote me and gave me inspiration and pride in myself (whether he knew it or not) when he said, "Your poetry is profound." Those words held my head up for fifteen years.
To Ms. Germane Paris from the *Observer News*, who told me I have writing skills and that I should write.
Thank you, City Councilwoman Jannie Blackwell, who told me that I could do anything I put my mind to because I was a great speaker.
Thanks to the artists I mentioned in the book; your songs and books lifted my Spirit.

I would like to thank my best friends who kept me laughing through my pain and who supported me and held me up when I was down.

To one of my best friends who passed away: Berthina Broaddus Dade may God bless your Spirit!
To my very best and lifetime friends/family, Victoria Felton, Rodnee, Ratisha.
To my friends; Wanda, Pricilla, Rea and to all the caring Gratz Street neighbors. Childhood friends; Denise Depass, Davetta.
To all of the O.D.D.A.T family of 1990/2000
To David McNealy, Jr. Nancy; may God bless your Spirit my friends. They passed away as I was writing this book.
I really loved you all, ODAAT Thanks for giving my family and me so much love.
May God Bless all the Spirits that passed away.

I thank all the people who have helped my family in so many ways, especially with housing.
Thank you so very much Mr. Smith from N.T, for helping my dreams come true at "The I Care Center."
Mr.Charles Highsmith: thank you for being the best principal in Philadelphia and a good friend to our family.
I acknowledge my sister Cinnamon and her family thank you for always opening your home to a family of eight anytime.
To Sister Margaret and Rev. Wells: thank you for helping us reunite our family and introducing us to recovery; Margaret Wells for your prayers.
Thank you Aunt Jerry and Ross, Kim Myers, and Ronald Atkins II, Rodger Atkins, Ronald Mckelvy for making me feel a family of love.

Everyone who has supported the Ali family I thank you all.
There were so many who showed us love through our drama-filled days; we will always remember you all, the living as well as the ancestors.

I acknowledge my seven grandbabies. I thank God I'm alive to see and love you all.

God blessed me with baby girl named Angel, my new grandbaby born with a veil on her face while completing this book.

Special Acknowledgement to my New Pastor Barbara Ward Farmer, for praying with me for a healing, supporting and keeping me strong in faith to go on with life, and for teaching me how to love God. She helped me throw all of my past pains, the old me in the trash and is teaching me to be a new creature in Christ and helping me restore my family, for this I love her.

Faith Tabernacle CLG – I appreciate you all so much.

CHAPTER ONE

OH, MY SON!

Get up! "You 're late again!"
Cyris pulled the cover off his face and sat up blindly wiping his crusty eyes and trying to focus on the figure that was standing over him. "All right! I'm up!" he said with his new deep voice.
Saturated in sweat; I snatched the covers back, "Don't just say 'okay' and go back to sleep either!"
He sat up with his eyes still closed.
My husband walked in. "Hey Cyris, isn't that the shirt you just bought?" he said while pointing at a white heap on the floor.
I laughed as I was just thinking the same thing.
"Yes Dad…"
Chris my husband of 25 years bent down and kissed me on my bootie. "Bye baby! I'll call you later and take it easy because it's supposed to rain today." He grabbed me in his strong arms looking good in his black trench coat. He whispered in my ear. "I love you baby! Thanks for last night!"
"I love you more!" I said. Then I squeezed his buns and asked, "Did you leave me a tip on my dresser?"
"But of course!" he responded "I can't see you begging bread!" meaning 'needing some weed money.' He showed me those dimples and whispered, "Can I come back and spend the night again tonight?"
I smiled my sexiest grin. "Yeah I think that can happen!"
He began to walk down the stairs but paused, "Cyris, I want to talk to you later ok?" he yelled. There was silence. He yelled again, "Cyris?"
Cyris yelled down to him, "Yes Dad!"
I hugged Chris around his neck as I asked, "Who's the man?" I answered myself with a kiss on his full big lips, "You're the man!"
He looked back at me and gave me that big dimpled smile that said, "I'm just one of the men!"

I returned to Cyris' room and looked around. "This room will get cleaned as soon as you come home!" I pointed to a light blue silk shirt lying on the floor by his bed and said, "That's a damn shame; you just bought that shirt and it's on the floor. Is that how you treat your stuff? You wore it once and now you treat it like it doesn't mean shit! You always do that, why? That's a pretty shirt too; you don't want it now? Shit I'll keep it! Why can't you be more like your dad and take care of your clothes?"
I slammed the door to make him jump. Quietly I said, "Bum ass!"

But I slowly shook my head thinking how much of a bum I was too. I opened the door to see if he had laid back down. I looked up to my six-foot son as he rose out of bed and stretched. I turned around and closed the door embarrassed to see his morning hard on.

I am forty-four but I look thirty-one and I sound eighteen on the phone. I'm a little big boned, "pleasantly plump," as I like to say. I'm a pretty light-skinned Native American woman with auburn hair past my shoulders that brings out my big light brown raccoon eyes. I'm 5'7" and I have been told on many occasions that I have the prettiest legs in the world. I am also a proud mother of five beautiful daughters and one son.

Cyris heard a noise: Boom, boom. And then, "Ouchhhh!"
He opened the door to find me sitting on the floor.
"What happened mom? Are you okay?"
"Yeah I'm okay baby. Here grab my arm."
Cyris ran over to help. "Put your arm around my shoulder mom. I'll help you to the chair in your room." He hated to see me in any pain. If I hurt he hurt; if I cried he cried; he'd die if I died.
"Ouch! Ouch! I sprained my ankle. I missed that last damn step." With my face just as twisted as my right ankle I rubbed it with alcohol, still yelling, "Damn, this shit hurts!"
"Come on mom let me get you in your bed."
"Get me the ice pack out the freezer baby."
He ran down the stairs two at a time. He opened the freezer and grabbed the ice pack and some orange juice for me.
"You want me to stay home with you?"
"No! Don't even try it Cyris go to school thank you! Thank you anyway baby."
"Mom you can't even answer the door! Or make yourself anything to eat."
"I'll be fine; this is not my first sprain and it's sure not going to be my clumsy ass last." I laughed with another "ooh, ouch." "Pass me the remote and my medication bag and then you can make me some toast and I'll be fine."
The disciplinary school Cyris attended was only ten blocks away. He was always getting into some shit that of course wasn't his fault.
Cyris washed up in my bathroom and then came in my antique-filled bedroom. There was a rug on the wall of an Indian family; a large picture of Indian Chiefs; dolls; and a beautiful black suede shield with an male Indian on a horse. His arms were stretched out praying. But the most important piece was a dream catcher over my bed.
It seemed like I'd spent most of my life in that room.
Chris provided me with everything I wanted and needed. I had my computer, a color TV, DVD, VCR, a 240-watt boom box, all the CD'S

and books I wanted, all updated movies. My on-line computer helped me kill time so I didn't have time to think about killing myself.

Cyris looked at himself in the black and brown dresser mirror. "Damn I look good!" He does look good I thought admiring his pretty light skin and curly hair.
He said it again: "Yes I do look good!" He stared into the mirror rubbing the few hairs growing in his immature mustache.
He smiled hard. "Yeah boy, I'm going to be seventeen next week, than eighteen."

Cyris inherited my sad browns eyes. No matter how hard he laughs his eyes look like they want to cry. We are both anemic and can look like a vampire in need of a bit of blood.
"Cyris, are you sad a lot?" I asked him
"I do be sad sometimes but I try not to dwell on it." Changing the subject, he laughed. "I get all the babes though. They just love playing with my curly hair."
"You better enjoy being sixteen while you don't hardly have any responsibilities. You need to start thinking about what you want to do with your life."
"I told you, I'm going to be a rap artist and take care of you."
"Yeah that's good baby but God gives us all a back up gift. What else can you do?"
"I'm good in carpentry and electrical wires, fixing shit… oops! My fault mom, I mean fixing 'stuff!' And you know I love the drums and boxing but all I think about is writing."
"Well you better get going now."
"I need to smell good." He sprayed on some of my most expensive cologne.
"Hey! You don't need a lot! Damn, don't take a bath in it!"
"Someday, I'm going to be a famous rapper and I'm going to buy you that car you want, you'll see!" I'm so tight; I got about 100 raps and they're all hot! I'm hot; no one's won a battle with me yet."
"I know you're good Cyris. I do love to listen to you rap… when it's positive."
"Shit, I'll get me a house where we all can live so none of us will ever be homeless, and when you spend all of your money fooling around you'll always have somewhere to live." He smiled, his eyes twinkling mischievously.
I couldn't help but laugh. "Hurry up now and get out of here."
I looked at him as he laughed and saw his comedian personality come out as he did a little dance in front of the mirror. But no matter what expression or excitement was on his face, his eyes begged for understanding and comfort. They seemed to say to me, "I'm not even

here; I'm somewhere else, searching somewhere, for something unseen." I see in his eyes what I see in my mother's eyes and my own; despair.
"How do I look mom?" I turned my head back towards him shining a watery smile.
"You look nice in that black shiny denim suit. Can I have that when you throw it on the floor?" I giggled. "That orange shirt brings out your complexion too but you need to comb that hair!"
"Yeah, yeah, yeah. Bye mom" he said as he gave me a smile that showed his mouth full of white teeth. He bent over and kissed my cheek long and hard. "You sure now, you don't need me to stay home and take care of you?"
"No Cyris, I'll be fine. You go ahead to school and be good okay?"
He rubbed my face gently and said, "Don't worry about me mom!"
As soon as he left, I limped to my bedroom window to see if he was heading in his school's direction.
My ankle was throbbing and so was my gut. Maybe I should have let him stay home with me. My gut wouldn't stop jumping till I saw him home safe.

"Hey Cyris wait up!" his boy Jaheem said as he ran a few feet to catch up with him.
Jaheem was seventeen, short and quite the sneaky type. "Whatz up?" he asked.
"Whatz up?" said Cyris. "Yo man, I heard Bennie G got shot last night?"
"Yeah man, they shot him up bad!" He shook his head and held it down.
"Is he dead?" Cyris asked.
"He sure is." Jaheem replied softly. "They shot him five times in the chest in the bar last night over some damn woman. You know his brother is coming out soon from prison. His other brothers and his boys are on the hunt. Shit is going to get real ugly dog."
"Man that's some deep shit! I just talked to Bennie G. yesterday!"
He stopped and spread out his arms and than he held his head. "I was just talking to him!" he said again. "Damn! He was just on the corner yesterday and today he's gone."
Jaheem zippered up his Eddie Bowers black coat. "Man, his other brothers are hunting them niggas' down."
"Damn man, that shit is crazy killing over a piece of ass! You never know when or where you're going to die dog. Man! You got to watch your back at all times yo!" He pulled up his fur hood and put his hands in his pocket and he shook with fear in the cold.

To change the mood Cyris said, "Check out my new lyrics I'm going to break it down to you!" He unzipped his coat and threw it at Jaheem. When Jaheem went to pick it up, Cyris hit him upside his head from behind as he ran in front of him.

He started walking backwards-facing Jaheem, licking his lips as he pinched his nose and pointing at his fast-moving feet. He waved his hands side to side and his feet were taking giant steps backwards, bouncing around to the beat in his head.

"Check it out, mum, mum, mum!"
"Cyris is here ready to battle
Stand back now in my shadow
Don't ask me any questions because I don't volunteer information
I don't act well to bullshit/or procrastination
My crew builds their foundation/on intimidation
Don't test me/my bullets reach their final destination
I don't do well with religion/because I like fornication
Bitches drop their thongs/after one conversation
If you value your life/step aside as I pass through
Out of 26 religions there's one devil/what do that tell you?
Another battle I won, then one more/Who's keeping score?
I come like a whisk wind/when I defeat men
Battle me/ In the dust/I leave them
My level is uncharted once I get started/this is the dearly departed!"

"That was hot Cyris! I'm feeling you! Hey, are you going to be on J Street tonight?"
"Yeah! I have to stop in the recording studio, why?"
"Well…" he kicked the bottle as he was walking. "I got a hot one to drop; you wit it?"
"Yeah! I'll catch up wit you later!" They reached the school's entrance and silently walked through the metal detectors.
"So what time are you coming through?" Cyris asked.
"I'll be around about six or seven, you down wit it?"
"Yeah, I be needing some of them new Jordan's," Cyris said laughing.
"Alright I'll catch up wit you later." They shook hands and hit shoulders and walked into their separate classes.

Cyris came bopping in the classroom saying, "Whatz up!" to everyone on his way to his chair. About twenty students were already into their assignment.
"Hi cutie" he said as he touched a pretty girl's face that sat in the front row.
"Stop it!" she yelled, though she secretly loved the attention.
The teacher with his square glasses and his high pants said in his passive voice, "Cyris, don't come in my classroom distracting my students!"
Cyris took his seat as the teacher said, "Everyone copy these words off the board." Cyris started asking for a pen.
One ugly girl said, "You should have your own!"

"Shut up with your ugly bony ass before I take yours."
A cutie next to him gave him a pen. He hollered at the guy next to him for paper.
The boy behind him had his feet on Cyris' chair.
"Can you move your feet?" he asked nicely but he didn't so Cyris got up and pulled his chair up. He ignored Cyris and put his feet back up.
The teacher was yelling at Cyris to sit down and shut up.
"I am! Wait a minute!" he yelled with his eyes flaring.
"Sit down now Cyris!"
He looked at the teacher and gritted on him, than turned around to look at the troublemaker.
He stood up; he was much taller than Cyris and much bigger. "Shit, Cyris thought, "I'm tall, six feet but dude had to be around 6'4 gritting on me. In them blue jeans hanging too much off his ass and those big ass feet he looked like a fucking giant sneering down on me."
Cyris laughed. "Shit, this is disciplinary school," he thought. "All these dudes start trouble; that's what got them here."
He couldn't back down, he wouldn't' back down. That wasn't how the game was played.

"Whatz your problem?" Cyris said as he snatched the chair that stood between the two of them.
"You are; you're my problem! I don't like you!" and than BAM! Between a blink, he punched Cyris in the face!
Cyris fell on another boy who immediately pushed him off.
He was hurt. He got up and threw the chair at him. It hit him right across his head.
He charged at him. Cyris wanted to run but he was blocked in. The other students who began pushing each other to a get closer look surrounded him.
The troublemaker looked like a black bull charging at him with smoke coming out his flexed nostrils. Cyris moved back and kicked him in the face as hard as he could. He lifted up his head and rubbed his eye where Cyris' boot left a mark but he still kept coming. Cyris pushed the table between them.
Cyris tried to get out of there, but the boy grabbed him from behind and picked him up over his head like they do in wrestling. He threw Cyris over a desk at the front of the room.

He rolled onto the floor and tried to get up. People were yelling all around him as he reached for a chair for support. He pulled himself up but the chair fell from his weight. By than he looked up and saw this giant stomping him, laughing.
The teacher didn't even try to stop him. He just ran out in the hall calling, "Guards! Guards!"

He stomped Cyris in his head and his body. All Cyris could do was crawl into a ball.
The students moved out of the way as they were screamed, "Fight! Fight!"
"Kick his ass!" someone said. Another yelled, "Get up! Get up!"
"Well hell," he thought, "someone help me up!"

Two male guards came in and pulled the boy off. It took both of them to hold him and he still was trying to get loose.
Cyris slid between a desk and chair to protect himself from the last kicks. Everyone in the school was use to fights, especially the guards. Emotionless they peeled him off the floor. Cyris' lip was split and his ribs were in excruciating pain, but he stood like he wasn't hurt. His pride was hurt the most.
He was steaming. He was insane with anger. He screamed, "I'm going to kill your ass! You better not ever let me see you again! Never! Ever!"
While he wiped the blood from his lip with the back of his hand, he picked up his orange bandana off the floor and kicked a desk out his way. A guard grabbed his arms to escort him out.
He pulled his arms away from him saying, "You don't have to grab me. I can walk!"
He still grabbed both of his arms roughly from behind and led the two of them into separate offices next to each other. Cyris could see the other boy through the glass. The bastard smiled with a smug "I won" expression.
Cyris exploded. "It's not over bitch!" and he meant it! He was hurt pretty badly but the embarrassment was more painful.

"Cyris started it!" the teacher told the principal. "He wouldn't comply with my directions. He disturbs everyone. I can't have this in my class! He comes unprepared and he talks when I talk, and as soon as he walked into the class he was trouble!" He sounded like a snake. He hissed the "s" in his words. Cyris wanted to smack him!
The counselors suspended the two for three days. As he walked out the troublemaker turned around and hollered, "I'll see you here tomorrow in the morning punk ass bitch!"
The guard stopped him. "If you are on school premises during this suspension you will be arrested!"
Nonetheless he pointed at Cyris and said, "I'll be seeing you!"
Cyris jumped up and said, "See me now! Well!" with his arms stretched out and his head bopping to the side. "Lets take it around the block! I got your bitch!"
He waved at Cyris. "Come on!" but the guards held him back.
"I'll see you in the morning bitch!" Cyris yelled. "His size doesn't intimidate me," the guard held him back "I'll kill him!"

With his eyes blazing, red in the face and his fist balled he silently screamed all the obscenities boiling in needing of a release. He could still taste the blood in his mouth.

He wanted him to suffer his pain! "I hope I don't have internal damage," he thought. "I'm so mad I could throw a car at him!"
He started walking out. The guard said, "Cyris!" He yelled again as he was still attempting to get out. "Cyris!" The guard blocked Cyris' passage. He told the bully, "Go ahead now and don't be nowhere around this property or you're going to jail!"
A big black male officer bigger then the other guard was at the front door ready to escort the troublemaker out.
The smaller guard grabbed Cyris' arm and pulled him close to his face. He looked down on him and said, "You're not going anywhere yet; you just sit here where I can see you!" He pushed Cyris on the bench.
Cyris immediately got back up. "I don't want to sit down!" I wanta leave too!" He could feel his heart jumping out of his chest.
"Have a seat!" the guard yelled.
Cyris flopped down on the bench, folded his arms and started plotting. He was having difficulty holding back the tears as he blew hard air out his mouth.
He didn't say a word to them; 30 minutes later he was allowed to leave.

"So I have to see him before he sees me," he thought.
He was hoping he was out there. "I'll fight him again," Cyris thought. "I'm mad as shit! I want to hurt someone!" He walked slowly to calm his heart down. He was plotting in his head: should he roll up on him tonight? The streets were empty and cold but he was hot! He had to go back inside to get his coat.
I want to see blood dripping down his head, he thought, or bent over with his guts in his hands! Premeditated murder my ass. On the streets it's self-defense. Everybody's got heat!

He was talking to himself walking back to the 'hood. "That mother-fucker stomped me! My damn head hurts. That nigga's going to threaten me to take my hood, my life! Hell no! I'm no damn rabbit," he said to himself. "I'm not going to run and I'm no bitch to hide. I'll be there with my boys; I know he's not coming alone. No doubt he'll be strapped. Under these circumstances, I will be too. Then we'll see who's a bitch!
"I'm not a bitch or a faggot and I'll prove it! Not for popularity or because I was humiliated but because he knows it's not finished. It's just going to another level now. That's just how it is.
"I just didn't see that coming! I'm not scared of him. He went too far! Like my dad says: 'I don't care if you're Jack or the Giant, bring it!' I want his ass; I don't care how big he is!

"That bitch ass teacher said I started shit! I hate that bitch! When they let me out after the fight I took a bottle and broke it against the wall and scratched up his car good. 'Take that mother-fucker!' It felt good!"

He wasn't going home to hear my mouth so he went to make some quick cash. He went to the drug corner a couple of blocks from my crib.
"Yo, give me a bundle of weed and twenty-five zanie's. I'll handle that for you!" He popped two zanie's and said, "Damn I needed that!"
Twenty for sale and five for him. No one in the family really knew for sure that he popped pills and smoked dust, "Wet" yet! When he was asked he always replied, "Hell no, I don't smoke wet! Once or twice I tried zanie's but I don't be messing around like that."
My response was, "Okay Cyris I hope not baby!"
The family saw through him, he just didn't know it!

The young dealer sat in his white 2001 Lexus in his designer clothes. He looked at Cyris and said, "How are you going to sell shit when you got on that bright ass orange shirt and bandana? They'll spot your ass a mile away! Whatz up wit that?"
"I'll handle my business! I always getz the paper don't I?"
"Yeah you're cool! What the hell is that blood on you?"
"That my battle scars for today my revenge reminder for tomorrow! I'm about to go in the store and cop me a tee shirt now."
Cyris called over a kid about ten years old. "Yo young buck! Let me use your bike I'll give you ten dollars for a few hours. It's 1:00 now; I'll be back by five." They did this often. All the kids knew he'd ride any size bike and he'd always pay.
"Sure!"
"Ok here!" He jumped on the kid's wheels. It was small but it would do. He went back to the car: "Yo give me two more bundles!"
"No! Handle that one first and come back and I'll hook you up!"
"Come on, give me one more bundle!" He was going to snatch it as he was counting his bags.
The dealer got mad. "Cyris you play too much dog. That shit is going to get you hurt."
Cyris just laughed. "Come on man, I'm just trying to eat like you!"
He went back to the corner and saw Ray one of his boys.
"Hey, you got my heat on you? I got something to handle tomorrow!"
"You got beef?" asked Ray.
"Yeah man, this big dude jumped all on me for nothing man! I'm getting mad just talking about it!" He started balling up his fist and turning red.
"Yeah I got it; it's in the park! Come on across the street wit me. Nobody's going to touch your shit while I'm holding it!" He patted Cyris on the back. "Lighten up dude. Yo! You know I got your back tomorrow; holler at me!"

"Cool!" Cyris went into the store and bought a white T-shirt and stuck his orange one in his back pocket. He also bought two blunts and a lighter and jumped on the bike. "I'm going to get rid of this," he said to Ray. "I'll see you in a few."

At 5:45 pm, he was back standing in a crowd peeling off big dubs in craps on the corner by the store steps on J. St.
He was debating with another guy about who got the most girls. His friend Jaheem drove up in a gray 1999 Acura. "Come on Cyris!" he hollered. "Are you ready to bounce?"
The boys on the corner looked at him. He couldn't look like a punk and not get in what they all knew was a stolen car. Content knowing that he was about to get paid he didn't care.
"Yeah hold up!" He played his last roll won sixty dollars and copped another bundle of weed and some zanies.
He jumped in the car happy that his pockets were getting fat and said, "Let's roll!"
"Yo, let's stop and get some beer," Jaheem said.
"Hold on, pull over for a second." Cyris began rolling a blunt. "So what are you getting for this?"
"You clocking my dough?"
"No! What I want to know is what's in it for me?"
Jaheem parked at the end of the block to smoke weed before they headed out to a buyer.
"I heard about the fight you had Cyris!" he said.
"That was a big mother-fucker!" he said.
"I heard you got stomped with his big black timbs," he laughed.
"Yeah, well, that bitch will pay for that shit tomorrow!" and he flashed his 38 hammer. "You wit me or what?"
"You know I'm down for you!" he said. "I have to give you your props though, nobody would fight that dude but you did or tried to I should say!" as he laughed some more. "You get big respect for that in school dog! How's your lip?" He was still laughing but even harder now and he was holding his stomach.
Cyris started to get angry. "I bet he got a knot in his damn head with that chair I clocked the shit out of him with!" He popped another zanie and gritted on him. "That shit's not funny!"
"I'm just fucking with you!" Jaheem said. "Come on let's go get rid of this shit!"
"Where are we…" but before he could finish the sentence they heard the cop's siren coming from behind. Jaheem jumped out the driver's side and hauled ass. Cyris had the bundle of weed and Zanies and his.38, so he ran too. He dropped the shit in the bushes as he turned the corner; it was dark and he did it so cool that he knew they didn't see that move. Unfortunately, the two fast-ass cops caught him three blocks away.

Jaheem got away. Cyris wondered if one of the neighbors called the police because they were smoking blunts and had the music blasting like they were running shit. Or maybe they just panicked and they were really going somewhere else. They cuffed him and took him to the round house. Philadelphia Police Department let him make his only call.

"Dad, I'm locked up for car theft but I didn't know it was stolen. I was just getting a ride home."
Chris was sitting at his office desk working late, sharp as always in his blue suit and crisp white shirt. He was a strong-featured African man. He was frustrated because he was always receiving a call about some shit Cyris got in to.
"Cyris, keep your mouth shut! I'll call the lawyer and you'll see the Judge tonight or tomorrow. Then we will know what were looking at. Just don't think the worse!"

Cyris was sent to a youth detention center because the teacher pressed charges on him, someone saw him scratch up his car. He was also booked on auto theft charges. That's where Chris and I went to visit him.
Chris walked in first. He stood tall and walked with confidence, pride and greatness. He was a beautiful man but he had intimidating eyes. He was not smiling at all.
I had been crying my brown eyes red. I was limping from the pain I always feel in an air-conditioned room or when the nights are cold and damp. My arthritis was hurting my knees and back but I still smiled and hugged him tight Cyris thought Chris was going to be mad and that I was going to be very disappointed, so he was surprised by Chris' support. He was pissed about having to go through the bullshit procedures to visit an inmate. He tried not to show his anger and distain for the White Man's treatment of the Black Man. He was relating to the similar regretful choices he made in his youthful days. He was forcibly reminded as he listened to the banging of the doors and the clinging keys, the locks on concrete blocks, the orders and restrictions and personal violations of living in the poorest conditions in the cages of Attica.

We sat in the lunchroom in the corner in the back at a table with four seats so we could look around and see everyone else. Cyris felt like he was in quick sand.
Chris held his shoulders as he looked at his son and whispered in his ear.
"I will get you out of here just keep your mouth shut and just watch people Cyris because you tend to talk more than you listen. You learn more by listening and people can't figure you out if you don't talk so much. As far as this bull- shit case they have on you they're just trying to exasperate the situation. I called Judge Jefferson; he knows me and you didn't know that." He smiled as he sat down.

Cyris finally smiled.

Chris continued talking, looking into Cyris' eyes speaking softly. "I know him from some of the cases I brought before him when I was helping youths get back with their families and he was impressed with my delivery. He even asked if I was a lawyer." He leaned over. "Cyris, I know I haven't been spending much time with you because I've been working a lot. We'll start doing something's together when you come home. I'm going to do everything I can to get you out of here soon they are not going to charge you with the car theft!"
He stopped and looked at him intently. "Cyris, you are going to have to change your life style. I don't want my son tied up in the system."
"Dad, do you think I'll walk away from this?"
"You might have to do a few months waiting for shit to happen but I don't think you have to worry. I know a lot of people that owe me favors so you will have good representation. I told you this is where you will end up Cyris, if you kept hanging with those no count niggas, didn't I?"
"Yes Dad." He had to change the subject. He looked at me. I just sat there quietly.
"Are you okay mom?"
"No! I'm not okay! I don't like to see you in here!" I snapped.
Cyris glanced around in disdain looking into the watchful eyes on us.
"Cyris," I said, "you are so smart and gifted. You have to stop wasting your talent getting high and stealing cars!"
He bent over and whispered, "Mom I didn't steal no car!"
"I've seen you a few times in different cars. Maybe this time you didn't do the stealing but you got caught! What is wrong with you? Dad and I give you everything we can."
He started to get really defensive. "Mom, I didn't do nothing wrong!"
I slapped my hand on the table–Slam! "You never do nothing wrong Cyris!" I yelled. "You just always be the one that ends up in trouble though!"
Cyris was getting frustrated now.
"I don't know how much more I can take Cyris!" A tear rolled down on to the table.
Chris turned to me. "Calm down Angel, now is not the time!"
I looked at him sharply. "So I'm just supposed to swallow my thoughts and excuse my fears? Cyris, you have a father; most people don't have one around much less have one that is there for him and gives you shit so you don't have to steal! Your sisters love you, I love you, and you have a beautiful home! I just don't know what more you need to do the right thing! When you do shit like this it affects all of us!"
"Mom I love my family very much. I don't be trying to hurt nobody! See, you don't understand!"

I put both hands on the table and twisted my mouth and got in his face. "Explain it to me than!"
"Mom, I'm trying to do the right thing but sometimes things just happen!"
"Yeah, like that car just happened to be stolen and you just happened to be sitting your ass in it."

Chris kicked me under the table and shook his head so I folded my arms and sat back nervously biting my bottom lip.
"Listen mom, I'm sorry I disappointed you!" He went to get up.
I held his hand and pulled him back down. "Listen baby!" I breathed in deep for the air that had been stolen from me for a second. "You're my only son and I don't want to lose you!" I squeezed his arm tighter. "And I damn sure don't want you to go to prison." Then I started crying.
"He's not going to any damn prison!" Chris said angrily.
On the speakers a voice announced: "Visiting hours are now over!"
I looked at my son. "Cyris stay out of trouble and call me everyday okay?" I kissed him a few times on the mouth saying in between, "I love you so much, stay strong baby." I hugged him long and tight and then I put my face in his chest and just kept it there.
"Damn, I really let her down," he thought.
"Remember what I said: keep your mouth shut and watch people and remember no one is your friend in here!" said Chris. He hugged him and they shook hands goodbye.

Later that day the intercom spoke again. "Dinner is now being served." The inmates all got in line for the food. A big dark-skinned guy with a big mole on his face and wild hair on his head bumped into Cyris from behind. He didn't say, "Excuse me;" he just looked at him and said, "What the fuck you looking at?"
He told himself that he had to try real hard to stay out of trouble so he didn't say anything back. He just picked up his tray and walked to a table. He heard someone call out, "Punk ass bitch!" from far behind.
He came over to the table and said, "You're in my seat! Get up bitch!" He had two of his boys with him. Cyris rose up and hit him across his face with the tray.
He started punching him in his face with all of his anger. He couldn't stop, even after he saw blood coming out of his nose and mouth. His boys went to grab him and three boys from Cyris' hood got up and soon it was on everyone was fighting. Everyone who had a beef with anyone saw that now was the time to get it out! Bodies and shoes were flying everywhere.
The alarm went off and it took the guards fifteen minutes to break it all up. One of the guards said, "I've been here five years and I've never seen anything like this before."

The next day Cyris was called into an office. A white bald-headed short fragile, humble man about 55 years old was sitting at the desk.
"Cyris, you will be transferred to a facility outside of Philadelphia."
"Why? I didn't start that fight! Dude called me a bitch!"
"Oh, so you're going to beat up everyone that calls you a name? That's how you handle things?"
"Yeah! That's the only way I know how! He hit me first! What was I suppose to do?"
"You have to find different ways of dealing with things because there are consequences for our actions and every decision we make."
"This is bullshit! What am I supposed to do? Sit there and let someone beat on me and call me a bitch and I'm not supposed to do shit? I'm not a punk and if I don't do shit everyone will take advantage of me! What would you do?"
"First of all, I wouldn't be in here! Second of all, what if he used a knife or fork and stabbed you in the jugular, or choked your ass and killed you? Would it have been worth not getting up then?"
"Sure, I rather be a dead man than a living bitch!"
He shook his head. "Well, if you're going to survive in jail Cyris you have to gain respect with your mind, you have to out-think challenging people. I would have challenged him to something that would prove me to be the strongest!"
Cyris started laughing at him. "Don't nobody want to hear that shit!"
"You have to find ways to avoid confrontations," He said as he stood up. He was getting frustrated. He put his foot on the chair between Cyris' legs and bent over in his face. "Listen to me," he said and he looked him straight into his eyes. "Tell me something. Let's just say you went to prison! If five dudes came to rape you; would you fight to the death to protect your hood?"
"You're damn right!"
"And you'll lose and still be raped! What can you do to avoid being raped?"
"I don't know; all I know is I'll kill them all one at a time if I have to!"

The counselor looked at him shaken his head side-to-side and said. "You use your mind to think of how not to get in that position in the first place! First, stay out of prison! Some buy security; some walk with a crowd never to be alone, some pray for safety and become a Muslim, and some change their ways because they rub people wrong and they attract bad attention! Because people don't like them, they are continually picked on or in fights to be dehumanized or raped, and if you go in their trying to show off your strengths you will be challenged! So I would say, use your mind and fight with knowledge. Think about the consequence and retribution before you respond."

Cyris looked at the floor. “Whatever man. Can I go now?”

He opened the door and stopped him with his arm. “You must like words; let the words work for you, use your words to get ahead! You had to do what you did in the lunchroom as a man and we have to do what we have to do to keep order around here! You should have avoided coming here. Than you wouldn’t have been in that situation and if you don’t straighten up, you will be in a worse situation. You do have a choice!”

Leaning on the chair, Cyris titled his head and said softly, “I don’t believe this shit! Hey wait, why do I have to leave Philadelphia though? I need to be around my family!”

The counselor suddenly turned around and opened the door. “Guards, I’m finished you can take him back now.” He looked back at him. “You young kids… you don’t think about your families until you’re locked up and need them! Sorry, but the transfer has already been signed!”

“What about the other dude? Is he leaving too?”

“Yes. This was his last offense; he is going to another correctional facility called CFCF. Do you want to press charges on him for assault?”

“No!” he yelled. “This shit is not fair!”

“What ever is, life is not fair young man, you’ll learn,” he said.

Cyris wanted to smack his bald-headed ass. “This is some bullshit!” He yelled angrily as he knocked his chair over and pushed his arm out of the way, and went to his room.

Three months after being in an almost all-white correctional facility in the woods far away from home, with deer’s and snakes, he was in math class. He completed the assignment and decided to rap and write to cure his boredom.

The tall, skinny, young, blonde hair blue eyes white teacher tried to get loud and tough with her not-so-tough voice: “Get out of my class!” she yelled, pointing her shaken finger at him. “You’re too disruptive!”

Defensively he frowned and replied, “I ain’t doing shit!”

“Watch your mouth before you’re sent to the counselors’ office!”

“And he’ll tell me that I have to write, ‘I will not be disruptive’ one hundred times. Yeah, I know the drill! If you ask me with some respect maybe I will. I’m tired of grown-ups that think that they can talk to me any kind of way just because they’re grown!”

“You’ve not given me any respect, so why should I give you any?”

“I finished your boring-ass work! Now what am I supposed to do, stare at you?”

“Watch your mouth! Now you can get out!” she yelled as she pointed to the door. The halls echoed her words: “Get out now!”

“Hell no!” he yelled back. “Put me out!” Then he whispered, “White bitch.”

She looked surprised: “What did you say?” Cyris ignored her.

“Guard! Guards! Get him out of here now!”

This big black counselor came in and gripped him up and pushed him against the wall in the back of the classroom.
"Why do you have to be such a smart ass? You need to shut up! You always have to be the class clown?"
"Put me down!" he yelled. "Leave me alone! Leave me alone!"
"You need to learn how to respect woman and I am going to teach you!"
He screamed louder, "Let me go! Get the fuck off of me!" He struggled to break out of his grip. His face turned blood red. He dragged Cyris into a closet in the back and started punching him in his stomach: BAM, BAM!
"You got a rap for me?" He was laughing as he continued to hit him in the stomach until he couldn't breathe. He held his stomach as he bent over. There was no one to rescue him. He couldn't even yell anymore. He was choking and gasping for air. Defeated and defenseless, he was thrown into his room.
"Someone is going to get your ass!" Cyris managed to scream.
The next day he called his dad.
"I'll be right up there tomorrow!" Chris said. Cyris was a hundred miles upstate.
He didn't think he was coming; it was a six-hour ride. Sitting in his cell in the dark with his head in his hands, he thought about how he was going to get out of there. He thought about the privilege to be free. How did he get into shit? It was never his fault! And who the fuck cares anyway? How much he hated his life. How he's always letting everyone down, and why no one understands him.

"Did you hear that?" The male guard asked the other female guard at their station.
They paused to listen. "Yeah, I heard something. Let's go see." They started walking towards the sound and heard it again. The male guard stopped and tilted his head towards the noise. "It sounds like banging in the bathroom." He turned on the lights and there was Cyris, with only his boxers on; his feet kicking the walls of the last shower stall as he hanged there. His white tee shirt was tied around his bony limp neck.
The female guard screamed. "Oh my God!" she exclaimed, as she covered her mouth. The male guard hollered, "Come on, let's get him down!" They ran to him. He stopped kicking and went limp.
"Get the chair! Get up there now!" the male guard instructed. He was trying not to panic. "Come on, I'll lift him up!" he said calmly.
She screamed, "I can't get this knot out! It's too tight, I can't get it loose!"
"Try harder! I'll lift him higher!"

She started crying as she was trying to get the knot loose. “Oh my God! Why would someone do this? It’s never this bad! Oh my God he is not breathing! Oh my God!”
Cyris body fell to the cold wet marble, lifeless.

CHAPTER TWO

WHO IS MY DADDY?

"Hi! Are you Mrs. Myers? Are you Cyris' mom?"
I was coming out of the store limping. I had to get some cigarettes.
"Yes I am Why?" I looked at this young man as if to say, "you better come correct."
"Miss, I just wanted to know how he is doing and does he need anything?"
"He is fine," I told this sixteen-year-old, skinny young man with his red eyes, smelling like blunts. "He is just fine. What's your name?"
"Dean!"
Okay, I'll tell him you asked about him Dean."
"Is he coming out?"
If I said, "yeah," he'll think he ratted. "No, I don't think so. No time soon." I turned around and walked away saying to myself, "Pleeeeease, God, help him get out soon." He goes to court tomorrow, he has been in for a year and just getting to court, He could get a few years. I fear tomorrow. I wonder what he's doing.
Another man about twenty-two stopped me and asked, "Is your husband at his office around the corner or at the one on Walnut Street? Because I want to ask him to help me get a job."
"I think he's on Walnut Street today baby."
He smiled. "Okay thanks!"

Cyris wouldn't rat his boys out and he didn't expect them to. I walked a few step forward and stopped to light a cigarette. I heard his boy about his age say, "Them light skinned bitches always have an attitude! She look like Denise Huxtable from 'The Cosby Show.' You know, Lisa Bonett or something like that."
The one I just spoke with shook his head. "Nah she's cool, that's Ms. Angel. Everyone gives her big respect. She's real nice 'but' just don't fuck with her kids because then she goes off!"
I smiled as I took slower steps with my painful limp.
The other one said, "Yeah, but she sure is fine. I like her she looks like she doesn't take any shit!"
"Have you seen his dad?"
"Yeah! That is one mean-looking mother-fucker. He looks so militant and shit! I heard he shot at Channel and her crew when they came in front of his house to fight his girls!"
"Yeah! That's what I'm talking about, now that's how I'm going to be!"

"I know I'll kill someone they mess with my daughters too. I wonder what he do!"
"He's a director of that building around the corner, he helps people get housing and jobs. I did see him on TV once with the Mayor."
"They're not from Philadelphia; you hear how they talk?"
"Cyris said they were from New York."
"All of his sisters are fine as shit! I would love to get wit that!"
"Which one?"
"Any of them!"
I crossed the street I'd heard enough.

I walked in the bedroom and Chris was sitting on the edge of the bed talking on the phone. All I heard was, "How is my son?"
I looked alert. "What happened to my son?" He signaled me to wait and be quiet. I ignored him.
"What? Is he in trouble?" He flagged me again to wait.
I sat down slowly at my computer desk. My stomach started doing flips. I knew it wasn't good news.
Chris just kept saying, "Yes" and "No." I wanted to know now.
"What happened?" I screamed.
He put his hand over the mouthpiece. "Wait a minute Angel!" he hissed.
I'm getting mad now. I wish we had another phone. I lit up another cigarette.
Finally he hung up the phone. He closed his eyes and breathed out a long sigh.
"What? What happened?"
"Angel, Cyris was found in the bathroom. He hung himself."
My eyes opened wide with my mouth. "What? Oh my God! My Son? What? No!" I was shaking my head in disbelief.
"Wait baby listen! They got him down in time and gave him CPR."
"Oh! Thank God!" I covered my mouth. Then I asked, "Why? Chris why would he do that?"
"I don't know Angel!" he replied with frustration.
Still shaking my head in disbelief that he would take his life, yet relieved that my baby is alive. I could only ask over and over again, "Oh my God, why? Why?"
Shit… I didn't know why I wanted to die many days of my life.
I sanctioned suicide holding his hand. The tears started rolling, my hands started shaking, my knees were bouncing.
I jumped up. "Can I talk to him?"
"Not yet. He has to talk to some doctors and they said most likely they are going to put him on depression medication."
"Oh shit! I didn't think he would do something like that. That was some real "I'm out" shit! Not a small wrist cut crying for help. Damn, I shouldn't have said them things to him."

"They are so tough on the streets but when they get locked up all the bitch comes out!"
"That's not what I need to hear right now Chris!"
"Look Angel, the way he is going, I'm getting prepared to bury him."
I looked at him sharply. "What?" I screamed. "How do you get prepared for that Chris?" I breathed in deep and yelled, "I have to see him!" As I held my heart from trying to jump out of my chest, again I yelled, "I have to talk to him now!"
"They are going to let him call us tomorrow! You have to calm down!"
"Tomorrow? Tomorrow? Shit, this is an emergency! I have to speak to my son today! Get her back on that line! Who was that? What is her name? Where is the number?"

"Calm down Angel! He is all right. Let the doctors look and talk to him, then you can talk to him. What are you going to say to him anyway? What can you say? What can you possibly say?"
That hurt. I looked at him with so much fury I know he felt the burn. I went in the bathroom and smoked a joint.
When I came out I said, "Chris I'll be back later. I'm going over to my mom's house."
Chris said: "Ok baby I'm sorry! I'm just hurt and real disappointed. You go ahead and drive careful; put your seat belt on and try not to stay out too late, ok? And call me."
"All right." I kissed him lightly on the cheek and then I whispered in his ear, "See you later."
"Here take some money with you!" He handed me a fifty. "Give me a hug Angel" I laid my head on his chest and thought, "what would have stopped me?"
"I love you baby and don't worry he is going to be all right."
I hate it when he says, "Don't worry" like I want to worry or "Calm down" like I can!

I jumped in my black blazer jeep. I sat there waiting for it to warm up. He's suicidal like me? Oh hell no! I held my head as I wiped the tears from my face. Chris is right I thought; what could I say to him?
But I wasn't in his position looking at doing a few years in prison either. Wanting to die is not as important as much as asking yourself why you should live, because if you can focus on that than death won't win.

Damn, what can I do about helping my son stay alive? Maybe I need to look at some things in my life that made me who I am and what made me so depressed and suicidal. So depressed that death sounds better than life. So angry I could kill someone so to avoid it I have to commit myself in the hospital.
What can I learn from me that can help him?

I wiped my face again and blew my nose with my already soaked tissue and drove off.
Damn, how can I tell him he must want to live?
I can't help anyone in this subject; I still haven't helped myself!

The counselor in me starts to reason.
Maybe he hates or resents his father for not protecting him from the evil man that raped him as a little six-year-old child.
Maybe because he's the only boy, always getting yelled at by the girls. Maybe he feels left out. Maybe it's because his father doesn't spend much time with him.
Or maybe it's hereditary, this depression thing. Maybe he's bipolar like me.
Maybe he thinks he is going to jail for years for car theft and he'd rather die.
Maybe the streets are so challenging that he has to wear two faces to exist and the real one is the sad one. He always shows the clown face so you never know when he's hurting. I used to say that we laugh to keep from crying.
I've been on meds for eight years. I'm sure I needed them a lot earlier; I'm a little more balanced now. My bipolar ass isn't bouncing off the walls and snapping at everyone and everything, everyday. Not anymore.
Maybe medication will help him too.
Maybe he blames me for putting him in foster care where he got molested.
I blame my mom for everything and she doesn't even know it!
We need someone or something to blame.
How can I tell him to forgive us when I don't?

I have to stop the cycle. We are so much alike. We have so much anger that we store up that eventually explodes. I can't even relate to my husband's fear of dying when I welcome death. So now I consider my children's feelings and I stay alive, looking for my next smile.
Please God help me so I can help him! Help me stop hating and stop the pain. There's too much pain for us to deal with. There's always some drama in my life, drama after drama. "God! Please give me a break!"

I pulled up to mom's house and shut off the Jeep. I looked at her big white three-story house and it dawned on me. Damn, I don't know anything about my dad!
I wish he were here so I could talk to him. I know my husband wouldn't have whipped my ass so much if he was here, and my son would be a strong man. My dad was a Marine and a damn hard worker. They would no doubt be intimidated by 'My Daddy' and would do what he said!

If I couldn't talk to him about things at least I could hug him and get some comfort from his big arms and hands.
I looked up in the sky and said in my head: "I miss you Daddy." I wiped my swollen eyes.

Damn, after being clean for eight years relapse brings me back to the same place my drunken ass was years ago. Here I am going to get drunk with my mom. Am I ready for this?
Sharon, my mom is very pretty. She's a light skinned, tall, medium-built woman with a gut and no teeth, with a heart of gold for people. She was standing at the door holding her arms out wide. "Ohh baby, it's so nice to see you. I miss you so much, you finally came to see your mommy!" She was wearing her pink short set, pink curlers and pink furry slippers looking like an Easter bunny this early May 2000.

"Hi mom. I need to talk to you for a while."
After I told her all about Cyris. I said with much frustration, "Mom I don't know what to do to help him!"
"Well baby what would help you?"
"That's just what I asked myself in the car and all I know is; I need to let a lot of shit go."
"Like what?" she asked with all of her attention on my answer.
"I don't know; a lot of stuff!"
I knew of course that she was stocked with beer and booze.
"Angel, maybe he needs some counseling! Well, he'll probably get some now!"
"Mom he had counseling and it didn't help! He still does everything to escape to deny his reality! I want to tell him to change his ways of coping by escaping to God but he don't want to listen!"
"Not too many young men do!" Moms looked at me as if she wanted to ask me this question her whole life.
"Angel, what is so overwhelming that you want to DIE? I don't understand it; can you tell me that?"
"Mom, it is a mountain of added-up daily pain, unresolved issues and unforgiving memories that won't leave and I can't forgive."
"Like what?"
I wanted to say, "LIKE FORGIVING YOUR ASS!" Instead, I said: "I NEED TO LOOK AT WHO I AM AND WHY AM I SO DAMN ANGRY!"
"What helped you stop trying to take your life Angel?"
I laughed and said, "Well, nothing I tried worked!"
"Sit down and relax baby. You want a drink? I'll get us some glasses okay?"
I wonder if Mom or Dad ever tried to commit suicide. I hardly knew him; shit I hardly knew her.

Mom came back in and sat down. "Baby, God is the only one that can reach some people sometime!"
"You're so right mom! I think this is one of those times!"
"Mom tell me about my dad," I said as we sat in her black and blue living room. I admired her giant mirror-glass picture of a black panther. She sat on her fluffy valor chair. I sat in the corner, in the love seat by the window.
She jumped up and said, "Wait a minute baby I forgot the beers."
She had on the radio station; it was playing, "Missing You," by Alliyah.
I held my head in my hands trying not to cry loud.
Mom came back with two cans of beer. She flopped down and breathed out a long sigh like she just ran a mile.

"What do you want to know Angel?"
"Everything. I really don't know much about him. I do remember he was real handsome, light skin with curly soft sandy brown hair, bright brown/hazel eyes, and a strong voice and a nice smile, with real big hands and a tall thick body. I remember a few things but not much. I remember him taking me down South for a week to meet his full-blooded Cherokee mother, and that he only came around once in a blue moon."
"Well baby, he didn't stay around long. For five years he lived with me and it was heaven and hell!"
"I remember you cut him and we went in foster care; why did you cut him? And have you or he ever tried to committed suicide?"
"Slow down, I'll tell you everything! Well I did! I cut my wrist when I was with your father. I know he did put the gun to his head a few times but decided to hold on. He wouldn't do nothing like that; he'd kill other people but he wouldn't kill himself."
"What do you mean 'he'd kill other people?"
"Well, he had to kill people in the war! Baby, your father was in the Vietnam War, and when he came home, he had internal damage with his liver and brain from Agent Orange. He had the Dots too."
"What's that?"
"Well, it's delusions people get when they drink and he drank a lot! Agent Orange is a chemical the government used to spray out of the helicopter to poison and kill all the trees and bushes so they could see the enemy. But they didn't tell their own people they also got sprayed till years later when so many vets started getting sick and shit. He was emotionally wounded, seeing so many horrible deaths and bloody scenes. He had to kill innocent woman and children. He said he didn't want to but he had to or his own people would kill him for treason!"
She paused. "Yeah, Mark was sick in the head. He believed he was still at war and pulled out his weapon on a regular basis. He was a great provider, though; he worked hard everyday as a mechanic, in a hot, dangerous boiler room. He loved all my kids like they was his own!"

She smiled and got all excited remembering. "Oh, and you would wait for him at the window everyday to come home from work like you knew what time to look out that window!"
I smiled at her; I could picture it!

"My husband, the father of your sisters and brother, well, we were separated. He ran off driving trucks around the country. I knew he wasn't coming back and your father was separated too."
"What? My dad was a married man?" I said shocked.
"Yeah!"
"Damn, I didn't know that! I'm forty-two and you never mentioned that!
"I'm a married man's baby? Damn!"
"Everyone was very scared of Mark. His own family didn't like him, none of them because he was very mean and they feared him. All four of his brothers called him the devil!
"He would be making love to me one minute all passionately and than he would get up and go into the bathroom. He'd come back out and have delusions and visions and pick up his gun and call me 'Charley,' and I would have to convince him it was I Sharon, and that he was home with me.
"Over the years he gave me many painful memories with bloody lips and black eyes. I had a black eye on the right before the left one could heal."
I poured another drink, but it was stronger this time and took a long swig. I wanted to get drunk but I wasn't feeling it at all. I only felt anger and frustration sitting in my skin.

Mom was rocking her folded legs and she continued. "I was pregnant with your brother. He would have been one year older than you: Little Mark. He was seven months when he came out and died. A stillborn they called it! Not a miscarriage!"
"Mom, I used to talk to him from the time you told me I would have had a brother at age eleven until I got married and got to busy with my children. But for years he was my invisible brother. I used to talk to him and walk around with him." I smiled and closed my eyes. "He was always with me when nobody would play with me!"
"Really baby? I didn't know that!" She took a drink and lit a cigarette.
There was silence for a while. I was waiting for her to say something. Eventually I spoke first.
"Are you okay Mom? We don't have to talk about this no more if you don't want to."
"No, you wanted to know about your father and you should know!"
She switched her leg-crossing and started rocking her other foot.
I lit a cigarette and remembered how much I wished my brother had survived. It would have been nice. I bet we would have been real tight! I wouldn't have been alone as much either.

Then she frowned and spoke with so much pain that her shaken words came out fast.
"One day, Mark came home very drunk and wanted to fight. He knocked me down and kicked me in my stomach a few times, and that's how I lost my baby! Ok? That's how your brother died! Mark kicked him out of me! The sad part is he didn't even remember nothing the next damn day."
"What? What?" I looked surprised, hurt and angry; this was inconceivable! My brother? He killed my brother?
But I didn't say anything. I didn't want her to think I couldn't handle all the truth. I didn't want her to stop telling me everything, so I paused to take this in.

I couldn't believe my ears. The tears started welling up in my eyes and my heart started beating fast. I balled up my fist.
I took a real deep breath. It felt like he just died again.
I had to blame something or somebody, so I asked her, "Was he on any medication?"
"No."
"You mean to tell me the United States left him in this condition and they didn't help him?"
"He wouldn't take any medicine; that would be him admitting he was sick in the head."
She put her hands on her hip and sarcastically said, "He was a Man! Back than you didn't show weakness. That was a sign of weakness taking crazy people's medicine. The alcohol is what made his mind worse and he wouldn't stop drinking. It was always, 'I deserve a drink after a hard days work,' everyday, and he deserved to party on weekends."
I just sat there in shock. She said, "Angel, I don't want you to hate your dad!"
But I knew I would justify this shit, she still stayed with him and I still loved him and so does she.
He was sick! I have to tell myself that every time I get mad at him. He didn't mean it! He wasn't himself; he didn't mean to make my mom live a traumatic life. It was only because he lived a traumatic life and that's all he knew, violence.
I looked at her in disbelief again. Thinking, "Maybe you were drunk and fell."
She contained her pain with a smile. "A year later I had you!"
I held most of the tears back; the ones I wiped while she wasn't looking helped me get through the next sentences.

"Mark believed you were his brother's baby because I was with him first, and his brother's wife told Mark and my mother that I was still messing with her husband! So to get back at me, when you were born he didn't

come to the hospital. Instead he was out screwing a woman with open sores all on her legs. I found out later because when I came home the woman came over and told me that Mark had raped her."
"What?" I put one cigarette out and lit another with my shaken hands, followed by a long drink. "No, Mom! No way! I know you didn't believe her?"
"Yes I did!"
"Why? Why would you believe her?" My dad was no damn rapist! Why'd you believe that bitch? Why didn't you whip her ass? But I couldn't say that to her.
Mom snapped at me. "Because he was going back and forth to court for it all the way up till the time you all went in foster care! He was found guilty and went to jail! That's why you didn't see him! Damn Angel, I knew it had to be true because he had to have sex all the time! He was a sex addict! A Nympho! He didn't care who you were or what you looked like when he required sex! He raped me!"
My mouth dropped open. "What?"
"Yes, the day I brought you home he raped me!" she said angrily. All of a sudden she looked at me like I did it and she was going to hit me. Shit I'm not him I thought as I got up and walked around.
She gritted her teeth. "He busted my stitches open and I had to go back in to the hospital," she said as she shook her finger in my face, "and he had the nerve to come see me and do you know what he had the nerve to say to me?" She was waiting for an answer. "That's not my baby! And by the way, you have gonorrhea!"

She breathed in deep and than said sadly, "He also kicked me down the stairs with you in my arms. I slid down the stairs on my back protecting you." She shook her head in shame, wiping her tears before they could fall. "He was twisted when he drank. He was so jealous too. When we would go out to a bar, he would make me sit by myself so some man could buy me a drink and try to talk to me. Then he would come over and beat him up. Sick shit like that he would do!"

My gut was in knots. I couldn't breath right and I needed some air.
I went out side on the porch. There were two chairs and one wooden nightstand with an ashtray filled with butts. I slowly sat down all the while staring into space. My legs began shaking, than my hands began sweating. I had to sit on them so mom doesn't see how upset I was. I held my head down.
Mom came outside a few minutes later with our drinks refreshed and sat across from me.
She held my hands. "Angel, he had some good qualities too!"
I thought, "Like what?" But I dared not ask another question.

She continued. "Angel, despite all that I loved him so very much. He was just sick. Insane when he drank but sober he was a damn good loving man."
I was thinking under my frown. Don't the Marines teach integrity and control? What about not invading other parameters? What about values and honor?
She tarnished his name; this better be true. I was proud of my dad before this conversation.
I wish I didn't ask now. Before all I knew was he was a Marine, he was a provider and he was all mine, a part of me. Shit! I could be his niece! And both of you were still married? Shit! I'm a bastard baby, a cursed child!

"Damn mom, I don't think I should know all this stuff. All I really wanted to know now is why did we go to foster homes and nice things about him. I don't want to hear anymore now!"
"You want to know why you went to foster care? Well Angel, that's when it happened. I just couldn't take another fight!"
As she told me her compelling story of my family falling apart, I just sat in shock and disappointment in who he was, who I was, and who she was too.
I'm clinically insane, is this shit genetic? His sperm was fucked up and she stayed stressed, drunk and fighting while carrying me! Stressing out as a baby, having to listen to them screaming and cursing, crying while knocking my crib over... As I continued to listen to her story for the first time I began to consider her suffering. I felt her pain.

Now I remember! I was there! I was about five it was the winter of 1965. Mom was screaming franticly. "Enough is enough! I can't take it any more! You cock- sucker- mother-fucker- liver lip bitch! You hit me for the last time!"
We all ran into the living room to see what was going on. As we stood by the doorway, we saw that mom had grabbed the knife from the kitchen drawer and started swinging.
"Mom stop it!" we yelled in unison. Blood was airborne everywhere. Mark was trying to grab her and she cut his face, over his eyebrow so the blood was running down in his face. Soon half of his face was covered with blood. I was so scared!
My sisters were crying, and my brother asked mom to put the knife down. My brother Dennis was 14 skinny bear chest in his draws, large afro. Mark grabbed her and punched her in the nose. Blood started dripping from her nose, all down her shirt, she wiped it all on her hands. She picked up an iron and threw it at him; it hit him on his arm as he went to grab her. He fell as she ran around the long brown sofa.

Mom was screaming, "You stay away from me, Mark! I'll kill you! I will! Don't test me!" She kicked him a few times yelling, "I'll kill you bitch!" He just laid their looking like a wounded giant.
Mark was on the floor; he couldn't get up with his drunken ass. He just laid there saying, "Sharon, why you do this to me?"
"Oh, you don't remember just wiping my ass? Well, I told you don't fuck with me!"

Missy10, with her skinny fragile self in her flower pajama dress leaned down to help Mark sit up against the wall. Mom was walking back and fourth, cursing and screaming. "I told you, don't fuck with me! I'm not taking your shit any more, get up! Mother fucker, get up!" She stood over him kicking him.
Missy looked at me. "Angel go get two wet washcloths for Mom and Dad."
I ran in the bathroom and ran the hot water. It stayed cold for a long time. I looked into the mirror and saw anger. My curls were as wild as the situation. I had blood on my white tee shirt that belonged to my daddy. "She didn't have to cut my daddy!" A fear of what would happen next came over me; maybe we're next. I leaned over the sink standing on the toilet. I held that washcloth under the cold water waiting for it to get warm. Why do they have to hurt each other?
I handed mom the washcloth. She threw it down and said, "I don't want this cold shit!" She had already wiped her face with her blood-soaked shirtsleeve.
I went to my daddy and sat on the floor and said, "Stop bleeding daddy! Here daddy." I placed the washcloth on his face and wiped it gently as I cried out, "Daddy stop bleeding!"
Everyone else was keeping mom away from him.

Mom went into the bathroom. I heard the water running. She was in their yelling, cursing and banging shit around. When she came out after what seemed like a very long time, both of her eyes were black.
"Give me some ice in this rag Tina!" Tina age12, had pink pajama pants set on with one yellow sock and a wild pony- tail standing as tall as Dennis with a mole above her always pocked out lip. I was scared. I didn't know that if you got punched in the nose, then both of your eyes would turn black. I thought he just punched her in both of her eyes and her nose swelled. But he didn't.
"Somebody call the police!" Mom shouted.
Missy sat down on the couch next to mom looking very scarred, holding her hands between her legs and rocking back and forth. Tina had the rag on mom's face as she held her head back. My brother Dennis just stood there leaning on the wall. Nobody wanted to call the police! "Dennis you

hear me? Call the damn police now!" she demanded. He did, then he just stood by the door with his head down and his legs and arms crossed.

The police banged on the door hollering, "POLICE! OPEN THE DOOR!" BAM! BAM! I jumped shaking in fear and I held tighter to my Daddy's bloody hand. I held the cold rag on his face with the other hand the whole time.

One officer walked around the room looking in our bedrooms and in the bathroom. He followed the blood drippings that were all around the house on the floor and stared at the silent blood drippings on the wall. He looked over at me in disappointment while the other officer called for an ambulance. I looked at the blood soaked rag and my sticky red hands, and watched dad just sit there in a daze.

"Get up dad the doctor's here!"

I saw the paramedics come in. I tried to pull him up but I was too small. I just sat back down by his side. I wasn't mad at him for hitting my mom but I was genuinely mad at her for cutting him.

The paramedics were taking his blood pressure and one of them yelled, "We have to move him now; his pressure is very low."

They put him on a gurney and said, "Lift up on three." I backed up and stood by my oldest sister's leg. Mom was yelling at the police and the paramedics. "Get him out of here now! He's crazy, he needs help!"

An officer came over to her. "Miss what happened here?" She told them her story, which was short.

"He is drunk and when he gets real drunk, he thinks he can come in here and just beat on me for stupid shit! Look at my damn eyes! Get him the fuck out of here now!"

One officer asked my dad, "What happened here sir?"

"She cut me!" he said.

"Why?"

Well, that part he couldn't remember. "I don't know! Ask her dumb ass!"

Then they both started talking at the same time; the officers couldn't hear them. One officer said to the other, "Take the kids out of here. Take them into the bedroom for a minute."

The police called Children Welfare and gave them our address. They were there before the ambulance even left.

A strange white man in a black trench coat and a compassionate-looking woman led us four terrified kids from our mom's arms. We screamed so loud that all the neighbors came out their houses and looked out their windows to see what all the commotion was. Blood was now on all of us: on our clothes, our faces, and our hands.

Mom tried to grab us. She was screaming hysterically. "What are you doing? You're not taking my kids out of here!"

The officer grabbed her by her arms and forced them behind her back. She struggled to get loose but he cuffed her. I was standing by the

doorway to our bedroom, wishing I were invisible. Dennis and Tina yelled, "Get off my mom!" But before she could spit, we were all in the back of some stranger's car. Dennis was trying to escape.
The police couldn't control Mom. She cursed them out and spit in the face of one cop. They put Mom in the back of the police car and said; "Now you're going to jail!" The strange man had to lean on my brother to keep him down. He felt bad because he couldn't stop them; he couldn't help his mother.
"Mom! I want to go with my mom!" Dennis screamed.

Mom finished up her drink. "Mark had 62 stitches around his left eyebrow. My mother signed commitment papers to place me in the Psychiatric ward at Brentwood in Long Island N.Y, to keep me away from your father. They put me on a depression med called Lithium. I wasn't charged with any crime because it was self-defense. You girls went to live with my mother. My mom told me she would take care of my kids for me. But instead she sent you all to foster homes. She said she couldn't handle it!
Mom poured herself another drink and I poured me one too.
She continued. "I would ask my mom why she treated you different from the others. She would deny it but she never would take you with her anywhere. She would buy my other children stuff and not buy you anything. I knew it was because she considered you a bastard child. She was a Christian and she didn't like that fact I had you from a married man and I was still married also."
Yeah, well, I didn't like her either! I thought.
"Maybe because she watched her husband, my step father, sit you on his lap with your legs open and she had to tell you to close them. She probably saw the lust in her man's eyes for you then. I just didn't see it!"
She stopped talking and suddenly looked furious. "That dirty bastard!" she said with disgust. "If she knew so much, than she should have known her husband was molesting you! I wish you would have told me!"
"Maybe that's why we were sent away because she did know," I said softly. Damn, I wonder if she resents her mom for signing the papers for her to be committed to the criminally insane psycho cell, or for putting her kids in foster homes. I resent her! Damn this cycle shit is crazy. Well, Grandma is gone and I don't feel like forgiving her or her nasty ass man yet! I'm not asking any more questions either!

I cringed as I remembered that old, fat, itchy bearded face between my six-year-old legs, as I cried "Stop! Stop!" Tears rolled down my face with hate in my heart for him fucking up my sex life.
I couldn't stand to be licked! Always seeing his face down there with his itchy beard and cigar breath. It took me twenty-five years of counseling to find out all the enjoyment I've been missing.

Damn, my dad was a rapist and he murdered my brother. I understood her still loving his abusive ass because I love my abuser, but killing my baby brother, and then rape? He's not even here to defend himself either. Suddenly, I felt so disappointed and ashamed of him! I loved a man I didn't even know. You don't really know a person until you know what they have done or are capable of doing, and their secrets. Otherwise they wear two or three faces and this was a face I didn't want to see.

Wow! I saw Dad in Chris and Cyris in both of us and Mom in me.
This cycle was getting even scarier.
The truth really hurts. Damn!
I stood up. "I'm going home now!"

CHAPTER THREE
SOME "WELCOME HOME"

Everyone was asleep so I laid on the couch with my hands behind my head. I got back up to turn the lights off and put the night-lights on for a more peaceful atmosphere. Eventually, I went up stairs and woke Chris up and told him what mom said about my dad.
"There's two sides to a story," he said, "and he is not here to defend himself."
"True Dat!" I said.
He paused. "There are some similarities with me and your dad huh?" And he rolled over and went back to sleep!
My teeth grinded as I immediately thought about his drinking days, and how he use too give me black eyes. He's probably a Nympho. The pain stabbed my gut so hard I had to bend over and hug my stomach. It got worse as I thought about all the cheating he's done with nasty woman while he was drunk. This mother-fucker gave me the same venereal disease! And denied his child! Yes! You two are too much alike, are you a rapist also? Sure you are, shit you raped me too, damn this is too much for me.

My heart is beating a mile a minute. I held and massage my chest. Oh my heart hurts maybe I'm having a heart attack. I want to throw up. I think I'm going to be sick. I ran to the toilet and released the booze out of my puffy check and my nose.
Damn, It's all over the toilet seat, the floor and the wall. Trying to clean up my stink ass mess I thought to myself.
I should bang him in his damn head right now! I left the bathroom in discuss for him, like he was my vomit. Then more so at myself for putting up with that shit for all those years and I still stayed with him, he may not be beating on me but he's always cheating on me, that is abuse too. He could bring me home Aids and with my wanting to die ass welcomes it. What the hell is wrong with me? I need to be busted in the damn head, dumb bitch! I really hate myself.
I breath out a long hard sigh and washed my mouth, up and out my nose, watered my red eyes, I looked up into the mirror and all the desires hit me at once, wanting to punch it, wanting to take the time back, wanting to run far, far away, wanting to just lay down and die, wanting to stop the tears, wanting to be held, wanting the pain to go away, wanting some understanding, wanting some answers, wanting some damn peace for a change, wanting God to save me, wanting so bad to not be me.
I slowly went back down stairs sliding my shoulders on the wall and staggered on the couch. Oh my head hurt now!

I wondered did I stay with my abuser because I love him or needed him? Or was I really afraid of him? Or was I afraid to be alone with children? All of that and because I didn't think no one else would want me and take care of me like he did. Because myself esteem was so low I believed everything he told me when he said I wasn't shit, because I didn't want to be like the rest of the world with a broken family, because I believed one day he would be that good God following person I knew was hiding inside and things would be better and I would have the perfect man, because I thought as long as I kept praying one day God will deliver me and tell me what to do, because I wanted anyone to stay with me so I don't have to be alone with me, because I didn't love myself.
I can understand why my mother stayed and cared about my father and needed him. How can I hate my dad and still love my husband? This is deep.

The tears were flowing as I asked myself again, "Why should I dig into the past?"
Because I need to! I WANT to live for myself and not just NEED to live for others. Than I can give Cyris reasons to live and sincerely encourage him. I need some passion for life. I want to wake up and be happy to see a new day, instead of covering my head and going back to sleep. Is this past information going to help me to do that?
A voice inside me said, "Yes Angel but first you have to know why you wanted to die! Why do you hate so much and why are you so angry and resentful? Why do you feel undesirable and guilty, so self-destructive, and what are you willing to do about it?"
But this is more information than I bargained for; this ride will no doubt be very painful and too emotional. Am I ready to deal with this shit alone?

I went back to peeked in the room hoping he would wake up so we could talk. I went to the dresser and took two Tylenols out of the bottle loudly. I turned around as he rolled over.
I looked at my husband; as usual, he was sleeping through my pain and tears, just like these last twenty-five years. He knows I be in deep pain and he just rolls over and sleep like a baby and leaves me alone with my depressed, suicidal self. How can he be so inconsiderate? I know he has to get up early to go to work but hell I'm in serious pain here. Just once I wish he would get up and hold me and rock me and talk to me, or listen to me and hold me and let me cry out my pain. Just once. Instead he leaves me alone to deal with my gut level pain. How can you hate someone so much and love him or her so much at the same time?
It's too much of a burden to put on my children. Damn, I'm still mourning my best friend's death; Lexes passed in her sleep just a week ago from leukemia.

I don't want to get more depressed than I am now!
I stomped back down stairs like a little angry child. I sat on the black couch pouting. I was alone again with the 'Evil Sprits' telling me, "Go get drunk and die!
"Shoot yourself in the head in front of your mother's house! It won't even hurt!
You want them to know what they did to you don't you Angel? You want them to acknowledge your pain and accept the part they played, you want them to hurt like you are hurting don't you?"
I spoke to the sprit, Yeah! They continue to abandon me and act like I don't exist! Him and her still won't love me like I need to be loved, they are selfish, fuck them, fuck me! I have to do something! I can't keep living with this shit! This is too much pain for one human to hold alone. I could just take some sleeping pills, a lot of pills; I have a lot of them too.

Another voice is torturing me loudly, "You fucked up your son's life and probably your daughters' too, what kind of mother are you any way? They don't need you, someone else can take better care of them, they have been abuse also you just don't know it yet! If you live, you'll fuck up their children's lives also because you're sick in the head, look at you, what can you possible offer anyone now? You're a drunk, a crack addict, your own mother doesn't want you! Your church left you! Where is your God? Your husband definitely don't want you, everyone is a better choice to him then you, look at yourself, your fat, ugly, with a big ass bump on your nose, white as a ghost, your scary looking, and your weak and stupid, what can you do with your cripple ass, what do you have to offer anyone, you can't work, you can't go places, and you can't satisfy anyone sexual your finished, your useless, no one will miss you, what are you waiting for just take the gun and get it over with, shoot yourself, make sure you do it right this time. Do it!"

But then a reasoning voice said, "This is not easy rehashing old feelings." I know the severity of pain that it can take me through. Can I deal with it? Do I really need to? No! I don't have to go through all that mess!
No, the past is over! I need to leave it there, buried! I don't have to look at it! I just need to keep praying for Cyris. "God please help him because I don't know how!" That's all to it! Only God can help him now!

Still, a stronger voice in my ears shouted with intolerance, "You're a punk! Chicken shit! And you're a weak ass complainer. All you do is complain and feel sorry for yourself, grow the hell up! Nobody wants to be around a depressed, unforgiving, judgmental, selfish, self-centered loser. You are in pain because you stay in it; you're not trying to get out! You're not trying to get better! You just want someone to feel sorry for your ass, you are a sorry ass and your going to always be in pain if you don't stand up and do something to change your life, your thoughts, your ideas, your pitiful attitude toward yourself and life, and definitely your opinion of yourself. No one loves you because you don't love yourself, and no one forgives you because you don't forgive anyone! What do you expect, someone else to do for you what your not even trying to do for yourself? You want some magic to change your life for you? Wake the hell up girl, you're too old to be acting like a poor me baby. Shake your dusty ass off and start to heal and deal!

"You're just scared because you really don't want to look not only at your situations, but a good honest look at damn yourself! You should be ashamed of yourself because you have so much talent, you seen it at work, your not even trying to do anything positive, your not even trying to think positive, you have gifts people wish they had, you can really do a lot in life if you get up and stop laying down and allowing people to walk over you. You think you're worthless? Well God don't make no junk, everything he made has a purpose in life, everything and everyone. You are special to him if to no one else and your letting him down wasting away living in the bottle. Your saying he made a mistake when he made you? You think he's not hearing your prayers? Well guess what? You're not listening to him because he says in me you have all power to do all things, great and small. He said come to me all that is heavy laden and I will give you rest. Instead you go to a man, a bottle, a drug, a stranger, you go to God and beg, and then you leave and still carry your burdens with you, instead of leaving them there with him to handle. So he backs up and watch you try to carry it alone because you won't give your total life to him, you want to carry around all that pass pains and present hurts? Obviously you do because you're not given it to him, and you're not putting your faith and trust in him, and your not following him. You want a man to love you, and a mother, a child? NO human can ever love you like you need to be loved. GOD IS LOVE! You want love? You want to know how to love? Then go to God. Maybe if you reflect back at your life, you'll be able to recognize your sons' feelings and pain, and confusions about love and life!

"Then maybe you'll be more committed to changing and learning why you need to let go of some of that shit your carrying around and began helping him without guilt. It's the guilt that is destroying your health, it's the stress that is tearing you apart, it's the constant need for love and affirmations from a man that is making you feel less than. So let's do this together so we can stop recycling the same painful patterns of life."
I said out loud to all the voices, "I'm not scared! I'm not afraid! I'm not a punk either! I have good reasons to complain, shit, leave me alone! I held my head in my hands and began to cry out loud uncontrollably, instantly

I felt an arm around my shoulders and a voice said in my ear, "I'll be with you, always!"

I held up my head and looked around and breathed in and out hard. I felt relieved, confident, compelled to be strong and I said out loud, "I can do it! Maybe I do need to deal with this stored-up pain, fear, and resentments. I can do this! Lets see!" So I grabbed a pen and paper and wrote down this list:
1} Who am I?
2} Why did I always want to die?
3} What will make me want to live?
4} How can I help Cyris?
5} How can God help me?
"Okay, let's do this!" I said boldly to all of the voices.
Slowly I lay down on the sofa on my stomach. I kicked off my black sneakers, snatched off my black stinky sweater, puffed up my pillow under my cheek and closed my eyes.

I recall…

My two sisters and I went through four foster homes in a three-year period. My brother was in an all-boys home so I never got to see him.
My two sisters eventually went home to Mom, and left me with a nice old couple for about a six months in White Plains, NY.
I loved it there; it was so peaceful and beautiful, very middle-class. We lived next door to Moms Mabel, an old-time comedian.
Green grass and colorful flowers, and dirt roads and fresh air, crickets, grasshoppers, lizards, and pretty birds surrounded me. I had plenty of toys, and a foster sister my age that I was very close to. I met happiness in full color.
And then one day, when I walked into the living room after a good day at school, my foster parents said, "Angel, you will be going home in a few days. Isn't that great?"
"No! I don't want to go nowhere! This is my home! I want to stay here!"
My foster mom sat me down on the plastic-covered couch and put her arm around me. My foster dad stood there in his robe, drinking coffee with his sad sagging face that always looked like he was crying. I used to sit on his lap and hold his face up for him.
"Baby girl," he said to me, "We don't want you to go but its time you were with your family."
I was confused; why did I have to leave now that I was finally settled in! I was so happy there!
"Can't I stay a little longer?" I looked at both of them crying, squeezing the couch pillow. "Did I do something wrong? Don't you like me?"

I held my head in my hands. Mom held me, and then dad came over and held both of us.
My foster mom lifted up my chin and said, "I am sorry Angel but your mom wants you home now! We would love for you to stay but it's not up to us."
Suddenly I got excited. "I have a good idea! My mom doesn't know I want to stay and if you want me to stay, and you ask her, she'll say 'yeah!' Ask her if I can stay! Please! Please!" I yelled louder. "I want to stay here! I want you to be my mom and dad! I love you two!"
This was a safe stable house. In this house, there wasn't any cursing or fighting. These two people with such good hearts loved me and spent time with me. I finally felt like a part of the world around me, a part of everyone and everything. I didn't know my mom and I never really got along with my sisters. They never spent time with me so bunk them!
"Don't you love me?" I looked at the dad I had adopted. His eyes started to water as he hugged me and said, "Angel, we love you; we love you very much and we'll always be here for you! The agency says you have to go back home now, it's not up to us baby. But you are always welcome to visit us."
I didn't hear another word they said. Their mouths were moving but my mind was moving faster, thinking: I was going from suburban life to the ghetto strife! From grass and balls to concrete walls, from grasshopper, crickets and dirt blocks, to police syringes and gangs and gunshots.
They both hugged me as I cried angrily at my real mom for pulling me away from here. Sadness overwhelmed me as I remembered the madness I thought I left behind forever.

"I'm home! Hello!"
There was no home-coming party, no family standing together with there arms stretched out eagerly waiting my return. No "Welcome Home" signs. Only mom who came out of her room in her flowered robe, dragging her raggedy slippers across the hard wood floors down the long hallway to kiss and hug me. She told the Social Services escort "thank you and goodbye" Bye Mrs. Sharon, bye Angel, take care now as she waved down the stairs. Mom hugged me as we walked the never ending white hallway to a very small blue living room with two couches with flowered covers, obvious cigarette burn holes, a wooden table in the middle with two wax candles of President heads, one of G. Washington's sitting on one end and Lincoln's' head on the other end and a giant gold ash tray in the middle. No pictures just one small circle mirror on the wall.
White sheer curtains covering two small front windows with an iron chair next to it like it was someone's permanent spot.
Mom smiled at me and said, "You sleep in there with your sisters." She pointed and escorted me to the bedroom with one queen size bed, one tall

dresser, and one chair. She hugged me again and said I missed you so much. I'm glad you're home, then she kissed me again with a big lip locking, tobacco smelling, no teeth puckering, laughing kiss. Then she went into the little green kitchen and poured herself some red kool-aid. I stood there with my bags next to me on the floor in the bedroom. I was frozen as I watched her walk to her bedroom and she closed her door. Slam!
I waited in the living room sitting in the iron chair by the window anxiously waiting for my sisters to return from school for some joy, they came kissed me hi and left out to play.
I sat alone in the small, dreary living room, listening to the streetcar's music and horns, and the children's laughter outside. The windowpane was cool as I laid my face on it and cried lonely tears.
I was about 8. I felt like the "bastard baby".

My sisters had friends and boyfriends and were settled in school. I had to go into the classroom as "the new girl." Everyone stared me up and down and laughed.
I would ask mom at her bedroom door: "Can I go outside and play?"
She would respond with a fast harsh, "NO! There's no one to watch you out there!"
All I had was my imagination and invented toys.
I really missed my old friends; I don't have anybody to talk to.
"Hey, Missy and Tina, where are you going? Can I come?"
"NO!" my sisters would respond as they ran down the stairs.
"I don't need to hang out with you stupid ugly girls any way!"
I would sit on the steps and think, I'll meet someone. Eventually I did, my best friend Donna. She was cute and tough, always wearing two ponytails. She was a really dark skinned girl and she taught me how to play "skullies." It became my daily ritual after school, to cop a top and drop and kick butt. I was the best in my hood on Kelly Street in the Bronx.

I guess what I really wanted was everyone to stay with me until I adjusted. I wanted more excitement about my existence. I wanted to feel my family's love!
But I didn't know how to ask for it. I felt that if they cared about me, they would have wanted to spend time with me. Shit, they hadn't seen me in a long time. I was the baby; where was the love and affection and attention?

School was tough for me. I lived right across the street from it but I was late everyday because I didn't want to go. I was always tired and weak and just wanted to sleep.

I thought I was just lazy but later found out that I was suffering from Chronic Fatigue Syndrome.
My reputation didn't start off so good you might say.
One day at school I was sitting in the back of class, and a big brown cockroach came out of my book bag. This Spanish boy saw it on the floor by me and he jumped up and pointed at it and started screaming.
"Look! Look, a roach! It's hers!" he said as he pointed at me. Some kids jumped on their chairs like they never seen a damn roach before.
I started getting pissed! All this for a damn roach!
He pointed at me and said. "Yuck, she's contaminated! It came out of her book bag!"
Well it could have, but damn! I wish I were invisible that moment. I wanted to whip his skinny ass all across the classroom but his tough-looking sister was also in the class.
He said it again. "She contaminated!" Everyone pointed and laughed at me. No one heard the teacher say, "Stop it!"
He teased me the whole period; the whole class would stop and start up again, laughing at me. He kept turning around, whispering; "Contaminated roach! Contaminated roach!"
I couldn't take it anymore. "Leave me alone!" I screamed.
His sister jumped up and said, "What did you say to my brother?"
Nervously, full of embarrassment but stern, I said, "Tell him to leave me alone!"
"NO!" she yelled and laughed.
The teacher yelled at her. "Sit down and be quiet."

I left the class on the bathroom pass with no intentions of returning. I went to my locker to get my book for the next period and there stood four girls in front of my locker.
"Excuse me," I said politely but they just ignored me. Damn I thought, I'm glad this year is almost over, maybe next year will be better.
Than a handsome boy with a nice big afro walked passed. I stared at him with a sudden desire to touch him. He was so gorgeous, walking in his football uniform. Damn he was so fine! All of us were looking at him. I had never seen a boy so cute before. I continued staring with desire until the big, tall girl standing next to me said, "Come here nigga, don't walk past me!" She grabbed him by the neck of his jersey and kissed him on his mouth.
I said to myself, "Ew, what are you doing with her?"
She was mean looking with wild hair and she looked way too old to be going to this P.S School. She was ugly!
I had been admiring him on the field for some time but I had never seen him this close before. He looked at me and smiled. I smiled back. He walked down the hall with a few other players. Damn, that was the quarterback! And he smiled at me!

I turned back around to my locker and was about to open it.
"What are you looking at?" the ugly girl asked me.
"What?"
"You heard me! Why are you looking at my boyfriend?"
Shit I thought, I'm definitely not going to say anything to make her mad!
"I'm trying to get to my locker," I replied.
I looked at another girl and said, "Excuse me," but I want to say, "MOVE!"
This big-ass, over-grown, hair-need-combing, big boned bully got in my face; the other three girls stood around me so I couldn't move.
"I saw you!" she said. "That's my man; you want to look at something? Look at this everyone!" and she pulled up my dress and pulled down my panties.
I grabbed them as they got to my knees, screaming, "Stop it!"
The girls were cheering her on: "Take them off!"
Everyone in the hallway stopped in his or her tracks to see what was all the commotion was about.
The crowd cheered her on: "Take them off!"
I'm trying to pull up, and she's fighting to pull them down. I finally won.
I held onto them for dear life. Everyone was full of enjoyment in my humiliation.
The bell rang. She pocked me in my forehead and said, "I'm going to beat you up after school!"
I had never heard those words before and I sure didn't want to hear it from her!

I was no punk but she was big boned and I was skinny as a pole. They walked away laughing. I don't have anyone to get my back. I never thought about calling my sisters to get me after school because too much fear set in; this girl looked like she beat her man's ass like my mom did.
She did bully off that kiss. Shit, her man was scared of her! He said, "yes" to whatever she said!
I didn't want to go to class; I couldn't show my face. I couldn't leave the school because they watched the doors, so I went into bathroom for this last period.
I went into a stall and said to myself, "What am I going to do?" I didn't know anyone who could help me! I couldn't tell any teachers. I didn't know who the hell she was anyway and I had no names of the girls.
So I got on my knees at the stall and prayed! Yes prayed! "Please God don't let her be outside waiting for me, please!" I was desperate!
The bell rang.
I waited till I thought most of the kids had left the building. I came out and walked slowly down the hallway, waiting for most of the kids to run out first. Maybe she'll get tired of waiting for me and leave.
I peeked outside and saw just a few stragglers and some teachers leaving.

I walked closer to them and I thanked God for not letting her be out there. When I turned the corner of the schoolyard, I ran home as fast as I could.
I did that every day for that last few days of school. She would never be outside waiting for me. I thanked God she didn't see me and I didn't see her and I stopped wearing short dresses.
Mom would ask me, "How was your day at school?"
I would say "Okay." I never told my sisters; I wonder why? I couldn't wait to go outside and play and get out of the house where nobody talks to me or did anything with me.

Donna and I were in someone else's building and a few kids were laughing over in the corner as we waited for another friend to come down stairs.
One girl said, "You're a white girl aren't you?"
I said with an attitude, "No stupid, I'm black!"
It really hurt my feelings to be called white. I hated my light-like-white complexion. I wanted to be golden brown
"You are so white, look at your skin! You look white!"
"I'm black stupid, I'm just light-skinned!"
"What! White girl, you can't hang out in here."
I was pissed. I said, "Fuck you with your buck teeth, black-as-night ass, calling somebody white! I look better than you ugly- black-liver-lip bitch!"
They all laughed at her! I had learned that line from my mom.
Some boy said, "Don't nobody like white girls!"
The other four kids that were standing around in that small hallway agitated me more with their "woohh!" I walked up to the girl and just punched her in her face as hard as I could, a right hook! My first fight!
"Fight! Fight!" the kids yelled!
She came at me swinging her arms around and around. I backed up.
I grabbed her hair with both hands and swung her around and let her go and she went flying against the wall.
The kids said, "Oh shit!" They started laughing harder.
I kicked her in her stomach and said, "Don't ever call me 'white girl' again, you hear me?"
I kicked her again and again and I heard my friend tell the other kids that they better not jump in!
Then I charged after the dirty nosed boy that always bothered me and called me names. I came up from behind him and grabbed him by his neck and held him under my arms and walked out the building.
I squeezed his head and said, "I'm tired of your shit too! Are you going to leave me alone?"
"Get off of me!" he yelled. "Get off of me girl! I'm going to beat you up!"

My other girlfriend came running down the stairs and out of the building. I flipped him on the sidewalk and stomped him. He started rolling in the street.
I was running after him trying to stomp him some more but he just kept rolling away like a wheel. I got him good one more time; I almost fell as I stomped him!
Then I screamed, "Stop fucking with me! You hear me? I'm tired of you fucking with me! I'm going to stab one of you mother- fuckers!"
That was the first time I really wanted to hurt someone really bad.
That was also the first time I really hated myself, and the skin I was stuck in.
I said, "Come on Donna and Jean!" and we walked up the block.
Donna looked at me and put her hand into mine and said, "My girl's not white! That's my sister!"
Jean said, "You fight well; you didn't even need my help!" and she laughed.
Donna put her arm around my shoulder as we laughed and went to her building. Happily we played handball, an excellent game to play when you were frustrated. I was really good.
After that day guess what? Nobody ever called me white again!

Mom didn't help any though; she would bring me home these white girl ruffles and flowers, down-to-your-ankles dresses. She brought me four of them and I had to wear them for my last week of school; she said I had to look pretty.
I was pretty to her but a white girl to everyone else.

Watching the kids pointing at me and laughing on gym days in my skips was bad enough. I would sit with my legs folded trying to hide them.
"Mom, why can't you buy me some Pro-Keds? You bought Dennis some!"
It hurt like hell to be teased but I couldn't let them see me cry.

Two months later, I yelled out of the back window to our neighbor, who lived around the corner at Missy's boyfriend's Mikes' house. He came to the window.
"Hi Mike, is your uncle going to church today?"
"Yes!"
"Ok! Tell him I'll be right over!"
"Ok!"
I liked church. I really wanted to be in the choir. I knew all the songs.
I went every Sunday and then I'd usually go to Mike's house and watch TV with his momma. She was interesting to listen to and she had a snake tongue. I called it that because it was skinny with black strips on both

sides and a slit at the tip. They had on some good Sunday movies that we enjoyed watching together. I would watch and smell her Sunday dinner as it cooked in the oven. But this Sunday I went straight home.

My brother Dennis was home which was strange but nice; I hardly ever saw him.
No "hi, how you been, glad to see you." It was, "Angel, go clean your room! What is with you leaving your room like that?"
He began to walk closer to me. I thought he was going to give me a hug or a kiss so I smiled a big greeting but instead he said, "Wash your face!" looking at me in disgust. "Mom said you have to clean the bath room!"
I backed up and frowned and sucked my teeth.
I looked in there where two grown German Shepard's lived, a girl and boy, Duke and Duchess. They were walking around, making shit footprints all over the floor that had been covered with clean newspaper; now the room was covered with funky shitty paper, and chewed-up toilet paper, and shit-printed towels, and shit scratches on the wall. Never mind the ring in the sink and tub.
"Me?" I asked him. "Why can't you clean the bathroom? Dag, I just got in and you're ordering me around! You're not my father!"
He gave me this look like he was going to hit me. He said, "That's right! I'm not your father! Where is he? I'm your big brother! I'm the man of the house! What I say goes and you're going to do like I tell you! And don't bother Mom either."

He handed me his clothes and said, "Here, fold up my pants and make sure the creases meet together, and the pants are on the middle of the hanger close to the crotch! And put it in the closet where the pants are at, and be neat!"
"Damn, by the time you told me all that, you could have done it yourself!"
"Don't get smart with me Angel, just do like I tell you." He squeezed into some black leather pants and a gray sweater.
"You have to do the dishes too!"
"Why do I ..." I started to yell but he was already slamming the door.
I'll be glad when he moves his perfect ass out!
I bet my sisters told him to tell me what to clean because they knew I wasn't going to listen to them. "You clean them pots Angel!" I mocked them. It was always my day to clean especially on Sundays the big breakfast and dinner day.

It was a struggle to get through the never-ending weekends with mom and her friends. Cleaning fragments of broken lamps and glass ashtrays, or wine bottles that went upside her new man's head, calling the police

every weekend. Trying to block out the loud cursing voices and fighting all day and night, two nights straight.
Clean, clean, clean. I could relate to Cinderella.
I remember crying as I cleaned up the shitty bathroom. "I'm not doing that kitchen too! I'm leaving! I'm going to disappear somewhere."
I went into my room and hid between the mattresses and box spring and went to sleep.

I was full of resentment. Why had it taken so long to send for me?
I was here now, hello! Does anybody care or even miss me? Damn! Who was doing dishes before I got here? I didn't cook and I didn't eat much. I sure shouldn't have to clean up after everyone!
Those dogs were not my dogs; that shitty job is a boy's job.
Yeah, I was an angry little girl so I went to God in prayer, pleading to take me far, far away from here.

CHAPTER FOUR

I LOST MORE THAN MY VIRGINITY

After four years of being ignored I was finally happy I was getting breasts. I was getting attention now. It was the summer of 1972; no more school for a while. I was going to spend the night again at my friends' house. One night, the grown-ups were playing cards under the streetlights, playing a radio good and loud, laughing and drinking and talking in circles. All of us kids were exhausted from playing "hot peas and butter," and "ring a leaveah." In this kind of dark you could hide the belt in the open and they still couldn't see it. That made the game more exciting because more people would get caught and get whipped. That's when I learned pain could be fun. It was 12:00am and we started to get hungry.

Donna's father yelled, "Lets go kids!"
We ran up the four flights of stairs two steps at a time, knocking each other out of the way, straight to the kitchen where he had boiled some eggs for us.
He showed us how to peel the eggs without all the mess we were always making. He cracked it and rolled it and it all peeled off in its skin. Then he said, "I'm going back outside! I'll be back in about an hour or so; I'll be right out in the front with the rest of the grown folks!"
He pointed his finger in all of our faces and said sternly, "Don't go out this door for any reason at all! Don't touch the door at all! Don't even answer it; don't open it for any reason, except a fire! If you do, you will be punished and Angel can't ever spent the night again. You all hear me?"
"Yes!" we said in harmony. "We won't!"

Her brother John was 17, a very short light brown bald headed kid. There was her little sister Jacky 7, who hardly talked. Donna was 12, my age; she was West Indian. She had a dirty, ragged look about her, but she was sweet and she befriended me. I always wanted to do something with her nappy hair. We ate those egg sandwiches like we were starving; we grabbed our cherry kool-aid and went out onto the fire escape.
We talked about what we wanted.
Donna said, "I want a ten-speed blue sparkly bike!"
Her sister said, "I want a whole lot of doll babies!" with a big smile. That was the only thing she said all night. She just laughed a lot.
John said, "I want to play basketball on TV and make a lot of money."

I couldn't think of just one thing. I said the thing I needed the most so I wouldn't be laughed at. I yelled out, "I want me some Pro-Keds!"
Then we started with 'your mama' jokes, and played riddle games from the book I brought with me.
Donna and her brother went into the house and than she called me in.
"Angel you're my best friend right?" she asked me.
"Sure I am!"
"Come here I got to tell you something!" She gently put her arms around my shoulder.
We were sitting on her bed. Her brother and little sister went back into the kitchen.
"Would you do anything for me?"
I thought she wanted me to do her a favor: "Sure, what?"
"My brother is dying of cancer."
Damn we were just laughing, having a good time! Why did she want to bring up sad stuff now?
"What's that?" I asked. "I know it's bad. I heard my grandmother had cancer and she died but no one talks about it."
"John is dying; a disease is eating him up inside, and he has these seizures, and he has real bad asthma. He can't hardly talk; he wheezes and sneezes, he's allergic to everything."
"Poor thing!" I jumped up. "Can we go back out on the fire escape now?"
It was more fun out there! The streets were always more fun than the houses we lived in. I wanted to see the streets and tell some more funny jokes about the grown-ups we lived with.
"No!" She proceeded to pull me by my arm, saying, "Sit down for a minute and listen! My dad said the cancer is why he has no hair any where on his body at all and that's why he is bald and skinny."

I started laughing at the hairless young man who never knew a mustache.
"I'm sorry for laughing!" I was feeling sorry for him.
The doctor told him he's going to die soon!"
"Wow! When?"
She held her head down. "We don't know but it could be anytime. One day he just won't wake up, or he won't be able to breathe and just fall down and die. Whatever way, it'll be fast."
"Damn!"
Then she said, "He never had sex and may die never doing it."
My mouth dropped open. This was a little too much information.
I started laughing and singing. "John don't have no girl friend," trying to lighten things up.
Donna said, "Come here, let me whisper something in your ear!"
"What?" I laughed and pulled away as her whispering tickled my ear.
"Just come here!" She pulled me close and whispered again, "He asked me to ask you would you do it with him?"

"What!" I screamed. "Are you crazy?"
"Please! Please for me!" she begged in her praying hands position.
"No!" I jumped up off her bed; "I can't do it! I don't like him like that! And! And…" I stuttered, "I never did it before!"
She begged harder, looking more desperate. "Please, please," and began to gently rub my arms in a friendly gesture. "Please! So he can at least know what it's like! I would do it for you!"
I stomped my feet; she wasn't listening to me! "But I never did it before!"
He came out of the kitchen and I know he had been listening. I was so embarrassed. I turned around to go back out on the fire escape when he grabbed my arm.
"I like you a lot Angel, please do this for me?" he pleaded, looking more desperate then she.
I said quietly, "I don't think I can now! Maybe another day!"
"Come on Angel! Don't be like that! I won't hurt you!" He grabbed my hand and held it tight.

The little sister just stood there grinning, covering her mouth.
Donna said, "I'm not going to be your friend no more if you don't!"
I sighed. "Okay! Okay! I'll do it! But if it hurts you have to take it out okay?"
He gave me the biggest grin and said, "Okay!"
I didn't want him to die never knowing sex. I didn't want to lose my best and only friends. John couldn't even go outside much; he was always too sick and he could hardly breathe. He had to stay by some machine. I guess he could only dream about doing a lot of things.
I told his sisters they had to go in the other room. "Don't peek either!"
I was scared and curious. I was a virgin; the many men who had molested me had never penetrated me. I heard it hurts! The big ones I saw looked like it would hurt; they would just rub it on me.

I pulled off my pants slowly saying, "Maybe we could do it later!"
"Come on please!"
He pulled down his pants and draws; his genitals were skinny too! It looked like a finger. I covered my face and he opened my legs and struggled to find the hole. Finally after a few attempts he put it in. It didn't even hurt. I really couldn't feel it.
I just lay there under him; I didn't know I was supposed to move around. I bet they're peeking, I thought. I was so embarrassed! I wished he'd hurry up and get off me! I covered my face as I laid there beneath him. John started moving faster and faster and faster and than he stopped and laid on me.
"That's it?" It was over?

He was breathing really hard. I was scared he was going to die on top of me.
He was making wheezing sounds in my ear.
I closed my eyes thinking, "Please don't die on top of me."
He was all sweaty. I pushed him off of me. "Get off!" I shouted.
He hurried up trying to pull up his pants, and then I heard his sisters giggling so I ran in the bathroom. He ran to his oxygen machine.
Damn that's what doing it is like? I thought that's it as I went to touch myself and felt this slimy stuff.
Eeww! What the hell is that stuff? I frowned as I wiped it off with tissue. I still felt sticky from this slimy shit oozing out of me.
I heard a knock on the door. "Who is it?"
Donna said, "It's me, open the door!"
"Wait a minute!" I yelled as I pulled up my pants and opened the door a little to make sure he wasn't standing there.
She came in. "How was it? What is it like?"
"It was… I don't know!"
She jumped up and down saying, "Come on, tell me!"
"Close the door!" I screamed.
"Well, say something Angel!"
"It was quick and not what I expected!" I blurted out. "It didn't feel like anything! I didn't feel it. I heard it hurts and it didn't hurt. I've heard my mom making noises like it hurt!"
"Come on," she said, "Lets go back outside." She looked disappointed, like she was expecting it to be more.
"I'm coming, let me wash my hands."
She went out and I wiped myself off and washed my hands.
I looked into the mirror. "What the hell did you just do?" I asked myself.

They all were back on the fire escape. I hesitantly went back out. I didn't want to look him in his face now. We didn't ever talk about it. Never!
We just went back to telling jokes like nothing happened.
I looked up and saw the sky full of stars and I breathed in the good night air. I looked down and saw all the grown folks laughing and talking loud, having a mighty good time.
Than I looked around and saw my brother sitting on the ground leaning against the wall of our building like he was sleeping.
That was strange because my brother was too cool and clean. Perfectly neat afro so fine and smart. He would never sit on the ground. That just wasn't his style.
It was dark and his head was down so I said, "Donna, isn't that my brother down there?"
"Yeah, that looks like him!"
I noticed the gray-and-white-checker knit pant he was wearing. I had folded those pants so neatly!

"Something is definitely wrong; maybe he's drunk! He needs to go to bed!" I didn't see my mom but I saw her boyfriend Boo, because of his red shirt, he was really tall, dark, with his hair process and a pointed beard.

"Boo!" I hollered. "Boo! Boo!"

He couldn't hear me over the music. I was on the forth floor and there was a lot of people outside making noise. He was directly underneath the building.

I keep calling him until finally he looked up.

I said, "Look at Dennis!" He didn't understand me so I pointed, yelling, "Look! Look at Dennis over there!" He was at least twenty-five feet away from him.

He went over to him. I saw him pick him up and carry him into my building. About fifteen minutes later an ambulance pulled up and the paramedics ran in my building.

I ran into the bedroom where I could see the staircase to my building. I watched so I could see what floor they were going to. I saw my cousin, whom I couldn't stand running up the stairs behind them. I wanted to know what was going on. I kept watching them and they eventually stopped. It was my floor.

"I have to go!" I said.

They said frantically, "My dad said don't touch that door or else!"

"I don't care! I have to see what's going on!"

"No!" They pulled me back. "Angel just wait, wait our dad said he'll be back soon then you can go okay?" They were afraid I would get them in trouble.

I didn't want to do that. I was taught to respect my elders; I was really scared to defy him. He wasn't anybody to me but when a strong man's voice says, "Don't you touch my door!" you don't touch his door! In those days, when leaving someone's house after visiting, they walked you to the door and opened it for you; you never opened someone's door.

I guess I was more scared of everyone getting in trouble then wanting to be nosey.

Their dad was raising them alone, their mother died so he was super protective.

But now I could see people running down my hallway stairs in a frenzy.

I ran back to the fire escape to see who came out the building. It was so frustrating! I wanted to leave so bad!

They were putting my brother in the ambulance.

I saw my mom. "Mom! Mommy! What's wrong?" She couldn't hear me either.

I started screaming louder. "Mom! Mommy!" Louder and louder, I screamed. "What's wrong with Dennis?"

I had to get down there! I had to go down the fire escape!

I started down the stairs yelling, "Mommy wait for me!"
She finally looked up. "Mom, what's wrong with Dennis?"
She looked worried and nervous. She waved her hand and yelled back at me. "Shut up! Leave me alone!" She started crying, holding her head. Again she said, "Just shut up and stay up there!"
I had a right to know! It was me who told Boo to see if he was all right! I wanted her to say, "come here" so I could leave. I wanted to be a part of what was going on. I wanted to be there for her and Dennis. I leaned over the edge. She got into the back of the ambulance and they drove away.

Oh, I was hurt.
I crawled off the fire escape and got in the bed with Donna and cried quietly.
I was scared, mad, confused. Donna and her brother told me that everything would be okay.
But I didn't want to talk to them. I felt if I weren't here I would know what's going on with my brother!
I threw the covers over my head and whimpered in the dark.
When I heard them snoring, I got up and tiptoed back into the living room.
I waited anxiously at the window in a daze, waiting to see my mother come back.
I never heard their dad come in. He was probably knocked out drunk.
I laid down on the fire escape with a blanket and a pillow. Something was seriously wrong; I felt it in my gut! But I was more hurt by the way she screamed at me then by what may be going on. I curled up in a ball, hurt and alone again. I cried myself to sleep feeling imprisoned by the cold iron grates.

Morning came. I put my shoes on and ran home. No one was there except for Boo.
I asked him where everyone was.
"Everyone is at the hospital!" he said.
"Why? What's wrong with Dennis?"
"I don't know yet. You'll have to wait till Mama comes home!"
I went in my room until I heard the door open and slam shut.
I ran into the living room and I stopped at the doorway because they were all crying. "What happened?" I asked.
No one answered me. Damn, I should have been at the hospital. "What's the matter?" I asked again. "And where is Dennis?"
Mom looked at me. "Just shut up Angel! Just shut up!"
I looked at her like she was crazy.
She screamed, "My son is dead! Oh my God!" than she collapsed.
Boo picked her up and placed her on their bed. Sharon, Sharon he called her as he smacked her awake. He yelled, "Get her a cold rag Missy."

I stood there in shock; my sisters were on the couch crying, hugging each other.

Mom Jumped up and started screaming louder, long screams calling out his name, Dennnnissssss, Dennnissssssss, and chills ran through my body.
I went in my room and I walked around trying to understand what 'dead' meant.
I went back to the living room and sat on the couch looking at everyone's reaction. Damn, I wouldn't ever see him again! No longer in existence!
I should have left Donna's house and helped him.
Wow, they were really crying a lot. I just stared.
"My son is dead!" she was screaming over and over. "My child is gone! Why God? Why! It's my fault! Oh God, it's all my fault!"
I didn't know why she was saying that! She told me later that because she didn't know CPR she lost him. He had died from a drug poisoning.

Mom began her grieving. Mom isolated in her bedroom for years.
Because of this tragedy I figured I wouldn't ever get any attention now. I was right. I didn't consider her lost of her mommy, her daddy now her only son, or her pain, her loneliness, I didn't consider she needed her mommy, she needed to be the baby, all I new was I was the baby and she never talked to me, she never held me, she never took me anywhere, she didn't laugh with me, where was my attention, where was my mommy?
I lost my virginity, my brother, my sisters, and now my mommy.
Depression, separation entered our hearts deeper then when we were apart.

CHAPTER FIVE

MY FIRST SUICIDE ATTEMPT

A year later…

I heard my name over the school intercom.
"Angel, please come to the office now!"
I looked at my teacher and she said, "Go ahead!"
I ran to the office feeling important to hear my name on the loud speaker. I know I didn't do anything wrong, so it had to be good.
A gray haired lady came to the counter. "Yes, may I help you?" she asked me.
"Yes! I'm Angel, you called for me?"
"Oh! Your mother called, she said you have to come home immediately."
"Why?"
"You just have to go home and see; here is your pass. You go straight home now okay?"
"Okay!"
I got my jean jacket out of my locker and put some of my books in it. Well, at least she got me out of class before the teacher gave out the homework.
I paused to think. What did I do that Mom would call me out of school?
I was thinking of everything I did or didn't do, wondering what she wanted.
Maybe the school told her something like me being caught kissing by the lockers yesterday during class.

I walked into the house and everyone was in the living room. Mom was busy splashing blue spots of paint all over the walls. My sisters were sitting down on the couch.
"Sit down Angel!"
I dropped my book bag and flopped down waiting for her to say something else.
She blew her nose and said, "Angel, your father is in the hospital and the doctor said he is very sick!"
"Sick from what?" I asked quickly.
"His liver is bad and something is wrong with his lungs!"
"Mom I want to go and see him."
"You can't; he's in Intensive Care and they don't allow kids in there!"
"I'm not a kid! I'm twelve almost thirteen," I yelled.
"You're still too young!"
"I want to see my daddy!" I ran into my room and slammed the door.

Mom spoke thru the door, "Were trying to get permission okay? I need you to stay here until we come back. I didn't want you to come home and not get in the house. We'll be back soon okay baby?"
I was determined to get in to see him. I just had to get there but it's far to the hospital.
Two days later when I got home from school mom said, "Baby come sit by me on the couch."
She looked like she was crying. She hugged me and cried some more.
I sat down and put my arms around her. "What's the matter Mommy?"
"Baby your..." she paused for what seemed like forever. "...Your father died today!"
"What? No! No! No!" I shook my head: "No! No! No! I didn't even get to see him!" I jumped up as she tried to hug me. "No, leave me alone, it's your fault I didn't get to say goodbye! You didn't even get him on the phone for me!" and I stomped away to my room and slammed the door.

My sisters came into the bedroom. I screamed at them both. "Get out! Just get out! Leave me alone!" I got up and pushed them out the door and slammed it and flopped onto my bed. I was so angry. My sisters better not say shit to me. Shit, they still have their dad!
I got up and walked around knocking their stuff off the dresser. I kicked their shoes around. I sat back down and pictured him there with me sitting on his lap. I saw his beautiful smile saying, "Angel, I'm still here!"
I didn't cry I wondered why? I knew I was getting angrier by the minute. Now I have no Dad or Mom I thought to myself. All she does is stay in her room all week and act like I don't exist. Then she acts a like a fool all weekend and I wish I didn't exist.

I went to the dreary funeral and looked at his stone face stiff like my brother, and my dog Boo kicked to death.
I looked at this large man stuffed in this small box, thinking, "That's not my Dad! He's all swollen; it looks like him but it's not him." I began poking him in the face. His face felt like leather. I pushed in his nose and it stayed in. I tried to fix it but it stayed in. I was so surprised how hard and cold his face and hands were.
I hadn't touched my brother; I had just looked, numb.
I was intrigued; I wasn't mourning because it still wasn't real to me.
I never saw him in a suit before. This was not my dad! There were no feelings. It couldn't be him! I wasn't excepting this at all. It was just someone who looked a little like him! It was just a clay dummy in a suit. My Dad will come back to see me!

I kept looking at him, standing there by his head with my hand touching the pretty marble coffin, wishing my sheets and pillow were as white and

clean and fluffy as his. People just passed by me looking at him. I wasn't moving.
I looked around at everyone. I told myself this had to be him! Why was all his family here crying? I'd never seen most of these people who are they?
Wow that really is him I thought, so I guess this is goodbye daddy!
That's when I tried to take off his onyx and gold ring so I could have something tangible to remember him by. My brother kept the one dad gave him to give me even though I said to him, "No it's my ring!" He probably sold it to buy drugs; it had disappeared from his neck. He said he lost it. I hated him for that shit! Than mom said it was meant for her. Dad didn't want her man Boo to get jealous.
So he really didn't give me anything. I had nothing, not even a picture of him!
I wasn't even asked to go to his house with mom. Maybe we would have found something that I could hold on to when I missed him.
Nothing! I had nothing!

I looked at my sister Missy and thought, what the hell is you crying for?
I had to have it.
But it wouldn't come off! I pulled really hard and I didn't care who was looking; this was going to be my ring.
That's when my tears started filling up in my eyes; they just appeared, pouring down uncontrollably. Someone sat me down. I cried quietly.
If anyone was trying to comfort me and hug me I didn't feel it. I was numb and getting angrier, feeling the despair as I watched tears fall on my shiny black skirt.
I looked at my finger and it sank in; I wouldn't be getting that ring.

He had a veteran's twenty-one-gun service that I didn't understand. It scared the shit out of me when they started shooting those guns, couldn't someone have warned me?
I saw them fold up the flag from his coffin and give it to his mom.
I pulled my mom's arm. "Mom! Mom! I want my dad's flag!"
She pulled down my pointed finger and said quietly, "Shush! Sorry baby, but it goes to his mother." His mother was being pushed around in a wheel chair.
I didn't even get to hug her hello or goodbye. I guess it wasn't important, neither to her nor to me.

Oh I hated watching the grown ups drinking and eating and laughing after the funeral.
"What the fuck is so damn funny? My father is gone! He's DEAD!" I yelled and ran back in my room.

Mom came in the room and said, "Baby, your dad is with God in heaven. Now he will be happy because he won't ever feel pain again, no more suffering and he will live forever in peace. We're just remembering the good times with him baby. I loved your father with all of my heart!"
"Death sounds better than life, Mom!" and I rolled over and hugged my tear-soaked pillow, wiping the snot on my sleeve.

My memories of my dad were short. The happiest one is when I went down south to North Carolina for two weeks on the farm and met his full-blooded Cherokee Indian mother.
She proudly showed me the picture of her grandfather and his father, a Chief, in full headdress and paint. They looked so nice it was so beautiful.
I was so proud to be me. I am a great granddaughter of an Indian Chief, who was born on a Cherokee reservation.
While I was there I ate candy canes and learned how to milk a cow and ate grits and gravy with smothered pork chops for breakfast for the first time.

The memory I wish I could forget is the day I went to visit him. He had an apartment in the Bronx, in the basement where he was the super for a year.
My two sisters Missy and Tina took me to see him. I was so happy; I hadn't seen my dad since that week after I came home. I was going on twelve, still skinny as a pole and as light as a bulb.
I jumped up into my daddies' great big body and his greater-than-life hands were stretched out to me. He was smiling his bright smile.
I hugged my daddy and I didn't want to let go.
He peeled me off to hug my sisters. I rolled my eyes and flopped down in the chair by the wall and leaned against it. We were there for about a half an hour sitting in his kitchen.
"So, how are all my beautiful girls doing today?" he asked while tickling me.
I smiled. Don't keep calling 'us' your girls, I thought. I'm your girl!
The apartment was so small; the living room was too small for all of us to sit down so we sat at his square yellow table that matched the dingy yellow walls. It was a cute little apartment for a single man.
I liked the mess it looked like my room. I told him all about school and my friends.
Dad had on a dirty blue T-shirt like he had been working in oil. I could see his muscles through the shirt. I was so proud to have such a big, fine daddy.
Missy was 17 then. She is short, skinny and pretty, with long hair and light skin. She always wore dresses; she was always saying she was a lady. She was a good girl, never in trouble. Tina is two years older than

her and Missy is five years older than me. Tina was built nicely, very shapely. She had a short haircut that made her sort of mean looking but she was sweet as pie.
I noticed some red juice stains on the table.
"Dad, do you have some kool-aid?"
"No, baby, I'm all out." He was drinking something red; it must have been wine.
"Tina, take my little Angel to the store across the street and buy her a blouse and some soda. You girls want some soda?"
"Yeah I do!" Missy said. "I want a Pepsi!"
"Yeah! That's my dad! He's going to buy me a shirt!" They have their own dad I thought to myself. Their daddy can buy their own shirt.
I was excited; it'd been a while since I had something new and not my sisters' hand-me-downs.

When we went outside I started skipping, trying to hurry to the corner to cross the street.
I could see the all the stores right there across the street in the Bronx on the Grand Concourse.
"Wait for me Angel! I'm the one with the money!" said Tina laughing.
I was thinking maybe a red or pink blouse, no blue or maybe yellow, yeah!
Out ran Missy screaming. "Wait! Wait, Tina!"
We looked back. She was running wild, wiggling in her shoes. "Stop! Wait!" she hollered.
"What? Tina asked. "What is wrong with you girl, why are you running?"
Missy grabbed Tina's hand. "He, he, he tried to rape me!"
"What?" Tina said. "Who? Dad?" They also called him 'Dad.' "No way!" looking surprised and confused.
A noisy lady was standing on the corner and she looked back at us and stared. I gave her a nasty look. "What are you looking at?" She turned and crossed the street.
I was confused; why was she saying this about my daddy? I knew she is just jealous!
"He wouldn't do that!" I shouted. "Don't say that about my father you liar!"
Missy started crying. "I'm not lying!"
"What did he do?" Tina asked, looking mad.
Missy with her asthma-breathing ass said, "He started kissing me, then he tried to pull my panties down."
I looked at her in disbelief. I was furious, "No he didn't you liar! Why are you saying that?"
I truly believed she had concocted this story because she was jealous. He was going to buy me a shirt and not her. She always thought that she was

his favorite child, even though she wasn't actually his, so I knew he wouldn't do anything to hurt her.
She rolled her eyes at me and continued acting all emotional with Tina.

Everything went silent. I didn't hear the car horns or people talking, just quiet.
I started walking away with my head down. Than I just ran. They had to run after me because I didn't know my way home.
We got back on the train; none of us said a word.
I looked at my sister like I wanted to scratch her eyes out. That moment I hated her.
I didn't even get to say good-bye to my dad or tell him what she accused him of. I wanted to hear his side of what happened. Why didn't I run back in the house? My eyes watered through my angry piercing tears. I don't believe her and I didn't even get my new shirt.
Mom said dad was sick and was going into the hospital. She said he though Missy was mom. She assured us he would never hurt Missy. His mind was going from his war experiences and drinking.
I wish I had better memories dad but you never did anything with me other than that. I loved you so much. I needed you so much!
Dads mean the world to their kids, especially girls and they just don't know how much. If they did, maybe they would realize that 95% of the kids that try to take their own life, or are always in some trouble, are yearning for a closer relationship with their dad.

Is that what Cyris is crying out for? How can I make Chris spend time with him?

I wanted some damn attention. Mom stayed in her bed all week and I hardly saw my sisters, my brother and now my father was dead!
I felt so alone and unloved. I was dating this boy who was always cheating on me with my friend Diane. He started spreading rumors that Diane and I were more than friends, that we were lovers. I became too embarrassed to go outside. I had no one to talk to, no one to scream at or beat on, no little sister or brother to take my frustrations out on. I was totally isolated and I cried myself to sleep many nights.
I was now13, the unlucky age. I felt all alone and unwanted, unloved. I just hated what life was offering.
I went under my mom's kitchen cabinet and found whatever said, "Poison! Do not swallow! Can cause DEATH!"
I mixed up some Comet cleanser, ammonia, bleach and water into a cup. I drank it all. It made my eyes squint and it burned the shit out my throat. I laid down thinking, "Wow! I am going to die. I will be in Paradise, living in peace, and looking at beautiful things. No more tears or pain! I'll see my brothers and my daddy!"

But all I ended up with was a bad stomachache.

Unsatisfied with my first attempt, I found a sure fire way to succeed.
I held it up to the light and said, "Hmmm, this bullet should do the job!" So I swallowed it and I waited for it to travel inside my body to a place of no return. I waited for it to explode in my stomach but it never did. I was told if a bullet goes into your stomach you'd die. It didn't work.
The next week I was still sad. The alcohol I was sneaking in wasn't helping, so I slept a lot to escape into darkness.
I had to end this miserable life!

One day, I looked in the medicine cabinet but I saw nothing I could use to help me die.
I can't fail this time I thought. I have to show her how much her ignoring me hurt me. She'll realize once I'm gone. I looked on top of Mom's dresser when she went to the welfare office and I found medication that said, 'For Sleeping.' There had to be about 60 pills. Finally, I'll fall a sleep and never wake up! A nice painless way to go! I laid down across my bed and named everyone I wanted to say goodbye to and fell asleep.
Obviously, I woke up the next day; the next night I should say. I slept since 12:00 noon to 12:30 am the next night, and mom never even knew! I was so disappointed to wake up so I went back to sleep.
The next day I decided I would camouflage my sadness into a clown's playground. With my artificial smile and my phony laughter I continued to live a regretful life, never getting rid of my compressed anger, sadness.

Neither mom nor my sisters ever knew what my heart has been through and how close they were to losing me. I couldn't do anything right! 'If a person really wants to die they will succeed' is not true. If you're a beginner and are ignorant or if it's just not your time, then nothing will work.
No one was watching me. Teenagers need to be watched! Talked to! Hugged and inspired to live or they die inside from sadness! It's hard to live a life of despair with no support; it destroys the Sprit.
But it's even harder to come back to life when you live with dead people.

CHAPTER SIX
ABANDONED IN NEW YORK CITY

Brooklyn streets are so big!
"Oh, these flowers are so pretty! What kind is that Mom?"
Diane was in awe. "Ooh, this Botanical Garden is so beautiful. I'm going to come here every day now that we only live five blocks away. This is great!" She looked at my mom. "Can I come and move with you here Ms. Sharon?"
"Sure Diane, what will your mom say?"
"She always says as long as I'm with you, she don't worry about me!"
"Okay Diane but you will have to go to school here."

We became inseparable. I even gave her my one of my new boyfriends. I was tired of him so I took her right to his door, introduced them and walked away, it was easy because I never gave him a shot.
People called us "Salt and Pepper." She was cute, with clear brown skin and a big ass, chinky eyes, small breast large mouth. I was the opposite; light skin and little ass, large breast, big brown eyes and small tiny lips. Together we would sing our asses off! I sounded a little like Natalie Cole, and she sounded like Patti Label. I was the dance chorographer. a damn good one too! I'd say, "Come on, let's go to the Apollo to Amateur Night." I was confident they would like us.
One day we were singing 'Sweet Thing' by Chaka Khan watching ourselves in the mirror in my large bedroom. It had turned out nice since Tina came home from the army and has put all of her stuff in it. There was her color TV, a stereo, some lamps, and a thick purple and blue quilt. I didn't mind the intrusion as long as she understood that this it was my room. I enjoyed lying back at night listening to "Summer Madness," by Kool-n-a-Gang, gazing into a blue light bulb. It was so relaxing.

"Come on, girl, we can do this!"
"No!" Diane said. "I'm not going to be able to sing in front of all those people! What if they boo us? Ooh hell, no!" She wrapped a black cotton scarf around her head to the back into a bun.
I was jumping up and down on the bed saying, "Let's get paid chicken shit!"
Mom yelled. "Come in the living room Angel and Diane!"
"Were coming" I lit a cigarette. At fourteen, I had permission to smoke. She just said that I was going to do it anyway.
We walked out of my bedroom into the living room and I sat on the arm of the chair.

“Get off my chair like that!” Mom yelled.
I flopped in the small gray seat with my legs dangling over the arms. I put the ashtray on the floor.
Mom was excited. “I’m going to go to work in the mountains upstate New York with Diane’s sister and her husband! Missy and Tina will look after you two. Tina will pay the bills; I’ll send her the money every month, and Missy will be right down stairs if you need her.”
Softly I asked, “Exactly when are you going mom?”
“In a few days! They’re going back upstate and I’ll be riding back with them!”
I looked at her surprised “So soon? When will you come back?”
“I’m not coming back! But I will send for you as soon as I get an apartment!”
“Send for me? Oh really! Okay is that it? Can I go now?” I walked out of the house. Diane grabbed our coats and followed me.
“Angel come back here!” mom yelled.

I ran down the stairs stomping and jumping two, three steps at a time. Outside in front of the building I was screaming. “She’s just going to up and leave just like that! She’s never worked a day since I was born and now when I need her she’s leaving!”
I just started going to a new high school. I had finally got into the classes I wanted, typing and cosmetology. Two more years and I’ll graduate! Shit, she wasn’t at my middle school graduation! Why did I think she’d be here for my high school one?
I had new friends! I even had a girl who uses to bully me befriended me! My neighbor Kim, who I knew from the Bronx, she was the one who burned my ear with a match because I wouldn’t come outside and play with her. And she was the one that encouraged me to stay in school.

“Mom never cared about me!” I said to Diane, as I paced in front of the building. “I hate her! I hate her ass!” I screamed while puffing the cigarette and blowing out hard.
“Don’t say that Angel!”
“Why do she have to leave now? We just got here! She’s selfish! She’s just thinking about herself!”
“Don’t say that Angel you don’t mean that! You should go back up there and talk to her!”
“And say what Diane? ‘Mommy, please don’t leave me?’ Fuck that! She can go wherever she wants to go! I don’t need her! She already took the job. She made her decision, so I will make a decision for myself. I’ll do exactly what I want to do! Fuck her, I hope I never see her again!”
“You don’t mean that!”

"Oh yes I do! Yes I do!" I was furious. I buttoned up the black leather coat Diane handed to me and waved, "Come on, let's go to the club house and get high!"
I tried acid that night. I wanted to fly far away. That wasn't for me though so I started smoking weed daily.
Mom left, and so in defiance I quit school. I needed pleasure for my pain, not work.
One night, Diane and I were going to go to a club in Manhattan. We bounced from Brooklyn to Manhattan, to the Bronx to Queens, like it was nothing. I was in front of the mirror doing 'the bus stop,' but I made up some different moves and I added a freeze. We practiced our hustle moves. I was a born dancer.
"Shit Diane, I should be a dance choreographer. People are going to love to watch us tonight!"

She had on a black silk shirt, jeans and short black boots. She never wore makeup, just lip-gloss. Not me; I packed it on. I had a white scarf twisted around my head and a white silk shirt, a short black skirt and black heels. We had our moves, our fake ID's, and some cash we made from braiding hair. We were ready.
"Come on, I'm ready!" Diane said.
"Okay, let me grab my coat."
Tina came into the hallway yelling, "Where do you think you're going miss?"
"Out!"
"Out where miss?"
"Just out!"
"No you're not!"
I sucked my teeth and looked at her like she was crazy. I turned to go down the stairs, and she had the audacity to grab me by the arm and pull me back up. "No you're not! It's too late for you to be running the streets! It's after 11:00 and you have on too much make up! Look at that skirt, it's too damn short! Take it off!" She was screaming at me, judging me up and down.
I grabbed her by the neck with one hand and ran her against the wall. I lifted her off her feet and said, "Leave me alone, you're not my mother! You can't tell me what to do!" I was mad as shit. I wanted to beat her senseless.
I just held her there up in the air, gritting my teeth. She was turning red and so was I. I watched as she gasped for air.
"Are you going to leave me alone?" I asked.
She tried to move my hand but I was holding her up higher, with my other fist balled up. I yelled again. "Are you going to leave me alone?"
I let her go and ran down the stairs in case she did some of that army shit she learned. Damn, I didn't know I was that strong. She walked back into

the house. She never attempted to stop me again. Eventually she left, moved out! I don't know where she went, probably back to the army!

Missy was down stairs in her apartment catching hell from her abusive baby's daddy. I didn't know how bad it was until later. I never bothered her. I just went to play with her baby now and then, until Missy punched me in my back with all of her might because I wouldn't listen to her either. So to avoid punching her ninety-five pound ass into another planet, I stayed away. Diane and I can take care of our own fourteen-year old asses.

Everyday we would hop the train to Coney Island Play land, where we flirted for free rides. I loved the 'Hellhole' where you stand up strapped to a wall shaped in a circle and it goes around fast, so fast, and then the floor falls out from under your feet. Little did I know that was the beginning of a hellhole of a life, with some blessings added in?

Even in my dreams there was no peace. I was always dreaming about some scary shit like snakes and big ugly bugs coming after me. Oftentimes, we didn't have any food so I had sex a few times with the man who owned a store so I could get some grub.

Old English 800, a type of malt liquor and weed came freely to my house; it became the 'Hang Out house'. At the end of the day my legs would hurt so badly. I didn't know why. I would rock and kick and rub my legs on the cold walls and cry myself to sleep and it would start all over again the next day.

We would sleep all day, hang out all night till daybreak, stumbling home, giggling and throwing up, falling to sleep on the floors, at someone's house or on the train.

I was dating a guy name Damon for about a month. He was a friend of my sister's boyfriend from child hood Mike. He would come to my house to play cards and kiss me. I liked the way he smelled. I loved kissing him. His tongue was perfect rolling in my mouth; he was a short, cute chocolate man. The sex was great. He was my first chocolate boyfriend.

I say "man" because he was twenty-one, and I was only fourteen but I lied and told him that I was eighteen. We did it twice.

"Come over my house with me tonight Angel, come see my crib," he said.

"Okay! Diane I'll see you later! You going anywhere?"

"No! I'm going to chill out here and play spades, get high with the squad here!"

"Okay, then watch the crib. I'll be back in a few hours" as I giggled out the door.

"It's Saturday night and I'm going to hang out with my baby," I was singing.
He was a black belt. I was a green belt myself; I never finished anything!
We had a lot of fun on the subway, kickboxing and slapping each other in the face.
"Oh this is a cute crib," I said when we got to his place. Mike was with us but I hoped he was leaving!
Mike said, "I'm going to get something to drink for us. I'll be right back!"
"Okay!" Damon said.
They were talking over by the door while I lit up a joint and walked around, being noisy.
Mike was real tall, light and not too bright. He was cute with curly soft hair and a nice conceited smile with dimples. He dressed real nice like most young men over eighteen did in 1974.

Damon came and sat on the black leather love seat, looking good in a black sweater, tight black jeans, and cowboy boots and hat to match. I was walking around checking out his African art pictures on the wall.
"Pass the joint!" he said.
I kept some weed. To me weed went better with sex. I just felt more sensual.
I laid back on the couch listening to 'Hey Girl' by The Temptations. I was feeling really romantic.
We started slow grinning to the song and he started kissing me. He got hard quick.
Mike came back with some fat guy. I don't even remember what he said his name was. I wasn't interested either. Why is he here? I thought. Damn, you two have to go!
"We're just going to have one drink and were leaving!" said Mike.
"Well okay! Barcardi and Coke," I said as they pulled out the bottle. That's all my mom drank so that became my favorite too.
I drank mine down as we laughed about the man on the train with holes in the toes of his shoes in the winter snow.
"I know his ass was cold!" I said, as I laughed a stupid giggle. Then I blacked out.

When I opened my eyes, Damon was on top of me just pounding away. I looked at him, then I closed my eyes and realized, wait, this hurts. Come to think about it, I don't remember taking off my pants. Shit, I'm naked! Let me see, we were dancing and kissing and… damn, my head hurts. Maybe I had too much to drink, maybe the weed had dust in it or something, I held my head as he breathed harder and pounding harder, like he was coming and I never got started.

I was dry and he was hurting my tight noncompliant pussy. My leg was all the way up in the air, as he stood up on the edge of the bed. Then I heard someone say, "Hurry up man, it's my turn!"
I turned to look and there was Mike in his draws, and the fat unknown fuck too in his underwear. I pushed Damon off of me.
I pulled up my pants fast as I could. I was shocked, shocked especially at Mike.
"How could you?" I screamed. "I'm like family! Your supposed to watch my back, not stab me in it! Damon! How could you do this to me? This is what you think of me? What the fuck! You all were going to run a train on me? And you Damon; I can't believe this shit; you were going to get it any way. You were going to share me with that man?" I pointed in disgust. "Who the fuck is he anyway?"
That shocked, stupid fat fuck said, "The pill was suppose to last longer!"
"What!" I stretched out my arms in anger: "You mother-fuckers drugged me? What, with some date rape shit? I don't believe this shit!" I'd heard of it. I knew not to put my drink down in clubs because I heard that's what happens. But I never thought it would happen to me.
I pulled down my sweater. I couldn't find my bra or my boots. I just grabbed my black leather coat, picked up my panties and put them in my pocket and I ran out the door. As I ran down the two fights of steps I heard Mike saying over the balusters from the third floor, "Wait! Wait Angel let me talk to you! Wait!"
"Fuck you!" I screamed. I ran to the train station about four blocks away. I kept looking back afraid they were going to stop me. I ran faster holding my coat closed with my shaken hands.

I was so relieved that I had a token. But even more relieved when the train came and they weren't behind me.
Doors please hurry up and close. I stood there holding the rail tight, shaking and crying; waiting for my stop. Through my red watery eyes I saw people staring at me. Kids were laughing at me now with no shoes on.
I ran so fast, I didn't even feel the cold snow soaking through my socks. I was so heated I probably melted it because my socks were soaked. I ran in the house out of breath.
"What happened Angel?" Diane asked anxiously.
I screamed at Diane, "Come on, we have to go down stairs and get Missy I'll tell you both!"
I ran into the bedroom and put my sneakers on. I was mad as shit. I have these raggedy ass sneakers with holes. Mom never sent me any money, not a damn dime for clothes, food, nothing! We ran down the stairs and banged on Missy's door. Then I told my sister and Diane what happened.

I went under her cabinet and got out the can of lye. I poured it into a large mayonnaise jar with some coke soda. I put it carefully in a paper bag!
"Let's roll out!" I said angrily. They grabbed their coats and Diane grabbed a butcher knife and back to the house we went.
I was huffing and puffing, I wanted blood! I was contemplating what I wanted to do to them for degrading me. I wondered which one of them concocted this up. Who and when did they have this discussion, back at my house, at his apartment, at the door?
Devastated and furious, I was cursing them out in my mind with premeditated murder in my heart. I wanted them dead! But I'd settle for burned up pricks!
I began questioning myself. Did I present myself to be loose or stupid? Were they expecting me to be accepting and participating if I woke up? Oh, I wanted my sister to leave that bastard and I intended to cut off my so-called boyfriends prick! I'll burn it off! Yeah! That's the target!
We were quiet on the train. Diane tried to pull my hair down in place. I looked like I just ran out a bed. Well I guess I did.
I was glad I paid attention on how to get to his place. I thought I would surprise him someday and he'd find me there after work ready for him. I never thought I would need to know so I could kill his ass.
Why did they do that to me? My eyes stared watering. But my anger wouldn't allow me to cry now, not yet!

I banged on the door; we heard voices. "Open the door!" I yelled. They got quiet, like they wanted us to believe they weren't in there. Missy said with her soft voice, "Mike, I know you're in there; open the damn door now!"
I started kicking the door and Diane joined me. "This door is going to open one-way or another!" I screamed.
Damon opened the door and looked at us like, "what you want?" The fat man was gone. They tried to say it didn't happen like that.
"You was drunk Angel and you wanted to have sex with Damon. We was just watching," said Mike.
"Oh, your ass wasn't sitting on the edge of the bed in your damn draws waiting for your turn?" Damon stood there like he couldn't speak.
"You mother fuckers, you two disrespected me!" I opened the jar of lye and said. "This just didn't happen either!" and I threw the acid in Damon's face.
He coved his face. "What's is that shit? My face is burning!" He started screaming. "What did you pour on me bitch?" He tried to wipe his face with his shirt.

I threw some at Mike but he jumped out of the way.

Diane stood behind him and put the knife to Damon's throat. "You burn bitch!" she whispered in his ear. "No water for your eyes! Fuck you!"

I went over to the bed and poured lye all over it. "Now you can sleep on the bed you raped me on, you bastard!" I splashed it around so I could save some for more destruction. I kicked the cat. "Move your ass before you get some of this wrath!" I poured it on the couch but the damn leather wouldn't burn like I wanted it to. I became even more frustrated and started throwing shit at them, causing major destruction.

"Now pull down your pants!" I looked at Damon. "Pull them down! Now! Mother-fucker pull out your dick or she's going to cut your ass!"

Damon started begging. "Please stop! I'm sorry, you made your point!"

I was enraged. "I've just begun! Now take that shit out!"

"No Angel, I rather you burn me anywhere else!" he cried, grabbing his shit with both hands tight.

He knew all the karate in the world wasn't going to save his ass from these three angry women and the lye in my shaking hands.

My four-foot tall sister was looking up at her six-foot tall man, trying to curse him out but since she usually didn't curse she sounded funny.

"I hope you die! Bitch ass fuck! And you'd better not come back to my house either fucker! You stay here and live with his trifling ass!" pointing at Damon. "I'm finished with your sick, sneaky ass. How could you do that to my sister? You're a sick fucker, you mother fucker, don't come around me! That's it Mike it's over between us, you hear me?"

He tried to hold her. "Come on baby wait that's not what happened!" he said softly.

She pulled away. "Don't think you can kiss me and make this shit up either! That's my sister you hurt!"

I was proud of her. I loved her; she had my back!

She pointed her little baby-size finger, screaming with her asthma-riddled voice. "You call if you want to see your child but not for a while! I might kill your ass!" She backed up near Diane who waved the knife she never used.

"I don't care where you burn me at but you're not burning my shit!" Damon yelled.

"Diane he made his choice, cut his fucking throat!" I said. But Diane was shaking and wouldn't cut him.

"Cut his ass!" I screamed. "Cut him now! Fuck it, give me the knife." But he jumped out at Diane to grab her, so I threw some lye on his pants. He backed up to look. The shit still didn't burn through!

There was none left. I was pissed but I knew I better get out while I was ahead!

As I backed up I screamed, pointing at them, "You bitches are crying now!" I opened the door and imitated them. "'Please stop! Please don't!

I'm still going to get someone to shoot your asses! Don't ever come around my way ever again Damon!"
I turned to the girls. "Come on let's go before there be chalk marks where his body is!"

CHAPTER SEVEN

I MET CHRIS

"Look Angel!" Diane said.

"Damn!" I said. "What are we going to do now?"

There was a big pad lock on our apartment door. "I guess the rent didn't get paid," I laughed. "We can't even sneak in now! I should've known something was up when mom sent for her shit!"

"Our clothes are in there! I'm ready to break this shit open!"

"With what Diane?"

"Angel, isn't there any way we could break in? Maybe we can find someone with one of them lock breaker thingies. Well, if we get some carfare, we can go to my youngest sister's house in the Bronx. I don't want to go to my moms house!"

"Okay, so where are we going to get some more money from?"

She thought for a minute. "In the morning I'll ask the pimp that lives next door. They'll be back by then!"

My current boyfriend had gone into the Army so I couldn't get any money there and the others were all broke. The other option was to wait until one of their payday.

"Okay I guess we'll have to wait. Well goodnight!" We balled up in the corner under the steps and used our coats for a blanket and arms for pillows.

"You want to ask the neighbor if we can stay there for a few days?"

"Hell no! I'm too ashamed and too proud to ask anyone for shit. We'll be fine! Come here and let me keep you warm!" She pushed her big ass against me and I held her from behind. I laid my face on her back, trying to keep my face warm for a few hours of sleep; it was already after 4am in mid-November.

We had to hold one another for comfort and warmth, in order to tough it out in that hallway for about a week. That's how long it took for some dude to hook us up enough cash so we could figure out our next move. We couldn't stay with her sister; shit, her sister couldn't stay in her own house because her jealous man was whipping on her ass so she ran away.

We used our girlfriend's bathroom or the pimp's to wash up. We got some clothes from the girlfriends we didn't mind getting clothes from. All the shit we had given them in the past to look good, they owed us.

I wasn't going to let them know we were homeless; I just told them we couldn't get to our shit right now!

"Come on Diane, let's go to the Bronx and see one of moms' friends. Maybe I can get some money from her and we can stay there for a few days. She's good people! She works for the telephone company; she makes cheese. She'll hook us up with some pocket change so we can at least eat or maybe she'll break bread like Jesus did! Either way the trip will be worth it!

"She was giving me $5 a day to go to school when I was staying with her one time, between mom's many moves. Eventually, her husband raped me and I had to leave."

Diane shook her head from side-to-side. "Damn Angel!"

We made our way to the Bronx. Mrs. Jean opened her door and stood there in her black valor pants set. She was short, dark, with long black hair down to her shoulders covering her big cheeks.

She smiled. "Hi Angel, isn't this a coincidence!"

"Really, why? Diane! This is Mrs. Jean: Mrs. Jean, this is my best friend Diane!"

"Hi Mrs. Jean!"

"Hi Diane, come on in and have a seat!"

We followed her inside. "Angel I'm glad you came by. Your mom called me just last night. She wants you to come and live with her."

"What? She called you last night?"

"Yeah, she told me she wants you to come home to her now!"

We went and sat down on her plastic-covered couch. I grew to hate that damn plastic shit. I still cringe at the sound. Everyone wants to preserve their shit; they should take such care in preserving their children.

I looked at Diane and said nothing!

Mrs. Jean spoke first. "I will give you the bus fare if you want to go!"

I responded fast. "What about Diane? She needs bus fare too, she's going with me!"

"I'll get her a ticket too!"

I looked at Diane. "Do you want to go Upstate New York and see what's up?"

"Yeah I'm wit it, let's check it out!"

I looked at her seriously. "If I don't like it I'm coming back to the city. I'll live in the street before I live with her madness I'm telling you! I do have a few boyfriends that want me here!"

"Hey, you can come to my sister's trailer with me if it doesn't work out!"

"How you know that's an option?"

"She'll let us sleep anywhere; she'll make room and probably get us a job too."

"Really? Okay lets go tomorrow! You have my mom's number?" I didn't even have her number. She could have at least written me. Shit it's been almost a year.

"Yes I do Angel, let me go get it!"

I hung up the phone and turned to Diane. "Okay, I spoke with mom and I have all the information. I told her we're coming tomorrow! We're going to stay here with you tonight; is that okay?"
"Yes sure! I'll pull out the couch and get some sheets; there are some hamburgers in the kitchen!"
"Bet I'm starving!" Diane said with no shame to her game, she was hungry no doubt, and me too.
"I'll help you make the bed Ms. Jean."

I made up the bed and yelled to Diane. "Hook me up a sandwich!" We ate and went right to sleep. It's been a while since we had a good night's sleep without jumping or worrying about who was coming up the stairs. My back was hurting. I needed a good hot bath soaking everything but sleep was calling me.
We were knocked out cold. We didn't wake up until after three o'clock in the afternoon the next day.
Mrs. Jean came in the room. "Damn you two sure were tired! I didn't want to wake you!"
I yawned and stretched and ran into the bathroom laughing and singing, "Ha, ha, me first. Hey Diane, cook me something to eat while I take my shower!"
" Who do you think I am?" she asked me.
"You're my bitch, now do like I tell you! I'm hungry!"
I came out the bathroom. "Oh I'm sorry Mrs. Jean, I thought you was still in your room. I didn't see you come back out! Mrs. Jean, we need a washcloth and towel!" I got in Dianes' face and kissed her on her mouth. "Now feed me!"
She laughed. "Shut up! I'm hungry too so I will cook us some cheese eggs!"
"That's great and toast and a lot of butter and I have to have my butter melted and a tiny bit of jelly."
"Oh, so now you want to tell me how to cook! You can do it yourself!"
"Have my food ready for me when I get out woman!" I hit her with my towel on her big ass.
"You want something to eat too Mrs. Jean?" Diane asked.
"Yes baby it will be nice to have someone cook for me for a change!"

It was about five o'clock when we finished eating. "We hate to eat and run but we want to head out since it's a four-hour ride," I said to Mrs. Jean. "It's going to be late when we get there. I called the bus station and the bus leaves at six, so let's pick up something for the road."
Diane looked at me. "Angel, you sure you want to go to the Mountains?"
"Well, I don't have anywhere else to go right now. I can't stay here. So I'll go check it out!"

We took the Greyhound bus out of Manhattan into Kerhonkson, New York. Diane's oldest sister had a trailer next to my mom's; they all worked together at the same hotel.
Welcome to the boonies, I thought. We got to Kerhonkson, Upstate New York and the bus driver said, "This is it!" The door squeezed open slowly.
"Where are the streetlights?" I asked. I couldn't see shit! Nothing!
He laughed behind me as I slowly walked down the stairs. It was pitch black. I wasn't going to front I was a little scared. I couldn't even see my hands in front of my face! I heard crickets and something in the trees moving. I heard howling. We were the only ones getting off!
I looked back at the driver. "You're not going to leave us here in these dark ass woods are you?" I stood in the doorway blocking it from closing. "Excuse me sir, umm… where do we go? There's nothing here!"
"Just go down the road for about a half a mile. There' s a cabstand and a phone!"
Diane looked at him. "How long is a half a mile sir? Like, how many blocks would that be?"
"Well, it would be about three long New York City blocks okay?"
"Okay thanks but could you like drop us off there instead?"
The bus driver laughed at her. "No mama! I am going to make a U turn and go back on the expressway. You'll be fine; just walk straight down that road!" The doors closed in my face and he pulled off.

Diane and I held hands for fear of what would jump out those dark trees. "Damn, haven't they ever heard of street lamps?" she asked, squeezing my hand. "Oh, my!" We sang and laughed, skipped and we ran some to get there quicker because we were really cold and scared. "I'll race you!" "Bet!" And we ran to the cabstand out of breath.

A gray haired Jewish lady who looked about seventy-five was sitting in the corner, sipping something hot in a smoking cup. The cabstand was a small 12-by-12 shack filled with paper.
The cowbells that were hanging over the door rang as we opened it. She jumped up and came dragging her long flowered dress over to the counter, "Can I help you girls?"
"Yes Ms. we need a cab to the Deeds trailer park. How much will that be?"
"That will be ten dollars!"
I looked at Diane. "Damn that's all I have left is ten dollars; well at least we'll get there!" I looked at the lady and said, "Okay let's go! Where's the driver?"
"Oh, you have to wait about fifteen minutes; he'll be back!"
"What, you only have one driver?"

"No we have two but Vinny is off tonight and Joe will be back soon! Grab yourselves a chair!"

"Diane you got some change to get a soda out of the machine for us to share?"
"Yeah, here!" She was shaking, trying to be cute in her short black leather jacket.
Desiring the lady's hot drink instead I whispered, "She could share that little heater she has by her feet! Shit it's freezing in here!"

"Hi Mom, we made it!" I looked around the trailer. "Well now this is cozy! This trailer is really nice mom!"
Diane nodded. "You always could hook up a crib Mrs. Sharon!"
Mom hugged me long and tight. "Put your bags in the first room to your right baby!" She hugged Diane tight also. "How are you?"
"Damn," I whispered, "look at this closet-sized room!" It had a small bed, a closet, a lamp, a dresser and that's it! Only three people could stand in there and it would be crowded.
I put my bags down and went back out into the front room. Mom smiled. "Angel, this is George!"
"Hi!" I extended my hand to shake his. He looked young; he was short and skinny with his pants hanging off his ass. It looked like there was food hanging off his wild growing mustache. He was very handsome though, with soft curly hair and smooth brown skin.
Moms' boyfriend I thought to myself. He gets to have a home with her before me? Resentments grew as I stood there thinking; while I was cold you were warm? While I was hungry, my mom fed you? While I was homeless, you had a home? While I had no money, you both had jobs, living large? I hate you already!
"Nice to meet you George!" I smiled a fake smile as I shook his hand.
He stood there looking like he was someone's child and needed to be told what to do next. He was perfect for mom's controlling man-beating ass. Yeah just her type!
"Damn how old are you?" I asked boldly.
"I'm twenty-seven!"
"Are you serious?"
"Yeah, what, you don't believe me?"
"Damn mom you got yourself a young buck!" I had to comment. Damn near half her age though!
His mouth dropped open. "You're more beautiful than your picture!"
I looked at this possible pervert. "Thanks," but I was thinking, yeah he'll be pushing up on me.
"Your mother talks about you all the time!"
"Yeah that's nice!" He was way too young for her but who was I to say anything?

"We're going next door now to see Diane's sister. We'll be back!"
We went to smoke some weed. We knew her sister would have some.
There wasn't much I had to say to my mom. I ended up pretty much spending a lot of time at Diane's sister's trailer or in my room trying to get a word in with God.
I read some of the Bible every night but I don't think he heard me because I was still alive.

Two weeks later;
I was sitting at the dinning table facing the window by the front door reading. I had argued with my mom about not going to the all white-school on their yellow bus; it wasn't for me. I was from New York City and we never rode like that!
"I'm not getting on no cheesy bus with a bunch of wild and crazy white teenagers. You're crazy mom; I'm sorry but I'm not going. I'll most likely be the only light skinned girl there and you know they don't like us light skinned people because we remind them of their rapist history as we read their books." I had convinced myself that avoiding them was more important than using them.
My first act of predictive: knowing we were in the Klan's territory. I really feared what I read.
I went back to reading, "The Bluest Eyes," by Toni Morrison. I understood wanting blue eyes so bad from the lead character, a young black misguided girl. She wanted something that she perceived would make her beautiful. To look at something else, to distract people from seeing her black-as-night, talked-about skin… the author is a talented, profound and explorative woman. I began to appreciate books.
I realized what I perceived as beautiful was golden brown tropical color, smooth and clear skin. That was what I wanted very much, to wake up one day and look in the mirror and see that I had changed into something beautiful to look at, I tried sun tanning, and tanning lotions nothing worked.
I didn't know the one thing that made me beautiful was already there. I didn't believe on the inside; I always went by what I saw. I now know the color is in me!

Something moved outside.
I looked out the window into the dark of night. I thought I saw something but I wasn't sure. I went back to reading but I sensed someone's presence in front of me.
I looked up and a big dark tall figure walking towards the door. I jumped up and made sure the door was locked.
I was petrified. It was pitch dark and nobody came there except Diane.
No damn lights out there! "Knock! Knock!" No damn peek hole either!
I called Mom then asked, "Who is it?"

"It's Chris!"
"Who the hell is Chris?"
Mom came to the door. "Who is it?"
"It's some body name Chris."
"Oh! He's George's boss. I wonder what he is doing here?" It was about eight o'clock. "Just a minute." She opened the door with a polite smile.
"Hi Mrs. Sharon!" He looked at me with interest and said, "Hi!"
Wow! He had a mouth full of beautiful white pearliness and dimples too!
"Hi!" I shook his extended hand and smiled. I blushed and went to the table to get my book. I was surprised to see another black face up here!
"Come in Chris!" Mom said.

But before mom could close the door all the way Diane walked in.
"Hi Ms Sharon!" than she turned and saw Chris. She looked as surprised as I was to see a black man other than mom's young buck George.
She smiled at me and said, "What's up girl?"
Giggling, we sat down on the couch like the two little girls we pretended not to be. She whispered in my ear. "Who is that? He is cute!"
"His boss!" I whispered back.
"Is George awake?" Chris asked mom. "I hope I didn't come too late!"
"Yes! He is in the back. It's not too late for us young folks!" she smiled.
"I need to talk to him. I need him to do something at work early tomorrow morning!"
"Okay have a seat, I'll get him!"
He looked West Indian, or like an African Massai warrior. He had thick perfectly shaped eyebrows and full printed lips that looked like somebody drew them on for him. Wearing tight butt hugging jeans and black mock sweater, black leather jacket and black boots.
The beautician in me wanted to ask, "Can I comb your hair?" looking at this two-foot Afro. It was big and wild but it was windy outside so I let it slide.
He sat down across from us on the other couch.
"Hi I'm Diane!" She couldn't wait to be introduced.
"Hi Diane," he smiled at her. "Are you two related?"
She giggled. "No! But we are like sisters."
Mom came back and said, "He'll be right out!"
I must say I was looking good in my green-and-white striped mini dress. My baby hair was slicked down the side of my face with my two curly ponytails and my lip-gloss was shining.
He was talking to mom and I was just staring, listening and thinking.
He spoke so eloquently. He had a cocky but confident smile, like he could talk his way in or out of any situation.
I was intrigued with every educated word. I was captivated by the movements of his full lips, and jealous of his radiant golden brown skin. I began to imagine his Mandingo wood swinging long, no doubt with

those size twelve feet and his long pretty fingers that could do the job on their own!
My oh my! A six-foot Massai warrior, with his high cheekbones and proud leader's posture encouraged me to sit my back straight. It was exciting me so much just to look at him. I had to take a deep breath because his words were stimulating like music. His voice was so rhythmic and harmonizing, so soothing, and his bass was throbbing through my blood. Mmm…I started to get wet.
I felt warm moisture down below. I was hoping no one noticed me folding my legs tighter. I had never felt this way before about anyone. I thought I could watch him walk and listen to him talk forever. He was like Farrakhan and Jessie Jackson and Martin all put together.
He sure was something special.

Diane started giggling in my ear, "He is so damn sexy!"
"He looks like Germane Jackson a little don't he?" I whispered back.
He looked at me. "Well, you didn't tell me your name!" He smiled at me flirtatiously.
"I'm Angel!" Damn I'm actually nervous! Men don't do this to me. I was only fifteen but in New York City, I lived an eighteen-year olds life and felt mature enough to listen.

"What is your sign?" I asked to categorize him.
"I'm a Virgo," he said as I stared, wanting to feel his muscles just once.
"Really! I'm a Virgo too and a Leo. I'm on the cusps as they say. I'm tough and gentle!"
Diane smiled. "I'm a Virgo too!" she giggled.
He smiled. I couldn't take it any longer. I had to say something. "Damn, you have some pretty ass teeth!" I hid my smoked-stained yellow teeth by keeping my lips together in my grins.
My record had been that I only dated men over seventeen and up to thirty and only light skinned men. I'll see a man I wanted and I pretty much always got him. Come to think of it, the only man I saw and wanted but didn't get was that football player the quarterback. It's not that I couldn't have him. His attentive smile told me I could. I just wasn't trying to pursue him; I didn't want to get beat up!
But this man… I felt tingly all inside around this man.

I enjoyed the challenge of catching me the finest men out of the crowds.
I was a female player but not for money. I played them for attention. I had kept at least ten boyfriends at a time, at all times. I had them taking me wherever I wanted to go and doing anything I wanted to do.
But this man was so different from anyone I ever met. I knew I couldn't control this man like I did all my other boyfriends; he would be my strength.

I knew what it was, he was as cool and sophisticated, militant and clean as my brother was, and I hadn't seen that maturity level before in anyone else. I was drawn to his sprit; it was so readable. It said. "I would give you the world, and protect you in my arms, and love you for eternity because you have touched my sprit." I saw a daddy.

"Nice to meet you!" he said as he extended his hand to shake mine again. I shook his hand thinking, you just don't know how you have just been sized up and chosen already!
George came out dragging his feet, tying his robe's belt in a knot.
They shook hands. "Hi Chris, what's up?" He took a seat. It was a sign of nervousness when we all lit a cigarette at the same time. Poor Diane, she didn't smoke and almost suffocated. She sat by the window and turned the knob to crack the window open.
Chris and George were talking as Diane and I were looking at them dead in their mouths. Chris was explaining his task for George and using these big words. Someone was incompetent, discussing expenditures because he had a charitable function, and what machines were inoperative and needed repairing, and what required perfection and discretion, and his expectations in the kitchen department tomorrow...
We sat there with our hands under our chin and our eyebrows straight up.
Damn he sounds good, I thought. I caressed my arms.
George could do the crossword puzzles so I knew he understood most of his words. Diane kept hitting my shoulder. "Angel what did he say? What did he say?" From the way he put it in a sentence I broke it down for her, feeling all-smart myself.

I knew she wanted him. We giggled and I kindly said, "He's mine!"
She looked at me seriously. "No way he's mine!"
She was my very best friend but I knew she was a tramp. She would've taken him into the bedroom right then and there if I had turned my head.
Well, we will see whom he chooses I thought. After all, he is one available, sexually attractive black man, and we both were horny and bored.
I leaned over and whispered, "Diane you can have him. I'm still missing my ex, Jammie. My heart still hurts for him!" But I thought to myself, Chris what's your flavor, chocolate or strawberry baby?
I prided myself on being able to get any man I wanted so a part of me wanted the challenge but at that point, I just wanted to be alone in these dark woods to think of a plan to get back to the 'Big City' my home. I just wasn't feeling this at all! I loved the trees and the fresh air, the beautiful star filled skies but I was bored and lonely as shit. I missed the fast lane; I missed the excitement of the New York City Streets.

George entertained us with the rhyme, "The Signified Monkey," by Rudy Ray Moore. Oh we had a good laugh from that. George looked at Chris and then at Diane and I. "I like this guy. Ever since that day he came over and washed dishes with the crew I knew he was a good man. He is the boss and he doesn't have to do a damn thing but tell us what to do but this guy, he cooks, cleans, and washes dishes if we get behind.

Chris asked Diane and I if we wanted to go see the hotel.
"Sure!" We ran and grabbed our coats for our boredom breaker.
He took us both by the hands as we walked down the hill through the yards of snow to give us a tour of the Grant Hotel where they all worked. It was right across the road from Mom's trailer. Chris was the Assistant Steward so he had full access.
"Oh it's so elegant and beautiful in here!" I said with amazement.
The hotel had two dining rooms that looked like what I had read in books and seen on TV.
I looked up to see big chandeliers; they were like glistening crystal rainbows with gold trim. Everything was white and gold. All of the tables were adorned with crystal glasses white and gold-trimmed plates, and gold utensils that were shining as the bus boys prepared for the next day's function.
The entertainment room was rocking with music and dancing and flashing lights. The kitchen was huge; the pots and appliances were silver, and it smelled so good from the party's meals. It was so interesting to me because I didn't know they made such big things. Stoves, pots, ovens, spoons, tables, sinks, washing machines… It was amazing.
"That's it ladies!" he said: "I'll invite you two over to eat one day when it's slow."
We walked back up the hill to the front door. He gently kissed both of us on the cheek and said, "It was a pleasure. Good night ladies!"
We said in unison, "Thank you! Good night Chris," and we giggled with pleasure.
"That Hotel was real nice right Angel?" Diane asked.
"Yeah that place is beautiful! Good night!" She went into her trailer and I went in mine.
I though a lot about him that cold lonely night as I tossed and turned in bed, squeezing my pillow between my legs wishing it were he.
He was so respectful, holding doors open and shit.

"I really like this girl I met tonight!" Chris said to his roommate Glen as he got undressed in their little country cabin. "She is so beautiful and sweet, kind of young-looking though. I saw her through her mother's window. I was just staring at her; I was frozen in that snow by her beauty. I knew then I wanted to know more about her. But I was too

nervous to knock on George's door. You believe that, me nervous? She's going to see me again tomorrow. I can't wait! I'm going to find some excuse to go back there!" He played, "I Don't Want to Lose Your Love," by The Emotions at least five times that night.
"You look like you're in love at first sight and shit!" Glen said.
"I'll just play this song over and over again, just to visualize her face until I fall asleep! I just don't know what she done to me! Goodnight, man!"
"Goodnight, Chris!"

I jumped out of bed at ten o'clock. I usually didn't get up till three because I stayed up until at least three every night but I knew I had to get cute. I kind of knew he was going to come back sometime today. If he got vibes like I did, he'd be back and I wanted to look good.
I didn't want no relationship, I just liked flirting, Diane and I had to see who he choose before we choose for him.
I put on my red leather skirt, black stockings, and a black rayon shirt I stole. He came by late that night for a minute to ask George another question and left because George was in bed asleep. Mom answered the door. I was disappointed because he didn't know what to say to me to stay awhile.

Thanksgiving day came two days later. Tina came up to visit with her Christian husband and daughter, 3.
I was ecstatic. I had to look really good so I put on an all-red jumper; I also stole that.
George invited Chris so he didn't have to spend Thanksgiving alone.
At least that's what he said, but he really was trying to hook us up.
Chris made some eggnog with a lot of Barcardi. I loved it! I would be talking to my mom and my sister but always glancing at him, trying to listen to him speak. He would be talking and our eyes would meet and we would both blush.

He took me outside on the homemade tree swing behind the trailer.
"Well, tell me something about yourself Angel, How old are you?"
"Well I'm 18!" I was lying of course but I couldn't dare tell him I was only 15. I was so used to lying about my age that it came out naturally. "And your age is…?"
"I'm twenty-seven!" he said quickly. I smiled in disbelief; here he was lying to me already.
"You don't look like you're no more than twenty-three!" He really didn't.
"Where are you coming from?"
"I was born and raised in New York City. I go to school in Brooklyn, Sarah J Hale. I'm going to be a beautician." I smiled proudly.

“Me too!”
“What? You’re going to become a beautician, too?”
“No silly, I was born in New York too I’m from Manhattan!” He leaned closer. “Do you have a boyfriend?”
“I have a few friends but I’m not serious with anybody, I just broke up with my first love Jammie!”
“Angel are you just visiting or are you staying here?”
“I’m not sure yet; it depends.”
“Depends on what?”
“Depends if there’s anything here for me or not!”
He came closer to my face and said, “Maybe there is!” and he kissed me.
I squeezed the ropes on the swing tighter. His big juicy lips were as good as they looked and so warm and cushiony soft.
Then he hugged me and I just melted in his arms; his chest was a warm bed with the smell of peace. I grabbed him around his neck and he picked me up and swung me around and put me back down.
He grabbed my hand and said, “Let’s go! Let me get you out of this cold!”

We went back in the house with our big kool-aid smiles.
George looked at u s. “I told you she was so beautiful and she would get your nose!”
I’m starting to like George.
I was smiling the rest of that day, talking and laughing with Diane and my sister. He had to leave so he asked me to walk him to the door. He kissed me very gently on my lips and asked, “Can I call you later?”
“Sure!” I replied.
Diane came outside to go to her trailer and said sarcastically, “Damn, Angel you always get the good ones! I thought you weren’t over Jammie!”
“It’s something about him I can’t shake Diane! He touches my Sprit!”
It wasn’t long before we were sneaking passionate sex on mom’s couch. It was in sections and it kept coming apart, so Chris had to hold them together between his down strokes. His muscles bulged, getting me more excited with each penetrating and gripping move.
Then we would lie under the covers on the floor and watch ‘West Side Story,’ and I felt like Maria in love. I couldn’t explain it. All I knew was, I had to tell all of my other boyfriends in the city that it was over! I had Chris now and I didn’t want anyone else. I had about five “friends” I cared a lot about and they cared about me; one wanted me to marry him and live on the army base with him. They were waiting for my return as I had promised.
It wouldn’t be easy so I went into the city and broke up with every one of them.

I visited Diane's mom and returned alone. Diane stayed in the city.
I contemplated living on the army base with one friend as he stood tall and strong with confidence, trying to convince me to stay with him. Was he the best man for me thought? Or I could've lived in the basement of another man's mother's house. He was a very nice poetic young man, fine as shit. That's why I cheated on Jammie because he cheated on me and this man had made me feel really good with his words.
I had decisions to make and I just had my heart broken when my boyfriend's best friend told me that Jammie was cheating on me with his old girlfriend, the one I took him from, as well as pimping gay men. I heard this from his best friend so I believed it, not considering he always wanted me too. I was still in shock, remembering the time he took me to a gay man's beautiful house, saying he had to live there now since his mom put him out.
I asked him about it and he didn't deny it convincingly enough, so we never got back together. I really loved him. I had been with him almost four years as I attended George Washington High School in Manhattan. My two girlfriends, Yvonne and Davette, and I would go to his house "playing hooky" in the Washington Towers, and we would have break dancing competitions all day. Jammie's hazel eyes kept me blinded to any truths; his devilish smile kept me intrigued and his dancing ass was my heart. I loved to watch him break dance. I wanted to get back with him but he went to jail. I really thought I would marry him.

It hurt like hell not to be with him but Chris made me feel so different, more mature, beautiful and safe and I liked it a lot. I decided to stay a little while longer.
About two weeks later, a week before New Year's, I asked, "Mom, can Chris and I go get some beer in town?"
"Yeah, and bring me back some more Barcardi and a six-pack of beer, and cigarettes," and she handed me a twenty dollar bill.
"Okay!" I figured I'd let him purchase it so I wouldn't be asked for ID.
We had to take a cab there to the bar that was three miles away. He knew which bar not to go into. We sat at a two-seated table with a small lamp in the back and we got to know each other a little better. We were listening to the Bee Gee's sing, "How Deep is Your Love."
I played a few games of pool as he held me from behind as he showed me how to hold my stick as I measured his.

We came home two-hours later. Mom and George were good and drunk. Mom came out looking wild and mean. She was screaming and storming towards me. "Where the fuck you been bitch?"
"We went to the bar!"
SLAP!
I screamed in surprise. "Mom what you do that for?"

"You're only fifteen! What the hell is you doing at the bar, hanging out like some whore? And you cock sucker, why you take my daughter there?"

He stood as a stunned deer.

I was totally embarrassed. You big mouth woman I thought, you're making me mad now!

I frowned and staggered over into the living room, screaming to be heard.

"Mom you said I could go! You told me to bring you some Barcadi back, here! Don't you remember?"

I was hoping she would feel stupid but instead she continued:

"Your asses been gone for hours! What you been doing?" She got on her toes to reach his face as she spit out, "Are you fucking my daughter with your old ass? You know your ass will go to jail! I'm calling the police!"

Before he could respond, I came to his defense.

"Mom why are you saying that? What are you doing?"

"I don't care if you are George's boss!" she yelled, breathing dragons and spitting fire. "What were you doing with my daughter cock sucker?"

Now she's playing the protective mother role? I thought.

I was beyond embarrassed; I was angry and resentful. You hypocrite with your jailbait man I thought.

Then I just blurted it all out with no control! I never could hold my drunken tongue.

"You can't tell me what to do! You didn't raise me! I raised myself! You're not my mother! You abandoned me! You can't tell me what to do anymore!"

She went to leap at me but I jumped out of the way. Chris grabbed her and I continued getting shit off my chest. I couldn't wait to let her have it; I'd been holding it in for a year.

"I had to buy my own food and clothes. You took my father's checks that were for me and never gave me shit! Not even an allowance! I had to steal snacks and fuck for food! Where were you than?"

"You lying bitch!" she screamed. "I sent money for you!"

"No you didn't! If you did, I didn't get shit! No 'Dear Angel' letter came to me! You didn't even buy me a pair of draws when you were home; I had to steal them too. You brought me one coat and you wore it!"

I backed up a little; she was pushing closer. I knew she was going to swing on me if he let her go.

She was as strong as an ox when she drank. I was glad Chris was stronger.

She was red hot! "Get the fuck off of me!" she screamed. "I'm going to kill her ass!"

I had all this shit bottled up that I just couldn't shut up! It just all came flowing out like vomit.

But sure enough, she got loose and threw the lamp at me. It missed!

Ha, I smiled as I ducked.
"I'm a get you bitch!" She slapped me real hard. Chris couldn't stop that one.
"Stop it Ms. Sharon, Calm down!"
"Fuck you!" she yelled.
I bit my tongue not to speak another word. I sat down.
She always pointed her finger when she talked. She had her other hand on her hip. "Let me tell you something, you little ungrateful bitch! I took good care of you!"
"Bite harder Angel, shut up, she is your mother;" a voice inside me said. I was also drunk so the lips were loose. "Yeah right! When? When? You stayed in your room all week and hardly said two words to me unless it was, "Angel get me something from the kitchen or the store!"
I continued. "You shut me out, than you fought with Boo all night, every weekend, and kept me awake verbally abusing me, calling me every name in the book! Yeah, you took care of me! What have you ever done for me? What did you ever buy me beside those corny ass Christmas toys? Why did you leave me in New York for almost a year now? I had to fuck for food and sleep in the streets while you were taking care of this new creep George. Mommy where were you when I needed you?"
I was screaming and crying out of control. Chris and Mom stared with their mouths hanging open in disbelief. So much stink was in the air.
"Well guess what? George, you're young ass man tried to hump on me when I had to sleep in your bed, yeah!"

"Calm down Angel and don't say another word." Chris said. He asked mom nicely to sit down, with a gentle push.
She was standing over me thinking what to say next, looking at me wondering what was true, denying and crying and screaming. "Why are you saying that? That's not true Angel!"
Chris was trying to stand between us but she just slapped his hands away. She pushed him aside. "Oh, so I don't do anything for you? Then get out my damn house you're so damn grown!"
"That's right I am grown!" I jumped up. Shit I couldn't move. I was trapped between the long couch and Chris, than her and an end table.
She reached over him and said, "Oh you want to jump in my face, bitch?" and started to swing at me. Bam! She got in a good right hook in my face.
I ducked as Chris pushed her back far enough so I could see a space that I could get by.

I heard George's voice in the background. He was there with his mustache in his mouth with dry food stuck to it as usual. He was staggering by the hallway wall to stay out the way. Shit, as long as it wasn't him getting fucked up tonight he was cool.

He wasn't trying to stop her either; he just puffed on his non-filter cigarette like he was watching a damn movie or something.
He did say, "Sharon leave that girl alone!" once.
She was punching my head like it was a boxing bag. Chris couldn't hold her off of me any longer without hurting her.
My head hurt from her punches but I couldn't shut up! I wanted her to hurt too!
He finally pulled her off of me and swung her over the other side of the room on the couch.
I could see in his eyes that he really wanted to protect me at any limit. He screamed at her with authority. "Don't move! Don't hurt her no more Sharon! Keep your hands off of her!" His one eye went cross as he frowned with disappointment.
She did move but only to grab a cigarette with her shaking hands. She was breathing hard, gasping for air between her words. "You had enough, bitch?"
"Did you have enough?" I screamed painfully from the gut. "You feel better? You're nothing to me! I had to raise myself in the city while you ran around with that young ass piece-of-shit-of-a-man you got! You never cared about me! So don't pretend now!"
Sarcastically I said, "I'll get out of your house; oh I mean, you and George's house!"
Oh, he didn't like that! He really wanted her to whip my ass then but he sure wasn't going to say shit to me and especially not to Chris. He just opened up a beer instead.
I stood there in the middle of her living room in her trailer in her cold presence. Huffing and puffing, I screamed to the top of my drunken level with tears rushing down in to my mouth and coming out through my salted words. "You would put me in the street again and keep him here? While you're up here fucking a man twenty years younger than you, another Army Psycho? It's you're fault I'll be sleeping on the streets! And you prefer it that way, don't you?"

I ran into her bedroom and closed the door to use the phone for a cab. Chris will give me some money to go to New York!
Before I could say a word on the phone, Mom came storming into the room like a bull. She snatched me by my throat and started strangling me.
The cabstand lady heard nothing but screams.
She threw me down on the floor between her bed and the wall. I couldn't flip her over or get her off of me! She was sitting on top of me and there wasn't enough room to maneuver.
I couldn't breath. I pushed her face up by her chin; and blocked her hits with the other hand. With her knee penetrating deeply in my side, I wanted to bang her in the head with the phone but I dared not hit her!

“What you say to me bitch? You want to fight me?”
I’m shaking my head “no” in surrender.
She was spitting in her holler. “I’ll kill you bitch! I brought you in this world and I’ll take you out!” She was piercing me with murderous eyes.

Chris grabbed her off of me by her hands and held her away from the door so I could get out. I ran straight out the house crying and screaming with hatred in my broken heart. “I’ll get out your damn house. No problem!”
It was dark and snowing and I didn’t know where the hell I was going. I just had to get out of there!
“She doesn’t care about me; she never did! I hate her! I hate her!” I said out loud looking back at the trailer through the snowdrops. I ran down the steep hill towards the hotel. Chris looked up and down the road for me, calling out my name, but I couldn’t hear him.
The world began spinning and before I knew it I had fainted, rolled down the hill. I had almost reached the doors of the hotel.
He saw my body lying in the snow. Franticly he ran down the steep hill. He tried to wake me up. “Angel can you hear me? Angel wake up baby! Angel!”
I was drunk and burned out and emotionally exhausted. I knew it wouldn’t work with me living there with her and her man. He always looked like he wanted to eat it; and there was definitely too much anger for her inside of me.
Chris put his coat around me and proved his strength as he carried me up that long steep hill to a co-worker’s house. Chris lived in the staff area of the hotel. The hotel needed him close by, him being the Assistant Steward. He couldn’t bring me there, so he took me right across the road from Mom’s trailer park. It was the only house in that trailer park. He kicked the door and asked for help.
His friend from New York opened the door. “Sure, bring her in here and hurry up,” he said. “She’s shaking bad. I’ll get her a blanket.”
My teeth were chattering. I woke up in Chris arms and I looked into his sad eyes.
His tears began to fall. He couldn’t hold them back any longer. He held me up and said, “I got you! It’s going to be okay!”
I put my head back on his shoulders and then I heard this voice. His friend said, “Lay her down over their on the long couch!”
I was a shaken, confused, young, immature, fifteen-year-old girl. He didn’t know what to do next.

I didn’t have any change of clothes to be warm. No coat. I had nowhere to go.
This night I hated her so much.

I heard his friend say, “Chris! You’re going to have to take off your clothes and keep her warm. Get under the covers and hold her!”
He took off his shirt and held me with his soft warm body. I had my clothes still on so he took off my wet sweater and sneakers and got under the blanket where he held me tight all night long.
I was warm from head to toe. He rubbed my head and rocked me back and forth saying, “I’ll take care of you!”
All I could say as I cried more and more was, “I want my daddy! I want my daddy!”
I said this over and over until I finally lost consciousness.

CHAPTER EIGHT
IT WAS SELF DEFENSE

The next day, his friend said we could take over his apartment since he was leaving in a couple of days. I told him I'll stay there for a while until I decided what I was going to do. They both had to go to work. Chris' friend told me to make myself at home; there were some steaks in the freezer and eggs in the fridge. I liked the way that sounded.
"I'll come back at lunchtime to check on you okay?" Chris said to me.
"Okay!" They left. I was good and hungry.
I wanted to change my clothes; they reeked of booze and sweaty armpits. So I went to my mom's trailer. George opened the door and walked away to go back in their bedroom. I went into my room and packed the little bit of clothes I got from friends; the few outfits I picked up; and panties and Mom's hand-me-down sweaters with a cigarette hole or two. Of course I couldn't live without my makeup. I put my Bible on top and zippered up my bag.

I was waiting for mom to come into my room to talk to me but she never came out of her room. I went to the refrigerator to snatch some yellow cheese for my eggs. I could always depend on my mom having some. I found a can of beer for my hangover. I bet they didn't know this was under the bottom or else it would be gone!
I held up my beer in one hand and my bag in the other and said, "Thanks" quietly. I left and went across the road. Damn, I forgot my toothbrush. My mouth did taste like shit but I was not going back.
Quickly, I made some food and drank my beer. I lay down and rubbed my satisfied stomach. Then the tears just started flowing. It hit me what had happened last night and my heart was very sad. I didn't want to come here and hurt her feelings like I did but she didn't have to hurt mine.
As I cried, I asked God to protect and guide me in my paths. I started talking to Dad. "Why did you leave me? I need you here to take care of me!"

I stayed there with him for three days, refusing to go across the road and see mom.
Chris' friend went back to New York City after the fourth day and left Chris and I with the one-bedroom furnished apartment. It was like walking into an old woman's' house. When you walked in there was beige and green couch and a long wooden table with white doilies on it. Over to the left was a small white kitchen set with two seats and to the right, a comfortable sized bedroom with nice old fashioned lamps on

each side of the queen sized bed. Plus there was a tall wooden dresser and a very small bathroom with no shower.
The landlord came by looking for his rent. I guess that's why he had left today. At first, the landlord said we couldn't stay but Chris had a good ass job, and a convincing attitude so he talked him into letting us stay. We kept quiet. I sure didn't want any reason to get put out, knowing that I was right across the road from mom who could come here and make a memorable announcement of her presence.

I was feeling very peaceful for the next three days. I would clean up and wait for Chris to come back. He would bring home cooked steaks soaked in beef juice so tender you didn't even have to have teeth, and some big buckets of strawberries or peaches, sorbet or fruit cocktail that we chilled with whipped cream. They were amazing evening-ending pleasures.
He took good care of me; the best part was that he brought home a cooked dinner for us every night so I didn't have to cook much.
He held me tight every night and I needed that so much. I fell in love with this place and time, and maybe him.
But I was still plotting what move I was going to make next.
This man was my knight in shining armor. He rescued me. I owed him! But if this didn't work out, I'd go back to New York and impose on family or friends. Or I'll go live with Missy or my cousin. I could always get a job braiding hair.
Chris' warm body was definitely needed in those cold ass mountains. I was so warm inside and loving every bit of being held by him all night after he educated me with his wealth of lovemaking experience.
I'd never felt a body that well built. It gave me a comforting and safe feeling.

I was enjoying my new relationship with a man twelve years older and smarter than me too. When I smoked some joint, I believed myself to be profound in a debate of any controversial discussion. I had to win and I usually did with my persistent ass. But I hadn't met anyone mentally challenging since that five-percenter dude in Brooklyn. Now he was deep, I learned a lot from him about life and the body. But at that time I just wasn't letting go of my makeup and weed so we broke up.
There was so much passion and consideration from Chris, something I never had.
Wow my first home!
We enjoyed relaxing, just holding each other, listening to some country music on the old-fashioned radio box. He would come home at night exhausted and would just want to lie down.
That was the night mom knocked on the door. Bang! Bang! Bang! Police style!
"What do you want mom?"

I acted like I was sleeping wiping my eyes. It was 11:00 pm on a Friday night and I didn't want to argue with her.
"I'm still your Mother!" she yelled.
"Yeah, So?" I stood in the doorway.
"Are you going to invite me in or what?" and she kindly pushed me out of the way.
"Yeah mom sure!"
I could smell the liquor all over her breath and her clothes stunk of cigarettes. She looked like she hadn't slept in days; she looked mean like a bully looking for a fight.
So I wasn't suggesting she sit down.
"Do you want to come home?" she asked.
"That's not my home!" I said. "I have no home!" I walked over to the refrigerator for some water. "For now I will be staying here! You want some juice mom?"
"No I don't want any damn juice what is this? Soon you'll have to leave and than where will you go?"
"The landlord said we could stay! Look Mom, I'm sorry! I shouldn't have said those things to you!" I said with my head down.
"You belong over there with me! You love me baby?" She hugged me.
"Yes mom! I'm sorry I disrespected you!"
"So come on, this man is too old for you; lets go home!"
Chris jumped up and came into the living room and stood behind me.
"No mom, I don't want to! I don't want to go over there with you. I'm sorry but right now I want to stay here."
Mom got mad. "You're only fifteen you know! He's twenty-seven!
He turned around and looked at me. "I'll take care of Angel!"
Mom started laughing. "No! I'll take care of my child! I'm still responsible for her!" She pointed at Chris. "That man can go to jail! Do you want me to call the police? I will!"
"Mom don't do that! Just give me a few days to decide if I'm going back to the city or not!" I was embarrassed that she brought up my age but he completely blocked it out.
"You can't live here! I'll decide where you are going!"
"Mom you don't have to worry about me. I'm just fine as you can see!" I moved away from the bedroom door so she could go in and see.

She looked around. "Yeah, this is cute but you're too young to be playing house!"
I frowned. "I'm not playing! This shit has never been a game to me, not knowing where I'm going to lay my head down! It's always been real to me after I woke up and you were gone! You left me, and now you bring me to this dark ass place with nothing to do. You expect me, a city girl, to get on a cheese bus to go to some all-white school? With no new clothes much less designer clothes or thrift shop clothes, just your hand-

me-downs sweaters? What were you thinking?" I remembered feeling so alone when I entered new classrooms. I wasn't going to face the unknown. I had expectations of it being like the white school shows on TV, and little me with no back up cue cards. I never even gave it a chance it was just, "Hell No!"

"Mom your man got his free feels off on me. I don't know for how long until I caught his ass as I was waking up and screamed for him to stop! He told you he thought I was you and you went for it, again! In your bed, Mom you made me sleep in it with you and your man at my age and than you went to work and left us alone! What did you think was going to happen? He's always trying to kiss me in the mouth and you think I want to stay there? No thanks!"
She grabbed me by my arms. "You're coming home with me now! You're not living with this grown man! I'm going to call the police! You talking all that shit about me leaving you! You know your sisters were taking care of you!"
"No they weren't!" I began to raise my voice: "Where did Tina go? Why was I left alone for almost a year? I took care of me!" I waved my hands in the air "You know mom, I don't want to have this conversation! You've been drinking. I can't talk to you! I'm staying here and that's all to it!"

She looked at me with anger started raising her voice so the world can hear, "I'm your mother! And if you want to come home you know where I live!" And she walked out the house.
I couldn't keep my mouth shut as I stood at the door. "'Mother! Yeah right! I'm still on my own and I'm going to be all right with out you!" {I was angry because she didn't put Gorge out for touching me, or for me to come back knowing now that I would come back if he wasn't their.}
She stopped and turned around. "Yeah! Okay! You go ahead and play house, Miss Know-It-All! You go ahead and take care of yourself!"
"I been doing it since you left me and I'm still alive!"
She got real mad at that and threw a rock through the window. "Fuck you Angel!" She stormed back across the road to her dismal trailer.
I went to the window and leaned my knees on the couch as I watched her walk away.
"I have to find something for this damn window now. Damn, now we have to deal with the landlord."
"Don't worry about the window or the Landlord," Chris said. "Leave that to me. I'll take care of it! You don't worry about anything you just rest!"
She was out there yelling and cursing as she staggered across the road. I could hear her and George yelling from my broken window. I just shook my head, breathed in the cold night air and looked up into the sky. There

were millions of stars. “Chris why? Why is there so much beauty up there and not down here?”
He grabbed me and hugged me. “I see beauty right here in front of me!”

Another week went by and I decided this had gone on long enough.
Chris was working late and I was bored so I went over to see what George and Mom were up to. I had to make sure they were both alive and they hadn't killed each other. Plus, I wanted something to drink. It was the weekend so I was sure they had something!
When I arrived they welcomed me in like they had no issues with me at all.
“Come on in and join us!” Mom said with a joyful smile. They were drinking heavily: a case of beer and a fifth of cheap vodka. They were laughing and playing with each other.
George was the funniest guy in the world, right between ‘drunk’ and ‘too drunk.’ I started drinking beer and vodka with them.
I didn't know not to mix beer with vodka ‘A boiler maker.’ Everything was fine until the fifth was empty, and the beer was running out and there were no more cigarettes. The house even seemed to be drunk.
Smoky Roberson was singing, “I Second That Emotion” on the 8-track tape. I was singing until, BAM! George entered the living room, pacing the floor and talking about when he was in the Vietnam War and how they only gave him one square piece of tissue and with one finger he wiped his ass! I started cracking up!

“Man, you'll shit on yourself when you see a man blown up right before your eyes or the enemy is running after your ass!” He turned right before my eyes from a comedian that should be on TV into an angry, ready-to-kill crazy man. He bent over into a hunting position and stared me straight in the eyes. He spoke like he was possessed. “Them mother fuckers was under the ground! And they would just pop up! The Con would slit the man's throat behind you and disappear back in the ground before you blinked! That's what I seen! You don't know nothing about nothing until you been in a war!”

“Oh No!” Mom shouted. “I don't want to hear this shit! Shut the fuck up George!”
He kept talking. “I killed my share,” he said. Then all of a sudden she grabbed his face and dug her nails in deep and scratched him all up. It happened so fast all I could say was, “Oh shit!” Another army nut, she sure knew how to pick them!
He went into the bedroom cursing. “I'm going to kill your stink ass and your daughter too. I hate you! I'm going to cut your throat from ear to ear! And then I'm gonna gut your daughter open like a pig. They're

going to find you two on that road. Road kill! You don't know who you're fucking with."
I was shocked! "What the hell? It's time for me to leave!"
"Oh yeah?" Mom was saying to him. "You just try it, cock sucker!" and she hit him in the head with a hammer. "Bang!"
He grabbed his head and saw the blood on his hands; it started dripping down his back.
"What you do that for? I'm bleeding shit you bitch!" He jumped towards her but she backed up quick.
"Go ahead!" she screamed. "I'm gonna bust your head all the way open! Don't fuck with me George!"
He went to the bathroom and got a towel. All I heard was, "You see my blood? Well, you're going to see yours too!"
I said to myself, "If this man hurts my mom or me; I'm going to kill him!" I jumped up and got a big butcher knife and sat back down on the couch. I put it behind my back. The same mom I hated, I was ready to defend.

My head was spinning. I was seeing doubles; I couldn't get my focus. But the tension ran through my body causing me to tremble with anxiety looking for an escape. I was always wishing I were somewhere else; I never wanted to be where I was!
Mom came out the room first. He came out with blood dripping from the large gash in his head. Then he grabbed her from behind.
Mom was struggling to get him off; she fell and he fell on top of her.
"Get off of her! Get off!" I shouted. I grabbed his ass by his feet and dragged him a few feet away and I kicked him. "Stay away from her!"

She got up and was heated; she grabbed the lamp and threw it at him. I ducked. It hit his arms as he protected his face.
He went to grab her again and I saw my opportunity to defend us, so I jumped up and stabbed him in the back with that butcher knife. I was holding on tight with two hands.
The blade penetrated his flesh and touched the bone.
A strong force snatched the knife out of my hands and threw it into another room. It landed under a table behind him where I used to sit and read.
I stood there in shock. "How the hell did that happen?" That was supposed to go right through! The knife was too far to get to if he attacked me. Fear set in. I couldn't run out the door because I'd have to get past him. I couldn't get another knife because he was standing in the kitchen.
He looked at me in disbelief.
I looked at him and said with all my anger, swinging my fist at him, "If you hurt my mom or me, you're a dead man for real! That was just a

taste!" Hoping he didn't come after me, he looked so scary with his bloodshot eyes and foaming a spit filled mouth like a diseased dog.
I was surprised; instead of running towards me to strangle me, or stabbing me back he ran out the house.
I sat down. Damn Angel, I really tried to kill him! No longer in existence, is that what I wanted?
Something snatched that blade out of my hands! Shit! He threatened to kill my mother and me and I didn't even do anything to him, oh yeah I'm sure she beat his ass for feeling on me, I'm sure she blames him for me not being here and I was talking shit about him last time I was here!
I was convinced he was challenging us to a duel of death and I knew his abilities so he needed to know ours!
With our emotions spiraling we staggered into that situation.
I might have insulted my mom. I was offensive and arrogant. But I still didn't want anything to happen her!
He deserved it! What kind of response did he think he was going to get intimidating vulnerable, emotionally damaged women? Panting and ragging like a lunatic?

I said to mom "You know he's going to have to tell the police when he goes to the hospital, He'll need stitches and in his head too you know!"
I suddenly stopped to think about what I did to him. "I can't stay here! I can't be here when he comes back! I'm out!"
Mom looked at me and pointed her finger. "You're not going anywhere! Don't worry about him!"
I looked at her. "Mom, I just tried to kill a man! I got to go back to New York! I'm not going to jail!"
"Angel, you're not going to jail, just sit down; you're staying here with me."
"No, I'm not. I can't ever stay here. I can't stay here mom let me go."
"If you go back to that man I will call the police myself"
"You wouldn't do that!" I slammed her door, "I should have kept my ass home!"

Wow someone snatched that knife out of my hand; I felt it pulling out of my hand and threw it across the room. That was deep, was that you God protecting him and me from killing him? Thank you! I don't think I could live with his death on my conscience. I didn't dislike him that much. I don't want to go to jail either for attempt, please God help me get out of town. It was self defense right?

CHAPTER NINE

WHAT DID I GET MYSELF INTO?

Chris had just gotten off of work. I ran into the house and told him what happened all out of breath.

I begged him to take me back to N.Y.C.

We packed what we could. "Okay," he said, "let me think. We have to get into town to the bus station!"

We didn't have a phone so he said, "Wait here, I'll be right back! I'm going to the hotel and ask Tony for a cash advance. I'll tell him I have to leave for a few days, that I'm having a family emergency!" He kissed me. "Relax, I'll be right back; make sure you have everything you need!"

He called for a cab. The cabstand didn't have a ride available until two hours due to the weather a snowstorm, and it being a weekend.

We walked down that long dark, cold wind blowing stormy road staying in the middle, holding bags in each of our hands, light leather jackets, no boots, snow going down our sneakers, listening to howls and the wind whistling and burning our ears, not saying a word, crunching in the deep three foot snow with frozen toes and frozen noses and finger tips for what seemed like hours till we got into town.

Some white men were standing by a pub asking each other, "Is that a white woman with a black man?" They came closer and saw I wasn't white but they still weren't too sure. Chris gave them a I'm already pissed off, don't fuck with me look.

I pulled on Chris arm. "Let's go, we have a bus to catch!" I said it loud enough for them to hear. We were leaving town NOW!

He looked at me and said, "Okay for you I'll be cool. Come on inside and get warm!"

I looked back hoping they wouldn't follow us. I was petrified, thinking of I know they're the Ku Klux Klan. It was the middle of the night and we were near the bar we knew not to enter, 'Whites ONLY". I knew Chris was not going to back down though, no matter what they brought!

We were going to die that night if he continued to get furious and began talking back to them in defiance. I was proud he was a stand-up guy but I didn't want him to be foolish and stand up to more then three men!

He looked at the men as we passed them. "What the fuck is their problem?"

I prayed they didn't hear him. Oh please God!

They began coming closer and a police car pulled up.

They turned and walked back into the bar. I sighed, finally glad to see police.
The police asked me my name and I told them. They said my mom called the police on me because I was running away from home with an older man!
I told them that she put me out, and he was just taking me back to my sister's house in New York. They left us alone. I sat down in relief and drank some coco and ate a buttered roll in the dinner while he purchased the tickets next door. The cold wind sobered me right up.
On the bus I was thinking with my head pressed against the window.
Mom; she's a crazy woman but I love her. Unfortunately I'm turning out just like her! A violent drunk! That's what I hated about her!

Chris was taking me into Manhattan to his mothers home.
Back in the city I felt at home.
Chris introduced me to a lot of people on the way their, it seemed like he knew everyone. Everyone seemed to really love him like family too.
He was generally happy to see everyone he saw from the time we got off the bus, on the train, he knew someone walking to his building and everyone around it, on the elevator.
I was tired of saying "hi" so much and smiling till my face hurt. I just wanted to rest.
Chris' younger brother Gary answered the door of the nineteenth floor apartment in the project on 114$^{St.}$ and Fifth Avenue. He was handsome; he had side burns connected to his beard, a big ass smile and big lips with super thick black shinny eyebrows. He was dressed in all black and had a jolly and hyped personality.
"Hey what's up?" They hugged as I stood behind Chris smiling. I was waiting for my acceptance as a welcomed guest and not an intrusion.
"Wow! Who is this beautiful young lady?" Gary asked. He tilted his head to the side, which I discovered he always did when he talked.
"This is my baby, Angel!" Chris put his arm around me and smiled.
I smiled at Chris and than at his brother. "Hi!" I said with my sexiest voice. I had on jeans and a red fitted shirt. Chris had on jeans and a red shirt too, but it wasn't planned that way.
"Come on in!" Gary said and he held out his arms. "Can I get some love?"
I giggled and hugged him.
"Have a seat!" he said and then they started talking.

I sat on the uncomfortable plastic-covered couch that gave off an annoying crunch with every move I made. It made me cringe so I sat as still as possible. I swore that day that I'll never put plastic on my damn couch! It reminded me that every time I did sit on one I was unhappy too.

Chris sat in the matching love seat. Gary stood up leaning on the fake fireplace telling him how everyone in the neighborhood was doing; who had died and how such and such was, who had AIDS from shooting up, who was in prison and who got out, who was in wheel chairs. All the people he grew up with were doing badly, or dying or dead. Chris looked so sad. I wanted him to just shut up. His body movements and emotions were entertaining to watch. Gary went from happy to sad to mad to grateful that them two were still alive after all they had been thru, living a life filled with drug dealing and using, and shoot-outs and fighting with gangs and hanging with cold blooded murders, controlling the street of fifth avenue. They hadn't seen each other in about a year and he was spilling all the beans, things I don't think Chris wanted me to know about.

After a few months there Chris began to get drunk everyday, threaten me; he said that I had better not ever leave him. "There's nowhere you can run; you better jump off the planet because I would find you and then I'll really make your life miserable and you'll wish you was dead!"
I began to fear him. He was angry he had to live in his mothers' house and he didn't have a job yet. He was beginning to resent me for making him leave his good job, here he was a grown man asking his mother to care for him and a young girl and giving him money, and his brother started acting like it was his house and we stayed long enough, he was getting depressed I can tell.

A year later I worked at a beauty parlor up Sugar Hill where I use to live on 145 St. Saint Nicholas Ave. The rumor was that Red Fox had slept on my roof for a while.
Chris began to get high off dope, something I knew nothing about. My brother died using it and I swore I would never touch a needle. He began staying out a lot.
I knew if I went to my mom's or sister's house that I may not be welcomed, and before I would sit down he would be there banging on the door.
"Get your shit! Let's go now!" No one would stop him and I didn't want anyone else to get hurt so I obeyed for now because I was pregnant. Where was I going to run? He'd find me! I needed to escape and I didn't mean drugs
I couldn't change him! I couldn't hang with him either; he was all I had now to take care of me. So we moved up state to Kingston N.Y, to escape the drugs but they were there too.
His drinking got worse; everyday, all day, he was beyond drunk by twelve and whipping my ass by twelve fifteen.

He would come home missing-draws drunk. Piss-in-the-corners-of-the-house-thinking-he-was-at-the-toilet-bowl drunk. How he even made it home half the time was beyond me.
I only knew one way to escape; he was becoming too abusive, strangling me up to my last breath and giving me one black eye after another.

Delivering my first baby was the first time I didn't feel alone and selfishly, that's why I had her! When everyone was constantly telling us we weren't ready or prepared for a child that I needed to get an abortion I refused!
But now we had a baby hearing this arguing and fighting and shit!
I was fighting back, demanding he stay home with us and not go out with that car full of women.
He said that without me he wouldn't be here so I knew if I was dead, the baby would be free from his short-tempered, addicted, abusive ass. And he would be free from what he perceived as a burdensome responsibility, working now and then, and he could go back out on the corner and hold up the lamp poles, watching the hoes.
I didn't want her to live, sleep, eat, this abuse even as an observer.
I couldn't take another day of pain and suffering. I'd rather be dead and live in paradise with no more pain and no more tears. I was a nice person; I shouldn't go to Hell!
God knew my heart and He would forgive me, wouldn't He?
Mercedes was a good friend who was living with us, and her sprit so loved. I thought she would be the perfect mother for my perfect one-year-old child. I watched her over-protected ass take good loving care of her. I knew a baby would make me happy; I wouldn't care about anything else.
I had someone to love deeply and someone who'd love me back without pain. Someone to keep me company so I wouldn't be lonely, someone who would make him want to get sober and do the right thing, and be that loving man he was when he was sober.
This beautiful baby would bring smiles to my tearful miles. I needed her.
But I still wasn't happy.

I washed and ironed his clothes fed him three times a day, I kept the house clean, I stayed cute and gave him sex whenever he wanted it whether I felt like it or not. I did all I could and I was the best woman I could be and it still wasn't good enough.
I was pretty and sexy; why would he want any one else? "God why don't I get any of this peace you be talking about in this book?"

"Yeah… um, Mercedes come here!" I was standing in our large yellow kitchen against the wall. She was short and skinny weighing about 90 pounds, brown skin with shoulder length Brown hair, very pretty and so sweet, my new best friend came to live with us because she couldn't get

along with her mom either, I sure could relate to that. Her grandmother gave us this apt because she was moving out.
I'd had a major fight with Chris about him wanting the rent money. He took it happily in my surrender. Convincing himself he would get it right back in time with his hustle. We all know a monkey can't sell bananas.

I was trying to stand up strong. I was standing in tears and a bruised body "Mercedes will you go outside and take Tunisia with you please?"
"Are you O-K Angel?"
Yes, I just need you to do this for me, I don't want her here when he comes back arguing."
"Sure I will! I don't want you to be alone though!"
I'll be al right, he'll fuss a little than he'll fall asleep, just keep her out at least an hour ok?"
I extended my arms and put her sweater on while I smiled at my twelve months baby's beauty, wiping my tears saying, "Wait Tunisia, stay still baby!"
She was wiggling impatiently.
I kissed her goodbye and hugged her tight while I whispered with my shaken words, "I love you so much baby this is why I doing this, for us!
"Here you go!" I said. "Mercedes take good care of her!" I knew what I really meant.
"Keep her outside for a long while now ok?" I kissed Mercedes on the cheek and said, "Thank you!"
For the responsibility you're about to take on but you just don't know it yet, I thought. We both were nineteen.

"Ok come on Tunisia!" She reached for her out of my arms that wouldn't let go. "I hate to see him hit you. I started to call the police on his ass you know!"
"Yeah but that will only make him more angry and there's no telling what he'll do to me when he got out or to you. You won't have to worry about him hurting me any more I have a plan."
"What?"
"I tell you later, you go ahead now!"
Tunisia was so happy to be going outside, it was spring and she loves to go outside. She wiggled to get down as she looked towards the door and smiled a big happy smile. I gave her one last kiss.
I knew in my heart Mercedes would take good care of her and when she gets older she could explain to her how bad it was for me, and how I thought this was the best thing for her and me.
My dumb logic said that he was going to disappear. Let Mercedes raise her in fun in the sun.

As soon as she left, I ran in the bathroom and ran some hot water in the tub. I went in the cabinet and picked out the sharpest razor I could find. I took off my clothes while watching the water fill up.
I slowly climbed in the bathtub, laid back and momentarily enjoyed a warm feeling for the last time.
"God please forgive me for my weakness and my sins in Jesus' name!" and I cut my left wrist deeply across all the veins I saw.
I heard that's how you do it.
I laid back as the water filled the tub hotter. I watched the blood flow faster in the water.
I turned off the water and thought about my daughter growing up with out me.
"She'll be better off! I'm not shit as a role model! I don't want her to be like me.
"She will not live a traumatic life being around all this violence." I said to the walls.
Chris was a loving father and would never ever hurt her but he was hurting this family with his drug use and abuse. I thought about my mom neglecting me. I heard every ugly, hateful, painful word from him and her in my head. Bitch! Whore!
Chris' last words to me were, "I hate you bitch! I don't give a fuck what you do! As far as I'm concerned you're dead! You can't do shit for me! I don't know why I stay with your dumb ass!"
I started crying but was relieved this time. I'm finally going to die, no more shitty life as I watched the clear water turn red.
"Why me?" I asked God. "Why couldn't I have some happiness? Why did I have to be around all these nuts that turned me into a nut? Why am I always crying and getting beat up and cursed out? Please! Take care of my daughter God please. Don't let her go through this abuse with no man, ever!"

I fell asleep. I dreamed two concrete walls went SLAM! Together and were slamming our daughter with her doll!
I woke up in the hospital with stitches and white bandages on my wrist.
"I'm not dead? Damn it!"
I wondered if that was Chris and I crushing our precious daughter that hard like concrete walls?
I had to save her but what could I do? I was young and miserable. I was a baby myself. She didn't deserve to be around neither one of us because we were evil and were spreading it to her. Chris was evil because of what he was doing. I was evil because evil was always present with me and I accepted it.
If I had a gun and some guts, I would have shot him and I to death for her happiness.

Chris found me.
He was over my bed in the hospital, holding my hand when I woke up.
I was disgusted; I had failed again! I had to live with you and why didn't it work this time?
I snatched my hand away and sat up and closed my eyes so I didn't have to look in his damn face.
"Baby, I love you so much!" Chris said. "I love you more than my life, more than our child's life, more than GOD! Without you I don't want to live; please forgive me and promise me you'll never do that again! I need you! Tunisia needs you! Please baby I love you so much! Why did you do this?"
I looked at him and rolled my eyes and closed them back.
He shook me. "Angel why?"
"Because death might be better than this fucked-up life!"
I looked into his eyes and saw the tears well up. It was the first time I saw him drop a tear since the night he carried me out of the snow. When the tears fell from his face, he looked so pathetic and really sorry. I surrendered.
I hugged him and promised to never try to take my life again!

He moved us to an even bigger three-bedroom place with wooden floors, wood panel, a fake fireplace, and a big side yard to hang my clothes and lounge and let the baby run free. We always made up in bed, and he stopped using for a while and returned into the loving, caring dad we needed. We made passionate love every night and snuck it in on some days. I was happy! Thank you God.

Mercedes was still living with us, helping me with the house and children as they arrived one after another.
She never said a word to me about my attempt or leaving my child with her.
She would stand up to him. He didn't yell at her about nothing. Things were cool for a few months.
But too much romance, wining and dining on the roast that he cooked in beer led back to boredom after the loss of another job.
I even sniffed coke with him once as we laid on the blanket on the floor under the red lights. Barry White was playing and the floor was trembling which made the loving more passionate.
Just for that night I accepted cocaine and him as is.

Bam! "Chris I'm pregnant again!"
"This wouldn't have happened if you were taking the pills everyday like you are supposed to!"
"I did take them everyday at dinner time. I didn't see you trying to buy no condoms!"

"You're getting an abortion!"
"No I'm not!"
"Yes you are!"
"No I'm not!"
I cried and prayed; don't let him make me do this God! Than I found a book that shows you what a baby looks like at three months.
I menstruated for two of my pregnant months so I didn't know I was pregnant until the third month. I was surprised to see the baby had a brain, a heart, a body with little everything fingers, a nose and toes.
I showed Chris the picture after making love one night, while he was sober and he too with his master's degree and his behavioral science awards was surprised and uniformed.
We were thinking it was shaped like a gooey sack, shaped like a deformed fish.
We no longer referred to the baby as an "It" but as a baby!

We agreed this would be the last baby. Two crying kids were more than enough, a year apart at that.
Chris was extremely helpful washing the clothes, going food shopping, and buying all the clothes and cribs, walkers, swings, strollers, toys. He provided for them and me considering he was a dope fiend. Surprisingly thought we needed for nothing because Chris sold the product and than he would hit. He had money to bring home for the babies and my personal needs. He bathed them, changed shitty diapers, played with them; he was damn near perfect. He would only do enough Heroin than he was real cool to be around.
They had everything they needed, thanks to his hustle, and his mom's large pocketbook and heart. She was buying more than his love. Shit, my biggest fear was that if she died he would go insane and he'd probably kill all of us and wouldn't even remember.
I would be devastated because she was the one that prayed for everyone and I used her to get to God. I loved her like my own mommy.

Bam! "Chris, I'm pregnant again!"
He started going outside everyday, all day.
He came home drunk and started tossing me around.
"What's wrong with you? What did I do?" I screamed.
"Whose baby is that?"
"It's yours; who else?"
He was looking at with me with hate, anger, and betrayal all over his face. He frowned his eyebrows and one eye went crossed. "Johnny told me you and Shawn had sex and that baby is his!"
I jumped up off the couch. "He's lying! He's lying!"

Slap! "You're lying! You remember that day I came home from work and he was there and you took too long to answer the door? I knew something was going on that moment!"
"We were asleep! And you did tell him he could stay with us a few days. If you didn't have trust in us then you shouldn't have let him sleep here. I didn't fuck that man! I never ever cheated on you Chris never! His girlfriend is one of my best friends; you believe some man who wants to fuck me?"
Chris swore it was someone else's child and treated me as if it was and he kicked me in my stomach in disgust. I protected my baby well, holding in tight as I curled in a protective ball.
"I never let another man touch me!" I insisted. "You really believe I would touch him? He's your friend! What kind of person do you think I am? You don't even know me!"
He screamed, pointing his finger in my face. "We will see! I want a damn blood test!"
"Who aren't you fucking? Feeling a little guilty Chris?"
"Slap!" I held my stinging face. "Fuck you Chris!"

If my child had another father I would tell him or her because I have no right to deprive the child of the truth of a whole other family that's there's to meet and love and learn from, blood that may be needed one day, or a transplant that only a family member can give. Shit, the father might become rich and I couldn't claim anything; there are a million reasons.
But the most important one was that it's just not right to the child to be lied to; that's stealing someone's identity!

"The test is there baby for your uncertainty, and to think you stood in front of the welfare board and told them you was my child's father and any that came after them will be yours too? Didn't you believe yourself?"
He just left me on the floor and walked out.
I just sat there holding my head down, rubbing my belly. I can't believe he don't know my character by now.

It wasn't until Kameena was five months when I saw Shawn's daughter, and didn't Kameena look just like Shawn's little girl, with big ears and big eyes, light skin, and a big ass smile.
I couldn't tell him anything; his mind was set and it had to be true.
"Don't say shit to me bitch!" He was starting to get more violent with me.
His cheating really took off. But I still married him.

I would run away to his mom's house in hopes that he would miss me and treat me better. I would stay a few days to regroup; sometimes the

visits would be shortened by his appearance at the front door saying, "Let's go!"
Where else could I go with my kids?
I didn't know.
Before we knew it, he was rubbing the belly: baby number four, a daughter.

CHAPTER TEN

THERE REALLY ARE ANGELS

Knock, Knock!
I answered the door. "It's so nice to see you! Missy, Tina, hi!" I gave them a "save me" hug. "Come on in! Tina, I'm so glad you came to visit me; I needed some love and smiles about now!"
Tina looked the same, just thicker. She was my height with a fatter face and pressed long thin hair. She was wearing jeans, sneakers and a yellow button-down shirt.
"Hi Sandra!" I hugged Tina's daughter tight and long. "I haven't seen you in how long? Three years it's been right?"
"Yes! It has been that long. How is my baby sister?"
"I'm okay." I lifted up my head. "I'm fine, just a little stressed! You drove here from Philadelphia by yourself?" We walked into the living room.
"Well, I did most of the driving. Bill is parking the car he'll be in. You look pregnant!"
"I am!" I said, as I rubbed my tiny bulge. "Come in here, have a seat!"
Tina's eyebrows went up. "Again! So soon?"
"Yes, again; what can I say? I was using a stronger birth control pill this time but I guess it wasn't strong enough. You see them things on the table? It goes down with juice every morning!" I didn't want her to think I wasn't doing my part, like I wanted to keep getting pregnant at my young age. I was only twenty-one and I was carrying my fourth child.
Missy looked at me. "Well maybe after you have this one you can think about getting the other kinds of birth control!"
"Well, the only choices now I used and the doctor says that I'm too young to tie them. I'll probably tie them anyway; some women is said to be getting cutie cancer from the coils!"

"Hi Bill, how are you?" as I kissed him on his cheek after a warm hug. He put the largest suitcase down. He was so nice and quiet; he talked about God all the time.
He always looked happy all the time, filled with lots of laughter, playing jokes, reminding me of a Bill Cosby-kind of dad. He had dark skin and a thick body with a fat face and Jeri Curl. Tina bossed him around; she was the boss of him and everything else. She had always been like that.
I smiled at my sisters and noticed my niece. "Sandra how have you been? It's been so long! You've grown so much. You look so pretty; come here and give your auntie another hug!"

"Angel we want to take a shower and change our clothes; is that okay?" Missy asked.
"Sure of course! I'll tell you what. I was on my way out the door to take the kids to the park down the street. We'll be back in an hour or two, so that should give you two enough time to do what you need and want to do!" I laughed with Tina and her husband.
"Where is Chris?" Missy asked.
"He went to New York to see his mom."
"Oh, how is she?"
"She's fine; he just misses his mommy!" I giggled. "The towels are in the bathroom closet. Help yourself to anything in the fridge. Come on Tunisia." She was about three and Aqusia was one. Kameena was two. I picked her up to sit her in her stroller. "Come on Sandra." Sandra was 10; she was a cute girl with two big rabbit front teeth. She had two pigtails with big pink balls and a curl in the front.
"Come on kids lets go bye- bye!" They were so happy to be going bye-bye.
We were really hot after playing on the swings. The sliding board was hot enough to cook on so they couldn't play on that; I looked around. What else could we do?
I noticed water in the back of the park. I didn't know that was back there.
"Let's go!" I ran and skipped and pushed the stroller with a dance. I wanted to jump in the stream. No one else was there; we could see far left and far right and there wasn't a soul in sight. I wanted some kids for them to play with while I took a quick swim.

"It's so hot! It has to be about 100 degrees out here in this sun!" Sandra said wiping her forehead.
I took a cloth and dipped it in the water and cooled off the babies. I gave them juice with some ice so it was good and cold. I placed a little blanket down for Tunisia to sit on because she didn't like the grass to touch her. I don't want her running around. If I said, "Stay!" she stayed. She was the sweetest, well-mannered, well-behaved, smart-ass child I ever met. People always gave her shit just to hear her say, "thank you." You have to make most kids say, "thank you." Kameena, and Aqusia were well-taken care of by Tunisia so they'd be entertained.
I looked at Sandra. "Do you want to get in with me?" I kicked off my sneakers.
"No!"
"Why? Girl, you better come on and cool off!"
"I can't swim!"
"Really? I love to swim! Oh I swim well! I'll teach you!"
Sandra stuttered. "I can't get wet!"

"Don't worry, the sun will dry our clothes fast. It's really hot. I'll get in first. Oh this feels good!" I backed up a little until the water was up to my waist. "Come on in!"
"No! I'm scared!"
"Don't be scared! I'll hold you. Look at me, see?" I stretched out my arms. "Come on in girl!"
She slowly walked in but when the water came to her knees, she froze.
"I want you to move your arms like this!" I said as I moved mine in a circular motion. "And move your head with your mouth closed. Now go like this side-to-side, and kick your feet like this," and I swam towards her and stood up. "See it's easy! Come on in it feels so good!" I looked at my kids. "Hi kids, see Mommy!" I waved. "You stay right there now, don't move okay?"

Sandra walked in slowly. The closer she came the higher the water went up her body and she became more scared and backed up.
I grabbed her back. I held her hand and said, "Calm down, I got you!" I could see the fear in her face. "Okay! Turn around; I'll stand on your side and hold your waist while you move your arms and kick your feet, okay? Now lie down. Now swim back to the ground." She kicked like crazy, slapping the water with open hands.
"Cuff your hands!" I laughed. I looked up at the kids. I looked around making sure nobody will steal my babies. All I saw was miles and miles of grass. The park seemed so far away.
"Wait!" I said. "Wait!" I showed her the hand movement again and said; "Now lets do it again! Hi kids!" I waved and they smiled. "Sandra lie down and don't kick so hard. Move your hands in a cuff to feel the water, like you're grabbing it and pushing it behind you."
She kicked so hard that we started going backwards instead of forward. I stepped back a few more steps and there was no bottom and I realized I was in a current.

Sandra was still splashing like she was out of control because I was no longer holding her. She had her mouth open and water was going in. I tried to swim closer to her to push her forward a little so she could feel the bottom but I was being pulled to the right with the current. I couldn't help her this way so I thought I could swim around her and then I can pull her forward.
"Calm down Sandra I'm coming!" But I was going to try to save myself first at this time. I was gasping for air; the water was choking me. I couldn't talk. I was losing my breath and I couldn't swim out of it. It pulled me harder away from her. I was going down stream.
I was drowning. She was drowning.
When I popped my head up I saw my oldest daughter crying. "Mommy! Mommy!"

I saw no one to help us, or stop her, because Tunisia was coming towards the water!
I couldn't get the words out! Trying to get the words out I screamed, "Get back!" I waved.
The water kept going in my mouth and I didn't make any sense. My eyes were burning and clogged with green seaweed. Oh God help me. Help us all! Please!
I was going down. Water was all in my mouth and nose; there was no air left. I was being pulled down so hard that I couldn't do anything else. There was nothing I could do to fight.
I was going under to stay; someone under there wanted me.
I knew at that moment we were both going to die and what about my kids? It was my fault Sandra is over there drowning; I can't go home without her even if I could save myself, I no longer saw her she went under to stay.

Someone grabbed me from behind and lifted me up. I came up coughing hard.
I thought wow! How can you swim in this current?
He carried me to the ground and laid me down. I was still coughing.
I looked and I saw another boy, they were both about seventeen. One of them put Sandra down. He pushed down on her chest three times and she started to cough.
"Sandra, are you okay?" I yelled franticly. The boy backed up. She was spitting out water as she coughed, gagging.
I went and picked up crying Tunisia and I looked up to say, "thank you," but they were gone! Disappeared!
I looked far to the left and far to the right, and behind us, in the water and no one was in sight. They couldn't get out of sight that quick. I turned around in a circle looking again and saw no one. I wondered how he came from behind me. There were only woods on the other side of the stream.
Where did they come from?

Sandra was crying and yelling. "You let me go! You let me go!"
"I didn't know there was a current there and you kicked me into it!" But she didn't understand what the hell a current was. "I couldn't hold you! You were kicking me and swinging too hard!"
"You let me go!" she cried.
"No I'm sorry baby, I was wrong!" I held her and we just sat there for a while.
I thought about how dumb I was to leave the kids there alone.
"Where did they go? Sharon where did they go? Where are they?"
I turned to look around again still looking for some life. This was bizarre and then it occurred me!

I smiled real hard and looked up. "Thank you Creator, for sending us angels!" A week later, a boy about ten drowned and died in that very stream.

I also knew angels were with me the day evil was in my ear.
Chris and I were getting along very good most days but when we did argue and said the most painful, hurtful things we could think of saying to each other; we played the "I'm going to hurt you more than you hurt me" game. It's a very dangerous game that you don't even know you're playing.
His favorite words were, "Die bitch!" Or: "As far as I'm concerned you're dead!" Or: "I'll get you back; you know I will!" I was sure he would too.
Mine were, "I hate you and everything you do to me is going to come back on you; you'll see!" I would say shit like, "You weak ass dope fiend. You wouldn't be beating on me if my father or my brother were still alive! I'm going to pay someone to beat your punk ass up for me!"
The Evil in my ear said, "Say more hurtful things! It will feel good!"
Chris and I always made up with sex. There was no talking; nothing was ever resolved. It was just pushed under the rug as they say, with his hoping to never see the dirt again and me wanting to clean it out so I could throw it in his face to remind him it was still there.

He was irresistible when he was sober. He was so sweet and considerate and helpful and he treated me like a queen, like I was the most beautiful woman in the world, like I was the breath he breathed. He would give me the world and all his heart. I watched him play with the kids or battle the storms trying to detoxify and I'd fall in love with him all over again.
I saw his efforts; I knew his abilities, strengths, and I wanted to encourage and support him because he was someone very special under that drunken sprit, under the devil's heel.
I took the damn birth control pills but between the fights and the making up, the babies kept coming: four girls a year apart.
And here I was pregnant again! I was totally against abortions and that messy diaphragm couldn't always be planned ahead of time.
I went to see the doctor. After the examination he said, "You have to have an abortion because the baby will come out deformed. Angel, you could die."
The Evil voice said, "Kill the baby! You have too many kids now!"
"What kind of infection?" Chris asked:
"It's Pseudomonas from your iguana. It's an infection that cannot be treated while she is pregnant."
Chris looked at me. "Angel we could always have children; I need you! I love you! I can't lose you baby! We need you! You have to have this abortion!"

This would be our fifth child. It really would be a lot for us to handle. Our baby had just turned two months old. Chris only heard that I could die. That's it! He didn't want to hear anything else.
"Oh hell no! You're not dying so I guess we have to listen to the doctor Angel!"
I thought the doctor was biased. He actually believed that I was just a twenty-two year-old girl who shouldn't have a fifth baby and be on welfare and he just didn't want to support us with his tax money while I laid on my ass, getting pregnant by a man with no job.
My man could keep a job; he was just in between jobs. And I didn't like being on welfare!
I looked at the doctor and then at Chris. "This is the son I've been waiting for. He will be fine and so will I!" I walked out. I smelled the evening spring mountain air from up the hill as I held on to Chris' arm. He supported me home as my legs became weaker and weaker. I got another doctor.

"God please help our son be healthy," I prayed. "I believe that you want my son to live, so let it be! Keep the Devil from taking my son with his recommended abortion, please!" Once again, my instincts were confirmed to be true. We did have a son.
I knew it! I knew it was a boy! I knew it was the son I asked God for!
Thank you God! I was so happy. "Thank you angels for telling me not to have an abortion, no matter what that doctor said!"
Our baby had a bad case of jaundice and had to be hospitalized under florescent light for a few days. His lungs were weak so he had to be transported by helicopter to an Albany hospital.
Dr. Evil said, "There is a chance he will die within the first week."
But my faith was stronger than his diagnosis.

CHAPTER ELEVEN

WHY DO I LOVE CHRIS?

Mercedes asked me, "Angel, why do you stay with him?" as we ate at the table.

"Chris is so good to me when he is not drunk and I need him. He can be so sweet; there's nothing he wouldn't do for me. He loves his children and he is very good at taking care of them. You see that! Sometimes it's like being in paradise with him. I feel lucky he stayed with me and didn't run away like most babies' daddies!

"He has so many qualities; he is articulate and meticulous, and funny and talented. He plays drums, the bass and percussion drums, and piano and the bass fiddle. He can box very well, and people respect him, and he is fine and dresses his ass off. I love his walk; I love watching him move, and listening to him talk. And he loves me, and he is my best friend. I feel blessed to be with him. And; the sex is great! Really great," I laughed.

She just looked at me. "Well, I know he better stop hitting you because I'm going to bust something up side his head! He is not going to keep beating on my friend!"

"I know, I hate him then too," and we hugged. I put my head on her shoulders thinking about the quart of beer he poured on my head just last night.

It was a blizzard outside, down in the bottom of the mountain where we lived. The supermarket was up the very top, five miles away. Chris went into the blizzard and walked those five miles to get the baby's milk and some food.

I was so ignorant. I never even thought about Chris with another woman. I believed, because he loved me so much he would never lay with another woman.

It was so easy for depression to get in me. I started feeling really sad thinking about him sharing his body with someone else. The only reason I knew about it was because of the Gonorrhea! How many other woman have he been with? He had unbuckled his pants and pulled out my stuff and shared it. I wonder did he suck her…, oh my, I can't handle the thoughts, the visions.

I never thought about another woman until the doctor said to me, "You have contracted Gonorrhea!"

So that's why he told me to go to the doctor. "Oh, you don't remember how your pants got off?" I said to Chris. "You don't know which woman you fucked? I don't want to be touched by you ever again!"

My mom had come to visit us. She was sitting in our kitchen at the table quietly, never moving.

Stunned, I confronted him in the bedroom. "Okay! I went and got the shot in my ass and for what? And for who? You broke your vow to me; we are no longer one! You violated our space! I hate you! I hate your ass! You have the nerve to accuse me of shit!"

"Come here Angel!"

"No don't touch me!" I pulled my arms away, wiping my tears so he saw only anger, not weakness! "Don't ever touch me! You're disgusting! You gave me a disease mother-fucker! You fucking bastard! I hate your ass!"

"I'm sorry," he said. He threw me on the bed and started kissing and feeling on me.

I pushed him up. "Stop it! What the hell are you doing? Go the fuck back outside with your dirty disease-carrying bitch! You'll get no pussy here! Ever!"

"I want you now! I'm sorry! I love you Angel, let me show you!"

"I don't want to have no damn sex! Besides, my mother is in the kitchen and I'm still angry and hurt; Are you crazy?"

Out of fear of angering him and getting another black eye, I tried to speak nicely since mom was here. "Listen Chris, I'm going in there with my mom we'll talk about this later, okay?"

"No!" He pushed me back down and I struggled to get up. I yelled, "Get the fuck off of me!"

"Don't be mad at me okay?"

"Well get off of me then!"

He held both of my hands down behind my head with just one hand. He pulled down my jeans and panties and pulled down his and Bong! He was long and hard as a rock. He jumped on top of me and forced my legs open and pushed his hot, throbbing penis inside of me with long, deep, hard strokes. He pulled my hair back with his other hand and sucked my neck real hard.

"Get off of me Chris! Now get up!"

I got loose and punched him in his back a few times. He just held me down with both arms and continued to penetrate my dry, resistant piece of ass.

Exhausted from struggling, I just laid there with tears rolling down the side of my face soaking the pillow. He kept whispering, "I love you!" As he crawled and climbed up me, deeper and deeper I gasped for air.

"I love you," he said over and over in my ear.

He held his head back and pulled up my legs higher and pushed in deeper till I felt it in my stomach. He screamed, "Oooh shit!" and pushed in deeper and then froze. He bit his bottom lip and squirted a big nut, a long continuous throb. Then in slow motion he fell on me, and he grabbed my face and kissed me deeply on my lips. I turned away sighing.

I didn't kiss him back and he turned my face back towards him and looked me in my eyes. "I'm sorry, I won't ever get that drunk again. I won't have sex with anyone else. You're all I want!" He was looking down on me with his pitiful, puppy dog eyes. "Do you love me?"

Just to get him out of my face I said, "Yes Chris, I love you!" I hope he knew he just raped me!

The sadness overwhelmed me. As soon as he got off of me I ran in the bathroom and locked the door.

Chris went out the door. I came out of the bathroom and sat down in the kitchen. I told my mom and she didn't know what to say. "Your father gave it to me too! He always cheated on me! He would screw anyone!" Gee Mom thanks I thought; Just what I need to hear now. My desire being only for him I stayed faithful. I could have dealt with the cheating if I could lie under another man for comfort but he was my only desire.

One night, one question, gone badly.

I made some spaghetti, Chris' favorite. "Chris and Mercedes come on and eat!" I yelled. He sat down at one end of the table and I sat at the other end facing him. Mercedes sat in the middle.

As I buttered my bread I thought, why not ask now? He hasn't said shit to me since he came in the house. There was so much tension at the table. My heart was in an avalanched state. I couldn't keep quiet. I had to ask! "Where you been last night? You didn't come home till 6am!" The kids were in there room watching TV they had already eaten.

Before I could say another word, he stood up and flipped the table up in the air. Spaghetti went everywhere; the walls were covered. It was on the stove and the floor, the cabinets, the table and me.

My mouth hung open looking at the broken glasses and plates. The broken table leg was on the floor lying on the yellow and now orange tablecloth.

I looked at him in total shock. He was steaming with his fist balled. His eyebrows went down and his eyes crossed as they always did when he was mad.

He yelled a few obscenities and threw up his hands. "I don't need this shit!"

"That was my damn food too! Shit!" Mercedes yelled. "The man done lost his damn mind!" She leaned on the side of the wall that the food hadn't touched with her arms folded, one foot in front of the other tapping it. "What was that all about?" She was one hungry, angry woman. It was funny but no one was laughing.

"What's wrong with you?" I yelled boldly with my arms folded. "I'm not cleaning that shit up either!"
He walked towards me fast. I backed up to the wall. He grabbed me by my throat and squeezed so tight I couldn't breathe.
I looked him square in the eye. "Go ahead, kill me! I don't care!" I sounded like a man. "Go ahead! Kill me!"
Mercedes tried to pull him off of me but he was too strong and she is just a tiny thing.
He let go just as I passed out. I woke up to Mercedes cursing him out.
He pointed at the floor standing over me. "Now clean this shit up!"
I got on my knees and picked up some broken glass and put it together slowly. He went to lay down in the living room, which was right next to the kitchen. He laid his ass on our couch on his back, with his hands laid across his chest like he was laid to rest.
I was breathing hard trying to catch my breath and calm down. Mercedes was shaking her head. "This shit doesn't make any sense." She helped me up. She held the table as I screwed the leg back on.

I looked over at Chris. He was already snoring!
I ran some cold water in the biggest pot I could find. I tiptoed over to him and took the pot of water and threw it right in his damn face.
He jumped straight up and started grabbing his throat, gasping for air like he couldn't catch his breath.
I jumped back and continued backing up into the kitchen just in case I needed a weapon. I thought, he is going to die! He can't breathe! Wow! I looked at his face. His eyes popped wide open and he turned blue for a while.
My first response was to go pat him on the back but my feet wouldn't move. He began coughing.
"See how it feels not to be able to breathe?" I yelled. "Mother fucking asshole! Don't fuck with me any more! I'll kill you! I'll kill your ass!" I was ready to run but I was frozen watching him coughing for relief.
Astounded that he didn't come after me; I thanked God.
I went into my room and slammed the door. I sat on my bed for a while, scared. If he came in here hitting me I was going to crack his head wide open with this iron.

We moved to Philadelphia to a huge three-story home right down the street from mom on Old York Road. We started getting real close. I visited her everyday or she would sit on the porch with me while we watched the kids play.
I prayed and read the Bible everyday. I went to church and asked God for some peace and happiness.
It was in that house that it happened.

I dreamed that I saw people being slaughtered like pigs directly across the street from my house where a three-story abandoned building stood. In my dream, there was so much loud screeching and screaming, and dead bodies were all over the streets. There were so many children of all ages, and men and woman with their faces torn off, with blood flowing down the street like a river stream.

The screams just ran through my body and made me shake inside and out. I held my ears to cast out the loud, painful screams. Skin was burning off people's bodies and there was a pit where people were on fire.

I could feel their pain. The smell of flesh carried further than the screams. I was scared the torturers were going to get me too.

I ran on my side of the street and looked back. I saw Chris going towards the pit to look closer.

I ran screaming out his name. Stop! I ran back across the street and grabbed him by his arm and pulled him across the street with me stomping in puddles of blood. We started walking towards Erie Avenue two blocks up.

Still holding his hand, pulling him as far away as I can. I looked up in total shock.

I couldn't believe my eyes. It was really happening, and it was so powerful and beautiful to behold. My heart started beating even faster. "LOOK! LOOK! CHRIS, LOOK!"

I saw an army of thousands and thousands of figures of men in white on horses and a shiny man in white leading them on a white horse coming out of the sky, riding on the clouds with thunder and horns blowing loudly. The strange evil things were roaming. It was nighttime on the side of the street where the pit was. I looked back and saw that the sky was black and red. And on the side of the street where the horses were coming with God's son, it was daylight. The sky was bright blue. In astonishment I said, "Wow, the end of the world is really here!" I held Chris with my left hand as he was on the curbside of the street

I held up my right hand and I prayed with all my heart and soul and tears were rolling fast down my cheeks.

I said The Lord's Prayer slowly, to feel each and every word, and loudly, so He could hear me.

It was a horrible sight to see: so much blood and so many bones in the streets. The children's screams shivered through my body but when I saw Heaven open and the pureness that was descending; there was joy.

I felt blessed. I knew I was going back with them. I was ready to be taken away. I wasn't letting go of Chris' hand either.

Than I woke up! I knew we had to change and leave here. Hell was right across our street right next to "Nate the Snake," one of Chris' get high buddies and his wife Barbara, my weed partner.
I would have more nightmares. Snakes were coming in and out of me. I wish I knew what this dream meant! I was soon to find out about the snakes and Hell!

I woke up to the slamming of the door. Chris came back in the house with two other men and went in the basement. The kids were in their rooms upstairs on the second floor in bed. They had two really large bedrooms next to each other. That meant lots of room to run, jump and play. Upstairs on the third floor, in the smallest and most peaceful room in the house, I taped Scripture all over the four walls on boards. Whenever we argued I went up there to pray and be still, and to sleep on the garbage bags full of clothes if I had to. The room stayed empty. I never put a thing in it but my bags of bedding.

Later I was looking for our son Cyris.
I saw him at the top of the stairs on the third floor. He knew better than to go up there!
"Cyris, what are you doing up there baby? Come down here now!"
My two year-old son stood by the window, near that blessed room and said, "Look Mommy, I see God! Look Mommy, God is right there! Come here, look!" He pointed out at the star-lit sky.
I ran up the stairs in amazement. I never told him that God was in the sky. We were still working on praying over food and bedtime prayers. We hadn't talked about God.
I looked out to where he pointed. It was behind my house, where I saw the horses coming from Erie Avenue. "I believe you baby!" I gave him a big smile from my pounding heart, overjoyed in amazement. I hugged him and the tears started flowing. My son sees God! "That's right baby it's God!"
He had never gone up to the third floor before. No one went up there except me to pray. Sometimes, Chris went in the bathroom up there to get high alone.
This boy is going to be real special if he gives his life over to God I thought. I put him to bed and kissed him and the girls goodnight saying, "You girls be quiet now and go to sleep. I love you all. Sleep with the Angels."

I was feeling good about our kids. They were all so individually beautiful and always doing something amazing.
I tiptoed downstairs to see who was in the house. I peeked through the cracks in the hardwood floor where I could see everything in the

basement where Chris had taken two men. I had to move around quietly to find the right crack to get a good view.
One man pulled out his works and was cooking heroin or cocaine or both in his spoon. There was silence except the only three words I heard "My turn next!"
But before Chris could get his turn, the man squished in the last drop from his syringe and SLAM! His face hit that cold hard ass concrete floor.
"Oh shit!" I said. I thought he cracked his skull.
Chris was smacking that man's face hard, saying, "Wake up!" He heard me and hollered, "Angel, get me some ice, quick, hurry up!"
I ran into the kitchen and got a tray. "Get me a towel too!" he yelled. He turned to the other man. "Help me hold him up, while I pull down his pants." I grabbed the kitchen towel and ran downstairs as Chris kept saying; "Hurry! Hurry up! Hurry!"
When I got downstairs the tall, skinny, toothless man was back in the chair, being held up by some strange man I never seen before. He was dark and short, and scared as shit, shaking.
The lighter skinned man was limp, sitting with his head down. His pants were off and his legs were wide open and I saw his limp penis.
I didn't know what the hell was going on. This was some freaky shit!
Chris grabbed the ice and put it in the towel. "Hold him back in the chair!" He opened his legs and as he fell forward; Chris put the ice under his balls.
The other man said, "He's not breathing!" He walked closer to the wooden stairs. "He's dead Chris!" He backed up ready to run. "Yo man I'm out!"
Chris looked at him in disgust and yelled, "Keep your ass right there! Don't you fucking move! Now help me hold him up!"

"Oh shit!" I said again. I covered my mouth out of fear that Death was visiting our blessed home. "He can't die in our basement! No! Oh my God! Wake him up!" I prayed with my hands together over my lips.
Chris managed to lay him on the cold, dusty concrete and started pumping on his heart and breathing in his mouth. That was the first time I had seen CPR. The man woke up like he just came out of a nod and wanted another hit.
Oh! We all were so relived. We all breathed out at the same time.
"Get the fuck out right now!" I screamed. "Don't ever come back to my house ever again! Get the fuck out!"
Chris helped him up to his feet. The man was pulling up his pants, asking where the drugs were, now in a nod from his recent hit.
I couldn't believe my ears. "YOU DIED!" I screamed at the top of my lungs. "You died and Chris BROUGHT YOU BACK TO LIFE! He

saved your life and you want more?" I screamed again and again. "Get out!" Pushing them towards the steps, I yelled, "Move faster!"
Chris didn't say a word to me, just to them. "Lets go fellers!"
That man died in my basement and Chris brought him back to life!

I had always begged, "No Chris, not in my house!"
His reply was always the same. "Come on baby, he/she is hooking me up!"
I hated it whenever he brought someone in our house. I was scared someone was going to die. I was not prepared for any shit like that, so I would constantly yell; kicking the doors loud and hard, screaming, "Get the fuck out of my house!" I was supposed to sit there all cool while he and some bitch was in the bathroom for what seemed like hours and not say nothing? Please!
I cursed people out so much they stopped coming. I blamed the people that were getting him high. I wished they all would die! Just not in my house, with our kids and me!

Chris stopped bringing them home. Thank God!
He knew that I'd blow his high and make him spill his shit. I'd embarrass him. I'd do anything to get them out of my basement or bathroom. He became paranoid of me whenever he got high, so he found other places to do it.

Chris called a hot line and asked them to pray with him as I slept.
I woke up and smiled; pleased that he still prayed so I got on my knees with him and held his hands and quietly prayed with him and for him.
"God, I feel like an avalanche is coming. Please I ask you God to give us guidance, strength and support, and some peace. I beg you Father. Please fill me with knowledge, wisdom, and understanding, so that I may be a person you can be proud of, and help Chris stop using drugs!" I was told in Church, "Where two or more agree there the Father will be."

I believe he heard the prayers of two sinful addicts desiring a change.

CHAPTER TWELVE

ESCAPE TO PARADISE

"Wow! I won! I won! I won a trip to Florida!" Three days and four nights, including hotel and food.
Our choice was Orlando, Miami or Fort Lauderdale. I wanted to go to Orlando.
Wow, now that's paradise. We had to get out of Philly before he dies.
I knew if I went there, then God would help us. God and Chris always found us a home. I prayed and prayed. I went to church in jeans.
One day, I asked God to answer me: should we go, because if we did then I was going to stay there!
I opened the Bible and it said, "Go, and I will prepare the way." I closed the Bible and opened it again. I came to the same page: "Go, and I will prepare the way."
Oh this was cool. Could I do that again? I closed the book tight so the page would be harder to get to and I opened the Bible slowly again, and sure enough, there it was.
I laughed and cried. "Okay! I got the message! Thank you Father!" and from then on when I wanted answers I used that method and it always worked.

I called Orlando and I got the Salvation Army's number and told them I was coming there on vacation and wanted to know if they had room for us to stay there for two weeks to wait for our vacation room. I gave myself some room; I really only needed one week. I told them we had six kids ages 2,3,4,5,6,7, and they said, "Yes!"
I was surprised. I was waiting for them to say; "If you don't live here or are not homeless already here in Florida then we can't help you." I was prepared to beg. But they kept their word and were waiting for us.
I introduced our six babies, starting with the oldest and ending with the youngest: Tunisia very smart; Kameena is very compassionate; Aquasia is mean; Samara the jokester; Cyris is over active; and Laqwana is very neat. We had four beautiful light-skinned girls, one chocolate sweetheart and of course our son.

We paid $600 for our vacation packages. I mailed that off hoping it wasn't a gag. I waited impatiently for a month for the response that everything was arranged and they would be expecting us.
We packed six kids and six suitcases, and took buses and trains.
We were on our way to a new life.

Chris thought I was crazy but he wasn't going to let me leave him behind and he wasn't going to let go of his family so he went along with it.
I felt in my gut it was the right thing to do for our children and us.
I knew God would protect us and guide us. I had faith.
I saw palm trees and swimming pools and pictured myself in my sexiest bathing suit, smiling on Chris face while other men looked at me. I saw the many beautiful sunsets Chris and I would share, and Disney World right there for the kids.
I saw all of this as I lay my head back thinking about our Paradise as I tried to get comfortable in my seat on the bus.
My family is going to be so jealous I thought. I opened my eyes and watched Chris cover up the sleeping kids with their jackets. He put their stuffed animals under their heads for a pillow; all of them had to bring one.

When we arrived, the Salvation Army had our beds prepared. Chris had to sleep on the men's side. I put the kids in bed and as I laid in mine, I looked around. This place is clean and big I thought. It was night time so I couldn't see much outside but I did see my palm trees. I could smell the fragrances of flowers all along the walkway to the door.
"Wow, I can't believe it, we're really here!" I smiled hard and said quietly in the dark, "Thank you God! Thank you so much!"
In the morning, the kids and I couldn't move fast enough. We were filled with excitement; we wanted to see this new place.
Chris and I talked to the agency about how long we'd be staying. I did tell them two weeks, and so I told them when we come back from our vacation we would need two or three more weeks. I called the vacation people. They had messed up and had given away our cabin. They said we would have to wait a month.
"What? We're here in Florida already! We're not trying to hear that!"
They insisted there was nothing they could do except gives us a refund within two weeks.
I wasn't that disappointed because we were already here. Chris was down with what ever I wanted. I was happy enough just being here.

There was a gorgeous place called Lake-E-O-la. We went to it everyday. It was our ritual. We ate lunch with the ducks because like all shelters they put your assess out early.
I got on public assistance quickly and with food stamps we were able to buy us all some lunch everyday and plenty of snacks. I got about $500 cash every two weeks so we saved most of it.
We loved feeding the tall as the two-year-old baby ducks cheese balls and the ducks loved it. We were surrounded by at least twenty-five at a time.

We were all so happy. We were one big happy family. We didn't have anything material but we had each other and this beautiful lake, with a goal to get our own home. We would line six kids up and they walked and stood in lines like ducks everywhere we went. We stayed in the shelter for about a month.
One night Cyris was sleeping with me and I rolled over to hold him and my baby was burning up. He had a very high fever and I was afraid he was going to die!
I was a twenty-three year-old mother trying to prove that I knew what I was doing but it was the middle of the night and I had nothing to give him. What do I do? I thought.
I ran downstairs to the office and they gave me some ice. I rubbed my crying baby all over his head and behind his neck to make sure his head don't boil. I learned that you put ice under their balls from Chris so I did.
He was limp. "Wake up baby" I silently told him "open your eyes."
He was so red and hot, sweating. I prayed, "Please God don't let him die." I cooled off his body with the icy rag for about an hour until he cooled off a little and went to sleep. I stayed awake all night monitoring him.
Thank God he woke up, he was fine the next day.

As we all stood against a wall in the lounge room waiting for Chris to come down stairs this tall lady, with long dark hair and spooky black eyes came by and said, "You have some beautiful children! They are so well behaved. Can I look at her hand?" She grabbed our oldest daughter Tunisia hand. She smiled and said; "She is a very smart girl and she will have many achievements. She sees greatness, prosperity."
"Yeah, she was in a gifted class and she wins first place at everything she enters." Tunisia and I smiled at each other. "All of my children are smart!" I said. "Look at my hand! Here, look at mine!" I push my hand in her face.
She looked at it and then at me. She looked frightened.
"What?" I asked. "What do you see?"
"Nothing… I have to go," and she literally ran away from me.
"Wait! You can't just leave me hanging like that! Come back!" I called.
She never even turned around; she was gone.

I wondered what she saw. It bothered me.
I looked at my palm and than at Tunisia's. She had five long deep lines. I had about ten lines crisscrossing each other. Some were deep and some were light but there were a lot.
"Damn, how can she not see anything?" I whispered. I looked at my other hand; it had about ten crisp lines there. Damn.

They were all significantly deep and going around my hand never ending. My lifeline went straight, then stopped and turned into another direction. It wasn't straight like Tunisia's.
I started looking at all the kid's hands and their lines were simple too.
My palms were real busy, and I wasn't even counting the fifty little tiny lines in each hand. Shit!
The Bible said not to go to any psychics. But I wanted to know now! Could I read a book about it?
I was really considering going to see one now. "I'll respect you," I said to God. "I know you got this." I really wanted to see her again. I really needed to know what she thought she saw. Was she going to tell me she saw death?
Shit, she could have made something up but she ran. And she was so accurate with the way she described Tunisia. Maybe she really could see something. She sure did look terrified. I knew it was bad news, that's why she couldn't just tell me! But she should have said something! Maybe I would have been aware of what not to do or where not to go or something that I could prevent… whatever!
That stayed on my mind for days. I looked for her everyday but I never saw her again.
I looked harder at my hand everyday and then I saw it! I saw it, there it was!
I had wings! I had angel's wings on the palms of my hands! So that's why your evil ass ran!

We were in rooms upstairs. On the main floor we had to walk pass other people's rooms. I'm noisy so I always looked in. There was an elderly Indian woman with her daughter in a room, and she was trying to help the old woman get out of her chair and on to her bottom bunk bed. I thought it was so nice to see someone caring for the old lady.
One day in the hallway that old lady stopped me. She admired my children. "Are you a Cherokee Indian?" she asked me.
"Yes!" I said proudly. "My grandmother told me I was. She looked just like an Indian."
She started coughing. "Are you okay?" I asked.
She was short and bent over. She looked so fragile. She had gray and black hair that was parted into two braids. She had a sincere smile.
Her daughter was a little heavy, with one ponytail hanging down her back. She told me that her mother was very sick and was suffering from cancer and wasn't given much time to live.
"I'm sorry to hear that." I looked at the old woman as I patted her back. She was coughing hard and long. I could tell that each one hurt her chest as she collapsed forward.
After she wiped her mouth, she said in her gentle voice, "We are Cherokee Indians also."

"Yeah? That's cool!" I said excitedly: I looked hard to see if I had any of their features but I didn't. I did see that their eyes looked sad like mine. Chris came down from the men's side looking good and sober. I reached out to kiss him good morning; mmm, he smelled like snacks. I introduced them and we went to breakfast.

Later that day I went to their room to visit them.
I wanted some answers. I never met a real Indian before except Grandma. I was drawn to them. "Come in and have a seat!" said the daughter with her welcoming smile and a gentle nod at a chair.
The elderly woman inquired about my grandparents. I told her what my grandmother said about getting the book, "Trail of Tears" and reading it. I had brought it with me. I was proud of myself for remembering. We talked for about an hour.
"You should visit North Carolina's Cherokee reservation," she said to me.
"God willing I will one day," I responded.
"You know something?" she said to me as she reached out to hold both of my hands. She placed them in her warm, soft hands.
"What?"
"I love your sprit!" she responded softly. "I feel like I've known you all my life."
I smiled at her, wishing she didn't have to die. She was so nice and her daughter jumped every time she coughed or needed something.
"I want to give you a name!" she exclaimed.
I was elated. "Okay!"
She thought for one second and then said, "I have chosen for you a new name, a name that describes what I see in your sprit. You are to be called, 'Cherokea,' because your sprit flows like the water stream that will quench thirsty dreamers."
"Thank you!" I smiled proudly. "I love my new name."
I walked down the hall with my head high to find my sweetheart and the kids. Eventually, I'd get more of my ancestors' information when I visited the Reservation.
Wow, "Cherokea!" I liked that name. It sounded good and the meaning was deep.

I saw people standing in the Community Room in a staff meeting. In walked an elderly Hispanic man.
"Good morning, my name is Santos. I have a few apartments to be cleaned. Does anyone want some work?"
A voice inside me said, "If he has houses to clean then maybe he has some to rent!"
I went up to him. "Do you have apartments for rent?" I asked.
"Yes! Yes I do"

“Really?” My eyebrows went up. “How many bedrooms and how much is the rent?” I asked.
The short plump man scratched his head with his pen. “Well, I have a four-bedroom house on Rio Grande for $400 a month, and a two-bedroom…” But before he could tell me more about the two-bedroom house, I interrupted him. “Go back to the four-bedroom.” I was surprised; this was just too good to be true. “When can we see it?”
“Tomorrow; I’m too busy today!”
“I have six kids and a husband!”
“It’s perfect for them; it has a big yard in the back.”
“Great, give me the address and my husband and I will call you tomorrow so we can see it okay?’
He handed me his card which felt like gold in my hands. “Here is my number.”
“Thank you so much.” I gave him a big smile as I walked away.
I looked back and said, “I’m going to call you early okay?”

“Chris! Chris!” I saw him and the kids in the park playing tag.
“What’s the matter? Are you okay?”
“We just may have a new home tomorrow!”
“What?” He looked surprised.
“Yeah baby, I just talked to a man that is renting out apartments! Here’s his card.” I started jumping up and down. I kissed Chris on the cheek giggling. Then I started chasing the kids acting like a monster. I screamed, “I’m going to get you! Ggggrrrrallll!” They screamed and ran laughing. I was so happy.

The next day Chris called and we meet the man at the house. God please let us be able to get it, I don’t care what it looks like. We’ll fix it up. It will be ours and it’s somewhere to start. I hoped it was nice though.
We had $600 that was returned to us from the vacation people, plus a check for $400. We had enough for a security deposit and one month’s rent.

The place was beautiful.
There was a large palm tree out front and grass was growing around the large white house. A beautiful flower garden was in front of a long screen patio.
There was the living room; the kitchen; two bedrooms to the right by a bathroom; and two large bedrooms with another bathroom to the left. The backyard was so big; the swings would go over there near the back. A washer and dryer would go here on the back porch, and oh, a garden over there. I can do my laundry and look at the kids or at the amazing sky.

It was Paradise. God had prepared the way, just like He said He would.

CHAPTER THIRTEEN
CRACK COMES TO FLORIDA

Chris got a construction job right away. I started going to college, studying to be a paralegal.
Each of us had a nice new bike. We had a nice comfortable home. Chris filled it up with everything we needed, and Mr. Santos hooked the kids up with candy through the window. He was the best landlord you could ask for.
After about two years, my family came to go to Disney World; my mom and my two sisters stayed with us. My sisters each had one boy and one girl. Tina's husband came; Missy's new husband didn't. They loved our house and I was so proud to show it off. There was a gorgeous lake where we would all go and lay back and watch the sun set. Our house was so beautiful. All the flowers were blooming and the grass was never so greener. Everyone had a great time.

We spent $1500 getting extra beds and handmade blankets, new sheets, and towels, lots of good food, and a water cooler. My brother-in-law commented that the bathroom was so nice you could sleep in there. Therefore, we didn't have the money to go to Disney with them. It was a choice; they would have been just as content sleeping on the floors. "Hey, we can go any time; maybe next income tax time," I said to them. "Yeah, that's when we'll go."
My kids were great about it. They really didn't act like they minded at all. I cared more about having everything so right; that was more important than spending $1500 for us to go to Disney World. We would need a lot more money, but I really didn't want them to hate me.
Yes, it was paradise! Chris was the best husband in the world. The kids were the greatest! And I looked damn good; my body was in top shape!
I knew he was a good man; he just had to get away from those people that were influencing him.
Chris would put on my wig and show us his legs and sing that Ike and Tina Turner song, "Proud Mary," shaking his ass fast. He would make us laugh for hours.
He would take care of the kids while I attended to my paralegal studies at Orlando College at night. He was great with feeding them and giving them baths. In Florida there is no dirt, just sand, and I saw what some kid's legs and arms looked like in the Salvation Army because no one was washing them before they went to bed. They were scarred and scabbed up and had black marks from old infected wounds because of the sand flies. I vowed every night that my kids would take baths.

I was so proud of myself; I was dressing professionally, typing 80 words a minute and maintaining a B average considering that I was raising six children with my biggest child being my husband.

I was just so excited about living.

I met a sister that became my best friend. They called her Sweetness. She was a big boned woman, with dark skin. She drove trucks long distances for a living. She had a big silver van that had furniture in it, a couch and tables and shit. I wasn't privatized to viewing inside such a thing, much less hanging out in a mobile van. I was impressed. I thought it was so cool to have her park in front of my house and I'd sit in it and wish I could own one to show off!

We would drink wine coolers and smoke some weed and just laugh with her friends until our faces hurt.

Chris didn't complain much; he didn't smoke weed. He wasn't drinking or getting high, either so I know he did feel a little left out.

One morning, I welcomed the new day, pleased with the beauty I saw and still shining from the pleasures with Chris from the night before. I yawned and stretched at the front door, smelling the misty grass.

I felt fantastically happy until Chris said, "Angel, I got a call from Barbara and Nate. They lost their job and their apartment." They were the ones living across the street from us up in Philly right next door to my Hell.

I shrugged my shoulders. "Sorry to hear that!"

"Well, they want to know if they can come here and stay with us for a while until they get their place."

"Chris, we've already let thirty-eight people live with us over a ten-year period. Don't you think we did our share of helping people out with their problems? No! I don't like Nate anyway with his nasty ass! Grinning like he wanta to eat me."

Chris and Nate used to be gone for hours getting high and doing I don't know what! He had that sneaky look with his perverted eyes, and I believed he was a bad influence around my man. That's why I really didn't like him. He was a good person when he was sober and a great thinker; I think that's why Chris tolerated him. He would give him a verbal challenge.

Chris visited people but he hung out with very few. I think that was why Chris hung with him so he had some intellectual conversation. With Nate, he could talk about politics and war, the economy and reparations for the black man.

"Well you and Barbara hung out. She's supposed to be your friend," Chris said to me.

"No, we're not friends. She's cool but we're associates. She is my sister's friend. We smoked a little weed together sometimes, that's it! We waited and hung out together and sat on the porch waiting for our men to return home and then we'd go home. We never hung out!" I went to the coffee table and lit a cigarette. "And Nate still gets high and you're not getting high anymore so you can't have him around you. No! I don't want him here and that's all there is to it!"
Chris stood by the opened door. "That's why they want to come here, to get away from the life like I did."

I didn't think they could fine heroin and cocaine and needles here. It was too nice in our neighborhood with big beautiful houses everywhere you turned. But I still didn't want them here.
"I'm not taking any chances; everything is perfect for us now." I looked at him in despair. "Don't destroy what we have here, please!"
Chris looked at the floor. "I already told them yes!"
"What?" I got up from the couch and sat at the edge of the chair.
"Come on baby, we can help them get away from that life and start over. They both keep jobs."
"Well they don't seem to have one now do they? And why the hell are you even asking me? Shit, you told them 'yes,' and now you say you don't want to let them down and say no!"
"Sorry baby, I just couldn't say 'no.' they're homeless. I would want someone to look out for me!"
"Yeah but would they?" I paused. What could I do? He already told them they could stay. "One month Chris, that's it! I don't care where they go but they have to get out of here."

Two weeks after they arrived, they were eating more than we anticipated. We were constantly running back and forth to the market.
One night, I was getting dressed for school. I had to be there by 6:00pm. I looked for Chris to say goodbye.
"Chris!" I yelled!
"I'm in here! I'll be right out!" he called from the small bedroom we gave them next to ours.
All of a sudden, I got a bad feeling in my stomach. I knocked hard on the door. I heard them talking and then silence.
I started getting angry. They were taking too damn long to open the door.
I yelled and knocked harder. "Open the door!" Then I heard the door unlock. I walked in the bedroom and I smelled something strange.
Chris and Nate were smoking something off a bent can with holes poked in the middle. Chris puffed from the drinking hole and smoke started coming out of the can.
"What the hell is that?" I asked.
"Don't worry about it," Chris said. "Go ahead to school!"

"I can't leave the kids here now!" I screamed. "What is that shit, crack?"
"Yeah!" Nate said in between puffs and coughs.
I didn't know too much about crack, only what I'd heard on a news show, where a man said it was so addictive and that people would do just about anything for it.
"Damn, I knew this shit was going to happen! Chris, please don't do this to us, please!"
He frowned. "Look, I don't say nothing to you when you're smoking weed and drinking your wine coolers with Sweetness and your friends, now do I?"
"Chris damn it! Please don't do this!" I started tearing up.

I was hoping Chris would understand. "Okay," I imagined him saying. "I won't do this! I love you and I won't take you through any more pain and suffering with drugs. You're right; I will not do this to you Angel! I won't do this for our family! Nate she's right, I don't want this shit! You have to leave now. You're bring poison into my home and into my life and I can't hang with you!"
But he didn't hear a word I said.
So I said it. "Nate you have to leave. I want you out!"
Chris looked at me. "This is my house too! I say he stays!"
I thought to myself, what am I going to do? I can't go through him using cocaine with the needle again and this might take him back to it. Is he going to put everything in the pawnshop again? Oh no, my paradise had been invaded and it was slowly becoming a nightmare, and there was nothing I could do about it! I had to show him how much this would hurt us.
I had to think of something to make him stop. So I sat down next to Chris and Nate. "I want some!" I said. "I said I want some!"
They didn't respond.
"Don't ignore me!" I screamed. "I want some too then, if this is what you're going to do then I'm going to do it too!"
"No Angel, go to school!" Chris snapped.
"Here Chris." Nate passed it off and watched. Chris held the matches upside down like an expert.
"I heard women sell their bodies for this!" I said to Chris. "You want me to start selling my body? Because if you do it I'm going to do it too! You sure this is what you want to do? Is this what you want in our lives?"
Chris just puffed and ignored me as he breathed out very hard.
I screamed again, "pass it to me Chris, I want to try it!" then he passed it to me.
"You do it like this Nate?" I said sarcastically.
I took a few puffs and started choking. "Come on pass it back," Nate said waving his extended hand.

I pulled Chris' arms to turn him towards me to get his eyes off the can as Nate was putting another rock on.
"Look at me! We don't have to go down this road Chris. Listen, you stop and I'll stop."
He ignored what I said. "Pass it back now Nate!"
I told Chris to pass it back to me. I took two more puffs and passed it. The feeling was different from anything I ever experienced. I liked the taste; it was minty and it smelled minty too. I felt tingly all over. My head was spinning. I couldn't get up. I just sat there and then it was gone!
"That's it! The high is over? Give me another puff!"
They passed it back to me and I continued to puff. I thought, if I can't beat him, then I had to join him.

I really didn't understand addiction and there was nothing I had tried that I couldn't say no to. I was just a pothead and I wanted to see if he would put it down for me. So I said" I hear woman sell there bodies for this drug, you want me to get hooked on it and sell my ass for you?"
But when he didn't respond or stop me I felt like I wasn't worth shit to him. I wanted to make a statement. This was something we could do together. I didn't do cocaine or heroin and we couldn't drink together. In my gut, I believed it was the beginning of another roller coaster but I wanted the control.
Barbara came in with more. I hated looking at them.
Chris apparently had given her money because she passed it right to him.
"Oh, so you all were in here while I was asleep getting high?" I asked. "How long have you been doing this?" Of course, I was ignored. The crack was the center of attention.
"This is my first time. Now be quiet I hear something," Chris said nervously.
Nate started laughing. "Oh he's just getting paranoid; he gets like that."
I took some more. I looked at him. It had the same effect on him that cocaine had only without the needle.

The next day when I woke up I saw Chris going out the door. He wanted more.
"No, let's not get in to this," I begged.
"Just one more. I'm not going to get hooked on it." He put on his coat and returned quickly.
I watched him smoke it in the bathroom. I smelled it and immediately wanted more. "Give me some!" I said.
He just looked at me. "Look, my job is finished. I have to wait for another job and I'm bored waiting. I'm not going to get hooked, okay? I just wanted to relive some stress."

The next few days it was just smoke and smoke.

I would try to get the kids ready for school but it became more difficult to get up after just getting to sleep.
I needed some as soon as I woke up, so one day, I went out and asked around in an apartment complex and found the dealers myself. The income tax refund came and literally went up in smoke. In two months we were hooked.
Barbara and Nate got an apartment, stayed for three months and lost it. They ended up in a hotel that welfare paid for.
Smoking is just a tease; you always want the good dizzy hit that rushes through your body for a second. So you keep smoking, hoping you get that good hit again and you never do.

At night, I would look at my kids and think.
'God will give you all a better mommy.' I was tired of wearing another black eye. There was no money for food. I didn't recognize myself in the mirror anymore.
I weighed 100 pounds and wore two pairs of dirty pants because they were too big for me. The vicious cycle was tearing us apart. We'd get some money and smoke it up!
We needed everything but bought nothing! We had no lights, no heat, no deodorant, and no meat! I didn't see any other way out.
All the flowers in front of our house had died and the house had a dark shadow over it. It began to feel evil; it was once white but it had turned gray.
Even the palm tree died and the grass went bald. I hardly sleep in my bed.
This drug was in control. "Don't sleep!" it said.
We were on the bottom and the avalanche was still coming down.
I was tired of putting the kids through this.
I would keep myself locked in the bathroom screaming, "Leave me alone!" My mom used to say that to me from her bedroom door.
If I hurt their feelings I'd just say, "They'll get over it!" I never considered them when I wanted a hit. If they were out of sight then they were out of mind. I didn't even care if they needed to use the bathroom. All I knew was that I couldn't put it down until it was all gone.

My landlord entered our name in the newspaper. All these people responded; they wanted to give the kids toys for Christmas.
I was too proud to take handouts though. "We don't celebrate Christmas!" I told them.
I took their only chance of happiness away at that moment. That was a shameful moment. I told them it was a sin to celebrate Christmas. It was a pagan ritual, I told them it how they worship a Sun God. Nobody gave Jesus any gifts, and they would have to understand my decision. So they continued to make dolls and game boards out of cereal boxes.

I drank all I could to get as drunk as possible so I could sleep and come down from this sleepless drug. Sleeping pills helped a lot but the drug would never let me take the pill. It told me, "Try to get one more hit first."

The kids had no music; no TV, no outside, and they had to listen to us yell derogatory words to each other.

I neglected them to the point that I knew they hated me.

It became too difficult to stop and bathe them or feed them.

I would yell, "Wait a minute!" but that really meant hours or just "leave me alone!"

I shut them out of my life. To keep them out of the way, I confined them to their rooms like they were in jail. I had to protect them from the evil that was beyond their door. Just like my mom did to me as she laid in her bed all day, everyday.

I wouldn't let them go outside for days or weeks at a time because I didn't have clean clothes for them, or because I knew I wasn't going to be able to watch them because I was going to be getting high.

Sometimes they had store-bought sandwiches. We had ravioli or macaroni and cheese or hot dogs and beans. We'd have anything, as long as I didn't have to cook: lunchmeat, tuna fish, cheesesteak hoagies, potatoes made all kinds of ways with soda, bread and mayonnaise or Oodles of Noodles. For treats there were Little Debbie snacks. The poor kids were so hungry that they would eat a sandwich while making another.

Once I really got started, I would wake Chris up or harass him for more and more money. After we ran through my check, his mom would try to help us, giving him any amount of money he asked for. I knew that was always something to fall back on monthly, so we didn't have a problem spending all of my check.

I couldn't stop. Chris would give me every dime he had until it wasn't anymore and then he would say, "See, you're not satisfied until it's all gone!"

"Yeah, well, you started it, now give me the money!" I respond.

Eventually, we had to move. "Goodbye Mr. Santos. I'm sorry I can't pay the rent. We're going to a hotel. Thank you for being such a good landlord. I know God will bless you! When I come back to Florida again, I will look you up and pay you what I owe."

His reply was. "Just take care of those beautiful kids!"

I felt so bad disappointing him, our friend. He looked so sad like he was about to cry for me instead of being angry with me.

We moved to the same hotel that Nate lived in because welfare paid the rent there.

We wanted to stop using crack but we couldn't.

Our children were 4, 5, 6, 7, 8, and 9. Tunisia, the nine year-old, was the mommy now. She took care of everyone most of the time; all I had to do was keep Chris happy so he didn't go off on anybody. I had to keep them quiet for him when he finally got to sleep. Tunisia was so creative; they made up games and made soda bottle dolls with strings, glitter and buttons and they'd put on some of my old clothes, cutting them up and tying knots where the stitches would go to make it fit.
Thank God for imagination.
I would go into their room and sit on their bed at bedtime and talk to the kids for hours.
I would plead with them, "Please, don't hate your dad and me." I thought my past pains were a good enough excuse to want to be in oblivion but it was my present.

I wanted them to understand my pain and who I was.
I told them they were to never use drugs but the whole time I was telling and showing them that drugs were the way to deal with pain.
I don't mean to hurt any of them or be this way. I would tell them not to hate their dad for hurting me either. He didn't mean what he said; he was just angry and confused.
I didn't realize that I was teaching them to find excuses and love your abuser anyway, even if they're your family.
I wasn't even trying to forgive my mom. I needed her to be mad at. I could forgive Chris for his abuse because he made me feel good making up but I couldn't forgive my own mom for leaving me, and having to listen to her verbal abuse. Never giving me any attention, making me feel like I wasn't important to her. I wanted forgiveness and understanding from my sweet kids but I knew I didn't deserve it.
"Pray for us okay? Pray every night for all of us. Things will be better for us all soon, you'll see!" I never promised them a thing a day in their lives! I knew I couldn't keep promises so I would always say, "I'll do my best to get us out of this mess."
"We love you both Mommy!" they would say to me. They would sit there on their beds in a circle listening to me babble for hours. They all sat there looking at my new black eye.
Then they all would give me a big hug. I was the baby in their arms.

I was so busy hating my mom and myself. I hated to see that I was just like her, saying the same things like, "Leave me alone and go to your room," and screaming, "NO!" harshly. I was neglecting my kids like she had neglected me.

As a matter of fact, I was less than my mom because I neglected them twice as much. My mom at least kept food in the house and she didn't have any black eyes.
She didn't beat me at all. I got smacked a few times and a cut in my head from an ashtray upside my head once but that was it. She hugged me a lot and would sometimes tell me she loved me no matter what.
I wondered if they would think about these days and resent and hate me. I would hate, resent, and be ashamed of me for sure. I had put my man and drugs before their needs and I showed them neither strength nor control.

It was 5:00am on a weekend. After spending hours on my knees, looking for some crumbs we might have dropped, I paused in my crawl.
I saw myself in the mirror and I was disgusted at what I saw.
It was a pathetic sight. I was so ashamed of myself. I sat down on the rug and cried.
What has happened to me? I hated myself for not being able to stop using crack and I just couldn't face the kids in the morning with no food or money, and another black eye.
I crept in their room and kissed them all goodbye.
Chris would hear the squeaky door opening so I climbed out the window and ran eight blocks to the lake. I'm going to jump in and swim as far out as I could I thought.

When I got there I was so tired and out of breath. I sat down to rest on the bench. I had to get my strength so I could swim far out and drown.
I was out of breath, breathing hard holding my chest, it was hurting, it's all that damn smoking and cigarettes. "Ok I'm ready!" I was about to stand up and I heard a voice say, "Don't give up!"
"What?" I said out loud.
There it was again! "Don't give up!"
I looked around the dark lake. I didn't see anyone around. "Who said that?"
"Don't give up!" I started crying. Then I said, "But I'm tired! I'm so tried!, I hate myself and I can't kept living like this!" I breathed out a deep sigh. I looked out as far as I could see and it looked so beautiful, the sky and moonlight on the water.
My thought was that in the morning they would find a body in the water and my children may never know what happened to me! They won't have to worry about burial money. Well, I'll swim towards the light far out there!

I took in a few deep breaths to prepare myself and suddenly, this tremendous peace came over me. I felt so relieved.
I felt so good like I just took a good hit with that breath. I had to just sit there for a while longer. My head was spinning and I felt my body lifting

up off the bench floating. I just steered into the moonlight in a frozen state

I don't know how much time went by but I remembered this feeling one time in my life before.

It was when I had Aqusia. I had been carrying so much stress. Chris was accusing me of having sex with a man that was living with us. He tormented me throughout the whole pregnancy. When she came out, she came out like roadrunner and flew off the table. Chris had to catch her and I was content he was there for us.

I remember letting out the biggest sigh in the world. Oh, I was feeling so peaceful all over.

The nurse wanted to press on my stomach. "Don't touch me for one minute!" I said to her. "Don't nobody touch me!"

The nurse said that I had to push the afterbirth out and when she pushed it out, I was in heaven. It was a big relief, like the weight of the world was lifted off my shoulders. I had delivered all my pain.

I just laid there in this peaceful bliss while they cleaned her off and Chris put the afterbirth in a bag, as instructed by the old nurse. It was the most peaceful time in my life the best high I ever had. She was the most beautiful baby in the world! Nurses from other floors had to come and see how beautiful she is. That feeling was better than any drug.

As I sat on the bench, I opened my eyes as the sun was rising over the water. I thought it was the most beautiful scene I ever saw.

I said, "Thank you God." I got up and I walked home slowly, breathing in the Florida air. I was the only person in the world for that moment, just God and me and he was talking to me, I felt so special.

I felt like I was floating not walking. "Okay, I won't give up!" I whispered.

The houses were more beautiful to look at, the birds were singing just to me. I climbed back in the window and went right to sleep.

Chris found a rehab for me to go to at a hospital. I was glad to be getting some help. I knew if I could stop then everything would go back to like it was, my paradise would return.

Chris agreed he would go when I came home. We had a plan.

I had to talk to counselors while I was there. I had group therapy too.

"Angel, when are you going to open up?"

"I talk!"

"Tell us what was it like for you out there."

"It wasn't so bad. I wasn't, 'out there.' I didn't trick for no drugs and I'm not homeless."

"Angel, you need to get honest!"

"Damn what do you want from me? Okay, so I use everyday, all day and so do their father. I have six kids and I want to stop using so things can go back to normal, that's it!"
"Why do *you* want to stop using Angel?"
"I want to stop using for my kids, they need me to be sober!"
A white man who was about 25 told me I had to do it for myself.
He told me that whatever I said was confidential.
"So, who is taking care of your kids?"
"Their father is!" I said with a "who do you think?" expression on my face.
"Well, isn't he using too?"
I had his back: "Well, he still takes care of his kids!" I was getting frustrated now. "Leave me alone! They are fine. When I do my sixty days than I'll go home and watch them and he'll come in."
The head counselor called me into his office and told me that he was required to call Child Services because the kids were not being taken care of since Chris was using.
I got angry. "See you want to hurt me, not help me. I tell you shit and you use it against me!" I ran out of his office and down the stairs. I didn't know how I was going to get back to the far away hotel but I knew I had to leave and warn Chris.

When I got down the bottom of the steps Chris was standing there talking to the guard, getting ready to visit me. I couldn't believe it!
I grabbed his arm. "Come on we have to go!"
He pulled his arm away from me. "No, you're not going anywhere!" He gritted his teeth. "What are you doing Angel?"
The guard was staring right into my face so I didn't want to tell him why! I just responded anxiously, "We have to leave! Now!" I waved my hand for him to come closer.
"What's going on?" he asked.
"Chris, they know you're using drugs and they want to take our kids!"
He called a cab. I went back to the hotel and stopped at a neighbor's and got drunk. Then I saw the kids. We had been put out of our room while I was gone so the kids were in the room with Barbara and Nate.
We had to sleep outside on a bench. There wasn't enough room inside. Chris stayed awake while I slept and then he slept while I kept watch. The second night on the street, he asked me what time I thought it was.
"It's probably about 12:30am." He got up and looked in the hotel's office window and saw that it was 12:35 am.
"See, that's my Indian skills," I said. "I don't need any watch." We laughed and drank some wine. It was then that he flipped out and started treating me like shit on his shoe all day.

He was upset because we were on the street and because I told the people that he gets high. He knew it was just a matter of time before they came to get us. The next night we were going to sleep in his friend's car. He beat me up so bad that I couldn't talk, not only from my mouth being swollen but because I was so sad I went inside of myself. His anger just elevated because I wouldn't talk and I wouldn't look at him. I just stared right through him.
He yelled, "Answer me! Look at me!" He grabbed my face and pointed it toward him. "Look at me I said!"
He slapped me again with those big hands that took up the whole side of my face and again! And again! And again! Harder each time. I was safely escaping within my mind.
He wanted me to return to him, so he believed that smacking me more and more would bring me back to this reality. But I just didn't want to attend! I didn't respond. I wasn't even there, so I felt nothing.

He threw me into the car and when I still didn't speak to him, he got out of the car and opened my side and told me to get out.
I couldn't move so he dragged me out. He dragged me around the car to the driver's side.
I backed up against the tree slowly.
I slid down and sat there on the ground holding my knees, and then I came back to reality and began to cry.
I held my head as he yelled obscenities at me. I saw the evil in his eyes and he frightened me so much that I began to shake uncontrollably.
Than I felt the really hard smack that hot sting that lasted forever.
I screamed in pain. "Leave me alone!" I jumped up and just started punching him in his face, wild and crazy.
He grabbed my hands but I struggled for release.
We were rolling around on the ground. Then he stood up and kicked me in my sides a few time and said, "Don't ever put your fucking hands on me ever again! Now get up!"
"Leave me alone! Pleaaaaaase!" I wailed as my teeth chattered. I looked to my right and there stood Chris yelling at me. "Get up now! Get your ass over here!" He started walking back towards the big blue Cadillac.
It was dark; there were no house lights close by to light up the road. To my left, I heard a few dogs barking angrily getting closer to me. Just last week I was bitten by a German Shepard, and a few days after that, two Dobermans chased me and one bit the back of my leg. I guess that's why I couldn't move. I was paralyzed, traumatized, and petrified.

Chris grabbed me by my neck and pulled me up to my feet. He dragged me into his friend's car where we could sleep for only one night.

I was having a nervous breakdown. I couldn't stop my body from shaking; holding my hands didn't help. I was so tense and my muscles were tight. I became as stiff as the dead.
I didn't sleep. I just sat there all night wishing I were dead, feeling nothing.
Child Service came to our hotel room but we already were gone.

"I'm leaving you," I said to Chris the next day.
That's what it took for me to wake up into my own reality.

CHAPTER FOURTEEN

DELIVER ME FROM THIS EVIL

I had to go back to Philly with my tail between my legs. I was a failure.

It was difficult trying to organize six little kids for the trip. The trip was twenty something hours long and we had to switch three times for different buses without Chris' help.

Two weeks later, Chris came to Philly with his stories of sleeping on the streets in boxes and shit.

"I missed you all so much, please let's stay together!" he said.

I was happy to see him so I took him back.

My sister couldn't handle my big family in her basement anymore so she dropped us off at a shelter three months later. We went through the shelter system and were moved around a lot. We still continued to use crack. Everyone in the shelters was using it too so we couldn't get away from it. Chris looked for work and a home. He made sure we had food because we didn't eat the shelter food too much. He would wash the kids' clothes and help me take care of them. He wasn't drinking much so he was cool to be around. We would drink a beer now and than.

After four shelters and six months, that's when I decided that I couldn't drag our children through anymore of this madness.

"Chris, I'm going to put the kids in foster homes!"

He got angry. "No you're not!"

"Yes I am! We can't take care of them like this no more!"

"No Angel, my kids are not going in any damn foster homes! Didn't you tell me how you were molested in one? What is wrong with you? Are you crazy?"

"Chris listen to me for a minute! They screen the homes better now I'm sure, and God will take care of them. They will have a roof, their own beds and food, and a stable environment, something we haven't been able to provide for them with this crack shit! I have to put them somewhere safe so I can go get some help! I'm not going to wait till they take them from me, you understand? I have to go away for a while. I'll get a place for them and get them right back; it shouldn't take more than a year the most. I suggest you take that time to go into a program also."

He walked away with his back turned. "I'm not going with you. It's your idea so you do it!"

"Well, we can't take care of them!" I said frustrated. "And they can't stay at my mom's house. I'm sick of the shelters; we have no home for them

Chris, and we're fucking smoking crack everyday, all fucking day and I'm sick of it all!"

The next morning I went to my mom's house and spent the night on the floor with the kids so we could talk. I sat all the kids down in a circle on my mom's floor.
"I'm going in a drug program. That's where people go when they want to stop using drugs but I can't take you all with me and there's no one that can take care of you all." I looked at their faces. "I want you to have hot baths and meals every night. I want you to have a home and your own beds and I have to leave to get that! And you kids will live with other people for a while until I get better. Mommy doesn't want you to be hungry anymore. Moving around in all theses different shelters and having to walk the streets all day, waiting and hoping for the Housing Authority to call me which could be two or even three years... I can't have you all dealing with Mom and Dad fighting, so I'm going to get some help."
Chris looked at me in disgust and he walked out the house and didn't return for hours.
"How long will it take?" the oldest one asked.
"I honestly don't know but I will see you and talk to you all so you'll know what's going on with us."
They shook their heads like they understood. "Okay!"
"Where is dad?" Aqusia asked, "And where is he going to live?"
"He will be looking for a house for us. He'll stay here at Grandma's for a little while. It shouldn't be too long baby. We're going to get us a nice house soon. I just need to go to this hospital first."

The next morning I gave them baths, ironed their clothes and did their hair real nice and walked to the 'DHS' Dept of human services office. As we walked down the sidewalk I overheard two women walking by say, "Look at those pretty kids. They look so nice. At least she got all of her kids with her."
They knew me from one of the shelters. Little did they know; I was on my way to give them up!
I started crying ready to change my mind but quickly asked myself, when will it end? I stopped to get them each a pretzel and a hug for breakfast.
I sat in the office waiting for the authorities to take them one at a time. I tried not to cry in front of them but it was hard. We sat in a line, all on one long black couch. I told them I loved them so much and I wanted better for them and this will be better.

I sat the baby I called "Moo Moo" on my lap, and told her that Mommy will come and visit her all the time. I wiped her tears and hugged her tight. I wiped my tears on my shirtsleeve. I know what used to go on in

some foster homes. I figured that there would be more advances made twenty years later, like they screen the people better. Shit, it was my grandfather, a family member molesting me. I ran up to them and gave them another big hug and told them it won't be long.
I didn't know they were going to live in a warehouse for a year.
Nobody better not touch these girls God will protect them. I begged God to protect them. I believed with all my heart he would.
I never thought to ask him to protect my son from being sexually abused.
I just didn't think that kind of thing happened! He was only five.
After saying my goodbyes to the girls' one at a time, I held my shameful head down the elevator.

I sat outside on the bench and watched a strange white man take my son to his car. My son didn't even look back. He ran and skipped like he was going on an exciting trip. Too late to say, "Never mine!"
I was all alone, and I felt like a big failure.
The tears wouldn't stop flowing; they were like the waterfalls in Love Park. I sat across from the falls staring into the drops. The cold breeze made me feel like I was abandoning my children, like mom abandoned me. I couldn't keep them comfortable and warm from the cold breeze.
There in the street with my head bowed, hands together and eyes closed, I didn't care who was watching. I prayed to God.
"Please God don't let nobody rape or molest my girls. Please Father keep them safe, and help their father and me stop using, help us get into a program and help us get another home so we all can be back together soon, please, In Jesus name I pray, And forgive me for being so weak and stupid, I'm sorry I failed as a mother after you in trusted me with them." I sat there till dark came.
I was angry with myself and very lonely, and pissed with Chris for getting us into this crack shit, and for letting me do this by myself. He knew it had to be done.

I was angry with mom; she could have told us we could live with her for a while longer. I know she didn't have the room but shit, make some! I made the kids a bed on her living room floor.
But really, why should she get up five in the morning to take a two-hour ride on that dangerous subway to work while the two grown men are sleeping? And six kids all over the place with her TV on too long, and her water and electric bills rising, her phone always tied up, and no one buying toilet paper for all these asses but her… hell no! She didn't have to put up with us fighting, either!
Chris and I were running in and out her house all day and all night, spending and wasting money that could go towards bills and food.

Oh hell no! She sure wasn't going to feed us all, even though I got food stamps. Hell, half went to the drug man. She wanted everyone out. She had a right to.
I have to remember, it wasn't her fault or her responsibility we were homeless. I believed if she just gave Chris a little more time that he'd get us a place like he always did!
Her peace and quiet was now compromised and her bathroom was never available the one week we stayed with her. What's a person who has grown children and is through raising kids to do?

After grieving without my kids for days, I got up and made that call.
First I fell on my knees and I looked up. "Father God, please help me. I'm tired of living. I want to die. I want to die! Help me! In Jesus' name, hear my cries, all of your closest beloved humans sinned. This drug is more powerful than I. I have no strength over this drug. Remove it from me."
I got up, wiped my tears and called the Detox programs.
Chris was gone. I don't know where he was or what he was doing. But I was going away! So I didn't even care!
After my seven days in Detox, I was told I had to wait for a sixty-day program bed.
I went back to live in Mom's house in my room. Chris was still there. I was so happy because I was on my way and I had something to look forward to and fight for! I dared her to tell me I couldn't stay there. I was her baby! This is my room!
Chris agreed to go with me to meetings everyday for ninety days. On the ninetieth day, I was asked by my sponsor to share at a meeting. I agreed but I was nervous. I got up 7:00 that morning even though the meeting was at 2:00. Mom was in the kitchen never having known sleep. It was Thanksgiving.
She immediately started cursing and saying that we were eating up her food and not contributing.
"We hardly eat!" I said furiously. "Oh I didn't buy this turkey?" and I threw it up side the wall and left. I called my sponsor but there was no answer. I walked around for a coffee but nothing was open.
I went back to the house and Chris was in the bedroom. I sat in the living room with my arms folded.
Chris bolted out of the bedroom. I could tell he just had a hit.
"Chris, why did you start using crack again? Why?" I yelled. "You were supposed to do this with me!"
"Well baby, I went to this job interview yesterday and they told me I was over-qualified and denied me. I was sure I was going to get it but I didn't and I felt really bad being rejected." He held a pint of liquor in his hand.
I snatched it and walked out the door. I went to put it in a trash but didn't see one. I held it all the way to the train station.

I was going to go to my meeting but the bottle told me it could make me feel better right away. The meeting wasn't for another few hours. But I couldn't do it. "No! I don't need a drink! I need a meeting now! I didn't have any idea how to find one!" I sat on a bench angry as shit. "Why couldn't he leave that shit alone? Damn him!"

I looked in the bag. What kind of wine or booze was he going to drink? Barcardi Rum.

The bottle looked like my only friend. "Smell me!" it said.

So I cracked it and smelled it. I never drank this straight; I needed soda.

I really don't need this I told myself. This shit is nasty straight but I don't want to be sober!

The drink said, "Just take a quick shot so nobody will see you. After about three or four straight shots, you will be feeling real good and calm and cool and collected and we can just chill right here, just you and me! We need to sit here and think! And drink!"

I drank the whole damn pint, talking to myself about how this was better because it wasn't crack.

After drinking the bottle sip by sip, I returned home and Chris was in the room still getting high. He had a lot, like he hit the damn jackpot.

I looked at it and then at him. This will be the death of me I thought, as I sat on the bed next to him. "Pass it to me!"

We stayed in that little room for two weeks. I didn't give mom any money, not a dime because I believed she owed me. Here take me as I am with my entire shit mom!

I never did see my kids that Thanksgiving, It was Satan's plan against me before I woke up.

I'm so, so tired of this life. I was missing my babies so much as the days went by slowly. Our arguments drove us to try to kill each other. I knew in my heart that if I held on they would be back with me! But I couldn't do it alone. This nightmare had to go away.

We'd never been separated. I wondered what they were doing, if they were okay, were they thinking about their dad and me, and did they hate us? I'd never have them back in my arms kissing them goodnight if I didn't stop this shit!

I got so mad with myself. I started hitting myself in the head, punching and punching, screaming, "You dumb bitch!"

I walked out of the house, mumbling up the street. It was a bright Sunday morning and people were dressed in their pretty nice clothes. Yeah! I thought, "I'll go to church."

I was dirty; I hadn't even washed the crust out of my eyes. I had just put on my sneakers and threw on a blue sweater.

Which way should I go? I had $5 in my pocket. I walked to the bus stop to go to the church I had gone to a few times before. It was called the

Deliverance Church, down on Broad Street. Every time I had gone there I left feeling good and stronger.
I was running late. The bus was taking forever to arrive. Damn, it had to be over forty minutes late now I said to myself, "I'll miss all the singing now! Shoot!"
But as I said that I heard singing from the church across the street. I walked closer. Yeah, now they sound good! Let me check them out!
I wasn't dressed nicely so I wanted to stay in the back but an usher escorted me to the front. I whispered, "I wanted to sit back there." She pointed me to keep going to the front and gave me a gentle push.
I walked up two rows and pointed. "Can I sit there?" I asked her quietly.
"No miss, go up further!" she responded with another gentle nudge.
I looked back at her thinking, oh, so you want the pastor to see me and embarrass me? Is that your plan?
I reluctantly sat in the second row.
"The first row and every other row are closed for the Holy Sprit!" she said to me. I'd never heard that before.
I looked around and saw the people staring at me, and when I would catch them looking at me they would smile. I stared back. I knew what they were thinking. As soon as the pastor asked who wants to be saved, they'd look at me like they always do when I dress this way.
I hated that look! But I was okay with it. I may stagger in a church at anytime; the Lord understands my heart.
"Go up front now sinner. I am saved, I'm just a backslider." I thought I had been forgiven a lot because I'd been baptized at least five times.
I tried to ignore the eyes behind my head.

I stood up and prayed as the pastor instructed. His sermon was about why Jesus called Peter "the rock." I'm a rock; well I use to be I thought with a smile. I'll cut off an ear for you Jesus, I laughed.
"Now let all the people pray with me," the pastor said.
I prayed hard! There was no one there but him and me. I was in God's presence, begging! "God, please save me. Forgive me for my sins and bad decisions. Deliver me from this evil drug and all the physical abuse." I wiped the tears from my newest black eye. "Please, I can't control myself. Will you make me strong? Help Chris and me get off these drugs. Please help us. I can't take anymore of this life. I know he is a good man underneath his dirt. Please let me see it and love it!"
I felt a hand on my left shoulder. It felt warm and comforting.
Oohh this is so nice I thought. Someone is praying with me. I assumed it was a woman because the touch was so warm and compassionate. She must know I'm in pain. When I said, "Amen," I wiped my tears and looked back to say thank you. But no one was there! The whole row was empty like every other row was. I looked in front of me and no one was there. No one was on my left side. I was on the edge of the pew and no

one on my right side was close enough to touch me. Who could've touched me?
Than it dawned on me. It had felt so good because it wasn't human. God heard me. I went back to mom's house crying and praising God. He comforted me to tell me it would be okay!
I skipped home and a young man across the street saw me. "Can I have some.of what you had?" he asked.
"Sure you can!" I said. "It's the best high I ever had!"
He stopped in his tracks and was getting ready to come across the street and I screamed, "It's God! Meet God! He will make you feel real good!" The dude backed up and walked away.
I laughed and skipped along, feeling special. He touched me! That was not my imagination either!
I would soon find out just how special I was.

A week later, Chris went to get our son for a visit but he didn't take him back to the foster home.
We'd had a real punching, deadly words kind of fight. He wished I were dead he said to me, he said he would kill me when he came back. I knew the big fight wasn't over. That was over whose fault it was that the kids were in foster homes. We both used drugs and we both caused our homelessness but I took them there so I was the bad guy.
"If anything happened to my children I'll kill you bitch!" he yelled with such venom. BAM! Another black eye and a busted lip, I tried to fight back but he is too strong for me, I only got in a few neck scratches. My weave was all pulled out and my clothes were ripped off. I screamed as he was leaving, "If you weren't beating me up and taking the rent money, we wouldn't be homeless, you started this crack shit remember?"
"I hate you bitch! I hope you die! The kids are better off with out a mother like you!" He slammed the door.
I sat in the room crying. I went into the bathroom and saw my black eye and busted lip.
I ran down the stairs, I wanted to run away. I didn't know where to go so I just sat down on the bottom step by the front door. I said out loud, "God please help me!"
Louder: "God, please deliver me from this evil!" I was holding my head between my legs and squeezing my ankles, rocking and crying.
Louder "God, please deliver me from this evil!"
Louder "God, deliver me from this evilll!"
Louder "God, deliver me from this evillll!"
Louder "God, deliver me from this evilllllll!"
Louder "God, deliver me from this evilllllllll!
"Oh God, please hear me! Help me!! Help Me! Pleaseeeeeeeeeeee! Oh God it hurts so much!"

I was crying out loud, holding my stomach now bent over because it hurts so much in the gut. I wanted to cut out the pain.
As I screamed and cried my mom never came out of her room. I wanted her to come and hold me but she never came.

I heard George come out of the bedroom, stomping into the living room. "I'm tired of this shit!" he shouted. "This shit has to stop!"
I agreed! I stomped up the stairs thinking, you're right, this shit does have to stop!
I went into the kitchen and got a steak knife. The butcher knife was too dull; it was big and intimidating too but still too dull.
I found a long curved steak knife that was sharp as a sword. It would just slide in I thought. Yeah, this should do the job!
I went in my room and put on the new white cowboy shirt and jeans my sister Missy just given for my birthday. She was the only one that ever bought me something. We had been trying to get closer.
I wanted to look nice when they found me dead.
I sat on the edge of the bed and I pulled up my shirt. I and stabbed myself in the stomach as hard as I could. I pulled the shirt down over it and laid back.
Wow, that didn't even hurt! It felt like a little sting. I could hear the sound my skin made, like it was tearing.
I should do it again just to make sure but it didn't want to come out.
I was so weak from the fighting and the screaming. I had no energy left. I just lay there so weak, thinking how I wished I could say goodbye to the girls.
How I wish I could have been a better mother.

They said they were happy with their foster parents. My baby had hurt my heart when she called her foster mom, "Mommy." She was only four, and this white lady spoiled her rotten buying her everything that Barbie made. I couldn't compete with that!
I convinced myself that they had better mommies. God would give them to someone who would never use and abuse them, someone that will feed them and keep a roof over their head. Someone that wasn't weak and stupid, someone they could look up to! Someone that would hug and kiss then goodnight now matter how old he or she was!

My son came into the room as I was dozing off.
"Mommy is you sleeping? Wake up Mommy!" He tried to open my eyes with his two little fingers. He felt so gentle and understanding. "Wake up mommy and play with me!"
I opened my eyes and held his little dimpled hand and said weakly, "Give mommy a kiss!"
He leaned over and kissed me. "I love you baby'

"I love you too mommy" What's wrong mommy?"
The tears just rolled down the sides of my face.
"I love you baby so much. You deserve a better mommy. All of you do. Mommy is going to sleep now. Cyris be a good man for mommy okay? Be a good man! Now go into the living room and watch TV with George."
I started crying harder as he smiled and rubbed my face gently like he loved to do. Then he said "ok" and ran away with his bow-legged run. I envisioned my unsuspecting mother in her bed flicking her remote as I was fading into darkness. "Goodbye Mommy Dearest!"

Chris came back. He saw the blood that had soaked through my new shirt and called for my mom. "Sharon! Sharon!"
"What! What! What is it now?" she answered angrily, like she didn't want to be bothered.
She looked in and covered her mouth. "Oh my God!" She pushed Chris out the room. "Call the ambulance! Angel! Angel, can you hear me?"
George came to see and so did Cyris. They stood at the doorway in disbelief.
"Is she dead?" George asked.
"Oh no!" Mom screamed. "What is this shit? Get the baby out of here, now! Take him out of here George!" She never came and held me; she didn't kiss me, or say a single encouraging word that made me want to live.
I could hear but I couldn't respond. I couldn't open my eyes. I couldn't move. I couldn't find any strength to talk. I was there but my body wasn't functional to anything I wanted to say or do.
I was screaming inside, "Please, will someone hold me? I'm cold!" But all I heard was her footsteps walking away.
She went back in her room mumbling some shit about what she didn't need.
"Is she going to be alright?" Chris asked the paramedics when they got there.
"We don't know anything yet sir, please move so we can get her out of here now!"
I heard the paramedics yell, "We're losing her! She hardly has a pulse! Let's go!" I remembered them saying that about my daddy.
Chris still said nothing to me. At that moment I knew it was going to be the last thing I heard: silence.
The police questioned Chris, "Were you here sir? What is your name? Do you live here? Who is she to you?"
Chris answered all the questions franticly. "I wasn't even here, was I Sharon? I left and came back and she was like this!"
"Well sir, how did she get that black eye?"

"Well, we did have a fight and she hit me. I didn't mean to hit her in her eye; it was an accident! That's why I went for a walk. I love her! I wouldn't hurt her!"
Mom and George convinced the police that he was out of the house when I did it.
That wasn't good enough for them. They arrested Chris and he spent the night in jail.
Maybe they had some sympathy for me.

I was in the psycho ward with a black eye and a stab wound.
Damn, I failed again! I don't believe this shit! I looked at my stomach. I had stitches from my pelvis to my breasts. Damn, what a cut!
I'm disfigured now for life! Damn, one full inch cut across and six inches long. Damn, they didn't have to cut me open like a pig!
They said I punctured my liver. I can't believe I'm still alive.
Why God, why didn't you let me die? I can't live with this shit any more!
I can't deal with life, as I know it. What am I going to do now?
I guess I'd have to get a gun and shot myself in the head next time."

My ribs were all sore from Chris kicking me on the floor. That bastard. Why would I want to see Chris? Why would he want to see me with another black eye? Wasn't he ashamed that everyone would know he'd done it? I'd be an ass to kiss him hello, so why would he come see me?
I didn't want to see my mom at all either. Why didn't she come and comfort me when I needed her? It was too late now. I cringed inside, hurt. She didn't love me.
I would never let my child scream and cry like that and not run to comfort her. What kind of lesson was she teaching me?
Depend only on God Angel, because no one else will be there for you.
That is what I learned. I needed to know that. She heard me screaming and crying. She saw me dying and she still didn't hold me.
Did she think this was the drug's and Chris' fault? No, it wasn't! It was because she wasn't there to comfort me and to give me some guidance. A sleeping pill would have calmed me down!
The kids were gone. I didn't have to stay with Chris anymore. That's it!
"It's over Chris!" I said silently.

They both came to my room. I had nothing to say to them.
Chris pulled out some wine and I wanted some, so I drank it all.
Mom held on to her pocketbook. I know she had a bottle in there. She just stood by the wall speechless.
"Chris you know it's over between us right?" I said.
"No it's not. It's not over until I say its over, and you're my wife. You're not going anywhere!"

"Chris in God's eyes I ask for a divorce. This is not a marriage and it's sure not love. I don't have to put up with you or your abuse ever again. So don't come back here and don't try to find me when I leave because I'm going on with my life!"

Chris looked at me. "I love you Angel. You know I didn't mean to hurt your eye and this wasn't my fault! You should have told me you felt this way!"

"Chris go to hell! Get out! Don't ever let me see you again or I will kill you! Get out!" I screamed louder. "Now!"

I looked at my mother. "Mom, I'm tired. It's time for you both to leave."

I went into the bathroom and shut the door until I heard them leave.

I requested no more visitors at all.

A nice heavyset nurse came into my room. "These pills will help you sweetie."

"What is that for?"

"The doctor prescribed these for you for your depression. They're called Prozac."

I took them for a week, cursed everyone out and went hysterical after a phone call from Chris. They gave me another drug called Depakote. That seemed to calm me down and it worked better at keeping me stable. I wasn't bouncing off the walls anymore and crying at every commercial. I was sleeping better too.

They said I was bipolar. I explained some of my episodes of painting and redecorating the whole house and than sleeping for months. Half the time I didn't want to wash up because it would make me cold or brush my teeth because it made me spit up.

I spent my time sitting on the floor in the corner. Chris bought me a carton of cigarettes and I'd have to ask the nurses for them one at a time and go to a hole in the wall for a light. I was feeling very crazy until a nurse's assistant who looked like Phillip Michael Thomas asked me to braid his long hair. After a few days of sitting in the TV room, he began to flirt with me.

I loved it! Here I was with a black eye and no make up! I looked like a ghost with a self-inflicted wound in the gut in the nut ward, and this fine man wanted to flirt with me!

He must've seen past the physical stuff. I loved the attention. Just the thought of someone wanting me thrilled me, and he was fine as shit!

I wasn't depressed for a while; I was just glad to be there.

I realized that all my life I went after the finest men in order to find my beauty because if they wanted me than I must be beautiful!

I realized that if I was lucky enough to find someone who liked my inner beauty and not the sexy clothes I was wearing or because he knew he was going to get lucky, then I was lucky!

He said softly, "I really like talking to you because you give me things to think about," he said to me. "You're a deep woman. I never met anyone so real like you. Most women would cover their face and wouldn't have talked to me at all. I respect your courage. It takes courage to take your own life but it takes more courage to face it!" He smiled. "I'll be back to check on you later."

I'd been faithful to my husband for fifteen years. Now I wanted to know if I could be with another man. So when I got out of the hospital I dated him a few times. He licked my cut up and all the way down on my stomach. He knew I was uncomfortable. He looked up at me and said with his tender voice, "Don't be ashamed. You're still beautiful."

That moment I knew that I could move on with my life without Chris. He wouldn't be the only one to confirm my worth now! I'll have to find more to boost my ego though, so I did fine muscle-bound, moneymaking cuties.

Chris had gone back to New York City. He kept calling me but I was in the bars living it up! I refused to answer his calls.

Nine months went by. I hadn't touched crack nor did I have a desire to do so. God had taken away the desire. My dedicated begging worked.

I was drinking to get drunk after a hard day of work at Kentucky Fried Chicken. Everyday, I'd come home and play music and reminisce. I hardly slept.

I was constantly crying and lying to myself about how I was going to get my kids out. I was sleeping on the floor, renting a room from my niece Sandra who was all grown up now with a daughter of her own.

Ring, Ring, "Hello?"

"Hi Angel, I'm in Philadelphia and I need to talk to you."

"No Chris, we have nothing to say to each other."

"I divorced you in my heart, are you ready to sign some papers?"

I was staying with my sister Tina on weekends. She always looked out for me.

"Angel he keeps calling here! Please talk to him." Tina would say with frustration. She did like him though: "He is a nice guy when he's not drunk," she would say. But she was fed up. "Talk to him so he'll stop calling every hour looking for you. He's getting on our nerves."

"Meet you for what?" I asked Chris.

"I have to talk to you about meeting with the kids."

"What about it Chris?"

"Well, they have to see us together so they think we'll be a family to the kids. We have a visit soon and I wanted to see you before we go okay?"

"Okay Chris I'll meet with you."
I knew we had to show them we were a family, so I'd go with him and be nice to him for the kids' sake.

We went to visit our babies. There were trees and a lot of grass and flowers around a little building made of brown bricks.
I tried to look my best but I spent the night at my new boyfriend's house. He gave me one of his clean T-shirts that had something on it about a cute woman with a big butt. I meet Chris on the corner of Germantown Pike and Chelton Avenue. When he saw me he smiled a big smile. Then he looked at my shirt and the smile vanished as quick as it came.
He knew it was a nigga's shirt. He looked me over head to toe.
He kissed me on my cheek and I on his.
"How are you?" I asked.
"Fine. Is that a nigga's shirt you got on?"
I was surprised, and he saw my face and snatched it right off my ass in the street.
He took me into a store by my hand like I was a little kid who was walking too slowly. The T-shirt was torn down the front and the sleeves were hanging off. He bought me a shirt.
I was pissed but it was funny as shit. He was so cute when he was jealous.
We had to see the kids and I didn't want them to see me sad or crying or wearing a black eye. So I played it cool.

We were led into a waiting room on the first floor. We walked in and they all jumped into our arms. "Mommy, Daddy!"
We were hugging and kissing with excitement.
"You come to take us home now?" Aqusia asked.
Chris looked sad. "No baby, we can't take you home yet because we don't have one yet. But we will. You just hold on baby. Daddy is doing his best."
She gave him the biggest hug.
Cyris now six had his arms around Chris' legs, and Laqwana was jumping up with her arms stretched out for him to pick her up. I immediately started fixing their hair. I was kissing them all over, again and again, tickling them to make them laugh and be happy with me for that moment they allowed us to share supervised of course.
I was watching Cyris and his dad talk and play on an ugly green couch. The baby was hanging all over her dad's neck. The girls were telling me stories about what it was like for them in their foster homes.
Tunisia said her foster mom had them on their knees scrubbing her floor as soon as they got there and she made them eat nasty foods so they hid it all in her sofa. They told me she hardly ever let them go outside and play, and when they did they had to sit still on the porch.

Then one day, her toilet pipes burst in her basement and she tried to make them clean it up but they refused and so she reported that they were incorporative and disobedient and disrespectful. My Aqusia told her adamantly, "I'm not cleaning shit!"
Tunisa had agreed with her sister. "Me either. I'm not clean up shit. You're going to have to do what ever you got to do to punish me. Fuck that!"

I was getting more disgusted and angry by the minute. I didn't even care they cursed, "Chris, do you hear this shit?" I hugged my babies while I had to think. Damn, what did I do to them?
I was even more upset because Aqusia had long shoulder-length hair and now it was so damaged. It was totally broken off from the middle down. I could hardly get it into a ponytail. I held back the tears. "Damn Chris, smell their clothes!" I sat back down and covered my mouth. I looked at my dressed-up two girls in their thrift shop-smelling clothes.
"Yeah, that's where she buys our clothes from and she don't wash them first," Tunisia said quickly. "I don't want to go to school anymore because the kids tease us."
The lady that was supposed to be watching us had gone somewhere else.
I was pissed. I jumped up and I said, "That's it, let's go!" I grabbed all of their coats and put them on real fast. "Let's go now!"
"Where are we going mommy?" the baby girl asked.
"I don't know but you're getting out of here! You're going with me! To another shelter, somewhere we can be together!"
Chris jumped up and grabbed my arm. "Angel what are you doing? You can't just walk out of here with them!"
"Well you just watch me! Let's go Cyris!" I snatched him off of Chris' lap and grabbed his coat.
I ran to the door and opened it. "Let's go kids!" They walked out holding hands.
"Hurry up, faster!" I shouted.
Chris grabbed me by the coat. "Stop right there kids!" he yelled. They were walking fast.
I snatched my coat from him. "Get off of me! What are you doing? What's wrong with you? They are treating our kids like slaves, like shit! I'm going to see that bitch! I'm taking them with me. We can stay at my sister's house or at the shelter."

I looked at him frustrated. "Look at them. They are not being well taken care of. Look at their hair falling out. It's a mess! They got on these stinky ass cloths and old fashioned coats! I can do better than this shit! Shit, with us on crack they looked, dressed and smelled better than this shit! Lets go! I'll take care of them!"

I screamed louder out of control now. "She's getting paid to care for them to provide for them, plus she gets her own check for caring for them, plus another check because she works for this damn agency! I don't believe this shit! I'm going to report her trifling ass. Where is the money really being spent while they're eating beans and scrapple? Shit, maybe her damn ass is using drugs! Piss her ass!"

Chris tried to calm me down. "Angel, it doesn't work like that. You have to go to court to take them out of here. You have to go to court first baby!"

I pushed him back off of me. "Court? What? No I don't! Why?" I shook my head. "Hell no! I put them here voluntarily. They weren't taken from me, so I can voluntarily take them out!"

"Okay baby, you do and it's kidnapping because by law the state is their parents now."

"How can I kidnap my own children? That's bullshit!" I brushed past him and kept walking.

"Baby wait!" He ran up to me and grabbed my hand. I turned to yell, "Leave me alone; you should be getting my back." Instead, I just froze and considered his feelings. I looked him in his eyes and saw that he looked so pitiful and helpless, angry, but with strength. "I'll help you do it the right way. You can't just walk out of here with them! The police will arrest you!"

"So what? They're the ones who are wrong. I'll tell them what they are doing to our babies, treating them like Cinderella and shit just to get a check. Shit, they'll have to find me first. Come on Chris let's get them out of here, please!"

"Angel no!"

I was crushed to hear that word! I looked at him in disbelief. "I can't just walk away from here with my own kids?"

He looked very serious. "This is no game! No you can't. You'll go to jail and then you'll have an even harder time getting them back." He rubbed the tears away. "I will help you get them out of there but not this way."

He held me tight as I was shaking mad. I went over to the benches where the kids were sitting and staring. They looked confused and sad.

I was getting ready to take a brick and throw it through the window but he stopped me.

"Calm down Angel. You can't get nothing done like this, and you don't want them to have ammunition about your behavior when it's time to review how you been responding to your visits."

The kids looked at us in disbelief.

Tunisia spread her arms open. "What, we can't go?"

I bent down and stretched out my arms to hug them all together. "No, babies, I'm sorry. I have to take you all back inside. Come here!"
We huddled in a circle. I got down on my knees and said, "You are warriors. You be strong and patient. God is going to bring us together soon. Just pray and wait and see. He will definitely get you out of her home." We hugged and kissed each other. We all stood hugged in a circle.
Laqwana and Cyris were mad. Their arms were folded and they started crying. "Look at what you did now," I said to Chris.
"I want to go with you Daddy," the baby said.
Chris stood there with his one hand under his arm and the other grabbing his chin tight, thinking hard. I saw his eyes staring but not really seeing; they were plotting, until he heard his baby's voice again trying to get his attention.
"Daddy, I want to go with you."
He walked over and picked up Laqwana. He let out a frustrated sigh and hugged her tight. "Daddy has to go find you a home and me a job baby and I'll be back to visit next week and every week after that okay baby?"
"Okay daddy," she responded. She is so understanding, than she kissed him on his cheek. I looked at them and smiled knowing how important they were to him. He was going to do whatever it took to get them out!

He took them back inside. I kissed them and reassured them that it wouldn't be long and I walked away in shame.
I yelled back at them. "We're going to get you all out of there real soon!"

I left and went straight to the nearest bar. I drank beer and Bacardi and played, "Make it like it was," by Regina Bell on the juke box: I sat across from him as he sat quietly watching me, not drinking but thinking. I wished Chris could make it like it was, that love and happiness between the pain. Like it was in Florida when he was saying, "Here Mommy, here is your new house, your new shoes, your new car, your blue leather coat… what else do you want, baby? I'll get it for you. Much passion."
Back then he kept our babies comfortable and fed and they were clean without a scratch on them. I'd watch him laugh while he'd cook us a roast and clean up everything, everywhere and under everything. I missed him holding me in his warm arms every night, all night, comforting me in my sleep. I miss all the fore play and the after-sex comfort.

Goodbye Chris, until the next visit. I had a job at KFC. I had four boyfriends; one was a light-skinned black version of Jean Claude Van Damm and he was a hand full of fun and pleasure. As far as I was concerned, I wasn't married anymore! I prayed to God to dissolve our marriage.

I searched for comfort in a young fun-filled man with strong muscles, with tight buns, who loved holding me up in the air while he made love to me, and then held me in his safe strong arms. I felt eighteen again and he didn't care that I had six kids. He wanted me scars and all.
I loved my single life. I met a few older macks with cash to spend on me and that fine-ass baby boy, all of seventeen that wished he could have me, and the man with my daddy's build and face and light skin with big hands and deep brown eyes and curly hair, standing six feet and more and the biggest penis in the world, but I still wasn't happy.
They were all mine with just one phone call.

I still hanged on to my bottle and men still wanted me.
Shit, Chris had cheated left and right on me. Therefore, I didn't need any paper to tell me I was divorced. In Gods eyes I was. I read in the book, "Trail of Tears," that Indian women threw their husband's clothes out of the house to end their marriage.
I'm Indian. I would do that if we had a house.

CHAPTER FIFTEEN

REHAB TO RELAPSE

One day, Chris came back to Philadelphia after staying in New York City for six months.

I had a place that I was sharing with my niece. I paid rent for a corner in the empty living room.

He talked me into meeting him so we could discuss visiting the kids together again. We'd show the white man a "united front," as he put it, so we could get them back when we got a home.

"Okay, I'll meet you. Where?"

"At your mom's house."

"Okay!"

I took a bus down to where my mom lived but we didn't go inside because I got a stomach cramp at the door and bent over in pain. I couldn't ring the bell. I couldn't walk into her house to remember me screaming at the bottom of the stairs. As soon as I opened the door I remember that's where I sat screaming in pain, as soon as I went up the steps there would be the kitchen with the knives. I never wanted to see that kitchen. I didn't want see my room that was like my death trap with glue.

I grabbed his arm and looked him in his eyes. I didn't have to say a word. We walked away and around the corner.

"Come over here" he said as he pulled me by my arm across the street.

"Where are we going?"

"In here for a minute!"

"Hell no! That's an abandoned building! What are we going in there for?"

"I had to sleep in there last night Angel and I left my sweater in there," he said in an embarrassed voice. "Let's just get it."

"You go ahead I'll wait right here. It's dark enough out here, so it's much more darker in there. At least I have one streetlight. Just hurry up!"

"Come on Angel, you scared? I'll protect you! You know I won't ever let anything happen to you."

"Yeah I know that but can't you just go? I just don't see why I have to go in there with you."

"Because I don't want to leave you out here alone and I don't want you to leave me. Please, it will just take a minute." He pulled my hand tight.

"Okay just for a minute." We walked up the squeaky stairs that were full of dust and paper, urine filled bottles and there were plenty of spider webs.

We went up to the second floor and Chris saw a man standing in a corner. “Get the fuck out of here, now!” he screamed at the man.
The man didn’t move.
“What! You got problems hearing? I said, “get the fuck out of here now!” Then he ran towards him and my heart jumped.
Chris looked like he was going to pull out a gat. The man ran out.
I was right behind the man. Chris grabbed me by my arm and said, “Wait!” He looked at me with his puppy dog eyes. “Please, just let me hold you. Please stay with me! Don’t leave me Angel I miss you so much! I can’t live without you!”
It was dark as shit and I couldn’t hardly see him only his white teeth, his scary eyes.
“Can we go now?” I asked. “We can talk about this outside okay? Let’s get out of here before he comes back with some friends!”
His eyes crossed as he tightened his teeth together. “I will kill somebody tonight, trust me! He seen my face! Trust me he won’t be back!”
I looked into his eyes and saw his fury. But he switched back to his pitiful look. “Angel, I don’t have anywhere to go. Please stay here with me.”
“Hell no! I have a home.”
“So what about me? You’re just going to leave me in the street like this?”
“I have an agreement with my niece no men in our house overnight. I sleep in the living room with her child next door. I can’t take you there and I don’t want you to know where I live right now!”

He grabbed me tightly by the hand. “Come here, this is where we will sleep here in this closet.”
“What are you crazy? You done lost your damn mind!”
“We both can fit in there and I can here if anyone’s coming! I put those clothes in there so I would be comfortable last night.”
Damn… I rubbed my face. What could I say, what could I do? I started shaking. “Chris, I can’t stay here! I have to leave. It is not fair for you to ask me to stay here!” I went to leave but he grabbed me and kissed me.
“Chris I have to go!”
“No, I’m not letting you go,” he snapped. “That’s all there is to it. Now lay down!” He softened his tone. “Please, one last time. Let me touch you, let me hold you… I miss you so much.”
I was mad as shit at him but in this dark cold place but I felt sorry for him and I wanted one last shot too. But not like this.
Out of fear I surrendered and laid down. I gave him his “goodbye” shot. I really missed him too.
I figured if I just let him have sex with me then he’d let me go home. But no, he wanted to hold me in his arms all night.
He said it again intimidating me. “You’re not going any where. Just stay right here in my arms. I’ll hold you all night and protect you.

Just give me tonight, then you'll never have to see me again, only to see the kids, okay?"
"Okay Chris" and I balled up and so did he behind me, with his arms around me in a tight grip. For a moment, I found a place I used to call home. I use to call him my home with feet I held his hands and fell asleep for about two hours.

With the first light of morning we were both up, drunk and exhausted. We instantly smelled shit. We found that the shit we smelled was all over our clothes.
I was so upset. I ran out of the building looking for where it was on me but most of it was on Chris. I wanted to go somewhere that I could buy a forty.
Chris took of his sweater off and tossed it. I washed my face with the snow on the car. I ate quite a bit too.
"Stop that, that's dirty!" he shouted.
"Leave me alone!" I yelled. I was so angry that I couldn't get the words out quick enough.
He put on his coat and tied his shoes as I screamed, "How low can we go? We are better than this Chris, shit!" I was tying my shoes tighter so the snow didn't go down into my sneakers. I had gotten so drunk last night that my head was hurting. I couldn't even argue with Chris that morning! Everything was "whatever!"
"Angel forgive me. I was drunk and I just wanted to be with you, to love you and hold you!"
I didn't want to talk. I didn't want him to touch me, especially not kiss me or hug me.
I just backed up. "Leave me alone!" I started walking towards a store that had large bright neon lights that shrieked "Beer!"

I turned around. "It will never happen again! Never! You'll never touch me again! You held me hostage in an abandoned, shitty, scary building! Are you crazy? Just leave me alone and don't say shit to me, ever! Don't come and don't call! As far as you're concerned, I'm dead. So you can leave now! Bye!"
"Wait a minute!" he said, still trying to get most of the shit off of his shoes with snow. "I didn't hold you hostage. I held you in love. I needed you to be with me so I did what I had to do so you would no I can't live without you! I bet that nigger that ran out of here took a shit in there! That wasn't there last night."
I rolled my eyes. "I still can't believe we are in this predicament. I'm in some human's shit! I feel like shit, and I'm being treated like shit! Our life is shit! And now you ain't shit! Goodbye!"
We stood in the middle of the empty street looking at each other. "Chris, I thought sleeping in the shooting gallery under a broken window with no

water, playing with pregnant rats was beneath us, but we got through that. This… I don't think so! Fifteen years later same shit, different place. I love you but I hate you more! Look at what you did to our family. I lived in hell with your cocaine abuse; than I begged you not to smoke that crack shit! I did it to be with you! Look at how that bitch cocaine took everything from us! Look at all the bitches you were out with fucking, coming home to my bed every night like you're a good man. Look at all the ass beatings I took from your drunken ass because a plate was in the sink. It's finally over, all the black eyes and hurtful gut stabbing words, it's all over Chris!"

"Oh, you said and done a lot of shit too Angel. Don't act like you're all innocent in all this shit."

"What! Have you ever had a black eye and busted lips where you couldn't talk? Did I ever bring you home a sexually transmitted disease, or fuck someone in our own house? Did I ever choke the shit out of you until you passed out? Nigga please, get away from me!" I was getting more hyper so I went and bought my beer.

"Look," I said to him as I walked out of the store. "I'm going to go home. I would appreciate it if you don't follow me either! I don't want you at my door okay? I want to get cleaned up!" I started walking fast.

We finally got our stinking shitty asses to the train station.

"Can I hug you bye?" he asked. I let him. He held me real tight and long. I hugged him back. "Goodbye Chris!"

"Angel I'm going into a drug and alcohol program today. That's why I didn't want to let you go. I was afraid I'd never be with you again. I've seen your hate for me in your eyes."

"Yeah, well, good luck. Bye!"

"Wait!" he pleaded. "Listen to me Angel for a minute okay?" He got on his knees. "I love you so much. You are my soul mate," he said as he held my hands, "and I want you to wait for me. I won't let you down, I promise. I'll make it all up to you, you'll see. Give me a chance to show you the real me. I can do anything I put my mind to and I want my family back more than life. I can't live with out them. It hurts so much not to be with them! Please let me get them back! Please take me back!"

"Chris please stop it! Just stop it! I can't even talk now, all I want is a damn shower!"

"Angel, listen to me. I'm not just telling you bullshit. I'm really going in and I'm coming out looking to get you a home. Didn't I always get you and our children a home?"

"Yes Chris you always did, I'll give you that but…"

"Angel, you are my breath. I can't live with out you! I don't care about nothing and nobody but you. I'll die without you. I don't want to live without my family! I'll get our kids out of foster care and I'll make you

proud! You just have to believe in me! Just don't give up on me okay? Please think about it because I will want to call you."
I sighed frustrated. I'd heard it all before. "Chris we'll see, okay? Give me some time. You're always more than a breath full to deal with. I just don't know anything right now. I'm just tired of this crazy shit. I'm tired, Chris, don't you understand? Maybe we're not meant to be together. I was really young when we got together and you felt you had to take care of me. Well now you don't have to anymore. You're free now, no nagging wife, and no kids. You are a free man, so go enjoy your life! I'm going to enjoy mine!"

I started to walk away but I turned back. "I really didn't even know you outside of the house. You were someone totally different than the man I thought I knew. Until I would come outside and see you... Wow, you would blow my mind with your flirting, your compliments, and your looking at everything that walked by. You made me sick watching you laugh with other women, dancing with them, and you never laughed or slow danced with me! You have so much to talk about outside but when you came home you'd have nothing to say but complain. What do we really have Chris? You lied to me, you hurt me, and you don't respect me, constantly cheated on me and now I can't trust you!"
"We're all the kids have Angel! We are a family and I'll do anything to get them back. Now we have to try to work it out for them!"
"Chris you can get us a house but as far as you and me are concerned, we can never get back together again!"
"I don't want to hear that shit!" he snapped. "You're my wife!" I walked away from him to go to my north sidetrack.

We left each other at that station. He went south and I went north. I was so glad there weren't a lot of people on the tracks to smell my stinky ass and to see me crying. I hated love. I ran down the stairs and looked over at the other side. There he stood looking at me.
He looked pathetic, with his skinny body and ashy skin, wearing a sheepskin coat as brown as the shit we were covered in.
I looked around the tracks and cracked my bottle and as it said, "fizz," I could hear the echo. I drank my beer quick. I stared back at him thinking; for the first time in fifteen years, we are going different ways. I wished that he would know all the pain and suffering he caused me. I was really afraid to let go of him and reach for an unknown future alone.
I waited for my train to take me away. His came first; I watched him wave and throw me a kiss. I felt sorry for him being homeless and alone. I hoped he was really going to a program and that they could help him change his life. I hoped he'd stop drinking that madman's liquor and stop being an abusive, angry man. Maybe he'd become a loving, dependable father and a respectful considerate husband.

Yeah right…that could take years. I knew I couldn't take any more rides with him. Goodbye Chris.

It felt good knowing that good men wanted me. Young ones too, I was free and I was never going to be with no man who beats on me.
I went to a sixty-day drug program in Philadelphia. I was there for two days when a woman there mentioned that she was beaten regularly. And then it just happened – I just couldn't stop crying.
I was shaking, my hands, my legs. My teeth were chattering because everything had gotten really cold all of a sudden. I could feel goose bumps. There was a stabbing in my gut and I felt like I was going to collapse. I was bent over and the people next to me grabbed me and held me up so I was taken into my room.
I hit the walls and threw the mattress off the bed onto the floor. Then I fell on it and started crying uncontrollably. I reached for my pillow and screamed in it a few times. No one came in the room to check on me. I needed a sedative or something; I couldn't stop shaking all over. I hugged myself tight and bit the pillow and rocked myself to sleep.
That's where I stayed all night. They opened up a subject that gave me a nervous breakdown and they weren't prepared to handle it.

My counselor took me in to see an abuse counselor the next day. She opened her door. There stood a big white lady, with jet-black hair and glasses down to the tip of her nose. She smelled like garlic.
She waved us in and pointed at the couch. "Have a seat over their sweetie." I felt so small sitting in it. I think that was part of her plan, to make me feel small at the door.

"Hi! I'm Ms. Gladys," she said as she shook my hand. She took her seat behind her shiny marble desk. She clapped her hands together and came right to the point. "I understand you got upset as the conversation began to center around abuse. Would you like to talk about it now with me? It might make you feel better to talk about it."
"Well, a lady said she got knocked down and came up with a black eye, and that her husband tried to strangle her. I saw myself, and it hurt so much that I just started shaking uncontrollably. I couldn't stop shaking." I paused and looked down at my hands, starting to shake again.. "My husband beats on me when he gets drunk, sometimes, not always."
"How long has this been going on Angel?"
"About fifteen years!"
She stood up and bent over her desk. "What? Why did you stay with him?"
I stood up. "Because he's a damn good father! He provides for us. He's a good man; he just can't control his anger when he's drinking. He said he's going to stop!"

She pointed at me as she came from behind her desk. She came closer. "Under any and all circumstances are you not to go back to him! You must not keep giving him another chance because one day he might not stop strangling you and you could die! That is not love! That's insanity."
I looked at my counselor and than at her. "We have six children together! I can't just leave him!"
She looked surprised. "What! Six? Oh, so you're in love with the dick!" She gave the other counselor a smug look. She just sat there and didn't say a thing other than "aah uhum"

"How old are you? Are they all his? And did you two ever give it a rest?"
I backed up towards the door. "Excuse you! Yes, all of them are HIS, all SIX! We are a family and we are asking for help! I'm here and he's there, but Chris does love his kids and me very much! He would die for us! He would do anything for me! He just needs help with his drinking! And he's probably in a program now!"
She scolded me, taking it personally: "You don't listen well, do you? That's not love! That's abuse, and whether it's verbal or physical, once an abuser always an abuser!"
I thought about it. Would he ever stop hitting me? I wasn't even considering all the other types of abuse I was getting.
"You have to have the courage to move forward with your life! You deserve to be treated with respect and care. Having sex with a black eye is not love. You young girls want to be grown up and keep a no-good boyfriend around because he pays the bills or is a good lover!"
"Excuse you. I'm twenty-seven and married, I am a grown up, and I didn't come here to be abused by you!"
"You're acting like an abuse victim protecting your abuser," she said sarcastically.

My eyebrows went up but I sat down at my counselors' request.
She sat down and folded her hands on her desk. "Some men are abuse victims by women neighbors or girlfriends. some were physically or sexually abused when they were young, or emotionally neglected by mothers or wives, abandoned by their mothers or fathers and they're angry, They were abused and never spoken to about it, men don't talk about such things. They just hold it in and wait for it to be released at a further date. Some men see abuse as the only way to get respect from women, or to get her to not question him so he can be free to do his dirt. They've been fathers with out guidance or training.
They're bitter with low a self-esteem, always having to prove their manhood in the streets. These men are very angry. They have high expectations. Or they just hate women because many women are abusers, and provoke them to rage because they like to push buttons, they have

there excuses and they need help, and if we don't change and stop excepting it, they won't change!"
"Damn, what are you saying? I make him beat on me because someone mistreated him, or I push his buttons out of pleasure?"

"You're the easy target! He hates himself because he is weak! That's why he drinks because he's too weak to handle his situations! It makes him feel stronger to beat on you and make you feel like shit so he can feel good! He makes you depend on him for all of your comforts so you have to take his shit! He needs someone to take his shit out on, and you allow him to use you as his target because you don't do anything about it!
"What are you going to change? What are you going to do for Angel? Get yourself together so you can depend on yourself! Love yourself Angel! Stand up for yourself! You only stay with him because you don't think anyone else will want you, or you don't have anyone else who can help you, or you believe you have no chance of meeting anyone, especially with six kids. He knows you feel like shit, so he plays on it and brings it up. Has he ever said, "Who'd want you?" Or, "I put up with you so you should be happy?"

I just stared at her and bit my bottom lip. I knew she was right.
"You're looking at yourself and wondering if he is comparing you to the other women he sees. And then you believe that you're not worth much so you should be grateful that he wants you. So you tolerate his abuse. Well baby, if you called the police on his butt, I bet he would stop! He'd know he could go to jail for a long time. That's assault and battery. There are shelters you could go to with your kids to get away from him. They could be scared for life after listening to you two fight. You don't think about them listening and how it's going to affect them. I bet you were affected by your parents!"

There was nothing I could say. She was so right. I did nothing. I just accepted it, like I didn't have a choice because he said he loved me. I needed him to stay with me, so I took the abuse.
She read me like a book. The kids had heard everything! They cried throughout all of the fights and I never stopped it! I'd just keep arguing. I was yelling at the kids to shut up and telling them to go to their rooms and close the door. They were listening to their mommy getting hurt and now they're going to hurt and hate. Here I was, thinking that I was protecting them and not remembering how I felt when I wanted to help my brother and mom and couldn't.
I played a major part in this family's destruction too, with my drunken, drugging, inconsiderate ass; I did enjoy pushing his buttons.
She held my hands and looked into my eyes as they watered.

I gave her a "Miss Know-it-all" smile. "Are you finished now?" I asked.
"Yes, You can go. Do you have anything else you want to say before you go Angel?"
"No, I just want to lay down." I just wanted to get under the covers and never come out.

I went into my room to cry.
I laid on my bed and threw the blanket over my face squeezing it tight around my shoulders, not able to cover myself completely.
I cried and prayed, shaken cold. I crawled all the way underneath the blanket with it still over my face with my butt in the air as I got up on my knees.
I needed to pray! I don't want to get on the floor. This is comfortable, and He wouldn't want me to be uncomfortable, right? I wouldn't be so fast to finish.
"God it hurts so much. Please make it stop!" I fell and laid flat. I was too tired and weak to pray. I couldn't move. I was emotionally drained.
Someone came to my left side and sat on my bed, rubbing my shoulders and back.
I didn't even look up. I thought it was my counselor consoling me since I was the only one without a roommate. Who else could it be?
It felt so comforting and warm. I cried even harder. I yelled into my pillow a few times, than I felt a warm since of relief, like I'd cried out a lump of pain that was in my gut. My head stopped hurting after twenty-four hours of pain.
Than I remembered that there were men in this ward and that anyone could come into your room. It was dark in here. The hand was starting to feel heavy; more like a man's hand so I looked up.
No one was there.
What the…? I looked around the room. I jumped up and ran to the door to look into the hall but no one was there either.
Wow, I was touched! Oh my, a sprit had comforted me! "Thank you! I feel better."
I went back to lie down and enjoy the momentary peace that had come over me.

I was suddenly inspired to write about how Jesus has always been a friend to me. I named it "If I only had a friend" I realized God gave me valuable gifts better than diamonds and pearls, gold, expensive cars, and I didn't appreciated them. He gave me a body, Sprit, and a mind and you know what I did with it? I neglected and abused it, I gave it to his enemy, his adversary, my body I tried to kill it, he said no I'll keep it, my mind I tried to burn it and he said no I will use it, my Sprit I tried to defile it and gave it to his adversary to control it but he still said I forgive you. I gave more love and respect to a leather coat or a diamond ring and a shirt given to me by a friend them I did to his gifts. I didn't even appreciated the fingers he gave me to write this but because he loved me he still gave me more, he gave me his sons life. He said he will always be my friend and I'll never be alone again and I ignored him and act like he wasn't even there and I begged for a human friend and they hurt me and left me but he still stayed knocking at my door waiting for me to open it. He had always been there for me but I haven't been a friend to Him. I ignored Him and never talked about Him. I didn't give Him any of my time and attention. I didn't go places with Him, and I didn't take Him anywhere with me. I sure didn't introduce Him to anyone. But I was always asking for things in His name as I had been taught to. Did I have a right to do that?

I finally got a roommate. She was a heroin addict. She was a skinny little old lady. She looked like she been out there for years; she had a hard struggling face. After two days of group, on the third night she sat on the edge of her bed with her lamp shining.

"Angel are you awake?" she whispered.

"yeah, What's up? I'm just laying here thinking about the day."

"I need to tell you something!"

I sat up and looked at this fragile woman with respect, "Okay."

"Angel, my family asked me to come here so I don't die. I am 57 years old and I've been getting high all of my life and I don't intend on quitting now. The rest did me some good. But I have a message for you before I leave!"

I was shocked. She was always quiet in Group.

"Angel, you are going through the irons of the fire to be purified like gold. You will do great things; you just have to hold on.

Why do you do you think you were the only one for two weeks with out a roommate?

Not because no one needed the bed. He was waiting for me to come in to give you this message.

You are very gifted and blessed by God and Satan is trying to kill you. He keeps his sprits of torment, insecurity, and guilt with you so you can't do what God has in store for you. So you must stop trying to take your life and live because you will be His testimony."

I looked surprised how did she know I tried to kill myself? I didn't tell her that

"God has heard your prayers and He wants you to know that He loves you, and He will teach you why you had to go through these things. Angel, you have more pain to suffer but it will make you stronger."

I sat there speechless with tears filling in my eyes as I heard her speak for the first time. I felt peace surround the room.

She rolled over and went to sleep and was gone before I got up.

I "graduated," as they say after 60 days and was sent out to do my "ninety and ninety with an out patient plan. I read the book by Zig Ziglar 'See you at the top' who said some thing that stayed in my head, "you are where you are because that's where you want to be!" I choose to stay in pain. That book opened my eyes to so much and gave me a lot of confidences. Then my counselor looked at my book and laughed at me and said only one out of ten makes it. I said confidently, "yeah well I'll see you at the top!" It was 9,9,89. I said today God turned the three 666 upside down, like my life. I know longer belong to Satan.
After nine months, I agreed to meet Chris after work. He was in a drug program but since it was the weekend, he could spend the night out.
"Angel, please stay with me tonight so we can talk!" I agreed and we sat in the park and talked for hours.

"Angel, I really want my family back more than anything in the world! I'll do anything for you baby; I have changed. I read the Bible everyday, and God wants me to be a father and to get our children a home. I was even baptized! I am a changed man; you have to believe me. I even stopped smoking cigarettes! Please Angel, I love you more than life. Give me… no give us, our family another chance!"
We laid under the dark cloudy sky in the grass at Temple's park as night arrived. "Chris, I can't take that chance! It's only been nine months since you entered a program. Nobody changes that fast. What if I take you back and you go back to using again? I just can't! I've been through too much pain. I can't and won't go through it ever again. I'm not going to allow you to hit me ever again! I can't take you hurting my feelings and verbally abusing me!"

"I've changed," he promised. "Let me prove it to you!" He had his Bible in his hands, proudly quoting a husband's duty to his wife.
"I'm serious about this! I feel great like I have a natural high."
"I hate to be the one to burst your bubble but that spiritual high you feel is temporary if you don't keep feeding it and most people don't! It goes away after the pain and suffering slacks up. And then we tend to pray less and less sincerely."
"You don't have any faith in me do you? How do you know how I'm going to feel?"
"Because I've been there many times that's how! I'm telling you to feed it! You have to keep fighting! The closer you get to God, the harder your battles get. Are you ready to fight?"
"I'm fighting for my life and our family I know that much! Do you always have to be so negative Angel?"
"No! I'm not trying to be negative! I'm trying to prepare you for the hardest temptations! I want our family together too!"

He kissed me and we made passionate love in that park. I slept under his arm all night. I missed him so much. I missed my home with feet!

The next day his program had a picnic to attend. It was a yearly event and he invited me.
I didn't want to go but the barbeque sounded good about now.
"Here take this $20 and go across the street and buy yourself a short set to wear to the park okay? Please?"
I went and bought a pink jumper short set with patches and big side pockets.
"Come on into the recovery house! You can use our bathroom." We went inside and he started yelling, "Female coming up the stairs!" He took me by the hand. "This is my room," he said and gave me a washcloth and soap. I washed up quickly; thank God for perms because all I had to do was part it down the middle and pull my hair back into a ponytail and I was ready.
The picnic was in a park in Philadelphia called Lemon Hill. Chris and about thirty men all had on T-shirts that identified their program. A nice Muslim man started a conversation with me, telling me how all Chris talks about is getting his family back together! Then he invited me to attend their group.
"Sure why not?" I replied. I really didn't have any intentions of going.
I was impressed with Chris; he was finally sober and he pushed the family issue. He kept telling me that the quickest way to get the kids was to stay together.
I wanted our children out. "Okay," I told him, "I'll try it!"

I began attending their groups and I loved it. Within one week I was facilitating the group. Apparently the guy at the park was a counselor. He had been clean for five years. He basically said I had good feedback and that I was a natural born counselor.
I looked forward to going to groups everyday after work. I was implementing what I called "Goofy Fridays" and "The House of Pain" room. In that room we got busy with pain and had a tremendous amount of group support. I was proud to be able to walk past the bar that enticed me with their loud music and the smell of beer but I'd say, "Not today," and I'd cross the street.

After nine months Chris came to me all excited. "Baby I have some great news! The founder of the drug program asked a nun to give us a home to live in as long as we needed it and this beautiful woman said, 'Yes,' so now we can get our children!"
"What?" I screamed. "Really? Oh baby really? Are you serious? Oh thank you Ms. Nun Lady, whoever you are, thank you so much!" I

hugged Chris. "Thank you Chris, I knew you would find someone to help us!"
"God is helping us because we are trying and now we are doing things His way!"
"Oh I'm so happy! So how soon will the house be finished? Who's going to do the work? What has to be done? How long before we can get the kids?"
"Slow down baby. I called the caseworker and she said we go to court in three weeks and if the house is together by then, then they'll send out an investigator. Then if the house is approved they'll release the kids!"
"Oh baby, will it be ready?"
"You bet it will! We just have to put in a staircase and a bathroom shower. We're going to get a house full of free furniture too. I already set it up! I told you to trust me."
"Oh Chris, I'm so happy!" I jumped up and down screaming, "Thank you God! Thank you!"

We were given a home for three years rent-free from the good-hearted sister on Norris Street. We were put into the newspaper, as the world watched our children run from foster care to be united with Chris and me. They hugged us so tight jumping up and down as we told them that they were home with Mommy and Daddy for good!
"Really? We can stay here with you two, really?" Oh, they were so happy.
The reporters from the paper were so impressed with the level of our love that they asked to come back again the following week, Christmas week, to put us as an inspirational story.
"Sure!" we said.
Before we knew it, we were on the TV news, in all of the papers.

The program gave both of us jobs. I created an outpatient program I started by writing names and numbers on matchbooks until I demanded an office. I charged the outpatients $10 per month; the ones that paid inadvertently paid the telephone bill and stocked the office with supplies. I began one-on-one counseling and within five years the program grew from thirty people to five hundred men and woman and they had houses N.S.E.W. Then I coordinated groups at ten different locations all around the city that I had to monitor and designate a group facilitator.
I was giving seminars at Temple University every year at our retreats. Chris was doing case-management and counseling groups and training group leaders. He was helping woman get their children out of foster care, representing the parents in court and getting them homes. He was also being the best husband and father in the world.

I was becoming important and very busy. God (and a very nice man) blessed me with two buildings to start my dream program to help kids in the community. It was called the 'I Care Center.'

The center was great. The members in my program helped run it. In the summer we had camp and dances and free food for the elderly and the needy and in the winter we went out to schools and talked to the kids about everything they should avoid. Listening to our experiences helped drive our points.

Three times a year Chris' brother Gary and I would get twenty-five to thirty volunteers to help other organizations get thirty kids to a hard-core challenge campground for ten days in the wilderness three times a year. I went to night classes and obtained my GED in six months. I obtained my drivers license and my drug and alcohol certification.

I was sitting on five very important and prestigious organization boards, and I was on TV programs like *Visions*. I taught at various training programs. The newspapers followed our family every year for four years on Thanksgiving and Christmas to put us in the newspapers for inspirational updates. The kids were doing great in school; we got the "Parents of the Year" award.

We had hundreds of people hugging us everyday, calling us and asking us for help. For eight years, Chris and I were very happy, no fights, no pain, just love and respect.

The kids was famous, everyone feared them because once a man slapped Cyris. Chris paged me when it happened. I was at group. "Come home now and bring a few back-up men," he told me.

I whispered, "Chris got beef. I need four men to ride home with me." Six men jumped up. I waved 'sit back down' to two that I couldn't fit in the car. I got in my car and drove the thirty blocks home.

That's when we found out it was just a slap and that he was not going to apologize. We looked up and no lie, three hundred people came running down our block to get our back! And everyone knew that we had big back up! You could see them two blocks long, still running from that far away place to our house because they thought something happened to Chris' family.

I waved at them to go back. "Thank you but you have to go back."

Cars were pulling up. "What's the problem Angel?"

"It's a misunderstanding everyone back up and go home." I heard the police sirens. I didn't want to get the program in trouble and I didn't want to punch the woman who said, "This is uncalled for! She needs to watch her kids better." If I would've hit her, everyone on that block would have been approached and she would have been jumped, so I ignored her and continued to say, "Let's go."

But a friend of mine heard her. "Angel, you want me to handle that fat bitch for you?" Another big friend said, "Yeah, we'll handle her for you; you don't have to do a thing."
I started laughing, happy as shit to see such a beautiful sight. "No, I don't want no trouble and no one arrested so just go and thanks!" I hugged some people and thanked them for their love and concern.
I looked back as I walked down the block. I watched as people continued to walk toward my house. I went upstairs to look out the window. I smiled proudly. Yeah, I was sure that this hadn't been seen in Philadelphia before for just one family.

Chris bought me about seven cars in ten years. I'd get tired of one and he'd trade it in and buy me another one. Everything my heart wanted he would provide. He cared for his kids and made sure they had everything they needed. I felt so good knowing that I was helping people not use drugs, steal or kill. Thanks to our Youth at Risk program, I was helping hundreds of teens get through some of his or her issues. I was on top of the world.
I was feeling needed, loved and part of a family, a close recovering family: I would never use and lose all of this, I was happy to be alive!

Then it all began. I walked into my building and I was crushed at what I saw.
In one of my buildings the pipes burst and flooded the entire building. All the floors were soaked into the wood and it buckled up. It was leaking through the cracks and down the three flights of stairs into the basement. It went unchecked for three days during a weekend in December.
When I walked in I was devastated. I heard it sounding like it was raining loud inside my nicely fixed up offices. The basement was flooded so bad that I had to drain it out with the machine all by myself. Cyris helped me pull up the little strips of wood and replace it with wood panel and linoleum bought with money out of my pocket.
I bought lots of sheet rock for the ceilings and gallons of paint, only to be told that all of the pipes were stolen out of the building after all that work. I got some information on how to write proposals and I received some funds to replace the pipes, which cost $1200. Before I could feel any relief I got a call; the other building's pipes were taken and hundreds of dollars of paint and supplies were stolen, as well as my computer.

I stood in front of the building and just cried. I called my partner and asked him if the summer food program checks come in yet. Shit, that's $700; we can fix this.

"No not yet," he said. "I'm still waiting. They said they sent it to the wrong address and when it comes back to them then they'll send it back out."
"Okay," I said as I walked away with my head down. Later that day, I went back around his house to see his wife and I found him high.
He had relapsed after five years clean. "You liar!" I yelled at him. "You got those checks didn't you?"
"Yes, I'm sorry. I needed the money!"
"Well what about the center? The kids?" I screamed. "I'm taking money out of my damn pockets, taking all of my husband's money to fix up these damages and you go and do this shit to me?"
I found out all sorts of information that day. He was high, which meant he wasn't honest. Through out the center's history we would hold dances. While I was busy keeping the police from closing us down because we needed a second exit for escape, he was stealing that money. The nice man that let me utilize his two buildings for three years went away. With no one to help and support me, I locked up both buildings in defeat! My dream came and gone. It didn't last very long.
I thought that losing my dream program was painful. Then I was told that I was fired because the drug program didn't have the funds to pay me.

I had previously resigned from all of the boards because I was too busy. I'd wanted to free up sometime to be with my kids and now all I had was time. I still went to group to show that I wasn't there just for the money. I got another job working at night with teens. But I was hurting everyday. It was becoming harder for me to walk. It was so painful. I felt betrayed by the family that said they loved me but ended up stabbing me in the back and taking my job, giving themselves raises.
I opened up a car wash and was making good money for three weeks, and just when I thought I couldn't handle another loss, the founder of the program shut me down. He said he couldn't pay for the water. The damn electricity has been in Chris' name for years and I'd done so much to help the newcomers eat like us, paying them $3 out of every $5. I was hurt and felt rejected and I felt he owed me. I really thought he, the founder of the program loved me like his daughter but he was stopping me from eating!

Then I got a call I never wanted to receive. I got a call telling me to go to my best friend's house. She was there in her bed, dead! I was devastated.
I was in denial until I held her stiff hand. I told everyone's staring eyes to get away from her. I kept my promise to her and took off her jewelry and gave it to her kids. She had leukemia and I knew she was going to die but I still asked, "Why did you leave me now Lexes?" I cried on her arm. "I need you! I love you so much! I'm sorry I wasn't here for you! I can't go

to your funeral; I will say my goodbye here and now. You go visit your family and swing bye and visit me. I'll be waiting for you!"
And behold my TV blacked out the day she was buried and she called me on the phone for a second! I heard her voice say, "Angel? Guess what?" Then we were disconnected. If she could sneak a call, out of everyone in the world besides her mom she would've called me! And she did!

Then my legs started getting worse, it started with just knee pains and I started walking with a limp. Then both of my legs would hurt so much I could hardly walk, all day every day, pain beyond Tolerable.
My knees, my calves, my thighs were so tight it felt like a truck was sitting on them. It was so painful I cried myself to sleep every night. When I was young I use to get leg cramps and they would fall to sleep but this was much worse and I found myself crawling up the stairs and not being able to drive or even walk to the corner. The pain was so excruciating I swear I wanted them cut off. I rather have no legs then to be in this much pain all the time. And then my back and arms, and neck began to hurt, I was no more good. It felt like someone was sitting on my shoulders, pulling both of my arms and I was carrying a grown man on my back and someone continually was punching my arms and the truck wouldn't get off my legs. I stayed in bed most days and if it rained I stayed in bed and cried all day. I wanted to die. I didn't deserve this pain.

The straw that broke my strong ass back happened when I was taking a nap before I had to go to work at midnight. Chris peeked into the dark bedroom. I kept my eyes closed, hoping he would come and kiss me awake, but he didn't. He left and quietly closed the door.
I looked at the clock 11:00pm and said, "Well, I have to be getting up soon anyway, I was still trying to kept my job with the pain and all."

A voice in my head said, "Pick up the phone, unplug it, and plug it in to the phone jack that is for the line downstairs.
"What?" I said to the voice.
"Just do it!" it demanded.
I did. The phone was ringing. I heard a female voice say, "Hello?"
"Hi baby," I heard Chris say. "What are you doing?"
"I'm watching TV, why?"
"I want to see you tonight. Can I come over?"
I looked at the phone, than put it back to my unbelieving ear.
"No, because you play too much. You're not going to take me on a trip! You can't keep playing with my feelings!"
"I'm not playing," Chris responded. "I really want to be with you. I need to talk to you!"
"Talk to me now!"
"Obviously, I can't talk on the phone now. Just let me come over!"

"Okay."
"I'll be there by one!" he said and hung up.
I heard her hang up. I stood there looking at the phone.
I sat on the edge of the bed. That cheating mother-fucker! I thought we were getting along great and he's cheating on me? What should I do? Oh shit! Wow, I never would have had proof if I didn't hear that for myself. He would have told me I was just being insecure and he that he needed some space.
Damn, another woman that he's going to be with when I leave to go to work. That bastard.

Oh hell no. He has to pay for this pain. My chest was tightening up.
I took out a condom! I wrote a note with it saying,. "Take this condom with you to the devil's bed you bastard! I hope you burn in hell for adultery and by the way, take all of your shit with you to go be with your whore! Don't let your shit be here when I get home or I will burn your shit! P.S. Next time your in another woman's house, call your bitches from a phone booth you dumb mother-fucker."

I acted like I didn't hear a thing on the phone and smiled and kissed him goodbye. He was watching TV and looked like he was going to get a treat or a snack, something that he shouldn't have. He had that look that said, "yeah, bye already, just go ahead, bye! Kiss, kiss and go! And stop distracting me from what I'm not really focusing on!"
I left and slammed the door and jumped in the car.
I cried so hard that I could barely drive to work. I couldn't work with that on my mind! I couldn't accept that he wanted another woman to comfort him and give pleasure and talk to. I went from "confident" to "devastated" in a matter of seconds!
He said he loved me! We were getting along so well…why? Why, damn it?
Crying uncontrollably, I called my favorite brother-in-law, Missy's husband and asked him to call me out sick.
I went back to the house to get some money. Chris jumped in the car and tried to tell me he was just going there to talk!
"Yeah, at 1:00 am, you sure have a lot to talk about in person!" I screamed. "Kiss my ass!" I pulled out my loaded Beretta. "Get out of my car and leave my house!"
Chris grabbed my arm. "It's one in the chamber so if it goes off and hits you now it's your fault!" I screamed. I pointed it at his legs and squeezed the trigger as I looked at him with disgust. "Get off of me now! Your whore can take care of you after I shoot your damn leg off! Now get out!"

He grabbed my hand quickly. He had his hand so tight around mine I couldn't move my finger. He was squeezing it so hard while twisting it. I had to let go and he disarmed me.
"Give me back my shit!" I screamed.
"Hell no!" he yelled and jumped out. He slammed the car door and went back into the house.
I followed him. He was not going to get the comfort of being home.
I went upstairs and took out all of his nicely hung clothes and threw them on the bed. I then tried to light a match to the stack I formed but the fire keep going out. I was still demanding that he hurry up and get out!
"I'm not going anywhere," he said. "You wait till I get some money and than I'll leave!"

He grabbed me and snatched the matches and threw me on the bed like a rag doll. Then he jumped on top of me and held both of my arms down with his knees. It hurt so bad that I began to cry. He looked at me with disgust, like it was always me acting a fool but for no reason. I smacked the shit out of his face once and he grabbed me by my throat. "Angel, leave me alone!" He squeezed tighter. "You hear me? I'll kill you! Do you hear me?"
My face was full of blood that was about to burst out of my temples. I gagged as I tried to unsuccessfully kick him off. I twisted and turned and tried flipping him over.
Finally he released what seemed like all of his power to give or take my life. "I mean it!" he screamed. "I'm going to sleep now! I don't want to talk about this anymore!" He took off all off his clothes. He was buck-naked and as usual he went right to sleep.
I sat there in the dark for a moment wiping my bloody nose from all the blood that had rushed to my head. I went into the bathroom and looked in the mirror and said, "What are you going to do now? Stab his sleeping ass? He's got your damn gun." I went down stairs because if I stayed in there I might have stabbed him in his sleep because as usual by tomorrow none of this shit will have happened. It will all get swept under the rug never to be relived with answers, not even a "forgive me," revenge time.

I must go get cute and find me a man! Fuck this faithful shit!
I went down stairs and put a long brown weave in my hair.
It looked real pretty. I put on some make up too. I had on a pretty strapless sundress, red with black hearts that went all the way down to my black sandals.
I should go to a bar and find me a boyfriend I thought. I sure do look sexy. I looked like a model from the head up until you got to my fat ass gut and flat ass butt!
I looked closer into my eyes. It'd been a long time since I really looked into my eyes; is that me in there? I looked artificial in the mirror. I

realized that I was tired of this fake hair, and my fake nails, and all this make up. I was tired of feeling fake, where was the real me? I wanted to change myself drastically because I hated what I saw! I hated it; it was not I! What I saw was not reflecting what I felt my sprit was like inside! I wore too many different faces and attitudes with each hairstyle I changed every week, always a new look but I never saw the real me.

Before I knew what I was doing, I started snatching the weave out of my head! "OOOOUCHHHHH!" I screamed. The tracks were drying so the front was tight and hurt immensely all around the headline. "Ooooucccch!" damn this was painful and torturous. I didn't even think of all the money that I'd spent on weaves and glue and nails polished designs… all the hours I just spent on my nails and hairdo.

I wanted to feel all of this pain. There was so much anger coming out in my pulling. It felt good in a painful way. I was punishing myself. I felt ugly and disgusting. I never thought to just cut it out.

I breathed out hard and felt this last tight dry track on the bottom back row that just ripped all my hair. It left glued patches. The glue held on tight because I put on way too much. I heard the tearing of my hair. I pulled and pulled until every last track was out.

In the drawer in the kitchen I found the scissors. Still looking in the mirror I grabbed the patches and lumps and bumps, and cut my hair as far down as I could. I got out the clippers and shaved it all off.

I looked at my new look and smiled. Now I was real! I was real, unmade-up, undecorated, with no fancy hairdo, or shiny colorful jewelry, no material to compliment my skin or cover my face… just plain old me! A changing me like it or not world because I loved it! It felt like a bold and strong gesture!

But I grieved the end of a part of me and my transformation through a painful birth. I was introducing a new beginning a better me.

I looked at myself in the mirror. "Hi Angel, it's nice to meet you!"

I laid on the couch until 8:00am wide-eyed like I was on crack.

Chris came down in a beige suit with a brown hat and sharp brown alligator Giorgio B shoes. He had no wedding ring on.

He looked at me and did a double take. He shook his head as if to say, "Yeah she's crazy!" and backed out the house. "It's over!" he yelled. "I'm through with you!" He went on to work.

"Fuck you!" I yelled back. "Fuck it! You're damn right it's over! I don't want your trifling ass!"

That night, he worked late again 11:00pm alone in the office with his secretarial whore, so I drove past the program's office screaming, "Fuck you all too!" I drove around for an hour, scared to ask for the drug but

finally finding that rock! I had $300 and it was all mine to spend, as I wanted. I figured it would last all night.
I tried to get high but I couldn't. After the third tiny rock I said out loud, "I don't want this shit!" I took the four remaining rocks and wrapped up the can I had poked holes into smoke out of. I put them in a plastic shopping bag and went outside and put the bag in the trashcan. I ran back upstairs and looked out my window proud of my choice.
I watched two men walk by with the going to cope walk. I started to tell them that there was $40 worth of crack in the trashcan but I said to myself, "don't help someone else kill themselves because you want to die." I drank beer after beer all night as my tears fell into my glass. He never came home. I paged him and he called me from her bed, talking about I was just laying down for a while in her sons room, yeah right I must really be stupid because I still let him come back to my bed the next night.

Most people will say, "I won't use drugs ever again because I don't want to ever lose what I have!"
Well I relapsed because I lost everything! I wasn't prepared for that!
I still had my kids but shit they were growing up and moving out. I still had my life but I was miserable with that and I didn't want to live. I had no gratitude, no one to run too, no one to talk too. And I was really mad at God, why do he allow me to go thru so much pain I'm a good hearted person and I tried not to brake his commandments, I treated people good. I didn't deserve any of that shit! The Church that just had baptized me and Chris didn't even come to have Bible study with us anymore, they just stop coming and I couldn't get to them, the church was too far and I was in too much pain, they abandoned me too no phone call how are you, no nothing.
The worst part was that I was always in so much physical pain. I couldn't get out anymore and I was confined to my room for months alone. I became lonely and board.
So I stayed drunk for three years as Chris stayed with me but he continued to lay with other woman. Only the alcohol made it all better. So I would drink until I didn't feel any pain. But I couldn't drink away the anger.
My fear of God and committing "big sins" prevented me from exploring worlds with other men, even to the point of having to discover the warm throbbing temptation in my hands.

I met a new friend; finally. The wildest, funniest girl on the block became my best friend. We had a deal: she would keep me laughing and I'd keep her drunk! While I was drunk the pain would leave so that was my pain pill.

Everyday, all day, we were laughing and drinking, playing pool, hanging out in the motorcycle club and every morning we were throwing up, and I was cursing out Chris, still taking his $500 a month for our beer, cigarettes, and entertainment.
I spent everyday on the stoop listening to people talk about everyone else's business. I just say, "That's a shame." I tried not to gossip.
I'd stagger around everyday with my gun cocked, ready to explode. Chris took it from me after I threatened him a few times. He hid it but I found it! I really don't know why he bothered to come home.
I had a fear of abandonment and I wanted it to be me who left him so I always screamed, "Then get out! Go find you a good, clean, sober woman who can walk and clean the house and cook for your ass who'll wear stocking and heels!" I made him not want to be there. After a while I did everything I could to push him away. He tried to say he cheated on me because I was using forgetting it was his cheating that pushed me over the edge to using. That phone call wasn't the first one it was the first bust.

"Make it quick! Stop threatening to leave after every argument! Just go! Why are you still here? Don't talk about it be about it Chris! Go let your stink ass bitches take care of you! Just don't let me run into you two, I want to kill someone!"

I committed myself into the hospital for a week in the psychiatric ward. I threatened the staff everyday and demanded to be released after three days I was very angry. I had to sign a waiver that said I was leaving even though they thought I should stay!
I had more havoc to reek. I had to seek out my victims carefully. I didn't want to falsely accuse a woman but the voice that told me to pick up the phone also told me which woman he was intimate with. So now he was going to pay for all of his years of abuse and pain. I would stay out all night and let him wonder where I was and whom I was with!

But who was going to want me now? Who wanted a 200-pound cripple who was unable to work at any level and was progressively getting worse and fatter? It was difficult to wear high heels. I was finding it more difficult to even stand long enough to cook. My hands, feet, and ankles were constantly swollen and throbbing. I drank just to get around and feel normal. It got to the point where I couldn't go a day without a drink!

I could've gone to jail and isolate myself no problem. I wondered if that would've been better for me.

CHAPTER SIXTEEN
BACK TO REALITY

It was day break and the birds were singing. The air smelled fresh from the dew on the leaves on the trees. The scent floated into my room and God said to me, "I gave the world's stinky ass a bath!"

Wow that was very emotional, all that thinking! So many feelings...so draining! I really wanted to die now! Damn, I am more depressed than ever. I understood mom better but I really hated Chris as well as my pathetic self. I hated how I was feeling. I hated who I was. I wished I were dead so I can end this fucked up hand of cards I've been dealt!
I really did learn a lot about my mom and myself. I really didn't know a lot about myself. Something's I wished I didn't know, like who I am. Well, it was easier to blame everyone else for my problems and pain but to learn I'm the problem and I stay for the pain and invite it in, and how weak I really am and sinful, and self centered, well that hurts, maybe now that I know, I'd have to forgive, let go, move on with my life and leave my entire past in the past. Maybe I could help Cyris learn how to forgive and let go. Because after all, who wants to hear someone say they understand if they haven't been through it?

I understood why I wanted to die and why I didn't care about life. Little did I know my lessons were just beginning?
I was drained but too excited to sleep. I jumped into the shower and was out quickly. I put on a comfortable robe and my red slippers. I looked out the window as the water fell off my wet head. I shook my hair in the air like a dog shakes off the water.

Cyris was coming home; Chris called from court and said good news. I was so excited! He'd been away for a year. He turned seventeen two weeks after he got locked up. A week after he got home was going to be his eighteenth birthday. My baby was growing up into a man.
I prayed he slowed down now.
I stuck my head further out the window. I could see them! Cyris was coming down the street with Chris. My heart started beating fast. I started jumping up and down. "Yippee! Yippee!" I shrieked. Ouch, that hurt my new sprained ankle...eh, so what? "Yippee!"
My son was coming home. He was really blown up; the depression pills made him fat. I couldn't believe this was my once-130-pound son who was now 225.
Chris kissed me on the cheek. "They released him in my custody. He's still on probation with a monitor on his ankle."

I watched him hug his sisters. Oh, they all looked so beautiful. I loved seeing them all together.
I finally got my turn. “I am so happy to see you baby!” I grabbed my baby, my only son, and my love of my life, my just-like-me baby. I looked at his puffy cheeks and squeezed them and smiled hard. I hugged him long and tight; I never wanted to let go!
“I missed you so much! Welcome home and stay home!” I whispered. “Stay out of trouble! Stay with me. I need you, okay baby?”
He held me as I planted my head on his soft comforting chest. He smelled like steel and in need of an oil bath. I couldn’t wait to help him get his hair washed so I could braid it for him. He still looked good just big as shit! He was nobody you’d want to just run up on believe me! His arms were all muscle and they swung hard and fast like his father’s and mine.

Chris interrupted my thoughts. “I’ll hook him up with his own room in the apartment building I’m leasing for my job. He can stay in my room for a while. We’ll see how it works! Cyris…” he called, reaching out for him to come and hug him. “I’ll help you get into a job-training program that will pay you every week. Here’s a few dollars for your pocket. Check it out, Cyris; you’ll have your own phone and TV. But you have to abide by all the residential rules or you will get put out!”
Everything was fine for a whole two weeks.

Cyris was straight until he was challenged at school and brought a knife for protection. Chris got that phone call and got that squashed for him because the people at the school owed him a favor. Then he got into an argument with a girl. He said, “I don’t hit girls,” and he had his sisters come up to the school to beat her up. Chris got the call; “Sorry,” the school said, “but we’ve done everything we could to work with him. Three students said he had a silver handgun in school. We have to cut him from the roster.”
There was a fire in Cyris’ room from a cigarette butt in the trashcan. The room was supposed to be smoke-free. Chris had to tell him to come home.
“He broke the rules over their Angel,” Chris said to me. “What can I do? This was not the first broken rule but it was the last.”

Cyris had to wear an ankle bracelet for a while. He was home with me for one week and he cut it off and was running the streets again. It took him two months to get skinny again, back to his original weight of 130 pounds. That “wet” Angel Dust will do it.

One day, I was listening to a spiritual song on the radio called, “Waiting for My Child,” by The Contenders. They were singing, “If you seen my child somewhere/send him home…” I couldn’t help but think about

Cyris. He was staying out all night, every night. I didn't know if my child was dead or alive, in jail or out of town.

I was about to lie down and relax that nice summer afternoon when I heard my son holler, "Mom! Mom! MOM!" From outside.
I jumped up and ran to the window. My heart was pounding like it always did at every sound of our kids raising their voice. Fear set in my heart and my stomach started to tighten up. Was it trouble?
I was alone in the house. Cyris was across the street with a big plastic trashcan. He was holding it up to protect himself from his enemy, a neighbor of his. The neighbor was trying to hit with a ten-foot pole. I couldn't run down the stairs because my legs were in a lot of pain.
"Stop it!" I hollered. "Put that pole down!"
The tough looking dude apparently didn't want to fight Cyris with his own hands, so he continued to swing the pole at him. Cyris was blocking every swing using the garbage can like a shield. The neighbor underestimated Cyris' cleverness and quick reflexes.

Than I saw Aqusia, she was fighting his sister in the middle of the street. She wasn't worried about her beautiful face getting scratched or her sexy designer clothes getting torn of or her long hair being pulled out; she wanted to see blood! Down the corner three guys were beating up Cyris' friend, a short stubby guy. He was very meek he didn't bother anybody!
I grabbed my gun out of its box and shot it off out the window. "Stop it!" I screamed. "Stop it I said, now!"
Everyone was ducking. I was fortunate that it didn't hit anyone. The dude stopped swinging the stick.
"Get in the house now Cyris!" I yelled. I had to run downstairs to get Aqusia because she didn't stop fighting. Cyris moved back but he didn't go into the house. He was helping me break up his sister's fight!
I got between Aqusia and the girl. They were bent over holding on to each other. "Let go of each other's hair!" I shouted. "Now," I said! The girl let go and then Aqusia let go.
The dude Cyris was fighting yelled, "Her gun is jammed!" But I gave him the "don't fuck with me" look. "You really don't want this to go any further, so stay back!" I said as I pushed them apart. "Get inside now!" I told my crew.
I told the dude's mother to keep her son away from mine because we could see that the bull shit they were going through would lead to chalk marks where one of there bodies will be laid out. She agreed that they didn't need to say shit to each other.

An hour later after trying to keep Cyris in the house, his friend came back on the block with about seven guys. They found two of the boys who jumped him and whipped their asses good. I was watching out the window, telling my kids that they'd better not go out there! Revenge was good to watch but it was dangerous, because one guy had to go to the hospital for stab wounds. He almost died and for what?

The next week, some woman started punching on Aqusia as she was fighting her daughter. Stress was building up in me.
"Oh hell no," I said out loud when I saw her. "I know this bitch didn't just jump in!" I ran down the stairs with no pain, just a mother's anger. I walked across the street. Before I knew it I was standing on my tiptoes to reach this 6'3" woman and punching her in her face. She fell down and I jumped on top of her. I commenced punching her in the face over and over again as hard as I could till I saw blood.
Chris told Cyris to pull me off. I didn't have on any shoes so as he dragged me off of her, I dragged my feet and scraped the top of my feet. The skin came off and it hurt so much that I started stomping her ass!
We both got up and she looked like she wanted to come after me. "Get off of my wife!" Chris yelled. He pulled us all into the house.
I looked back at her. "Keep your fucking hands off my kids! You crazy?" She looked a little drunk so what I was too.

Chris ran down the block breaking up a fight with another child, Jasmine. She was fighting every week now more stress. Laquana was punching some girl in the face and in the stomach and pinning her up against a car, so we left her alone to finish her job while we handled ours.
The police came to arrest me. "What did you hit her with miss? She has a big knot on her head."
"With my damn fist," I said angrily. "She shouldn't have touched my daughter." I was arrested and had my gun taken. I spent one night in jail and lost my license to carry a gun, because she said I threatened her with my gun.

When I got home I called my mom to talk for a minute. There was quiet on the phone. I sat down and lit my cigarette. "My son is always keeping me on pins and needles. He's always fighting now. He went back to hanging with the kids who were stealing cars and selling drugs mom. Cyris is back to his old ways and he cut the damn bracelet off his ankle so now they're going to put a warrant out on him! I'm really scared for him; he gets so high he can hardly walk! I had to carry him to his room many nights, drugs falling out of his pocket.
"Mom," I said as I blew my nose, "I really thought he was getting what he needed and he's still getting put out of schools. This time it was for fighting and for threatening people with a knife and guns. He went to our Youth at Risk retreat and I found out just how depressed he is, and how much he needs his father to show him love and attention, and to spend time with. I told Chris but he has like three jobs. All kids want their father to be in their lives. A lot of them can't stop their crime because of where they live. They really need more big brothers and sisters to spend

time with them, and to do things they never would have experienced. They just need to do something to get out of the neighborhood or the house for a while with someone who listens and cares. That means a lot to our youth.

"Mom, it was a shock to us when we heard him tell someone else in a meeting that he was angry at us because of shit that happened, like him getting raped when he was six by a man in his foster home. I immediately took full responsibility and plotted the man's torture and death." I blew my nose again and wiped the tears from my eyes. "I can't make Chris spend more time with him! Chris wants blood! Anger filled in his eyes because Cyris didn't tell us. He's so angry with the man who told us because it was in front of an audience of hundreds of people. And he's angry with me for putting him in there, and definitely at the man who defiled his son, whose life he has vowed to take! I can't take away this bad memory, but if I wasn't using drugs I wouldn't have put him in there and he wouldn't have gotten raped. I do have to take responsibility for that part! We can't get revenge now because Cyris won't stay still long enough to get to court if they find the man they are not looking for!"

"I learned a lot from the youths when we lived in one building together for twelve hours, getting intimate in the cold mountains for ten long emotional and physically challenged days. They learned to be considerate, understanding, team players, and most importantly responsible for their own actions and responses. For those few days, they had some people who thought they were valuable and who helped them find their worth and to think positive.

I learned as I listened intensely at the pleas for love from "Daddy." I filled my duties of the twelve hours as soundwoman in that time. I understood how much we had in common. The worst finding was that those kids and I had no respect or value for life." I stopped and waited for her response.

"I remember you going away for weeks at a time," Mom said. "That's what you were doing?"

"Yeah mom, and I learned a lot too. What we all had in common was that we were all trying to kill ourselves one way or another, and we were so full of anger that we wanted others to feel it or to know about it or to suffer for it. They really appreciated the fact that we weren't getting paid, that we were taking off from work and leaving our families and really working hard for them. We voluntarily sacrificed a lot just to show them someone cares about them and that they should care too! If our families would stop holding on to resentment and anger and really care about each other, then we could better prepare them for their relationships with others. We better sacrifice sometime and show our kids we care or else we're going to be breeding a generation of cold-blooded killers.

"There were no feelings for no one other than their one or two helpful family members, or the man or woman that we loved that gave us temporary comfort. Everyone else could die - we didn't care! I was a child in their circle, and I asked those kids to walk in their parents' shoes and just maybe they could find some forgiveness in their heart for them! Maybe they'd find some understanding of who their parents are, and who they are, and who they want to be! It was up to them and before they were going to judge their parents, ask some questions about what they'd been through!
I'm angry that I can't go on those retreats anymore. I really loved it! I always left really loving some of those kids. Some even called me 'Mom.''

There was silence on the other end of the phone. "Mom, you still there?"
"I'm still here baby!" she said. "I understand that you miss the life you had and that now you're not helping anyone. You can't help your own so you feel like a nothing, is that right? Every great leader had problems as a teenager. They can help everyone else except their own, and they all say that they're neglected and they raised themselves. So what should we all do differently to save all the teens, stop working? We come home and they want to run the street, not talk, and play them damn Nintendo games. They don't want to cook, clean or wash their own clothes, or their stink-weed-smoke-beer-sex-smelling ass! And half the mess they're out there doing, we told them not to do, but do they listen? No!

"Angel, you'll never know what they're thinking or doing. Maybe when they grow up, they'll tell you some stuff since they know that they can't get in trouble, but I'd be like, 'what my child? Oh, no, not my child!' Yes, your damn child did some foul shit! It was because they wanted to do it, not because their father or I wasn't there. When they need us, we were there but they always act like they don't need or want our attention, hugs or kisses, pushing us away too. They're always busy doing nothing! So much business to handle but still broke, living at home with Mommy. I want to know from those kids, when they're outside selling drugs and they have kids why they don't care if they go to jail or die and their kids don't have a father. Should the child fuck up his life and blame his father? Like you do?"

"Mom, there were plenty of times I had to sit there quietly, wishing I could say a few things too! You know what? I really took a good look at my life and I've seen so many things I have in common with you. I thought about my life and what made me so angry, and even now what pisses me off and drives me crazy. But I still don't have the right words! How can I penetrate him? I still don't know what to say to him that will make him not say 'fuck it' in his time of pain and despair.

I tried to tell him the Sprit never dies and it well go to heaven or hell and if you kill yourself you'll go to hell and be tortured, he says he don't care."

"I told him Death is not just going to sleep for ever and never feeling pain again, and that God don't appreciate us trying to take our life that he gave us, and that it's a selfish thing to do, I told him he should care about the people that he leaves behind and that he is not showing them see this is how much I'm hurting, or see how much you hurt me, or trying to hurt someone for the action. Because after a month after the funeral they all will forget about you, in a year you won't even be talked about so who are you really hurting, what are you really proving because most people just lose respect for suicidal victims or they feel guilty for a day or so than they realized you made your own choice, you could have stayed and worked it out. They say God don't give you more than you can handle so while your dead you want someone to cry for you well for a while they do but eventual some other problems come and your forgotten and everyone go on with there lives, and say oh that was a shame what he did, pass the joint. I told him that I was wrong to think death was a way out, never considering just maybe death is worse than life a walking dead with no flesh and tormenting because I do have to be accounted for my sins, so if I say alive longer maybe I can make amends so my suffering don't be so much. Mom what more can I say?
"Mommy, tell me, what do you think? How can I help him? How can I help my son with his depression? I told him that suicide is a selfish act and that I was being very selfish when I tried to take my life; I wasn't considering how much my children would have suffered. I just knew that I didn't want to keep living. It didn't mean that I didn't love them. I told him that I was wrong and I told him that that is not love and if he loves me, he won't do that again, I told him he has to learn how to love himself!"
"Angel, you see how many times you tried it? If it's not his time to go then he won't succeed baby."
"Yeah, I guess. Thanks mom. I'll talk to you later!"
I hung up unsatisfied, she don't know what to tell me.

I looked up out the window at the sky and said out loud: "God I need more answers!" Why should we want to live? How can we begin to love ourselves? What more do I need to know about death so I can help him and myself?" You hear me God? Because I say those things to him but I still want to die myself. I just want to stop hurting will death stop the hurt GOD?
What is death like?

CHAPTER SEVENTEEN

WHY DO I SUFFER SO MUCH?

I walked around my room back and fourth, thinking out loud and talking to the Indians in the pictures on the wall. I stared into the eyes of the tigers in another picture, and then looked over at the black and white feathered wheel of an Indian, sitting on a horse with his arms stretched out praying to his God. I put myself in this picture; I began saying, "What is with me? Where am I, spiritually? Stretching out my arms up in the air asking, 'why God?' Why do I suffer so much?

"I keep your commandments!" Actually, I guess I really didn't.
Thou shall not kill: I never had an abortion, I never killed anyone, I did try though and I am killing myself smoking cigarettes, and eating junk food, filling my heart with greasy fast food, and pork, and six cans of Pepsi everyday that gives me acid reflux, no safe sex, stressing... Okay, so I didn't honor my mother; I say "I love you" but I still did nothing for her. I gave little to no forgiveness in my so-called Twelve Step work. Thou shall not steal: well, I stole all my kids' time, running to meeting after meeting, being so important and helping the world all day, trying to give Chris my full attention and care all night. I was finally happy and I didn't want to see my kids' misery if there was any. I didn't want to know if they felt unappreciated or needed more time. Once, I stole my mom's $20 for drugs; I stole clothes and food and probably her sleep.
But I was saving peoples lives! When I spoke, there was silence with everyone waiting for my next words of wisdom. I had to be in meetings to speak truth and guidance and to give support and to give and receive hugs three times a day, five days a week. I'd come home, cook dinner, and kiss them all goodnight and tell them I loved them. Wasn't that enough?
"I didn't love myself, so I couldn't really love my neighbor. I loved what I was doing for them and what they said about me in gratitude. I loved feeling needed. I loved being busy and not having time to grieve and focus on the past and constantly hearing stories worse than mine. Whatever I was going through wasn't as bad so I could hold on. I loved the attention and prestige and accolades I received. That's what I loved. I didn't love anyone! I thought I was doing well because I didn't cheat on my husband even though I knew he was smutting around. I prayed daily; I asked what God's will was before I made decisions. I think I was pretty humble considering all that power I had over people's lives and their children's during the eight years of counseling."

"So why am I suffering so much? That's what I would like to know God I've been in so much pain that I want to die! What did I do to deserve this? I know it was you God that filled my mouth with the words to help people. It was you God that gave me the knowledge to coordinate and design all those programs and systems so naturally all at once; I was wearing seven hats, including "mom" and "wife."

"God, you have done a lot for my family. We all have come a very long way. I had everything! I was happy. I know it was the Devil who took it all away from me and now he wants me to give up and die. He wants me to curse and blame you God! But I can't ever do that so I don't even think about it!

"I know you have something for me, for allowing me to go through all this suffering with all this physical pain so that I can start over. Maybe you're slowing my ass down! Yeah, so you can teach me some things right? Because I was moving too fast! Just don't tell me that I just had the best years of my life and that's all! It's not about me now. It's over and the rest of my life will be just be living in pain under a blanket in a wheelchair being "Grandma!"

"Why me? I don't deserve this much pain though God! This kind of pain should be reserved for tormenters and murders and I am neither. My whole body hurts as if someone beat me down for hours with a baseball bat! Maybe it's because God is mad with me! Is that it? Are you mad at me because I stopped going to church? I told you God I don't trust the Bible translations or even all the stories. I know you inspired the stories but I always felt something was missing, and most of the churches aren't praying to God the Father anymore, only to God Jesus. I believe they are being deceived. Help me with this God! I heard that King James was gay! He took out at least fourteen books. I think Mary Magdalene was an apostle. Her story is not in there; oh no not a female Apostle – but Jesus came back to her first! She was his beloved one, she followed him with the other Apostles and spoke out also.

I think the Catholics hate woman. They only include embarrassing stories in the Bible, stories that depict women to be conniving, deceitful, jealous, and an all-around bad influence on men. Women are perceived as manipulators and down right whores. There's even a woman in there that murders her family men just so she can be queen! What examples do I have to follow?

Women are supposed to work hard for the family and to be unseen: covered in silent and obedient to a religion that doesn't even respect them. The historians blame man's downfalls on a woman tempting him with fruit. Like he didn't have a choice! Or better sense for that matter! I read stories about female positive leaders."

"In church, I didn't learn about the Angel Raphael, who walked and talked as a man from the book "Tobit." I could have learned and shown my son how Tobit and Sarrra begged God to take their life so they may be delivered out of their depression. An angel gave them their miracle to peace and happiness. I didn't read that in the King James Revised Version. That could have helped me understand death better, such as in the book, "The Wisdom of Salomon." He took out the commandment in chapter 1v.12, telling me to "seek not death and destroy not myself through the works of my own hand;" or 1v13, telling Cyris and I, "God did not make death and has no pleasure in the destruction of the living, as we believed God made death."

I would have known I wasn't crazy praying for my dead brother all the time, thinking it meant something, when it did. I read it in the second book of Maccabees, 12v.45; it says, "It is a holy and good thought to pray for the dead, and God would make reconciliation for the dead, so they might be deliver from sin." I could have been praying for many of my friends and other family members. Why did King James or Constantine take out the book of Baruch and Sufanna? A story about a beautiful and righteous woman who was accused of sinning (having sex with men) but Daniel proved she did not dishonor herself or her family and she was saved from death. Her accusers, two elders who tried to blackmail her into having sex with them were killed instead.

"I needed to hear that no matter what if you're innocent, then God will avenge you and help you. Didn't God say not to add or take away from the Bible? Yet we happily accept in our churches the King James Version, Edited and Revised! They abstract the truth so we don't get the whole picture! Why? Why is an important book like "The Wisdom of Solomon" taken out? That's nineteen whole chapters of wisdom, gone! And "The Wisdom of Jesus," with 51 chapters, and 16 more chapters to Ester! Why, God, why?

And why change names from "Apocalypse" to "Revelation?" The excellent "Song of Solomon" that we teach generation to generation – now it's called "Song of Songs!" What about the book of other the Prophets that we have not heard of in church, such as the Prophet Beloved of God, Esdras? Who gave King James or Constantine the right to decide which books enter the holy book? They couldn't be proven to be true? They didn't believe in those stories, they wasn't ready to be translated, whatever the reasons why don't all the Churches recognized them at all? Muslims do. Oh, I guess just being the King means you can do what you like!

"The Scribes and Pharaohs and Churches can appoint whomever they want to edit too! I want the truth! The full picture! Give me the Bible's books prior to King James playing GOD! Take me back to 1560: the Geneba version to start with... that's probably closer to the truth and understandable for an English speaker like me.

Why was I not taught that there's a third and fourth Kings book? Aren't they important books too? Okay, so they don't think we need those books; but we need three stories of the same, and letters Paul wrote to his disciples that was personal notes. There is nothing in there about Adam and eves life after they was cast out wasn't that book important? Why don't the preachers at least let us know that they're out there for further study, like the "Book of the Dead" and the Dead Sea Scrolls? What, I have to go to Catholic School to learn some of these things the Christians don't think are worthy to be taught? That's why I haven't been going,
I learn more at home and in the liberty then in church, plus I hate to be looked down upon because I may wear pants or appear a little unclean!

"I want to find a church that has all the good qualities of each religion put together: the fasting and cleaning and constant prayer and appropriate attire. Not packed on make-up and big fancy hats you can't see the pastor and expensive fancy clothes that makes a new comer feel cheap and tight dresses showing shapes of there bodies distracting the men and showing cleavage… just some meditation, real concern with God's love, and going out and telling the world about the glory of God! Giving charity, not just on Thanksgiving, and baptizing in the name of the Holy Ghost. Where the people pray to God and thank Jesus instead of praying to Jesus and thanking God. A church that goes out and knocks on doors to offer help, comfort, and company, and to keep their door open all the time to anyone… are there any churches like that? Any other church, like the 24-hour church, The Dream Center, in Los Angeles?"
I feel like God and Satan is just playing chess with us humans."

I looked out the window and up into the sky. "Children are said to suffer for their parents' sins. Is it because I'm a baby from two adulterers? Or maybe because one of my children prayed that I suffer because they suffered? Maybe I'm an angel and was sent by you God, to do a deed but I self-willed and stayed high never fulfilling my duties. Satan is trying everything to distract and disable me; Satan and his angels have succeeded.
Maybe you want me to sit still and learn and listen for my next big assignment. That's why I can't walk and why I suffer from all kinds of illnesses. They're to humble me so I'll be able to relate to every level of pain and suffering!
Maybe I'm like Moses who couldn't even read! After all his good deeds and prayers and obedience to the law, there was one time he took it upon himself to prove who he was. He was tired of all the complaining from his people so he said, "I want some appreciation and respect here," so he did it his way. "I will show you what power is," he said to them. But he never had power and was punished and banned from entering the

Promise Land. He died after going through all of that struggle and starvation and stress and he didn't even get to be rewarded on earth.
Now I can only sit here and watch everyone live a life without me heading towards the Promise Land.
Is that what I did? Is that how I will die? Am I being punished like Moses God?
Did I take credit for your glory?
Was I being like a god? Enjoying praise and worship?
Yes, I was and God doesn't like that, do you?"

'I know Satan isn't a talking snake; he was and is a beautiful praise Angel, only now instead of praising he wants the praise.
Like some of us, his sprit is what's ugly and monstrous, and snake like.
I thought about how Satan said we could all be like God! Through the power of suggestion, he is close to it, we do think we are God.
I'm sure I did get pumped up and arrogant and felt like it was my power to do things at times. I wanted the praise, the pat on the back… it felt damn good to tell hundreds of people what to do, which way to go, and when to do it. Ms. Queen Bee, head woman in charge!
I brought other women into power because I demanded that the drug program hire more females. I gave training on female empowerment. I bragged about how I got hundreds of votes for a female judge after my speech on why we need understanding black women on the bench for our misunderstood black males, our sons! I hope that if my son ever had to come in front of her, she would look out and remember me and thank me for speaking in her behalf."

"Did I get too big of an ego?
Eating and drinking with the Rev. Jessie Jackson, listening with great pride to him complimenting my self-designed braids, greeting with hugs and kisses Mayor Wilson Goode, and Mayor Ed Rendell, who knows me and Chris by our first names, and Congressmen, and City Council woman Blackwell, who hugged me and told me that I was something special after she heard me address an audience. Proudly taking pictures with famous actors, and holding rapper LL Cool J's hand and feeling false affirmation because he watched me walk away…
Was there too much self-importance in kissing Dick Gregory's struggled face…?
Standing with Mr. George Woods in front of the Uptown Theater on Broad Street reminiscing, looking into his pained face as he told me about the painful things he has seen, how hard it was for him to see the place destroyed, and me with my arrogant ass wanting to counsel him…
"And I flirted with the Dramatics and with the Whispers, and I desired Gerald Leveret and LL, all while I was married…

Wanting to join Ramona Africa's struggle for respect and equality as I took her picture but was afraid of the repercussions…
Or when I told one hundred people out of arrogance to do some jumping jacks and they did it! I felt control! Or when I prayed for revenge, I bragged about what I did when I got it!
Did I look up to Bernard Hopkins in Fresh Fields feeling exceptional, knowing how many people would love to be talking to him, standing as close to him as I did, listening to him tell me about his personal life, about his daughter, making me feel like family…? Did I think I was better then others? Did I look down on simple people?
Did I feel better then? Did I feel like a god sometimes?
Yes I did! Was it all about me? Yes it was!"

"Maybe it was because I didn't appreciate life and tried so many times to take it!
I never thought of what death would be like. Is it really a better choice? Maybe dead is worse! They say you can go to heaven or hell. I'd say, "I don't care," but I do!
I looked in the mirror and said to myself, "Look at yourself rambling, searching for answers. Where did you go wrong?"
I know! It's because I like pain! I'm so used to it coming that if it doesn't come, I hope that something will hurry up and happen. Or else I have to bring it on or I won't feel normal like I'm used to feeling – sad, addicted to pain and grief.
Angel, you are a crazy woman. Stop tormenting yourself.
I like people to feel sorry for me but they don't, so I have to feel sorry for myself.
Isn't that pathetic?
Well, I'm just being honest. I know I'm selfish; if nothing is in it for me, I don't want to do it but I will.

"I'm in pain because I bring it on myself.
I worry too much. The doctors don't even think it really hurts like I tell them it does. I don't eat right. I drink alcohol and smoke weed, so my body is not clean. I guess I can't be healed.
I looked closer at myself in the mirror. Guess what? I'm fat and ugly too!
I flopped on my bed. Oh well, I don't know… maybe I'll learn later why I've suffered. Or what the hell I'm to do about it!
I do appreciate just being able to walk to the store or fix my own food. Sometimes when I cry in my bed at night in excruciating pain, I wish that I had no legs. I really wish I could cut them off then to go through this kind of pain.
"Maybe it's just quilted in my body like an Indian healing man told me in Cincinnati. Maybe it's stress inside my body that's just had enough!

Sometimes I have to take sleeping pills to get to the third level of sleep so my muscles can completely relax.
God showed me the man in the wheel chair with no legs one day when I was walking with my cane." I looked up to my God's heaven and said, "What is this, some damn test?"
That's it; maybe it all just a test and the questions are, "Will you pass or will you fail?"

"Angel," a voice said as I tried to fall asleep, "You're not being punished. It's just something you have to go through for a reason that's not known to you right now. Your son will want to live when he finds something to want to live for and if he turns his life over to God. You say you thought about why you wanted to die but what would help you want to live Angel?"
"A lot of love, no more pain!" I answered the voice in my head. "And a considerate friend, and a closer relationship with God; my kids forgiving and loving me, and my husband's arms open to only me."

I looked at my palms and wondered what I can read. I do have angel wings in my palm, on my right hand: two wings, one wing is broken. Wow, isn't that deep? It looks like an "M" with an "X" in the middle. Wow! I knew I was special.
I prayed everyday for years the same prayer. "God! Please! Please fill me with knowledge, wisdom and an understanding of life! Send someone to minister to me! Send me an angel to guide me and to teach me things! Teach me the truth of your will and words, life. Please!"
I didn't know I would have to suffer so much to get Knowledge, wisdom, and understanding. I thought I would just wake up one day and bam there it is.

CHAPTER: EIGHTEEN

WILL CHRIS LEAVE ME?

"Hi Tunisia, it's so nice to see you baby. It's been a few days. Wow; you finally have on a dress and with those hips I know you been turning a lot of heads!"

Tunisia laughed. "I cut this skirt underneath this long yellow shear covering into a mini skirt. Do you like it?"

"Yes, That is a beautiful sheer blouse. Is that a real diamond pin? Excuse me!"

Her braids flowed down her back. They were tied with a sheer yellow bow. The outfit was finished off with black heels.

"You look so pretty baby. Let me look at you, Big Bird; oh sorry Tweety Bird!"

She was light skinned and very beautiful and so smart. At her graduation she had ten scholarships.

"Ha, ha, ha. You're so funny mom! Everybody gets so excited when I dress up. I guess I have to do it more often."

"I know it's hard to come out of your comfort zone in your sweats and sneakers and your only tail."

"You know sometimes I go to my classes at college in my pajamas!" We start laughing. "People don't care how you look there. I'm just trying to get to class on time and absorb all I can. I had to read three books in two weeks and write papers on all of them and if I'm not reading, I'm writing, and I hate group projects and everyone doesn't do their part and then I have to do it!"

"Poor baby, come sit down and rest yourself!" My room was very clean for a change. "Sit on the bed." She sat down on my green comforter and rubbed my knees.

"You still jog every morning Tunisia?"

"Yes, at least two miles. How are you mom?"

"Oh I'm okay. I should be doing better. I'm tired of drinking. I think I'm going to stop!" I folded my legs on the bed. I was still in the robe I'd had on for five days; depression does that no cleaning anything.

"That's good mom. So you're ready to stop huh?"

"I have to stop because I can't keep living like this! I wake up with a beer and I go to sleep with one. All day, sipping and guzzling beer after beer…I'm really tried of throwing up every night and having diarrhea every morning." I looked up and stared at my CD player. "I love you Otis Redding but I'm tired of crying with you. I'm still trying to figure out why I like to feel sad with you.

I sighed and looked at my daughter. "I pull out my gun a little too much. Yesterday, I scared the shit out of some girl visiting my friend next door.

I pulled it out on her because she said, "You don't know your man is not cheating on you!" and I flipped and pulled out my piece and pointed it right in her damn face. I grabbed her by the neck of her shirt and pulled her towards me. "Mind your damn business. I wasn't talking to you!" I pushed her backwards, than threw it down. "I don't need that shit!" I screamed. I pointed my finger and screamed again. "Mind your damn business bitch! You don't know me or my man!" and I threw up my hands to fight. "Come on! You got so much to say? Come on!" That shit could have went off and hit any five of us when it hit the floor. That was in my neighbor's small living room. She left the house quickly and I haven't seen her again. I'm glad she didn't sneak my drunken ass.

"I look and smell like shit under a disguise of perfume. The other day, my grandson said, 'OH GRANDMA YOU STINK!' Chris says it too and I really don't care but it hurt my feelings when he said it. I smelled my friend when I was sober for a day or two and I got an idea how bad alcohol and armpits and shit-mouth smell!

My locks are growing, but in this summer heat my sweaty locks stink too. I'm sweating alcohol bullets out of my pores, I have and tobacco breath and all my clothes smell like cigarette smoke mixed with weed. I reek of funk, anger, shame and despair so if you're standing in line by my drunken friend or me, remember one thing! We can't smell it! I'm a spiteful, resentful, nervous, dangerous, unpredictable, selfish bitch! To another addict, it's normal."

"Mom, don't be so hard on yourself!"

"I have to be baby!" I said as I twisted my locks. "I have to be sick of myself so I can change. I know I'm ready!"

"Mom, I know you can do anything you put your mind to. Now I'm going downstairs to mess with Aqusia. Is she the only one in the house with you?"

"Yeah."

"Do you need anything mom?"

"No baby, I'm fine thank you!"

Did I want to stop drinking for those reasons or because Chris was tired of my stinky ass and he really would leave me? I laid down with my hands behind my head and thought about last night.

I had picked up the phone and heard some snake-like woman's voice. "You should leave her Chris," she said. "She shouldn't be around you using everyday!"

I was waiting to hear what he was going to say. She continued in her soft 'I want you' voice. "You know you can call me anytime, day or night, and I'll be there for you. I know you're going through a lot and you need someone to talk to, or someone to just listen, so call me okay sweetheart?"

Well, I'd better stop picking up the phone. Then I wouldn't get my feelings hurt.
I was going to kill her as soon as I found out who she was, this bitch. She had some nerve.
"Thank you, I needed to hear that," he said, sounding all victimized. "I love my wife, but (there was that damn 'but!') I done all I can! I can't handle it no more! I just can't take any more of her shit. I'm moving as soon as I can. I already have the manager's room available in my building for me. I just need to buy some sheets and towels and things like that."
"I can pick you up some things today Chris and bring them to you!"
"Leave now bitch!" I screamed in phone. "Just don't let me see you in the street with this bitch! I will shoot both of your asses! That's a promise!"
"What?" she said.
I said loud and clear, "You heard me bitch! I will take your life!"
She hung up. I slammed the phone down and went into the bathroom where he made his personal calls. I pushed the door open; he was too surprised.
I pointed my finger at him. "Why you got to be such a sneaky bitch? You lied to me. Everything you say is a damn lie!"

He stood up in my face. "Move! She's just a friend. You're just paranoid!"
"You keep saying that and now I know I was right. That's some personal shit!" I pushed his chest. "Yeah, you said that shit about your other bitches too. Always telling me that I was just being jealous and paranoid and that I should trust you! I turned out to be right! I find out the truth one way or another! I don't know why I stay with you!"
"Shit, I don't know why I keep your stink ass!" he yelled.
I put my hands on my hips. "Baby, because you had the best of me, all shapes and sizes from age 15 to 42! And it was all good! That's why your ass is still here with six kids, keeping the pussy wet!"
"Yeah, well, that to is too wet!"
I got in his face and said, "Bitch, the best years of my life is yet to come, and you'll miss out on a great thing out there being a whore! You're going to burn in hell! And if I get too wet, it's because I don't get enough, so when I finally get it, it don't know how to act! I'm a faithful, grateful, humble, patient woman. I kept the houses clean and pretty. I treated you like a king…"
"What?" he interrupted. "King my ass! Now you're having delusions!"
"Yes, I was good to you, putting up with your stink ass for years! Up or down, I was always supportive to you!"
"No you weren't! You always want a debate! You never agree with me about anything!"

"Fuck you, Chris! I was a good wife, you damn liar!" I pushed him again in his chest to back him up out of my face. "I went through your worst days and you think I'm going to stand by and let some other woman reap the benefit of you being clean? And not being abusive, with a little money in your pocket that you would buy a woman anything she needed or that her heart desired? Oh hell no! I don't think so! I'll kill you both, so you just jump off the planet because I'll find your ass! You will always give me my money for my bills! If I'm miserable you will be too!"
"Move out my way Angel! I want to get out! I don't have to be miserable!"
I stood in front of the door holding on tight. I had more to say!
"Now you're thinking about leaving me for someone else? You'd better recognize!" I pushed him back again.
He stood there. "Move! I don't want to hurt you!"
"You'd better choose wisely!"
"Don't be threatening me!"
"It's a promise I'll keep! Know that you will suffer! I'm tired of you threatening to leave but still saying, having your little bitches on the side. I'm not having it ever again!"
"I'm not with no other bitches Angel! You're pathetic with your constant accusations. If there is destruction in this relationship it's because of your insecurities, what you perceive to be too intimate!"
"Maybe you're not cheating on me today! But down the road you not being happy here will always lead you elsewhere. You and your bitches are conspiring against me!"

He frowned. "Look who's talking?" he said with a "better-than-you" attitude. "Instead of supporting and reassuring me, you prefer to run into someone else's arms for some instant gratification, or is it just because you can? You don't have limitations with your female relationships anymore! Apparently, if you're still looking than something here is missing!" He laughed at me.
"Go and laugh! I hope life is better with someone else. Go be free! I hope your next bitch is a psychotic, obsessive woman and drives your ass totally crazy!"
He broke through my arms that were blocking the door. "You're the psychotic, obsessive bitch! You're the only crazy one here. You need to take your pills! I need to watch out for your ass!" He ran down stairs to go out the door.
"If I'm crazy, it's because you made me this way!" I yelled. I hated not getting the last word in. "I might be down now but when I rise and shine, don't come back around me begging like you always do!"
"You're still living in the past Angel. You always bring up old shit!"

"Because it's never resolved or because you're still doing the same shit with a different girl and I'm dead tired!"
"You don't give me no respect!" he screamed up stairs.
"Respect?" I screamed back. "You didn't respect me when you were fucking them bitches! I don't respect you because you still haven't punished the mother fucker that raped your son!" I didn't intend on saying that. It just slipped out!
He looked at me and said sadly, "I had people helping him and he ran away! What more am I supposed to do Angel?"
"More than you've been doing! You dropped the ball!"
"It was too painful for me! Did you ever consider that, Ms. Know It All?" Tears welled up in his eyes. He frowned in anger and said, "Did you know that every time I think about it I contemplate murder?"

"You just forget about him because you're too busy waiting for them other bitches to call you with their problems. Then you can happily resolve them with your inappropriate personal conversation from your married lips indulging in verbal ratification. You always want to be their hero. What kind of rewards do you get? Rewards with no limitations, I'm sure!" He went into the kitchen to grab a bottle of water. I went into the bedroom and flopped on the bed.
I got the last word now! Or so I thought! He came into the bedroom. He must've wanted more of my venom. "I know the truth," I said. "I know how you are. It's a pleasure to help them; you love feeling needed and it's a challenge to help others but with our family, everything we need done is a burden! You're always screaming, 'Leave me alone! Don't sweat me! I'm busy!' Yeah, busy doing shit that not even job related! If you weren't, you wouldn't be so damn busy and too tired to be bothered by us! And not too tired to fuck me! Shit! I'm in my prime! I gotta get mine!"

He looked me in my eyes. "So now I don't do nothing for my kids?" He turned around and put some of his clothes in a bag, mumbling, "I don't need this shit, and I don't have to put up with this abuse!"
"You do a lot for them financially, but you won't even get on the phone and talk to your son while he's locked up! Why is that? You think about just how much time you spend with them!"
He was steaming now. "I talk to them!" he yelled. "You don't know anything about our relationship! You need to stop judging me! He knows why I don't have a rap for him; that's between him and me. We had a deal!
"And you! I give you $20 everyday for your pocket. I'm there for your every need, catering to your every whim! I'm the one that gives them everything they ask for and need. I'm paying the bills. We all talk! They come to my job and visit with me and we go out to eat and talk, so you

don't know what you're talking about! I'm going to the doctor's office with Kameena tomorrow to make sure she doesn't have cancer! They come to me with their problems. You're not the only one! And I help them with their problems."

"Not as much time as you spend on the phone planning meetings to help others!" I mumbled. I slammed the door.

I know that Cyris comment was vicious. That's what he gets for telling me he was going to leave me! He made me feel like I was being abandoned again. He hurt me with rejection. I deliberately wanted to hurt him. I hope I accomplished that!

I heard his footsteps going back downstairs. I opened the door and started screaming. "And I'll stop drinking when I get good and ready, not because you want me to! Acting like you're better than me now!"

"I'll be out of here soon! I don't need this shit!" he yelled back. "I'll be back for the rest of my things so don't mess with my stuff."

I leaned over the banister. "Take your shit with you now!" I screamed. The front door went SLAM!

An hour later I was taking a bath with my radio blasting. I was trying to relax in an atmosphere of the night-light, bubbles and bath oil. I was singing along with Wilson Phillips. "Hold on for one more day..."

He opened up the door. "Don't say shit to me ever again. I'm finished with your sick ass. You need to take your medication; you're sick!" and he slammed the door.

I turned up the radio and sang even louder. I kept playing it because there are a few verses that I loved: "I know that there is pain/But you hold on for one more day/Someday, somebody is going to make you want to turn around and say goodbye/Until then, baby, don't let him hold you down and make you cry!"

I was singing at the top of my lungs. That really pissed him off.

We both knew there was a very thin line between our love and hate, both at its extremes. He opened the bathroom door and he yelled with his bass voice, "Don't test me! Turn that shit down!"

So I turned it down a little. I didn't want him to break this radio too.

We slept on the furthest sides of the bed. "Don't try to take all the cover either!" he warned.

I hated this. I wanted to hold him but I also wanted to punch him in the head.

Yeah, that was some argument we had yesterday. I sat up and started to get dressed. I decided to wear my pink pants set and my white sandals with a white head wrap. I was going to stop because I was tired. I couldn't stop drinking if I wanted to. I didn't feel as much pain when I was drunk. Shit, there was hardly any pain at all!

But I was wasting a lot of money every month. I added it up and with the money I'd save, I'd be able to get my big screen TV! If I stopped, maybe God would heal me like those preachers say.

I had to sacrifice something. I was feeling too guilty to pray because I was high. In order to stop anything I had to hate it first. I guess that day was as good as any other day!

Doing it for me. It was time!

Here I come program. I took my pain pills grabbed my black cane. It was June so I didn't need a jacket. I kissed Tunisia and Aqusia and I was out the door.

It felt really strange because I hadn't been outside in about three weeks. I stood frozen on my steps for a while, looking at everything and everybody like I was looking for the first time. I breathed in the good air. Wow, look at the birds fly.

I sat in my jeep listening to the radio to relax me before I drove. It'd been a while. I pulled up to the office and stared at it.

Damn, I was running things; I can't go in there and let them humiliate me or look down on me because I had twenty-four hours or less after all I had. Damn, I had to ask for help from some people that didn't know as much as I did. Okay ego stop tripping; your ass need to stop getting drunk. Go ahead Angel you can do it! Shit, your stink ass needs to go in there.

I walked into the small office. I'd been in only once, when they opened it ten years ago. On my right, there were five chairs lined up against the wall filled with three men and two women, who all stared at me. On my left stood a desk. They didn't have there before. The desk was as high as my neck.

A voice said, "Can I help you?"

I stood on my tiptoes and saw a female with extra long fake nails and a long red weave (in this heat?). She had way too much red lipstick on her black-like-night lips. I had to come closer to see her over the high wall.

"Hi. My name is Angel and I want to start coming to your groups."

"Just one minute!" and she called into the speakerphone, "Kane, come to the front desk." This handsome Roy Jones-look-alike came out. She pointed at me and said, "This is Angel." I shook his hand hello. "He will interview you!" she said.

"Hi Angel, what are you using?"

Damn, isn't there any privacy? Right here with the questions? I could feel all eyes on me. I dared not say anything about I it. I knew better because we used to say that we didn't care who saw us copping drugs.

"I drink and smoke weed."

"When was the last time you used?"

"Yesterday."

The golden-skinned man looked at me like he didn't believe me.
"Just weed and beer?"
"Yeah, that's right." I had taken off all of my gold jewelry because with all the sweating, my fingers would swell and they would break out into rashes. To other people in recovery jewelry showed your value. With only my wedding ring on people would assume that I had nothing coming out of the drug world.
I wish I had tried to put some on to show them I wasn't broke but most importantly, that I wasn't on crack! So treat me differently! I'm too damn fat to look like a crack addict with my two hundred pound ass. I was concerned how they would perceive me.

"Okay, well we have groups everyday at 1:00 and 6:00pm and you'll be required to attend five groups a week and take urine tests monthly. There's a $25 a month fee. Are you okay with that?"
"Sure! Can you write down your programs number please?"
"You will also be assigned an all-women's house so you'll always have someone to talk to or someplace to go hang out. Or if we have group in the houses you go there, okay?"
"Okay, can I pay now?"
"Sure!"
I gave him the money. "Thank you. Nice meeting you." I shook his hand again. "I bet everyone tells you that you look like Roy Jones!"
"Roy Jones, the boxer? He looks like me! I'm older!" He smiled.
"Yeah okay!" He just knows he's cute I can tell! I bet he hit a lot of woman in this place! With that boxer body, damn, he looks good. If I weren't married I would hit that. I knew I could too, in a matter of time and with some cleavage.
Stop thinking like that Angel. Shit, right about now you look like something the cat dragged in I said to myself as he wrote down the phone numbers.

I turned around to go out the door. Some people were coming in so I backed up and I heard, "Angel, is that you?" I knew someone would probably know me but it had been at least three years.
"Hi baby" I forget names so everyone was 'baby.'
"What's going on with you Angel?" A cute well-dressed man grabbed me and hugged me tight like I was a long lost child. He was an Alumni from the other program I was with.
"I'm going to start coming to your groups," I said with my head down.
"That's great, we need you up in here! They're good, but you, you give up the piece!" he said all excited. "Hey everyone this is Angel. She was my counselor! Hell, she was everyone's counselor! Shit, she ran things! This is Mrs. Angel!"

I looked around the office and Mr. Boxer-look-alike stared at me with interesting eyes. "Who is this woman?" his eyes asked. As I blushed at all the staring people, I saw more suspense in their eyes.
"Yeah, she knows the founder of this program. She worked with him, did she tell you that?" Eyebrows lifted. The women looked at me as if to say, "Are we supposed to be impressed? Look at you now and look at us!"
"It's so good to see you! Come here!" He pulled me to the side. "I was told you were selling crack at this house on Vampelt Street. They described you and everything, so I went there. There was a female there that was light skinned and her name was Angel too. I was so glad it wasn't you!" He held my hands. "You helped me so much I wanted to help you!"
"Oh baby thanks! I wasn't out there like that. I am a drunk and I smoke weed, that's it! Look, I have to go!" I gave him a hug.
"See you in group Angel"
I heard him tell someone else, "You know who that is?"
I jumped into my car proudly as if to say, "See, I have a nice Jeep too." It was nice that he was bragging about me. That's right let them know who I was! But at the same time, I was ashamed of my weakness for relapsing after all I'd said and done.
I hated the way some women in that office looked at me, like they were better than me because they were clean and they were running things now. Maybe that was just my shit, as they say. The more time you get, the more pride comes on your face that is sometimes mistaken for arrogance. I hated the fact that everyone had longer sobriety than me not as much as I did! They probably couldn't do eight years like I did nor face their founder! I worked with saying, "I am back with 24 hours or less."
I said to myself, "Damn you're arrogant Angel! That's why your ass used and is suffering now!"

It was a drug program that was an extension of the program I used to work for. I'd also coordinated their groups before they broke away. We had about twelve different extensions that Chris named "the umbrella." We had over three thousand family members, the largest in- and out-patient program in Philadelphia. I had to keep up with all the outpatients and made sure they had appropriate group facilitators I'd help train.
Now I had to go in front of people who knew of me and tell them that it was I who needed help.
Their program was 80% heroin addicts from Baltimore with different accents and attitudes. The Director, two alumni and two newcomers were the only ones who knew me.
It was basically all heroin and crack addicts; no one talked about being a drunk.

Heroin; a world I'd only slept in. All I knew was a needle and a nod that I took to be drug addicts. I felt so out of place. You can't give alcoholics the same feedback as a heroin addict. The process of degradation and dissipation is the same but the behaviors are so different.
I was mostly silent so they had to call on me. I didn't give anyone feedback at all. I didn't have any voice inside of me to tell anyone what he or she might need to hear.
Me! Angel! No feedback? I felt like I'd lost my skills. For now I just want to listen; that was my response.
I lost my confidence; I felt no one wanted to listen to a relapsed user who used to be counselor, and who couldn't even counsel herself.
The new comers were told at the door we are supposed to shut the fuck up and listen to learn because we obviously didn't know shit or we wouldn't be there. If I knew so much, I wouldn't have used alcohol or drugs. Like Jesus you had to help everyone else, save yourself. So my hands were tied!
I was drying out. I started reading the Bible again for sixty days. I just read and listened to other people talk. I wanted a new family and friends; everyone had a life except me. I resented that Chris had a job to go to and I was stuck in this room.
I was in here so much that I became uncomfortable away from it. I kept praying and asking for healing and guidance and the feeling I was getting was to go to God on a deeper level.

I was asked to share.
"Hi, I'm Angel. I am an addict and I need support!"
"Support how?"
"Well, I need support groups that I can attend to remind me why I need to stop drinking."
"Tell us more about yourself Angel. You sit here everyday and you don't say much. We would like to know who is sitting here with us!"
"I'm a mother of six beautiful children. I've been married for twenty something years. I was smoking weed and drinking beer all day, everyday and I want to stop, so I've been coming to your groups!"
"Why do you want to stop?"
"Because I'm sick of myself!"
"Do you use crack or heroin or anything else?"
"No, I don't."
"Is this your first time in recovery?"
This man just wouldn't let up. He was walking around in the group with his nice new clothes and white sneakers and teeth shining. I knew what he wanted. He wanted some dirt!
"Are you just tired of yourself?"

Okay I thought, I'd give a little more. "Well, I was a crack addict eleven years ago. For the past three years I've been a dangerous violent drunk. I was in recovery prior; I had eight years clean! I was here when the founder started this program. I was the senior administrative counselor and group coordinator and the outpatient director! I have love and respect for your founder. That's why I came to this spot!" I sat back with no more to share. But he was really intrigued now.
"Eight years, really? A counselor with certifications?"
"Yes!"
"I'm curious. Are you all curious group?"
"Yes," they all said in harmony.
"Why did you use Angel? It sounds like you had it going on!"
"It's a long story but to keep it short, it was because I lost everything! I was living in so much emotional and physical pain that I wanted to die. I had no support and my so-called recovery family, and my church abandoned me! So I said fuck it!"

"Tell us what happened Angel so we can learn from your lesson!"
He wanted me to share. Okay I will; than maybe he'll leave me alone. I did want all of them to know that I wasn't unimportant. I really didn't want to brag but I wanted them to know the level I at was when I fell, how high up the ladder I felt I was when I fell sober on my face. They needed to know it could happen to the best of us and that nobody prepared us for this loss. Unfortunately, since I had time and I was a good counselor, when I cried out for help the reaction was, "Oh, you're going to be alright!"

I held my head up and sat at the edge of my seat. I took a deep breath and released my fear.
"For once in my life, I was more than just a mom or Chris' wife. I showed I have potential. I transformed into a butterfly and I felt free and beautiful. I implemented the "Goofy Friday" and the spiritual groups, assuring others that there's more to life than just the pain to share. So it feels good to see it is still being done, like I was the start of something bigger than myself!
"I lost three offices, my out-patient office, my community center, and a Youth outreach program called the "I Care" center that I Directed for three years. That was my dream program. I enjoyed the daily challenge. Regardless of what we made it work! My job with the drug program discarded of me without warning. Then my body started hurting all over everyday, all day very much. I could no longer attend group three times a day but I still delegated responsibility as group coordinator. I couldn't attend church where I had just been baptized prior to studying the Bible every week. For a year with the pastor and his wife, my husband and the

program founder and his wife, all the leaders, we all studied and read together. And no one visited me.

"I was damaged in need of repairing; I felt like some fragments of my soul were divided into painful cubes. People say, 'Pick yourself up,' and, 'Do something else.' Well, with all the health problems what could I do? I lost my husband to other part-time women, and I lost my best friend to leukemia, which left me devastated. I wanted to die so my solution was predictable: suicide. Defeated now so shamefully I got drunk. In despair, I sat in front of my mom's house with an empty bottle of booze and a gun in the other hand. I wanted to shoot myself in the head in front of my mother's house for her much-needed reaction of regret. Instead, I brought a pen and paper and went into her house to my room and wrote down all my anger. As the sun set, the darker it got outside, the darker my sprit became. In near blindness, I continued to express what I believed my avenue of destruction was. I was an emotional wreck and stayed drunk and isolated for three years and now I'm tired! Tired of living!"
I smiled. "Back then I would say that if I died, over five hundred people would be at my funeral easy. But today, maybe fifty people in the family." I ignored the few people in recovery that really did love me.
I looked at my hands on my lap. "And if I did kill myself, nobody would probably come! I wasn't prepared for the abandonment. My program, my partner, and my husband stabbed me in the back. I depended on everything I was doing to define who I am.

"It gave me a sense of false pride to have a business card that said this is who I am and more. Finally, my life dreams came into reality and then slipped through my hands like I was being punished everyday one way or another, with family, or work, or my health, my church… now everything is gone. My husband cheating on me was the last straw. My self-esteem was shot, and the fear of being alone scared me. I felt rejected and unworthy. I used up all my usefulness so I wanted to shoot myself in the head and end it. But because of my children I couldn't do it! I couldn't take any more pain but I couldn't bring pain to them. I have six kids; they love me no matter what. They even got tattoos with my name on them and they're girls! That's love to me!" I sat back in my chair. "Shit, my son carved my name on one arm and 'Mom' on his other with a knife. If it weren't for their love, I wouldn't be sitting here today. I would have shot myself the day I used."
This was hard. I had to take a deep breath.
"I feel like I'm nothing, a nobody." My eyes started to well up with tears.

The facilitator spoke after a long silence. "It was not what you've done that made you who you are but who made you is who you are. He is the only one that can fix you." He walked closer to me: "You have to start over and ask Him again what His will is for you and you have to do it! Don't feel sorry for yourself and hold resentments, because the people that you are holding them against are not thinking about your ass at all. Learn to love yourself and stop expecting it from everyone else. Now you learned you can lose all that you love, but if you loved yourself, you would have been able to hold on. But you don't, and that's what you need to focus on: yourself and your relationship with God, if you want strength and a new healthy life!

"Angel, no one is gonna love you like you want to be loved, never! Ever! No one, not someone, sometime is not enough, not at the level you need. No time by anyone, anywhere, anytime! Angel, anyway you say it; you'll still find yourself by yourself. When you lose yourself and hurt yourself, you will be the last one left to console yourself Angel, so depend on yourself!"

Well, I guess he wouldn't have to call on me no more; it had all been said.

We closed out and I ran to my jeep and drove off fast. I drove three blocks and start crying like a damn baby that was just spanked for being bad.

I would have probably said more because I was getting hyped and angry. I was going to go off but he stopped me in time. He did well.

Yeah, it can happen to the best of the best. At least I'm trying; now I'll rest!

I went home and a song was on the radio that made me cry. "I'm Still Holding On" by Tramaine Hawkins. I started singing and the tears just keep flowing. I heard a knock on the door.

"Come in!"

"Hi Grandma!"

It was Aqusias' four-year-old son. He hugged me and kissed me on my cheek. "I just wanted to say I love you! Are you okay?"

"Yes baby, go ahead back downstairs now." I patted him on his butt and grabbed him. "I needed that," I said as I gave him a big hug. "Thank you and Grandma will talk with you later."

"Don't cry Grandma, it's going to be okay," and he closed the door.

In another group, another day, the same man asked, "You're still resentful aren't you Angel?"

"Yes I am!" I was sitting in my chair with my arms folded. I was surprised he noticed me. My opportunity to vent was near.

"Damn right I am! Absolutely right! My recovery family that I sacrificed for and put before my own family abandoned me! I don't want to sound redundant, but I am still angry! I have internal damage; I'm full of resentment and when I see some people it intensifies. Apparently, I need to deal with it before it controls me! We say in recovery, 'I don't want to lose everything, like my job.' It's unlikely that will happen if you do what your supposed to do or so I was told.

"I wouldn't use under any circumstances because I didn't want to lose my large recovery family, or the passionate episodes with my husband, or my good health, or my proud professional life, or my material things or my new relationship with a church and with God. I was finally happy and I wanted to live again. I cared about everyone. I had everything I wanted. I did everything to keep my kids and their respect so I had to stay clean! I couldn't handle losing everything!

"But I did lose everything and it wasn't due to me using or anything I did wrong! No one prepares you for that shit! The internal damage was hiding for a while. Losing my glory and fame, my hopes and dreams, my friends, love and support… I didn't think I would ever go down, only up! One by one, things were taken from me. I was devastated, alone, unable to eat or sleep, asking, 'Why me?'

"I live in constant physical pains all day. Some days are worse then others; in the winter, I can hardly walk. It's a pain that would make most men cry and wish to die! But I handle it with little to no complaints. I cry silently with a smile.

"I was doing good deeds. I was really helping people. I wonder why God stopped me? Why did He take away my programs and job and health? I couldn't walk anymore, and I couldn't drive to group or church, and now my man is leaving me and my son will probably kill himself out of depression. What did I do to deserve this shit? I'm suddenly alone, without functionality to get up and go out to meet others so I can tell my husband to kiss my ass! My values and fear of God won't allow me to go to bed for comfort and revenge with another man. The kids are growing up and moving out, having families of their own. What will become of me? Have I outlived my usefulness?"

I was starting to get frustrated and I slapped my chest. "I didn't do nothing, it wasn't my fault. Things were just happening one after another till I was stripped of everything that made me who I was, and what I was about! Now it's like I'm always at my own funeral. Every new day I mourn the death of who I was, and the life that died, and now my sprit is slowly dying! I'm a prisoner at home living in isolation, and I don't even get a call or a visit from the hundreds of people that once hugged me and said they loved me. I have nothing, no support, no love, no friends. My husband moved out and I wonder what he is doing all day and night. What happened to the twelve steps when I cried out the naked truth in meetings prior to picking up! Don't they still practice that step?

"My answer is that most of the recovering addicts are self-indulgent; they ignored my cries for support. I realized that nobody really gives a fuck! Some jealous people are actually happy that I used so they can feel greater than I. Hypocrisy behind the smiles of deceit, pleasure found in my demise…I see. Pretend-hugs like they care about me as they stare and whisper quietly." I sighed. "Thanks for listing to me share my frustration!"

I had to do it. I had to face the program that dismissed and abandoned me! I desired to see their reaction upon my upgraded appearance. After all the speculation and gossip that I was out there on crack, selling my ass, looking like shit! Chris said that I didn't have to go there and prove a thing. "If you were selling your ass under the bridge I'd still love you and get your back!" he said. That made me feel great but for my own self-growth, I had to face the staff and alumni. I came up with, without shame but strength.
I deliberately appeared at their large Friday night group and I found great pleasure knowing they had a population of less than one hundred. Yeah, their program was falling apart. They were in the midst of their demise indeed. That's what they get! I intended to let go of my resentments. I wanted to know why the mother-fuckers who said they loved me were not there for me? I remembered what the facilitator told me and I realized that it doesn't matter now because they didn't even know or care I resented them and had hurt so much! They didn't care about my ass, as he said! I said "goodbye" for good and dusted off my shoulders and wiped the dust off my feet as I left!

At my new family program I sat there watching the group facilitator's skills as he watch my body language. I admitted that I judged them all for the eight months I attended their groups. They were the best they could be with the time they had. Most of the things they said were predictable and controlling, which was not challenging even for a debate.
I enjoyed the discussions about God but I didn't feel any love. God is love, so they were missing it! I had a new recovering population to call family, but I actually didn't think they knew or cared that I existed. I felt invisible when I came and went. Compared to always being in the spotlight, now being in darkness, pushed to the side with the outcast and discarded was certainly a humbling experience.

"Angel, do you pray?" someone asked me.
"Yes! I pray everyday, all day sometimes. I realized I still didn't go to God when I wanted to totally give up, especially before or after arguments. I'd run and feel sorry for myself and look for comfort in all the wrong places and people and things. I looked for human attention and support and affirmation to feel worthy. I know not how to give these valuable things to myself. I know I have to believe and just because I'm not able to do great things now doesn't mean I'm worthless."

CHAPTER NINETEEN

ARTHRITIS>BIPOLOR>FIBROMYALGIA> INCARCERATION

After five years of testing for every damn thing and high hopes for answers, I was only disappointed with negative results every visit. I changed orthopedics for the sixth time and went to meet my new doctor.

I was tired and felt hopeless. After reading my recent test results, she gave me an exam, poking me all around.

I wanted to punch her in her face when she asked, "Does this hurt?"

"Damn right that shit hurts!"

"Our x-rays show you suffer from osteo-arthritis in your lower back, in both of your knees, front and behind, both shoulders, your lower back and in your hands. Both of your legs are crooked and you will have to wear a boot on both legs for six month."

"What? All that?" I couldn't believe it!

"Yes. I'm afraid that's why you're in so much pain all the time. Your legs are getting worse and you're putting too much pressure on your knees every time you walk."

Wow! I was in shock! "Damn, that's a lot of places! What can you do about it?"

"We'll give you some arthritic medication and some pain pills."

"Will that take it away?"

"No, unfortunately. But that's not all. After applying pressure to certain parts of your body, I've determined that the rest of the pain is caused by Fibromyalgia."

I finally got a name! Relief began to set in. "What is that?" I sat up straight up on the table and leaned forward to hear every word.

"It's a chronic muscle disorder. There are tender points where the muscles don't relax. You respond to all of the tender points."

I laughed out of frustration. "They should call it 'have mercy on me' points." She looked at me as if to say, "Oh, it really doesn't hurt that much."

"The good news is that this is nothing a few pain pills and muscle relaxants can't handle. You'll have some stiffness but you can live a somewhat normal life with some physical therapy."

"That's unlikely. I have limitations now," I responded. But I was relived and a bit more optimistic. Perhaps I could have a normal life.

I smiled. "Is there a cure?"

"No, but they are constantly doing studies on it."

"No cure?" I said, disappointed. "I wish you could feel the pain I feel daily. I feel like I was beaten with a baseball bat; it's like a fat man is sitting on my legs. My cries just flow down the street. How can I live with this for another week, much less for the rest of my life?" Oh God, please take this pain away. It was so unbearable at times.
There is so much insensitivity for Fibromyalgia patients. I see every year that I'm getting worse. Because I had less and less ability to walk and stand, I was isolated from everyone and became very lonely. Without a pain pill, I couldn't make it to the bathroom. I would be curled up in a ball crying, and those doctors think this shit doesn't hurt that much?
I went through their entire staff of doctors anyway. It took five painful years; every possible test exhausted us all when they came back negative. After they diagnosed me with bipolar depression, I went to their counselors and I saw that I could run circles around their residents. It was time for me to go to another hospital.

I went home and looked up 'Fibromyalgia' on the Internet. I printed out ninety pages of information. I even found a chat room. It was very comforting knowing that this pain wasn't in my mind, like some of my doctors thought because all of the tests came back negative. They thought I just wanted some narcotics. I meet some caring people online and they taught me a lot. They say it's not curable but some people do recover.
They say it's not progressive but I am progressively getting worse. Doctors are not doing much studying about it. Most doctors think it's a minor problem. I finally met a caring, understanding Doctor at Hahnemann Hospital at the pain center, there needs to be more Doctors like him but of course this country take all good things away so now he is closing down.
I've talked to people who are in wheelchairs; some kids are on morphine and can't go to school. I can get two good hours a day outside but some days I can't. Plus, I'm allergic to morphine. Pain pills help me be a little mobile but there is always pain present, even with the pain pills and the muscle relaxant they just make living a little more bearable.

I'm constantly screaming inside, "Ouch, ouch, damn, ouch!"
Some of my children complain of leg pains when it gets cold and that's how it began for me. I pray they don't get this painful disorder. An Indian medicine man said it was stress and guilt I carry. That's what brings my body so much pain inside, and only when I release the pain and guilt I will began to heal. How can I forgive myself for using crack and for putting our kids in foster homes where my son was raped?
We still couldn't bring the abuser to justice because Cyris wouldn't sit still in one place long enough to get the lawyers' assistance. We told everyone and nothing had been done so we plotted and prayed. It never left our minds but always crushed our hearts, all three of us. Who knows how the girls truly felt.

I always question how can I forgive my mom. I don't feel like she is a mother to me. She never reaches out to me to try to get to know me and tell me stuff to strengthen me. That's something moms are supposed to do but she's always in her bed with silent lips; eyes staring into the glaring TV, laughing now and then.

I sat by a male angel once. He said to me, "Maybe you can start being a better mother yourself and start being a less selfish and more supportive, non judgmental daughter. You'll find a very needy mother who needs her mommy also. And Angel, you'll see yourself, and that's when you'll realize that you don't hate her. You hate yourself; your drunken ass. You hate what life has done to you both, and how you both handled it in the same shameful way getting unforgettably drunk and depressed; abandoning your children for self-seeking life fulfillments. You're both sick thinkers and negative reactors. You're judgmental and angry and needy, selfish, not caring about self, life or God.

"You don't hate her; you hate what you did and need her to blame. You expected her to do what you couldn't do yourself. Now that you have been reminded, after you have walked in her shoes, hopefully you will stop blaming her for the same things you want forgiveness for! Therefore, you will not be forgiven as you have not forgiven others. You always said, 'in order to forgive, you first have to understand the other person's stories.' Well, now you know: love and honor your mother Angel!"

"Yes my angel, thank you for that lesson." If I can't help anyone else, I am helping myself. I never considered that she lost her baby, her nineteen-year-old son, and her husband left her with three babies. Her baby's daddy, the man that she loved deeply abused her and died. She lost her mother, and the only father she knew. She was an only child, young with no support, and a judgmental Christian mother telling her she was going the burn in hell no matter what she did.

She'd been through all kinds of abuse. She was a hostage because she needed her bills paid and meat on her kids' table. She went to bed crying alone many nights, missing her sons and her mother and I was not there to hold her. She was all-alone while her young daughters were out discovering what boyfriends were for. With the TV as her only escape, music and booze were her counselors, her friends, comforters, and depression medicine. Her kids always appeared to be able to care for themselves, so she had no problem staying in bed under her comforter for hugs. Where was her understanding? She didn't abandon me; she isolated herself from life and responsibility and from anyone that death could hurt. So she built a wall."

"I understand walls don't I? Is this your way of slowing me down to listen to You God?

Well, I'm listening now! Can you hear my screams?"

Two months later…
As I drove down the street on my way to the store I saw Cyris. It took my smile away to see him. I pulled over and watched him. He didn't even see my big black jeep ten feet from him. If I was the police his ass was caught. That made me so mad because this meant his ass was fucked up! On top of that he lied to me, swearing that he wasn't dealing! He thought he knew what he was doing wearing that bright ass yellow shirt and bandana to match. I spotted his ass a block away.
I beeped the horn three times. I yelled his name but he didn't hear me. He was getting a girl's phone number. I couldn't believe him; all he did was come home with about twenty phone numbers everyday. He never called any of the girls; he just liked knowing he got it like that.
Beep! Beep! "Cyris! Cyris!" I yelled. Finally, he came over. I was furious! "Your dad and I told you not to be on this block. Someone is always getting shot or killed or arrested every week! You lied to me! You told me you weren't dealing! You were just coming around here to go into the studio now?"

I screamed. "I SEE THEM DEALING IN THERE! THEY'RE NOT RAPPING! YOU DISAPPOINT ME! YOU WANT TO GO TO JAIL? YOU WANT TO GET SHOT? YOU MUST WANT TO GO TO JAIL!"
I screamed so loud and I didn't care who heard me.
His eyes were half closed. "Calm down mom," he whispered. He looked around to see who was watching.
"Don't tell me to calm down! Come over here!" He came a little closer to the passenger's side "Closer," I said.
He backed up quickly. "No mom, you're going to smack the shit out of me!" he said as he laughed.
"Oh, so this shit is funny to you?"
"No mom, I just know you want to hit me. I'm not going to come to you and let you hit me!" He backed up further. He wouldn't come near me. I was going to get out and he ran. He was lucky I couldn't run because I would have beaten his ass with my car club. I wanted to beat some sense into him. He was so high he could barely stand up; someone would take advantage of him like this! Maybe if I broke his legs he wouldn't come out and deal.

I went and got Chris because he might have to carry his ass home. When we returned, he was gone.
"Wait here baby," Chris said and got out of the jeep. He walked around a few blocks.
He came back after about ten minutes. Before he could close the door, I asked, "What's happening? Where is he? Did you see him?"

"I found him a few blocks away. I told him to give the rest of the pills and weed back to whomever he's selling that shit for and to bring his ass home right now! And I told him not to make me come back out here and get him."

Cyris came home and sat down on the couch, stinking from drinking.
"I'm not drunk mom!" he snapped.
Chris got mad. "Don't talk to your mother like that! Cyris, look at you! You can't even stand up! You fell down coming up the damn steps!" He was heated. "Why are you around their selling pills? And of all places on J Street? What is it going to take for you to listen to me? You already got a warrant out on your ass. Every night your mom is up and she can't sleep because your ass doesn't know how to come home. Look at you! You don't even take care of yourself; you look like shit. Are those niggas around there going to pay your bail? Are they going to visit you? Did they before? Huh, did they?" he screamed, spitting in his face that made me jump. Chris went in the poolroom and got on the phone.
"What are you doing now?" I asked.
"I called the police!" Chris said. "I'm going to save your dumb ass life!" He pointed at Cyris.
I stared at him in disbelief. "Why did you do that?" I screamed. "You're not serious are you? You didn't really call them did you Chris?"
His eyebrows went up and his eyes crossed like they did when he was mad. "Yes Angel, I did, so stop yelling at me! I'm going to save his dumb ass life before he get himself killed!"

Cyris looked at Chris in shock. "Dad, you dimed me out? You called on your own son?" He started to jump out the window but backed up, held his head up at Chris and said, "No! I'm not going to run!" He waved his hands up in the air and flopped into the loveseat. "I'll wait right here for them. I don't even care anymore!" His eyes began to water.
I went over to him and sat on the arm of the chair and rubbed his face. He backed away. I got up and sat down in the couch across from him staring in disbelief. I was holding his hand feeling inadequate, wanting him to run and hide and not deal with his responsibilities. He had courage that I lacked; I feared the life in the hand that I was holding would slip away from me, much like my own life was slipping away.
The hurt and disbelief was all over Cyris' face. I was speechless; there was nothing I could say that would have made a difference now. Cold silence lasted for an eternity as we waited for his impending incarceration and painful departure. I held his hand tighter. All I thought about was; if he went to jail, was he going to try to take his life again? Maybe this time he will succeed! Cyris was so hurt that his father was turning him in. He was huffing and puffing and holding back his tears as best he could. He turned red and I could see the veins popping out of the side of his head.

His fists were balled up so tight! I thought he was going to try to fight his father that night so I got up and stood between them.
Chris looked at him. "You're huffing and puffing like you want to do something to me. Come on, bring it!" He waved his hands. "Come on, you a tough man?"

I pushed Chris back into the poolroom. "Chris, you already called the police on him! Leave him alone now!" I begged him. "Please don't do this, please Chris! Let's send him away somewhere."
He threw up his hands in defeat. "For what Angel? Everywhere he goes he has a tendency to get into some trouble. Everywhere I send him... you know it Angel." He started counting on his hand. "I sent him to New York - trouble. Albany - trouble! And White Plans - trouble! Philadelphia - trouble! He's gotten into trouble since he came home! If trouble seems to follow him, maybe it's because he is the trouble! He finds trouble; it's like he goes looking for the troubled people to hand out more trouble! What am I supposed to do with him Angel? You tell me?" He was spitting and drooling like a mad dog. "There is nowhere left to send him! What? Hide him? Get him an alias? Let him sell drugs and stay high everyday, and I walk by like I don't see my son, as long as he is making money and not killing anyone? That's supposed to be cool? Let him walk in and out of my house all hours of the night, leaving the door open while we're asleep because he can't find his keys? One of those gunshots we hear every damn weekend is going be our call to him, laid out on the ground! Look at him!" Chris grabbed Cyris by his shirt. "Just look at him! He is dirty and stinking! He looks likes a damn crack addict! He can't weigh more than one hundred pounds and he is dying already!"
He poked his head. "You should care more about yourself!"
I looked at Chris and than over at Cyris' angry face. Through my tears, I saw my son needing help, not incarceration.

I stood up and asked, "Can we get him in a drug program?"
"He has a warrant out for his arrest you forgot? And we've done that too Angel, remember? Everyone loved him and he was one of the best counselors they had. He was an anti-violence facilitator for adults; he was so impressive exploring other options with them. Now he lives like he learned and taught nothing. I love his dumb ass and I'm going to help him! He just can't understand it right now!"
I hugged my son on bended knees. I looked up and wiped away his one stubborn tear that wouldn't fall. "Baby," I said, "you will beat this case and at least you won't have to run anymore. It will all be over soon. Just stay strong, please. I don't want to loss you Cyris!" I laid my head on his lap.

"Don't worry about me mom, "Cyris said sadly. "I'm going be all right!" He rubbed my head and wiped my tears with his shaking hands.
Chris came back into the living room. He pointed at me and said, "I had to call the police or else you're going to have a dead son on your hands, you hear me? Are you ready to burry him? Look at the condition he is in! He's using them damn pills, smoking that damn wet he thinks I don't know about! He looks pathetic. He stays plastered. I hate looking into his damn face! And then he has the audacity to tell me he's not high! It hurts me to my heart to see you like this Cyris! You're my son!" He bent over and grabbed his skinny face and looked him close in his eyes. "You're a king, not a slave! You don't listen to me. I've done all I can and you just say 'fuck me!'' He stood up and went towards the window. He looked out the dusty glass. He started pointing at himself in the chest over and over with so much anger he said. "Somebody has to save him from himself! That's me! That's my job! I'm his father! He can't run the rest of his life. He sure can't keep on living like this either!"

I was frantic. "Chris, can we…" but before I could finish, the police came stomping up the steps, about five of them for my one son. Cyris didn't say a word; he just stood up and put his hands behind his back to be cuffed. He kissed me with a long pause on my cheek. I rubbed his face.
"Ouch!" he said as the policeman cuffed him. "Hey officer, you don't have to hurt him! Don't be putting it on so tight! He's surrendering, shit!" He loosened up the cuffs. I was glad that I could still do a minor thing to comfort my son in a painful moment.
The officers had no rap for us the parents, so I yelled, "When can he call? Where will he go?"
"He'll call you when he can miss," an officer told me. Then the heavy door slammed shut.
I ran to the window and watched the cars ride away with my child. Will I ever see you again Cyris?

I couldn't sleep. Chris sat up and watched TV, trying to convince himself that he did the right thing.
"Angel, that boy is carrying guns. He is getting high everyday. He's selling drugs! He's riding in stolen cars. Every other day he is in a fight. I'm tired of losing sleep because I don't know if the next phone call is going to be someone telling me that my son is dead! He never could stay in any kind of school. He's not doing anything positive and he won't listen to me. I'm responsible for him! What was I supposed to do? I had to make that call! You understand Angel?"
"NO!" I screamed. "NO! I don't understand! Chris, I hate you for doing this!" I said with a heartbreaking voice. I sat quietly in the dark at the edge of our bed for what seemed like hours.

Finally I broke the silence. "I'm sorry but where I'm from, you don't rat out your family or friends! Shit, you didn't like it when your mother turned your ass in for your so-called own good! What good did it do you? I tried to see your side but as a mother, all I know is that car theft could give him a lot of time. He said he didn't even steal that car he's getting blamed for! I don't want my baby in jail. We should have sent him away somewhere, to boot camp maybe. It's more dangerous in jail than it is out here."

He was quiet with his head down. He was holding it tight like it hurt. "Good! I hope your head hurts everyday!" I pointed at his head. "If anything happens to him in there I'm not going to be able to forgive you I hope you know that!" I wasn't taking into consideration that Cyris deserved all his punishment for his sins. No matter what my son did, I didn't want him to suffer. I knew that was wrong but that's how I felt. I couldn't conceive that maybe Chris was saving his life. I knew Cyris made his own choices and got himself in his own messes. I just didn't want to blame Cyris; it was easer to blame his father. Chris didn't spend any time with him. He didn't want to deal with him so he'd rather the jails raised him. I didn't care if I hurt Chris. All I knew was at that time he was a rat! I hated him for not making Cyris stop!

Chris despises me, he says I interfered with his disciplining the children and the way they turned out is my fault, He says I took away his manhood and I didn't let him deal with them his way. Yeah I interfered with his discipline. Shit, he hit too damn hard. I couldn't stand to see him raise a hand to him because that wasn't helping anyway. He just rebelled even more, so, eventually, Chris just stopped. He never raised his hand to him again. He was drunk most of there life I was suppose to protect them. Then in recovery he only complained and wouldn't listen to them talk and explain there self, not even in our house meeting he did all the talking so I spoke up for them and he hate me for getting there backs and not his. So he blames everything on me now, If I would have stayed out of his way they all would be in college now not having babies. I was supposed to shut up. Well if he was teaching them and not dictating I would have.

The hugs didn't seem to help, either. He still didn't believe his dad loved him enough. Now he was really going to hate him. "Oh God, help this family please!"

Cyris went back to the youth study center for four months and was released due to insufficient evidence.

My son was back in my arms and this time I was going to save him!

CHAPTER TWENTY

HELL AND PURGATORY

I had been clean now for a few months and it shook me up! No drinking or smoking weed, and I even quit cigarettes. One day, I woke up and the desires were just gone!

I was told by my angel to tell everyone what I had seen. But my tongue was cut up into slits with blood dripping. It began to swell enormously and hung out my mouth so I couldn't speak if I tried. But if I couldn't tell everyone by speaking, then writing I believe is the way. So I will write what I have seen!

I couldn't sleep. I twisted and turned, fluffing the pillows and kicking off the blankets... so many thoughts kept running through my mind; something led to one thing that led to another, to something that had nothing to do with the first thought. In order to get it out of my head, I had to fill it with what I wanted to fill it with. I knew Satan didn't like it. He wouldn't let me keep praying. Insomnia was his plan.

So I began to say, "Praise the Lord. Thank you God. Praise the Lord, praise the Lord, praise the Lord." The other thoughts tried to bully their way back in and distract me with things I needed to do. I fought back to concentrate on my praise. I continued a few more "Praise the Lord, "Praise the Lord."

This worked for me a few times before but this time was different.

I was in my living room playing pool by myself because I felt good enough to walk around the table and I was home alone. All of a sudden, I heard **Bam! Bam! Bam! Bam!** I jumped back and froze. I thought it was the police so my heart started beating fast. Which one of my kids is in trouble?

I heard footsteps stomping hard as they ran up the stairs yelling, "Who's in here? Come out with your hands up, now!" in a loud command. I ran three steps at a time up to the bedroom floor to hide, breathing hard and scared as shit, uncertain where to hide. I jumped in the closet and threw some dirty clothes over me.

They were coming behind me. My heart was beating fast. I kept thinking, "What did I do?"

Who were they looking for, Cyris? Something told me to run, so I did!

Someone entered my son's room and looked under the bed screaming, "We heard you in here! You'd better come out now!" He opened the closet and started poking me with a long rifle with a knife at the end that stabbed my arm. I jumped out and pushed him down and ran out franticly.

He didn't look like any American police.
I reached a short hallway that seemed very far away on the third floor. As I turned the corner to enter my room to get my gun, a man in a strange soldier's uniform grabbed me with a strong grip by my arm and said, "Let's go now!" He pulled me by my collar and dragged me down two flights of stairs.
I was boiling mad about how tight he had me gripped. "Get the fuck off of me!" I screamed and snatched his arm away. He elbowed me in my nose and the blood came gushing out. My head began to spin and my eyes started throbbing.
"Oh hell no!" I yelled. "Damn, why'd you do that? Let me go!" I wiped my blood and screamed, "Shit!"
He pulled me up harder by my arms and gripped his nails deep into my flesh. Then he kicked me down the last level of fifteen stairs. I rolled all the way down to the bottom, bumping my head on the wall. I ended up balled up with my backbones snapped. I laid on the bottom where five other soldiers stood. One solder said with a strange accent, "The house is clean. No one else is here."

The one holding me ordered someone to check for water and supplies. Then he grabbed me by my red shirt collar. I had red stretch pants, red shirt, and red sandals; everything appeared red, even their evil eyes.
I thought about the unsuspecting but now non-useful emergency book bag I'd put together in my closet. If I ever had to grab and run and survive a few days in case of war too close to my home, I was going to be prepared. He threw me outside on the street and scraped the side of my face and arm. I lifted up my head and saw their knee-high boots and funny iron hats with a long thick knife on their belts that were full of torturing tools. One slashed my back with a whip; another was kicking my side and face with steel tipped hard ass boots, yelling, "Get up Get up!" He pulled me up by my hair to my feet and pushed me to walk. "Let's go!" they demanded.
As I was being pulled up by my hair. I saw my best friend's mother, my neighbor, across the street, pointing at me. "It's your fault!" she was screaming. "You called them here!" She too was being pulled out of her home.
"No, I didn't!" I screamed back. "No, I didn't!"
We went down the block. I watched all of my neighbors being dragged out of their homes. There was a lot of shooting and retaliating from the people!
Screaming babies were snatched from their crying mothers. "Please don't take my baby!" But the mothers could only watch as the soldiers cut their babies in two pieces for all to see. The soldiers said that the babies would be a burden on the trip.

We were chained to one other, continually being whipped because we fell over the sick handicapped bodies that didn't get up fast enough, or because we walked too slowly on the road to Hell, stepping over bodies on top of bodies. There was no place and no time to bury them. Sporadic fires were burning bright – yellow, red, and blue – high from the ground that was burning my rubber sneakers. Damn, the whole world damn near probably had on sneakers. But it was all in the plan.

The little kids were running in circles trying not to be caught, and screaming and searching for their mommies through the thick black smoke. Kids were trampled by horses and tanks, there were lots of tanks going every which way keeping people in order, and blowing up buildings. Big buildings were collapsing and bombs were blowing up near us, near every step we took. **Boom! Boom! Boom!**

I saw people blown to pieces that could have been me, one step closer. Blood was splashing everywhere and on everyone. There was dirt and smoke in my eyes and other people's blood mingling with mine. I depended on the brutal guidance of the pulling chain.

I tried to wipe my face with my shirt but found no dry spot to use. We were chained to others as we walked for hours until our feet were blistered, hot and raw, smelling like burning rubber mixed with burning flesh. We were still not allowed to sit or stop until we reached our destination. Finally, I believed I would get to rest.

We arrived at a place that looked like a meat factory. We walked through it, bending down under the hanging bodies where meat once hanged. As I looked at the sliced parts cooking, I threw up. I looked around and saw so many aching faces from every nation and denominations, all ages. There was no more partiality. We all were all treated the same and I felt the same for all of them – mournful.

I heard so many cries: "Daddy! Mommy! Help me! Oh God! Somebody, help me! Somebody, make them stop! Stop, stop! Please! I'm sorry God, please make him stop!"

I heard different levels of volume and languages of screams. I wanted so badly to cover my ears but was unable to because I was being pulled forward. I feared my own screams to come. I was taken outside again where I was tortured with different objects – hooks and whips, knives cutting through my flesh. I remembered the feeling when I stabbed myself but these were bigger knives and deeper cuts. It burned like fire and acid and they looked at me as if I'd killed their only child!

Then a few men tied wires around my neck and hands, hanging me from a fat wooden street pole. It was like I was on a cross with my arms stretched out like Jesus. I was outside by this huge meat factory like so many others, dripping a slow death.

One solder pulled the chain tighter around my neck so my tongue would protrude. The joy-seeking solder slowly cut five slits down my tongue;

they were so deep that the blood wasn't sure to run. He looked at me and his eyes were filled with instant gratification in my pain.
I thought about how many times I'd actually prayed when I was getting my ass whipped by others and now I couldn't even pray. I looked around through my puffy eyes only to see so many dead bodies everywhere. I knew pain like never before; I could never have imagined this pain. I knew I was soon to join them and I held my head down.

I never thought I deserved this kind of punishment. I know that Jesus said that he was crucified for our sins and IF we repent, then we don't have to go through the crucifixion and torture he went through. Then does that mean that if we sin and don't change or repent or not forgive them all before we die, then we will go through the crucifixion too? Hell yeah!
Believe me, I was in punishment for every sin I'd ever committed, forgot about or never considered. This was for those times when I didn't really repent or change or when I had hurt others. I paid for in it all in excruciating, wish-I-was-dead-and-can't-die pain.
There were people being tormented in all different kinds of techniques I'd never even seen on TV; real evil, thoughtful shit. I wept for them all, wishing that I could help someone, especially the children who legs were cut off so they would stop running.
The only words that came out of my mouth as I tried to scream were, "I'm sorry God! No adultery was worth this amount of pain!" Blood was splashing down my face from my where my head had been cut. Others' were splashing beside me and behind me; our blood was intermingling.
I screamed no words, just growls and moans, as I was being torn apart limb by limb. The soldiers' laughed in victory. "Please make them stop," my mind screamed. I was slowly falling into a dark death.
Suddenly the Guiding Angel appeared. He looked at me and said in a passive voice, "This is Hell!" As I was added into the darkness I knew I was dead.

"Let's go!" the Angel said.
The place where I was taken had people walking around with all kinds of images full of personalities and attitudes, even people that looked like they been in a car accidents. But I couldn't touch them. Some were mean and dangerous looking; some women had Holy Books in their hands walking by saying to me, "We can still save their souls here!"
There I saw my best friend Lexus the one that died from leukemia. My reaction was happiness, but I was astounded to see her in a pretty white dress. "See Angel," she said, "we're not dead like you think we're dead! Some of us can hear and watch everything and everybody we want in the world but we can't do nothing about it. We can't intervene when our family is in danger and we can't enjoy anything at all that brought us joy in life. But we're not in heaven or eternal hell yet!"

My tall strange guide explained. "Angel, this is Purgatory. It's between earth and eternal hell. It's where Jesus came for a few days. He had to die to get here to let the history of people's souls waiting here know that the time was coming and that people in Purgatory could still be changed in the sprit. The damage and ugliness you see will go away. Angel, if people in the flesh pray for you here, it shows God that you were loved and are still missed and thought about way after your death."

Lexus said, "We wait here until the end of the world to be judged. It's longer for us because we don't sleep. Some people hate each other, and there are plenty of evil sprits but they can't harm each other because we are just sprits. A lot of people get here and realize how important it is to forgive people so that they can be forgiven, so they do it here. Remember the prayer, 'Forgive us AS we forgive others?' We don't really pay attention to the way we were told to pray. We don't forgive others and we expect to pray and be forgiven like our prayers were heard and answered because the Book says, 'just ask and you will be forgiven.' We forget about the 'AS' part."

So I wasn't really forgiven for the adultery because I never forgave my husband for committing adultery on me. With hate and resentment in my heart, my prayers for forgiveness for leaving my children "AS" I refused to forgive my mom for leaving me went unanswered.

"Are there people you haven't forgiven Angel? Then don't expect to be forgiven! You do it more for your own growth and well-being. You forgive a little, than just a little will you be forgiven. Without love for another you can't enter heaven. You can't hate anyone in your heart. That's what brings evil out of your mouth and it defiles you!" She smiled at me like she told me the secrets to life. I wanted to ask her if she tried to call me. And was that her sprit I felt in my room and sitting on the edge of my bed many nights? And did she break my TV when her daughter was there? I had so many questions about this place and if she saw me crying at her door wishing she would answer me.

But I still couldn't talk. My tongue was still cut up but I wasn't in the physical body so it must been in my mind. My spiritual body was still cut up, in need of forgiveness and healing or at least a reality check. I couldn't even hug and kiss my best friend. I couldn't touch her hand for a good feeling. The only way I could show her I loved her was through really loving her sprit like I always craved to be loved, and forgiving anything I ever got mad at her for and not being there for her in her last days.

I turned around to see the Guiding Angel. I didn't see him and then she too was gone. I looked around and tried to scream for Chris. I was looking around at the maimed, departed sprits in unease.

I knew he was here. "Chris! Chris!" Only mumbles came out.

As I called out his name a strange man in a shadow said, "Who is Chris?" I was able to respond. "My husband! I want him!" The only way I could talk was with my tongue hanging out of my mouth, slobbering.

"I'll be your husband!" he said. I shook my head no and turned around and there stood Chris in a big gold coat and jeans. I ran into his arms and collapsed; finally, I'd found "my home with feet." I have found him, but I fell on the ground – I went right through him! Wow, I couldn't hold him either.

I laid there screaming in my sleep. "Chris, wake me up!" Since I always talked in my sleep, I thought he would hear me screaming and wake me but my mouth was sealed shut! I continued to try. "Chris! Wake me up!" I was frustrated because my screams wouldn't come out; it was as if someone was covering my mouth. "Chris, can you hear me? Wake me up! Shake me! Do something!"

As I was spitting out chunks of pieces of my tongue with blood clots, a sudden gush of warm water came flooding in and filled the room. Chris and I were engulfed by it. "Ohhh, wow!" we said. Chris and I were able to clasp hands and we began floating in what became an ocean of warm cleansing water.

I was healed. My body no longer hurt at all! I felt great! I was ready to do flips. I felt so good I cried. My tongue was healed and my sprit was healed. I felt such an overwhelming sense of peace. It filled me up inside my entire being. I was able to let go of Chris' hand because I knew he was in good hands. We were free! And I flipped!

I felt like a baby safe in a womb. I was being transformed into an angelic-like being, full of peace and love.

The Angel spoke. "This is the firmament; you must be cleansed in it before you can enter heaven. This is between earth and heaven!"

I woke up in the silent darkness of my bedroom in complete awe.

I shook Chris. "Baby! Baby, wake up!"

"What?" He jumped up.

"What is Purgatory?"

"It's a place the Catholics believe dead people go!" He went to Catholic school so he should know.

"Why haven't I ever heard of it?" I guess it is important to know what others believe. There might be some truth and proof to it. This was deep!

"Chris, wake up baby, please!" I pushed him again as he turned his head to go back to sleep. I jumped up and turned on the light.

He sat up fast and excited, ready to roll out. "What's up?" he said, as if something happened to one of his kids. He was ready to jump up and down stairs quick!

"Chris, I'm scared to go back to sleep!" I said anxiously.

"Why baby, you had a bad dream?"

"Baby, I was in hell! I didn't just see it! I felt it! I was in it!" I said as I rubbed the goose bumps from my cold arms. "Then an Angel took me to purgatory! I'd never even read of this in my little Bible searching for truths! There is no mention of it in the Bible!"

"Baby, the Catholics have a lot of scrolls that they didn't put in the Bible. Some are still unpublished today. The Christians don't believe in it that's why!" he said. "Angel, I'm tired. I have to get up in two hours. Come on let's get some sleep. I'll talk to you about it some more tomorrow okay?"

"Chris, I'm going to hell and I'm going to be tortured like Jesus for my sins! Damn, and I didn't even get to see heaven!"

"Baby; you're not going to Hell. Come here." He hugged me tight and rocked me. "You're a loving, good-hearted person. That's why I keep you," he smiled. "You're the best you can be right now and God loves you! That was just a dream. He knows you're a little crazy but He still loves you!"

I hit him and we laughed together.

"I'm scared to go back to sleep though." I poked out my lips like a baby.

He rubbed my face in comfort. "Say a prayer and go back to sleep! If you saw all of that and you're here to tell me about it then God will keep you safe. There's nothing to fear!"

"Well, I do want to know what happens to our kids. They weren't in the dream!" My dreams always continued when I went back to sleep but I was scared as shit. I didn't want to go back to hell. I was so scared that my hands were shaking.

I turned the light back off and Chris held me and cuddled on my butt with the pillow between both of our bony knees for extra comfort.

"I love you Angel!" he whispered.

"I love you too Chris. Thanks baby!" I grabbed his warm hands and held on tight.

He rocked me till I dozed off...

When I entered my dream we all were in line: Tunisia, Aqusia, Tunisia's husband, Jasmine, Kammena, and me! I wondered why Laquana and Cyris, Chris were not there.

One at a time, we were told to sit in a black wheel chair. It rolled itself through what looked like a cash register counter. We all rolled through one at a time. I was last.

We met on the other side with a paper in our hand; it was a list of all of our unforgiving sins. We looked at each other in disbelief. It was actually documented! Shit, I forgot about that one! Our faces were covered with fear and we were ashamed to show each other so we all held our papers close to our chest.

We were told to go through a door to our right to wait to be judged. Fear set in my heart, not just for me but for my children. Their papers looked as long as mine and I knew what I'd done: sins, long and many. All the

sins were judged and I prayed my good deeds were written on the opposite side. I didn't know the magnitude or even if it mattered; one was too many to not fear.
Suddenly, I had an idea on how to save us! I waved at all of them to come. "Follow me everyone," I said. "Come on, hurry up!" I found the Purgatory room, but now it looked like a movie theater where everyone watched their own movie of their family and friends.
"We can hide in here," I whispered. "This is Purgatory. We can work on some of these sins before we are judged! The angel told me that sins are forgiven here too, only this part of it is different I guess I was in the lobby before."
But all of a sudden, people started standing up out of their seats pointing at us, yelling, "Get out! Get out! You don't belong in here!"
We panicked, so we ran up to the front but others stood and hollered, "There they go! Get out! You don't belong in here!" Some guards came and grabbed us and took us out. We were screaming and crying, "No, we don't want to go in there! Wait, not yet! Please wait! We're not ready! We didn't know! We're sorry! Wait, please!"
The angel turned around and looked at me and I stopped yelling. I froze in my tracks and looked at him as if to say, "What's next and where are my other children?"
"Tell them what I have shown you!" he said. "Tell them all!"

I opened my eyes and saw Chris putting on his blue suit.
"Good morning, Angel. How was the rest of your night?"
I told him the rest of my dream and said I had to tell others. He kissed me gently with three pecks and went into the closet to his secret hiding place to get me my daily $20. "Have a good day. Go out and get some air okay?" It was a beautiful early June summer day. "I'll call you later Angel to check on you, okay?"
"Okay, baby. Bye-bye. Wait! Wait!" I jumped up and hugged him tight and thought about him already being in Purgatory before me. I didn't want him to die! "I love you Chris so much!"
"I love you too Angel. Are you going to be alright?"
"Yeah, I guess so. I'm just in shock! Those were some deep experiences I will never forget and I believe what I saw to be true! It was not a normal dream!"
"Angel, you are special," he said to me. "God is trying to tell you something so listen up! I'll call you later!"

It was 7:00 am. I got back into bed to keep warm. I looked around and thought how trivial material things are and how we kill for these things but was only going to pay for them in pain. It wasn't worth it!
I thought about the adultery, which confused me because the first sixteen years Chris and I were together, I didn't cheat on him! And when I left

him and prayed and said, "In God's eyes, we are now officially divorced," I had other men and he had other woman and when we got back together, I was faithful for the ten years. But then it hit me: "Angel," a voice said, "you're stupid! You had sex with married men!"
Yes I sure did. When I was a model and was trying to get free portfolios and get into shows, I had sex. If men bought me clothes I had sex with them and I allowed the owner of the modeling agency to lick me up while I looked at his wife's picture. I had sex with the man who gave me my own beauty shop. I used sex to get what I wanted, to get ahead and I didn't care if they were married. It wasn't personal; I never wanted to hurt the wife. It was just business and at age fourteen I didn't think about the word "adultery."

None of them gave me pleasure so they sure weren't worth the pain! Damn, I never asked for forgiveness for that either, I never even thought about it until now. Wow, I'd better repent for that now! Thank God I went down this memory lane. It might help me be less tormented. I definitely had no intentions of committing adultery in the future that's for sure! That was just straight-up torture and it wasn't even worth it! After we got back together after a year of separation, I got close to doing it only because he was doing it. With their penis in my hand I ran; only in my heart did I lust once or twice.
I used to say that if Chris cheated on me, then I was going to have to go out there and find me a man that I could cheat with just to get even to give me temporary comfort. I couldn't do that now! Hell no I wouldn't! Damn, that shit was a little too real.
God sees the hate in our hearts we have for each other, so let us be separated and divorced so we can be with other people without the "adultery" word! We can remarry if the adulterate has entered the marriage and we desire it. The lack of trust damn near destroyed me!

Wow, my heart started beating really fast. My sprit was saying, "Get up! Get up now! Go tell them! Tell them all as the angel instructed you!"
It was 7:30am. I sat there for a half hour and it felt like only a minute. Rationalizing and procrastinating, talking myself out of it. Saying, "But everyone will think I'm crazy or they might not care to hear it!"
"DO IT!" screamed my spirit.
I ran in the back room. I shook Aqusia awake. "Wake up!" I said, nice and soft-spoken so as not to alarm her. I wanted to pleasantly greet her so she'd want to listen. "I must tell you my dream! Wake up and listen to what an angel told me to tell you. You have to get up for school anyway!"
Tunisia lived with her husband so I called her.
"Please listen," I said and I told her everything from beginning to end; how I'd never heard of Purgatory till then and it does exist! How we will

be punished for our sins, so we'd better be mindful of what we do now. I told her the importance of forgiving to be forgiving, hoping that something is heard and to accept it as truth and not just a drunken rambling.

I ended by saying; "God wants a closer relationship with you all, okay?"

"Yes Mom! Mom I do pray and I do believe you!"

I was happy she believed me! She didn't believe too much. "I love you so much, baby! You know, baby, we cry out for someone to love us very deeply when we should be loving others deeply and not selfishly looking for it and loving ourselves, not getting hateful because we're not loved like we want to be loved. Remember, God is love; the more we give the more we will receive!"

I ran into my son's room and called his name softly. He heard me; usually I had to yell I was too drained to yell. I told him everything and hugged him long and tight. "Son, please think about your sins before you do them okay? And try to forgive people who have hurt you so you can be forgiven for all the people you've hurt and so you'll know your dirt!"

"Okay Mom!" He seemed to sincerely believe every word that flowed.

With a look of desperation to save his life, I said, "God loves you so much. He gave me this message for you so you can go to heaven. I want us all to go to heaven! If I don't tell you this message than it's on me. If you don't listen, then it's on you!"

I got back into my bed as I stared at the TV. I wiped my tears and thought about our country's past conflicts of religion and political greed and power. I turned to CNN to see if today was the day America would go to the higher level of its war with God's children in Iraq. I had questions! Will they try to disarm North Korea? Hell no! Will there be civil war here? And I thought how they didn't have any money for schools and after-school programs to keep the children busy and out of trouble and out of jail. After it's over, who will rule their country?

Where are our gas masks? Will a terrorism uprising affect my grandchildren and me with diseases in their blankets? Will there be bombs dropping in my backyard? Will different races be rising up against all western interests? My grandbabies can't get the smallpox shot because they have eczema? Oh my God! So they're supposed to suffer and die while we watch? Are all the involved countries going to break the greatest commandant of all – "Love they neighbor?"

"Good okay, not today. Maybe tomorrow. They are still practicing their maneuvers!" I said sarcastically to the TV. I wiped my eyes again and shook my head, thinking how no war is needed; the women and children will suffer the most because they have risen up arms too heavy for them to carry. Seven years old and willing to die fighting when they should be praying and playing in peace. I looked up to the ceiling. "God, how much time do we have before the army men snatch us out of our homes? When will the torment and painful sights begin?" I was crying for the lost souls in the Twin Towers here at home. "Peace please, children can't live at ease, Race, Space, it all a disgrace. Where are the missing men? Where will this country send their soldiers for World War III? Missile wows put up Missile toes. But who listens to meeeeee?"

The tears were just flowing uncontrollably. Why should anyone want to fight to live now? Why start anything? Why have babies? Is this the beginning of the end?
Then I heard a voice say, "The reason to stay alive now is to tell as many people as you can what you have seen and learned so they will not suffer as much. Time used positively helps you get to the time to forgive the living and be forgiving so you can be rewarded in the end!"

I stood up. That's why these people must know today! They must take this time to forgive. Where is the best place to do that? Somebody needs to hear to prayer for his or her deceased loved and unloved one. Somewhere, sprits are in need of forgiveness.
I threw on an African dress with no under clothes and slipped on my sandals. No wash up, no pocketbook, nothing just the keys and juice. I was good and thirsty. I drove to group fast. I was jittery in my seat; I couldn't wait to be called on.
Finally it was my turn. With much excitement and fear I told them my dream in a shorter version. "I was told to tell you this. Now I have to go and wash up and rest!"

An alumni from the program I was in before was there. He had about ten years clean and waited for me in the back as a lot of people stood in line, one, two, or three at a time hugging me and saying, "Bless God!" There was a compassionate Christian woman that was facilitating the Spiritual group. She kept saying, "Thank you Jesus!" as I shared my experience. I didn't care if they thought I was insane because this was real! I'm sure some people probably did think of me as insane. I was glad it was spiritual group what a coincidence!
Well, I was legally crazy but so was Eve because of the blame she carried. I probably would have thought someone was crazy too if I heard all this coming from a shaken, nervous dry-drunk who maybe just wanted some damn attention! Or I would probably think, "Why would God give a dirty mouth addict like her a vision?"
I was out of breath. I'd done what I was told to do! I was drained like I been through hell!
My friend came over to me as I was leaving the circle. "Come here girl!"
I almost collapsed but he held me up. "Are you okay?" he asked.
"Yes, I'm cool. Just help me to my car!"

He squeezed me tight and said, “I love you so much Angel!” He smiled real hard with his charming, flirtatious grin. “Angel, I’ve known you for ten years. You are so gifted to have helped the hundreds of people that came through the doors and you’ve helped me a whole lot. Remember when I wanted to get a divorce five years ago and you were in-group? I said I wanted it because I was saved and she wasn’t and she wasn’t trying to change. I wanted to give it up because I believed I didn’t have to be burdened. But you told me that I needed to remember the time I burdened her down with my addiction. For years, she wasn’t using and put up with my abusive tongue and me because I didn’t believe on hitting on no woman but this tongue is a sword! It cuts deep if you hurt me! But any way” he said as he tapped my shoulder, “You reminded my adulterous ass that I was just being selfish! You said what she was doing to me now was just ‘pay back reactions.’ You told me that if I believed in the Bible to read the part that says, ‘if your wife is an unbelieving wife, she can be saved through the believing husband – do not cast her away!’ You told me if I began to treat her good and forgive her, she would forgive our abused marriage and me. Thanks to you, we have been together for another five years, and we want to stay together. We are the happiest we’ve ever been and guess what? I don’t cheat at all. I don’t even have the desire to! Everyone is my sister in the Lord and I respect women more now. And you know, Angel, what a big flirt I was! I flirted with you all the time but when you speak it’s like I’d better listen because it’s always something I needed to hear!

Angel, you have a gift and you didn’t lose it – you just haven’t been practicing it!
“I haven’t seen in these groups the strength and love and insight you brought since you left. I remember you told this white man once, ‘I see you over there, hiding in the corner. Are you uncomfortable around all these black people?’ Everyone was thinking it but you said something! Then he said ‘no,’ so you told him to come closer and you read him like a book! You told the group that he needed support because he had a lot of pain in his eyes and that’s why he was always so angry but everyone thought he was just mean! Before then, you’d never even seen this man. You said as you looked him straight in his eyes, standing in the circle of the group, that he were raised up poorly and that his father was a war vet and a drunk who kicked him and his mama’s ass on a regular basis, and that he was a bum and he was mad because he tuned out just like his father, a drunk and a woman beater! I remember you asked him if you were right. And when he said you were right about everything and how did you know? We all looked at each other and said, ‘she’s damn good!’ That was when you only had about five years clean and you only got better with time.

"You helped me Angel, and I love you for it! I believe this dream is to tell you to start speaking again because for the last three years you haven't been doing what you're blessed to do with your tongue!"
I stared at him and smiled. "Thank you so much! I am so drained I can hardly walk and my back is killing me! Can you please help me to my car now?"
"I'm sorry," he said, "I'm just so happy to see you! Come on, I got you!"
He put his hands around my waist as I put my arms around his skinny shoulder and we walked very slowly through the park where we had group all summer long. I was very sore most days but I went to group every day.
As I climbed into my Jeep like a baby in a high chair, he came to the driver's side and said, "Are you sure you can drive? If not, I'll take you home!"
"I'll be fine! I'm going to just sit here in the air conditioner for a while and drink this juice. Then I'll drive home and go back to sleep. I feel like I've been through a ten-round fight!"
We laughed. "It sure is good to see you Angel! You know I love you right?" He gently rubbed my face.
"I love you too Marty! Thanks a lot baby!" He really gave me back some self worth.

Mom called me.
"Hi mom how are you doing?"
"Not too good baby. My cousin Johnny died today!"
"I'm sorry to hear that mom. How did he pass away?"
"He passed from cancer. He was in so much pain, his mother was a little relived because he's not suffering anymore and that he's with God now!"
"I will pray for you and his sprit!"
"Thank you baby!"
"You know mom, I had a dream that an angel showed me what it is like after we die and I was told we are supposed to pray for their souls. They are in Purgatory waiting for judgment, so no one is with God yet. The sprits can see us."
Suddenly, Mom shouted with anger, "I don't want to hear that shit! I don't want to think my mother is watching all this ugly shit! I would like to believe they are resting in peace! I always pray for my mother and I talk to her! You don't know what you're talking about!"

"Mom, I was told to tell people to pray for the dead that's all!"
"I know my mother is with Jesus in his bosom! She was a good woman. She is with my God! My Bible says; "to be absent from the body is to be present with the Lord," so go and tell your angel to read the Bible!" She hung up the phone, "Bam."

I was crushed. Tears watered in my eyes. I said out loud, "I can never talk to her about anything. That's why I don't say shit to her! She wonders why I don't call her no more!"

Maybe she needs to read 11 Corinthians 5v7, 8: "While we are at home in the body we are away from the lord." 8, "I'D RATHER/PERFER be absent from the body and present with the Lord/ at home with the lord." It's not saying I will be in the presents of the Lord "AS SOON" as I leave the body. V 10 says; "We must appear before the judgment seat of Christ first."
When is judgment? Read Revelations11v18, where it says: "When the trumpet sounds by an Angel at the end of the world, 'Judgment time' THEN the DEAD will rise up out of their graves!" Therefore you will be in the grave absent from the body and still not with the Lord yet waiting for the trumpet to sound.
If you study grave Rev 6v9, "When he opened up the fifth seal, I saw UNDER the Alter the SOULS of those who had been SLAIN because of the word of God and the testimony they maintained" now here is Gods own people who is dead, are they in his presents or in heaven? NO! They are under the alter and the slain can speak, so the SLAIN CAN SPEAK, REV 6v10 they called out in a loud voice, how long, Sovereign Lord until you judge the earth? They were given a robe, Therefore they are not asleep there souls can put on a robe and they was told to "WAIT" a little longer, until there fellow servants was killed also. So the dead souls are waiting? Where is under the Alter? Where are the dead waiting for this judgment? Are they waiting with the LORD in Heaven? NO! Then where? Read REV 5v 2...who is worthy to break the seals...no one in heaven or on earth or UNDER THE EARTH, so something is under the earth, and they have the ability to open things, and put on things, and speak, where is under the earth? The bible before the KingJames version will tell you it's named Purgatory.

Therefore my suicidal friends Dead is not a sleep and peaceful state or immediately being with God but "under the earth waiting for judgment" for how long? Until the trumpet sound by the angel, what will you be doing while you are waiting? Praying for forgiveness for all the dirt and harm you've done and sins committed and hoping the living is praying for your soul and forgiving you before judgment.
But everyone just says I like to debate.
She was raised Catholic. She should have told me about Purgatory. She should have believed and supported me! But I guess everyone is not ready to hear or accept the truth!
It couldn't have been my unconscious mind at work because I never heard the word "Purgatory" until then.
I believed the angel; and for once, I wish she believed in me.

CHAPTER TWENTYONE

THEY MADE ME DO IT!

Only two months since Cyris been out, we got a phone call at 1:00am in the morning.

Chris answered. "Hello? Hello, who is this?"

"Dad, I just shot two guys!" Cyris said, frightened and out of breath.

"What happened?"

"Dad, I'm hiding in a dog house!" He was trying to hold his cell phone with his shaking hands.

"Why did you do it?"

"They were coming to shoot me first! I ran, Dad! Dad, you have to believe me!"

"So who did you shoot?"

"Yesterday at least four dudes jumped me dad and today two of them saw me and talked shit about what they did and what they was going to do. They left and came back looking for me. Dad, they came back looking for me! They drove up a dark one-way street creeping up on me so I ran around the corner and picked my two pieces up and **BAM, BAM, BAM, BAM!** I shot two dudes! Both of them, twice in their heads and necks, point blank as they sat in their car at a stop sign!"

"Are they dead?"

"I don't know! I can't talk no more now! I'll call you back dad as soon as I can!"

"Cyris, you stay there until it's quiet and you can get out and go somewhere safe and call me back okay? I'll try to find out what's going on and I'll tell you what to do next!"

Chris hung up the phone and looked at me with his eyebrows up. I was sitting straight up in bed. "What happened? Who was that?" I knew one of our children was in trouble from the look on his face. He jumped up and started putting on his socks and jeans with no underwear. He threw his blue sweater over his head without a T-shirt.

"Don't panic Angel," he said calmly, "that was Cyris. He said he shot some people and now he's hiding." He said it so cool but it was rushed.

"Who did he shoot? Where? Is anyone dead?"

"He shot two people twice that's all I know!"

"Oh my God! Chris, where is he? Is he okay? Is anyone dead? What are we going to do?"

"I'm going to get him and get him out of town until we get some facts. Right now I have to protect him!"

We knew the guys had family and friends that would surely be coming to our house looking for him with their guns. Sure enough that night some guys came looking for him. They sent someone he knew to knock on the door to ask if he was home. I slammed the door in that trader's face. We met up with Cyris at the crack of morning and said goodbye as he got on the bus to New York.

"They are not going to blame our son for some shit until we find out what's going on and until we can get to his lawyer," Chris said.

I didn't know when I would see him again. I'd go there if I had to. I just hoped he stayed out of trouble. Chris told the New York family to look out and not to let him make any sales and that he would send him money.

He kept his word and sent him money. He had his own room and he was going to recording studios to brawl at a few rapping battles with the best rappers in New York. The right people were noticing him. Eventually, Cyris was offered to cut a demo. He was happy and living safely with a good perspective.

But I still couldn't sleep. I knew a phone call was coming about him.

One night, I was lying in my bed on the third floor of our house. I heard a lot of noise downstairs so I jumped up. It must have been about 6:00 am. I jumped up in my T-shirt and panties yelling, "Who is that?"

"It's the police!" I met them at the second level. "Why didn't you answer the door miss?"

"I was asleep and I can't hear the bell up there anyway!"

"Well you should get it fixed!" the detective snapped. "Where is Cyris? We have a warrant for his arrest!"

"What did he do?" I asked.

He told the six police officers to search the premises.

I sat down at the kitchen table as they walked around the house. My heart was about to jump out of my chest. I was so afraid that he was going to say MURDER! I was so nervous I was shaking, like I was guilty.

Two more plainclothes cops came in. I looked at their gold badges but they said nothing. They just watched like they were the bosses. They wanted to make sure they got Cyris.

I rolled my eyes at the detective that was getting smart with me. I went into our poolroom and asked them again.

"What did he do?"

"He did something very bad miss. We really need to talk to him now. Where is he?"

"I don't know where he's at!" I really didn't know where in New York he was; he could have been in any city.

I walked back into the kitchen and said, "I put him out last time he got in trouble!" I did put his ass out once so I wasn't lying. "Is anybody hurt?" I really wanted to know if anyone died and to know how serious this was. I still didn't know the facts!

He followed me. "I can't tell you that!"
"What you mean you can't tell me? That's my son! I have a right to know what he is accused of or being charged with!"
"No you don't!" he said. "You can't tell us where he is so we can't tell you anything either!" He had an 8" by 10" picture in his hand. "Is this Cyris?" he asked. Damn, I don't even have a picture of him that big looking that good.
"Yes, that is my son. What happened?"
He pushed away from the black marble table and began walking towards the stairs. I pulled his arm to turn him around to look at me. Desperate for an answer I asked again. "What happened?"
He ignored me so I frowned. "Can I have your card? I want his lawyer to contact you. Then you can talk to him!"
He gave me his card. "Mr. Hot Shot Detective" was determined to find my child. Did he actually expect me to hand him over? I don't think so!

"When you see your son call us so he doesn't get hurt trying to resist an arrest. You need to answer your damn door!"
"No hold up!" I put my hands on my hips. "And you need to give me some respect and watch how you talk to me!"
"We will be back. It might be five in the morning but we will be back!"
"Don't come running up in my house in the middle of the night scaring me! Somebody might get shot!" I responded.
My inner voice, "Damn, Angel why'd you say that? Is that a threat? Shit now they're going to lock your dumb ass up!"
They were going down the stairs and someone said, "Shoot to kill!"
I yelled down the stairs furious, at them saying, "None of you better not shoot to kill MY son! I know that much!" I wasn't thinking that they were probably talking about me, "shoot to kill," because if I didn't kill them, they were going to kill me.
I continued to yell. "I will have your badges! I know the past and present mayors, personally!" I shouted proudly. I did and I knew many other officials. Shit my sister is a detective; I could ask her what the deal is! "I know Congressmen and women, and two Philadelphia state senators and a few judges, so don't fuck with me or mine or there will be hell to pay! So you better come correct!"
I heard one ask another, "What did she say?"
"She said she knows your boss!" and they laughed!

I sighed of relief that they didn't take my ass with them.
Could my son have done this? He would fight anyone in a minute, he'd pistol whip you but to shoot two people twice in the head up close? Could he have done that?

He knows God said, “Do not murder,” and he said he was listening and trying to practice Islam. If he did do it, I knew it was only because he thought his life was in danger and he was high and panicked.
I guess I wouldn’t know until I could ask him myself.
Oh God, please help us.

Four months later…
The phone rang. “Hi Angel, how are you today? This is your oldest sister; you know the one you never call!”
“Hi! I’ve been busy here with everything that’s been going on!”
“What is going on?”
“Well, I was going to call you to get some information. I found out Cyris shot two people in the head out of self-defense. Thank God for letting those young men’s loss of life not be by my son’s hand; miraculously they are walking around just fine. I’m happy they didn’t die, not just for my son’s sake but also for those young men and their family’s sake. Cyris went to Albany to work. He wasn’t there a good two weeks and bought a bag of weed and got busted! They detained him and when they ran his name the warrant showed.”

“Wow, he shot them in the head and they’re walking around?”
“Yeah, well, God is good! The bullets went through one of them still has a bullet in him. My gut hurts everyday. I’m afraid of the outcome. I am shaking uncontrollably trying to hold this phone. I’m scratching my head my body itches… I have to take Valium to calm down. I need a drink… no, I want a drink… no I don’t want to be drunk. That will not stop this fear. Only hearing Cyris’ voice will calm me.”
“What do you fear?”
“I fear what Cyris will do now that he is facing some real time in prison.”
“You think he’ll hurt himself again?”
“I don’t think he will want to live in those conditions!”
“What is Chris doing?”
“Chris is so supportive. He tells me not to worry about anything, that he has everything under control. Yeah girl, they held him in Albany’s jail for three agonizing months waiting for Philly to come and get him. Chris went to visit him in Albany last week. I couldn’t even go because of my sore body. I couldn’t take that long ride. Chris encouraged him to stay stronger and to believe that God will see him through this. He calls me collect everyday. My phone bill is $300 because I have to hear his voice and know that he is all right. I have to let him know everyday that we love him very much and not to do anything stupid.

He just found out that between jail times he has a baby boy who needs his daddy!”
“What! He has a baby?”

"So he's told! Age two! Chris told him to do for his son what he wanted Chris to do for him! I think that gave him something to think about. What more did he want Chris to do?"
"Wow... well, you stay strong Angel and stop getting yourself all worried about something that might not happen. Give it to God and don't forget about the rest of your kids; they still need you too. Sometimes we give too much love and attention to one through a crisis but neglect the others. Then they do something to get some of that love and attention and then you have two crises instead of one! So give them all some love and attention and support and guidance in whatever it is they are going through or doing because it's important to them. Okay! I love you! Bye!"
"Bye Tina, I love you too!"

I sat down at my computer desk. He contacted a good lawyer and we would soon have some idea of what kind of time he was looking at with all of these charges. I was looking at a paper in my hand. Damn, two attempted murder charges because it was above the shoulder, execution-style; aggravated assault, two times; conspiracy because someone supposedly passed off; carrying illegal arms and illegal use of firing a firearm. Damn, so many felonies and misdemeanors. The list made me dizzy. I had to lie down.
His crimes were "thirty-two degrees below zero," as the Five Percenters used to say.
I held my head up with my eyes closed. "Please God, don't let him take his life! I love him! I need him. Help him please! Give him strength! My angel, are you still there?"
Damn, she was so right. I remembered how I felt, even though mom lost her son. I still wanted attention no matter in what area. I wanted acknowledgement that I still existed.

Finally I could see my baby. He was in Philadelphia! He was standing there in his orange jumper, light and bright with his large afro. He had bumps on his face from the harsh prison soap but he was smiling like he was getting a Christmas present.
Oh, I hugged him long! I didn't care that the guards will stop you if you hug and kiss too long. I was going to hold my child. Shit, this might be the last time I see him, I thought as I embarrassed him with too much comfort.
I watched him and Tunisia who took me to the jail hug. She talked to him like they did in their everyday conversation about who said what or did what in the street or the radio new songs and the newest rapper's gossip. What did he think about the newest videos? They both were laid back laughing.
I looked around as I left in my mind. It seemed like I was back home, watching the kids play when they were too young to be in here, in this

place full of orange suits. All of these people were waiting for a few minutes of escape back to their homes and looking into the eyes of their loved ones, looking for a reason to hold on for one more day.
I wanted facts but I couldn't talk freely with the guards looking down my throat. Shit, they might have these chairs wired!
The kids continued laughing about something. I began to get angry; how could they laugh? I wanted to cry! Didn't they know how serious this shit was? How could they not cry? "Because he has to laugh to keep from crying Angel. Cool out," I said to myself.

"Cyris these are very serious charges you're facing; six felonies and a limited time of ten to fifteen. If they offer you a deal, you should take it because they said you have been identified by the people that got shot." I looked him in his eyes as I grabbed his hands and waited for his response. "If you had to do ten years, can you do the time?"
He jumped back in his chair and laughed out a hardy, "No! Hell, no!" He shook his head. "No, I'm not going to do no time. Maybe two years but they can't prove anything! Check this out mom," he said, sitting back at the edge of his seat. "How did they see me if they got shot behind the ear and in the back of their shoulders and neck? They would instantly go forward not look back. I was there but everyone will say they were auguring with me first and I left. They will say they left and came back and cased me. If they got back in their Jeep and got shot from behind it doesn't mean it was me! One of them said in their statement that he didn't know who it was okay? So one said it was me… but he is not going to come to court, so I'm out of here."
"Look," I said, "That's enough!" I held up my hands. "That's enough baby!" I held his face and kissed him on the tip of his nose. "I'm just so happy to see my baby!" I smiled and hugged him again needing to touch him. "Stop picking your bumps. You're too rough and you're leaving these dark marks!"
"I try mom but look at these big ass… oops, sorry!" I gently slapped him upside his head as Tunisia laughed saying, "Oohh!"
"Mom," Cyris continued, "I have big heavy hands so it's hard to be gentle."
"Yeah, you have them big hands like my father. Then stay out of your face then. If you can't do something right, don't do it at all! You're too fine to have these dark spots all over you face! Now get some Noxzema okay?"
"Okay mom! Look at these muscles mom!" He pulled up his sleeve and flexed.
"Damn that is real hard!" I said as I felt his rock hard muscle.
He punched his stomach hard. "Look at my six-pack!"
"Yeah baby, you keep getting buff so you can knock a nigga out!" We laughed.

"Mom," he said, "I can't think negatively or else I'll get depressed. But it's going to be all right, okay? Don't worry about me; I hold my own! If I don't have to worry about you then I'll be okay."
"Well, if I don't have to worry about you, then I can rest."
"Okay mom, don't you worry about a thing. God's got this!"
"Ok baby bye!" I said with my tearful eyes.
He looked like he was getting ready to cry too, but he just sucked it up and showed me his strength with a smile. He threw me a kiss in the wind as I walked out backwards as the guard escorted us to the door.
I had given him something to read. Cyris laid across his bunk and read it.

Oh My Child…

If I could have done things differently
What would it be like so you wouldn't have turned out like me?
Unfilled dreams because I was too busy harboring resentment and anger,
Insecure and suicidal, reflections in the mirror – I see a stranger!
What happened to us? What caused us to say, "I really don't care?"
We both constantly go to God in prayer!
Spaced out, feeling unclean,
Crying within because of what we've seen!
I know that hurt that just won't go away,
We'll be traveling right, than we go the wrong way!
Thanks for sharing some of your pain with me,
I see it all in your eyes – the longing for relief; it's the reflection of me, see!
So now you're on the path of not caring who you hurt,
You selling and packing, I know the game I did my dirt!
I found out the long painful hard way at the end of the day,
I told you so you didn't have to go my way!
You were there you saw me cry, so again baby, why?
I learned every time – I didn't consider others people's history,
I didn't leave room for understanding to the answer to; why you did this to me?
I couldn't see past my own pain and needs,
I pray we receive some points for our good deeds!
We believed we could get away with getting that fast buck,
Bullets have no name even if you duck!

Now we stand before the Judge man,
"Your honor it's been hard for me you just don't understand!"
"That's not my problem; you have to take responsibility for yourself young man!"
Now for our wrong decisions, I have lost my son,

Oh my child, what have you done?
We're both soaking in our very own private cell?
Thinking how good we had it compared to this hell!
We must have a closer relationship with God if we want some peace today,
For yesterday is gone away and all we have is today; so lets find ourselves is what I say!
Remember my son, to show God some gratitude regardless of your situation, even in the smallest way,
When Evil is telling you to die and go away,
Remember Mommy's voice begging you to stay!

What will you say to your child now that you can see a criminal's reality?

LOVING YOU DEEPLY,
MOM

CHAPTER TWENTY TWO

I HOPE THE BITCHES WERE WORTH IT!

Just when I thought I'd won the battle and he'd surrender back to me, there was another whore in the picture, another secretary. He gets angry with me for cock blocking. That mother-fucker went through A-Z and it's the end for me.

Let me tell you how it finally ended.

I was weary and had no fight left in me. I surrendered in defeat in the fight for faithfulness. He was a damn whore!
He called me one day. He wanted to talk.
"Talk now?" I said to him. "You want to talk? 'Just listen,' you say but to what? To words that are as empty as my gut, to actions that contradict your words? Listen and than what? Believe? Believe in the words of your love that say the same thing every time? It wasn't me! I call you and you say shit like, 'ACT LIKE I'M DEAD!' and hang up on me! I listen to your spirit! Don't you know me by now? Don't you know who I am? I am a Spirit seeker! And you can't be faithful to me during this crucial time in your life. You feel you need various comforts. I'm filing for divorce in the morning so you can be free and I can be free to be me!"
He said: "Do whatever you want. I'm tired of you judging me. Let's just say for scenario's sake that I was a whore, you're not better than me. You still get high so don't tell me about how God is going to punish me. He loves me as much as he loves you!"
"You're a whore, a whore!"
"You feel better now?"
"Yeah, because that's as close as you ever came to confessing the truth."
I left town for a week and he came to find me, to beg me, overwhelming me with passionate sex, talking of spiritual counseling, saying things like, "I'd rather be unhappy with you then to be happy with someone else."
"Okay," I said to him, "I'll give this one more chance. Call that whore and tell her not to come around you no more!"
He called her. "Hi, I'm going to work things out with my wife. Don't call me anymore and don't come by my office. We will dissolve our relationship." He hung up and looked at me.
"Okay, well, we have two weeks to decide because the divorce papers will be in your face to sign by then."

Three weeks passed. The papers finally arrived but he was still involved with his whore and me.
He called me when he got his copies. "I'm in my room looking at the divorce papers. I have to process this shit. I will talk to you about it tomorrow, okay? I'm not feeling well. I'm just going to lay here for a while."
I wanted to say, "Process it between her legs," but my grandson walked in.
"Okay Chris, call me tomorrow so we can get together and talk about it. Bye."

Chris was lying down on his back with his hands behind his head. His stereo played "Three Times a Lady" by Lionel Ritchie. He closed his eyes and saw himself singing that song to Angel at her bedroom window. He visualized them having snowball fights and their passionate kiss after he threw her on top of a pile of snow. He saw her on TV proud of her on Visions program, remembering the excitement they shared. He recalled the day Angel's GED test score arrived and he opened it and told her she didn't pass. He remembered her disappointed face; but when he pulled out a framed certificate and a congratulatory card she smiled and cried with pride. He saw himself being baptized and then helping baptize her and they stood there, both soaked in their white clothes presented before the congregation and God as born again, a new beginning, husband and wife.
He saw her standing over him playing with a blown up condom. He saw her lying in the hospital after the stabbing, realizing that he almost lost her. A tear rolled down the side of his face; he jumped up and said, "I can't lose her."

I laid down, listening to "Release Me" by Wilson Phillips, thinking of how hard it was going to be to get over him, hearing his sexy voice and desiring him. He still wanted to kiss me but not in front of his people. I wished he desired only me as I only desired him.
I waited all day for his call. Finally at 5:00 PM, he called. I could hear women laughing in the background. "I'll see you later," he said to me. "I still have things to do!"
"I'll be over now. I want to see the papers!" I said quickly and hung up.

I arrived and was told he'd meet me around the corner. I slipped passed the guard and had a seat in the lunchroom where the short, bald-headed whore was also sitting waiting for him. I didn't say a word to her. I just sat behind her and looked at this whore in her $10 dress and I just felt disgusted. He can do much better than that, damn.
He wouldn't come in the back where we were sitting. He was acting like a teenager who just got busted. He demanded that I come out to him, but

I just laughed. We just made love the night before. He was mad and scared and didn't know if I was going to go off or not. But I was cool while he paced back and forth, telling me that I'm not allowed in his building and that I was not to come around him when he had business.
I just wanted the papers.

It happened so fast.
"Just sign the papers now!" I said. "I don't want to be married to you!"
"No," he said, "I'll sign them Monday after Father's Day."
"Now! Don't hold me hostage!"
He signed them to hurry up and get rid of me. He figured that he'd fix it later. He thought that he was signing a copy and that he had the original.
By the time we got back, she was gone. "You can still catch your whore if you run bitch!" I looked at him and the security guard and smiled. "I'm free!" I went home to get an envelope and then went to the store to get a stamp. As I left the store I saw her. She was going back to him.
I looked up to the Heavens. "God help me!" I wanted to punch her in the back. I wanted to knock her in her damn head in with my medal cane, stomp her face into the concrete and never stop. I told her that I'd take all of my shit out on her if I found out they were intimate! I would kill the little bitch.
But I didn't want to go to jail. If he didn't want me and couldn't be faithful, than what would I be fighting for?
So I said to her, "He's all yours. He's free now!" Not that she cared; I wanted her to know I didn't!
I walked on my way and prayed. "God, you deal with her and her adulterating ass for me. Make her suffer!"
Content they would both suffer, I walked up to the mailman and said, "I want to put these divorce papers in your trusting hands!"
I sat on the church steps to rest and to accept I was divorced. It wouldn't be finalized by the state for another two months so he was still married to me. He would still be sinning with his adulterating whore!

I went home and played Wilson Phillips again, over and over and over: "Hold on for some strength!" I was singing along very loudly. The music was blasting so loud that the whole neighborhood could hear it. They reminded me that I was not to let anyone step all over me! No one could change my life except for me; I had no one to blame for my unhappiness. I got myself in to my own mess and, most importantly, I had to keep hearing them sing this to me: "I know that there is pain but you hold on for one more day and break free from the chains." Release me, Chris! I'm not going back to you anymore! What is this power you have over me?
Oh, I loved those singing sisters! They didn't even know me, and they helped me deal with life through their songs. The radio station should

play these two songs everyday for us woman who deal with cheating men and pain.

I called my mommy. "Mom, I want to come and spend the night with you!"
"Okay baby. George will be right there to get you!"
"Okay Mom!" I brought two bags of weed, two 40's, and two packs of cigarettes, just for one day.
I hugged my mommy long and tight and told her that I was getting divorced. She began to cry for me. I felt like a baby for a moment.
After she sat down in her favorite chair and me in mine, she began to tell me how she was doing.
"My heart is bleeding, and I can't have bypass surgery until they can control my blood pressure. It's in a danger zone."
"Damn mom, your heart is bleeding? That's deep. I'm sorry, I didn't come here to upset you or stress you out with my problems."
"You're my baby! I'm glad you came to your mommy. You're supposed to come to me."
"I just wanted you to hear it from me. Since George works for Chris he will hear about it."

I didn't get to sleep until about 3:00am. Mom crashed on me about midnight. My drunk ass passed out but was up by 8, listening to Gospel. Mom dedicated a song to me, saying, "I give you to God."
I drank the last of the hot beer I'd left in the bottle, put on my new white T-shirt and kept on the jeans I'd slept in. I gelled my locks and the little baby hair down and sat on the porch. I waited for someone to come pick me up to take me to the BBQ birthday party in the park for my other grandbaby girl. She was turning one. I had seven grandbabies by then.

Chris called. "Hi baby, how are you doing?"
"Happy Fathers Day," I replied. "Enjoy your day," and I hung up. He wouldn't be getting any "I love you" card from me now.
Damn, I had to move into a new apartment. I hoped he would still help me, damn.
"I can't believe this shit. I'm divorced. I'm free to be a whore too." I kept saying that to myself all day and night. My best years were spent and gone – twenty-seven years with that man.

Mom brought some vodka. I had Pepsi and I wanted some. She gave me a strong drink.
Missy arrived to drop off her gift along with her son, who was twenty-five but looked seventeen with his pretty baby face.
George said, "Josh doesn't think anybody loves him. He doesn't like life."

"I don't want to hear that depression mess," Mom and Missy said at the same time.
I yelled, "I love you Josh!" and hugged and kissed him. They said, "I love you too Josh" and he kissed his mom but didn't kiss his Grandma.
Josh was in the doghouse. So many people were disappointed and upset with him so he didn't even know if he was welcome. He went back out on the porch. I went upstairs to tell his girlfriend that he was here. I went to the bathroom but he was gone. I ran to the corner with George. We looked down all four blocks and he wasn't in sight. I went into the kitchen to tell his mom. When I entered, I overheard her tell Mommy, "I can't stay long. I can't be around depressed people. Angel is depressed, Josh is depressed," but she stopped when she saw Mommy's face look surprised. She turned around and looked at me.
I grabbed my ice bag out of the freezer, slammed it and walked out. I grabbed my overnight bags and went out on the porch to call for a ride.

Missy came out and said goodbye as her husband came up the stairs.
"What's that matter?" she asked me.
"I'm going to take my depressed ass home! You need to be more sensitive to your son's needs!"
"You don't know the whole story."
"I'm not talking about what he has been doing. He has always suffered from depression and you never want to listen to him!"
Her husband came out and said to me, "Angel, don't you have your own problems? Then mind your business!"
I stood up and screamed out loud, "What? That's my damn nephew! I care about him! Maybe you don't care! He is my business. And nobody was talking to you anyway. I was talking to my sister! So mind your damn business!" He was my friend and I was mad that he turned against me. And I knew that Missy was his wife and I was hurting her.
"Come on Missy, she doesn't know the whole story. Don't pay her no mind!"
"I see the despair and deterioration," I screamed in her face pointing down on her, "and when he tries to kill himself and if he succeeds, I'll be the one in the funeral staring at you!"
"Angel, you don't understand! He does things to himself! He is grown!" Missy cried.
"Come on Missy, fuck her!" her husband said, pulling her away. "Let's go!"
"No, I don't want to leave her like this!"
He looked at me. "Angel, don't you suffer from depression? Then worry about yourself!"
I yelled louder, "That's right, I do, and what the fuck do any of you do about it? Nothing! No one calls me to see if I'm okay! You're two

insensitive mother-fuckers! And if you don't help him, you're going to have a dead son on your hands!"

He yelled at me because his wife was going to cry. Hell, I was crying and screaming by that point. "Angel, he is a grown man! It's time he grows up!"

"No, he is a depressed kid in a young man's body and he needs more love, something your insensitive ass can't give! You're both too cold and hard!"

He grabbed her hand and pulled her into his luxury car but she tried to say, "wait." His love was in his money and gifts. There wasn't too much hugging and affection going on in that relationship.

They pulled out and she sat in the passenger's side looking at me in disbelief. I yelled, "You should have gotten off your ass and given him a hug!"

I went into the house to calm Mom down. She was crying, saying, "My daughters never argue like this!"

"I'm so sorry mom. That boy lost everyone and everything and he feels alone and he doesn't feel any love. Now his pregnant woman is leaving him. I see his eyes and I know the look!"

"I don't like to see you like this Angel. Calm down baby!"

"I need a drink! Then I'm going home. I don't want to go to the BBQ now!"

"I don't want you to be alone Angel. Can I go with you?"

"No mom, I want to be alone!"

"But I shouldn't be alone now, I thought as she hugged me. Hell, I was always alone. I wished she had showed me this much love and attention and concern before. It felt genuine now. Shit, we could be real tight if I had felt this from her before or hell more often now. But I knew that she was just caught up in the moment.

"Don't worry about me. Call Josh; see if he is all right. I'll be fine; I'll call you later. I'm leaving so you can calm down. You need your peace and rest now. All I'm doing is making things worse, getting you all upset and making your blood pressure rise. I'm so sorry!"

"Okay, George will take you home now!"

"Okay, thanks. Bye mom!" I drank my drink and left to go back home to be depressed alone.

I went home and soaked. I felt guilty and mad because they didn't know how to love us.

Chris came running over to the house. He heard I was upset and he was real concerned about me. Oh, he was so cute! He spent the night and made love to me, saying, "I want you, only you! I've been hanging out with my spiritual advisor!" The following Sunday, we went to church together.

He had been calling me like crazy, coming to see me everyday and buying anything my heart desired. He helped me move and found every reason to call me.
I loved the attention but one day, I picked up the phone and heard him saying, "If my secretary calls tell her I'm with my daughter!"
"What! I screamed. "Tell that whore you're with your wife, you lying bitch! Get out of my house!" That damn phone caused me more than a little bit of pain.
He said he wanted me. He said that he still told everyone that I was his wife! He said he wanted to kiss me and hold me, watch movies with me, and let me do whatever I wanted to his body! He told me that he'd love me everyday, kiss on me, take care of all of my needs but he still wanted to keep his whore on the side! Just when I thought just maybe we could make this work and start over! He was still thinking with his dick! He would always love me; I know that he'd probably always be concerned about me but I had to let him go. He had to let me go and I had to focus on myself in order to survive.

She didn't take him from me. I knew I could still have him anytime I wanted to for sex; but how could I enjoy him with a condom? He would continue to provide for me and give me money for a new car, so what did she really have? A depressed man that just wanted some extra activities.
That divorce shit was hard when you still loved the man. I gave him a hicky on his neck and lower body to let her know that he still wanted me and he was still sexing me up! He was just using her. But I was angry that I had to take such desperate measures. She didn't give a fuck as long as he gave her a share. I was tired of playing these childish games.
Damn, what was I going to do with my life, my free life?
My idea came to me on July 4th. I wanted a percentage that was all, so I could at least buy me some clothes. I was no longer fat or depressed; I was on medication for it now.

He brought me cherries and a beautiful Indian picture and I just melted, especially when he woke me up with a gentle soft full kiss. I woke up in pleasure; I melted my coldness. Damn I loved that man! I have to let go.

CHAPTER TWENTY-THREE

I NEEDED TO HEAR THAT! I DIDN'T WANT TO HEAR THAT!

"Hi Tunisia, let me ask you a question, okay? You got time?"
"Yeah mom, I was just doing some laundry. What's up?"
She listened as I told her the history of their relationship and my intentions and dangerous violent thoughts and crazy ideas. Ashamed of blowing up her pager leaving all kinds of messages.
"What do you think?"
"Okay, Mom, now I listened to you. Are you ready to listen to me?"
"Yes baby!"
"Mom, when you are in pain, the best thing you can do is to go inside yourself and soothe it. Some people go to drugs and alcohol. You can do other things, like meditation, reading, whatever… just focus on yourself! The only thing you can do in life is hope, pray, and dream. Everything else is life happening around you. Remember, you have no control over everything external, only internal. You can never lose hope, hope that things will change for you. Something special is waiting for you. You can't lose that guide, that flicker that makes you believe that there is going to be positive coming out of every negative situation. That hope needs to be harnessed. It needs to he nurtured so you can believe there's a future for you! Life is drama! It really is. It is also other things. Sometimes, it's passionate fruits of life. It's all about what you focus on. You can convince yourself by looking at the good things than the bad things don't seem so bad! Always look at life as an opportunity to make each day like your last. It's never too late to make your life better. Live for yourself too; you can never make someone your universe, but what you can do is invite someone into yours, or have someone invite you into theirs to share. But once you make someone your universe, you're setting yourself up to be disappointed because that universe is not your life, and it will never be fulfilling enough.

"Love is the one thing that makes you human! Men… some men are so good to people that they cause problems in their relationships because they are a good person, because they're what a woman is looking for, need, and depend on. They might cause some kind of insecurities in the person they are with. Mom, you have a good man. Women see that and want what you have, so you will always have women pushing up on him. But you have to believe that he wants you because for all these years he still choose you! What is flesh temporarily rubbing against each other? Just remember that you have his heart and soul; no woman can take that

away from you. We are always given the opportunity to be with somebody, but rarely are you given the opportunity to grow and learn somebody and to love someone. You've done that for twenty-seven years and that can't be traded for all the whores or bitches out there.
"It's very easy to get married, but it's harder staying married and even harder to want to stay married after being married for so long. To have all these things makes you a fortunate woman; when you married him, you agreed to smell his stinking breath, his feet, and his butt. He agreed to smell your ass, your breath, your crotch, and your stinking breath! But also, you got to share the good loving, the good laughing, the good memories of the bad times; that's what's important. Always stay working in your relationship; that person will see what length you are going to go through to keep that relationship alive. A lot of people put their relationship on cruse control and everyday is the same event and they get bored. You have to stay busy working to improve it and your chances of him ever going anywhere is less.

"That's when the Devil's at his best; offering some adventure, some change, some fruits from his spot that looks real good on the other side of the wall but when we go over, we find a wall between the relationship that some choose not to climb back over while some choose to keep jumping back and forth wearing two faces. They're one way at home and totally different outside and you just want to strangle each other. Satan works from your fears, the inconsistencies, and your insecurities. He works from things that are not seen, as well as from what is seen. You've got to watch him. He is very clever and very miserable, and misery loves company. He wants you to be miserable too to take the joy out of your marriage, out of your relationship. He wants you to see only the bad parts, not the good parts. You promised God that you would work on your marriage no matter how hard it gets for better or worse; you said, 'forgive and forget!'"

I was in tears. I couldn't tell her that he is not trying to leave her and I made him sign divorce papers, I act foolish trying to keep him when he only brings me more pain. I'd be a fool to take him back.
"Thank you my baby girl counselor!"
"Mom, give yourself some good loving, the kind that will cause you to say, 'where have you been all my life?' Mom, this will be your mantra: 'I will focus on myself until I am satisfied with what I see!'"
"Okay baby. Thank you so much!" Damn, I needed to hear that!

I realized how pathetic I was; I was allowing the enemy, Lucifer, to play me like his puppet just to entertain his boys. He could depend on me to respond to the same button he pushed every damn time, no matter how many times he had previously pressed it. With each whisper, his angels were sitting heavily on my shoulders saying, "What happens if I push in this button, boys?" He would be with me one day or week then he go be with her for a weekend and I put him out and then take him back in, and do it again the next week, and he says I'm crazy for throwing his shit in the street, and going off hitting him and screaming looking like the devil when it's him that keep going back between her legs after he said we will work it out, give him some time to let her go, and the evil knows I'm going to flip when he is with her after just sexing me up and giving me hope for new beginnings.

I knew what it meant I wear two faces because I looked to the devil's angel to the right and have conversations and hang out. I'd look and lusted and desired what they offered and I'd let them entertain me. Then I'd look to the angel on the left and have conversations and hang out for a much shorter time and accept God's angel convicting me.

I didn't want to feel like the peaceful fish that swam across my computer's screen saver one day and then the next day be the different colored bouncing balls and then the next day be the rain and so on and so forth. I wanted to be grounded everyday and wear only one face.

Fibromyalgia sufferers and weed smokers lose their memories; we call it "fybro fog." Weed definitely kills the memory cells so I used to take dopamine substitute pills from the health food place call Ginko Biloba, but I would always forget to take them. The most painful thing I remember is that any good memories I had, I can't remember. It was like I was in the movie, "The Never Ending Story." I'd let the sadness overcome me and then I'd let each pain, each joint, take away a good memory and now my brain was almost empty. I wanted to live because it wasn't just about me and as strong as I had fought against taking an infant's life in an abortion, I should've fought as hard for my own!

Ring, ring, went the phone.

"Yes?" That was how I answered the phone; no more "Hell-low?"

"Mom?"

"Hi baby, what's up?"

It was Cyris. He was speaking in "help-me-right-now-quickly" tone. "Mom, they are offering me four to eight or we can take it to trial and I could get ten to twenty. What do you think I should do?"

"Cyris, this is your decision because if I tell you to deal, you're going to wish you fought because you think you have a chance to win. If I tell you to take it to trial and you lose and they give you the max because you took them through a trial, plus if they take into account the severity of the crime and she gives you twenty, it will be my fault! What do you think you should do is the question?"

"Okay mom I'll call you back!" Click – he hung up.

Damn, I wanted him to fight; what if they do give him ten to twenty? He'll only have to do a part of it, maybe ten years or eighty percent of that. Plus, he'd already done a year.
He will always wish that he fought I know him. One young man said he would deal with it on the street so he wasn't coming to court, and the other one didn't know who shot him. Maybe I should have told him to fight! But then again, Cyris did a bad thing; he should be punished for it, even though I love him. I taught him to be accountable for his actions and to think before he acted.
He ran away when they came after him; he should have kept running! Sometimes being a punk is a good thing! We warned him; his father constantly told him to avoid the jail piece but he didn't want to hear it. I told him about the drug dealing and what using was doing to him but he didn't want to hear it. He didn't believe he would get caught or get shot or go to jail, no not him!

People outside were saying he was throwed off; he loved the name and had to live up to it and when he got high he was dangerous and an irritant, so others wanted to hurt him.
Maybe he would grow up and be a stronger man. Maybe he'd even learn a trade in jail. He never could stay in school so he never really learned to write legibly. Maybe now he would learn some things and take responsibility for his actions.
Yeah in his mind, he probably was thinking, "Well they walked away from it. They still have a few bullets in them but we should be even because they had jumped me the day before!" He had a point but there had to be a different way.
I learned that revenge is the Lord's and if you asked him to revenge you, you should just sit back and watch him do so, if it was a justified request. Those men could have died and he would have been accountable to God for the loss of their lives. What was more exciting to him I wonder, knowing that he was not going to burn in hell for eternity for murder or that he shot people and had the power?
Could he do the time was the main thing on my mind.

Ring, ring, There was the phone again.
"Yes?"
"Mom, this is Aqusia!" She is a very beautiful young woman, built tight, with long hair down to her shoulders and big full lips like Cyris. She looked just like Cyris and she looked better than any chick in a music video. She could do all the West Indian dances.
"Mom, his lawyer came into the courtroom and Cyris said, 'I want to go to trial!'"
His sisters were undecided; one said to fight, another said to take the deal. His dad said that it was his decision.

"The lawyer told us that one person that got shot was locked up, so we shouldn't count on him not testifying against Cyris now. He already gave his testimony and identified him as the shooter! He looked over at the prosecutor as he was talking to another lawyer and we heard them adding about five charges times two and they added it up to about fifty years! He knew he wouldn't get that, but he knew it was going to be a lot of time so he took the deal!"
"What? He did? He took the four to eight?"
"Yes!"
"Wow, where is he?"
"He is still locked up!"
"What? They're not going to give him bail?"
"They said no because they said he was a risk of flight since they found him on a warrant out of state."
"Damn, I didn't even get to see him! I just knew he would be coming home with you all! His lawyer said he probably would! Damn!" I stamped my feet. I grabbed two herbal Valiums off my dresser and sat at the computer and said, "Aqusia how did he look? Disappointed?"
"Yes mom, I think you were right. He really believed he could fight his way out of this like he fought everything else! He really thought he would get out of this one!"
Damn, I don't want to hear that!
"Damn, I should have been there!"
"He understands mom, and Dad was there for him. He smiled when he saw all of us. That gave him a lot of life in his face and our support impressed the court!"
"Damn, I wish I were there for my son!" I started crying. "I should have tried harder to be there!"
"Mom there were so many people there. We had to stand outside for a half hour before we reached the door. You couldn't have stood that long and your wheel chair can't fit in Tunisia car!"
"I could have taken a cab and sat on the floor! I should have made a way!"
"You are too hard on yourself mom. We know you are ill so accept it! We do! I'll see you soon mom. I love you; don't cry, he knows you would have been there if you could!"
"I love you too baby! Bye!"
Oh God please give him the strength and the will to live through this!

CHAPTER TWENTY-FOUR

OH MY GOD

I took a sleeping pill and laid down and put the covers over my head. I slept all day and all night with nothing to eat or drink.

When I awakened, I needed something hot to calm down my painful gut. I went downstairs and made some nice hot cocoa and toast. I heard the phone ringing. I ran up the stairs saying, "ooh, ouch" because I spilled the hot cocoa on my legs. Just as the answering machine was coming on, I picked it up. "Yes? Yes?"

"Hello am I speaking to Mrs. Angel Myers?"

"Yes it is!" Damn, probably a bill collector!

"I'm am Ms. Betty Harris, the chief of staff from the Department of Psychiatric in CFCF correctional facility. I need to talk to you about your son Cyris!"

"Yes, Cyris, how is he? Is he back on depression medication?"

"Mrs. Myers, I am so sorry to have to inform you over the phone, but your son committed suicide in the shower last night. He is no longer with us."

"NO! NO! NOOOOOOOOOOO!" I yelled. "He's not really dead; you have to check him out! He did this before! He's just trying to get out!"

My grandson said, "Grandma I'm hungry!"

I pushed him to the side. "Shut up! Just shut up!"

"Hey miss, umm, Cyris is alive right?"

"I'm sorry Mrs. Myers. Is there anything I can do for you?"

I dropped the phone with my mouth open. The scream was delayed coming out.

"NO! CYRIS NO! NO, NO, NO, NO, NO, NO!" I jumped on the bed, screaming. "NO, NO, NO, NO! It's not true! She's wrong! No, this is not happing! No, No, No!" I shook my head NO! "This is not happening!" The tears came rushing down my face. I breathed in deeply and out deeper. I screamed, "I didn't even get to see him! Hold him! Talk to him! NO, not yet! NO, he can't be gone! Cyris, no, you didn't do this shit to me! NO, NO!"

I let out a high octave soprano scream that could've cracked a window. It was a never-ending scream; it just wouldn't stop coming out.

And then I fainted.

Aqusia had a cold rag on my face. "Mom! Mom!" I opened my eyes to see her red eyes full of tears. I didn't have to say a word; she just knew. Awaking to the reality and realizing that this was not a dream, I began screaming again. "NO, NO, NO, it can be true!"

"Cyris is dead, Mom?" she asked softly, needing conformation:
My grandson said, "Grandma are you alright? What's the matter?"
I looked down at the pretty hazel-eyed boy who was only four and screamed, "Leave me alone! Please, just leave me alone! I'll talk to you later. Get out my room!"
I was my mom when she lost her son; the cycle has completed itself.
Aqusia patted her son on his back. "I'll be right down," she said. She looked at me and said nothing. She just hugged me. We held one another as I shook out of control, as my guts were consistently being stabbed.
"Call your dad. Tell him to come here now! Wait! Don't tell him over the phone!"
But before I could get that out of my mouth he walked in full of tears knowing the tough job he had. He thought he had to tell me; she had called him first. He didn't know she had called me too.
I grabbed him and screamed, "Chris make it not be so! Make it not be so!"
He held me tighter as I tried to get lose, to jump up and down. He told Aqusia to get me some water; he gave me two Valiums. "Lay down Angel!"
"I can't lie down! I can't sit down! I can't stay in this house! I need some air!" I ran outside and fell on the ground.
Chris picked me up and sat me on the second step and held me as we rocked together. We sat there for hours, silently rocking, staring in disbelief.

I prayed silently. "God, please let me see him to say good-bye! Let me talk to him one more time. Please forgive him for taking his life!" I began to remember his smile and I saw him laughing, saying, "You're crazy! I'm not doing any time." I saw him holding his son, kissing him all over his face until the child laughed with pleasure, and me telling him that his son needed him and he said he knew that.
I saw him on stage rapping, living large like he wanted.
I saw him kissing me, telling me he would always be with me.
I went from sadly depressed, to angry. I went through that entire memory lane shit for nothing! I tried to stop his ass and for what? For nothing! I told him my dream! Nothing! It didn't help him, or warn him, nothing.
It didn't stop him! I didn't do shit, I got more angry! I transformed to fear; who was next, Chris? I remembered my dream of two walls will crush me if I run and don't pray for exceptance.
I switched over to concern; would his son want to be in our life? Will the man still die? Did he still have a bullet in him? Will Cyris go to hell?
I was soon back to denial again. This all is not really happening; this all is just a dream and I will wake up! NO! NO! NO! This is all just a dream! God wouldn't do this to me! He knows I needed my only son! I couldn't be like my mom in everything! Her husband left her, and her

only son died and her children were grown up and she was all-alone! She was sick and maybe dying too. Will I lose my mother, father, husband, son, like her. I may just die of starvation and sadness. I wish I were dead. Anything is better than always being in pain, physically, mental, emotional! Suffering from everything known to woman all my life, always crying, now I have to except being alone, I can't take it, the holy book says God don't give you more than you can handle but I can't handle this life anymore so what is the book saying, I can handle all this pain? Well I can't handle one more painful thing. Chris has diabetes and may die soon because his kidneys is failing him, so he will not be with me one way or another. I don't want to be here when he dies. I don't want to be here to live thru that. The Doctor said he only has about ten years to live and I haven't told the children. I have no one to talk too. I have no one to hold and comfort me.

"Cyris! Cyris!" I screamed inside my mind. "Why baby? Why'd you leave Mommy?" I was holding my face in my hands and shaking in anger, wanting to hurt something. I wanted to hit something someone!
"Angel, can I spend the night with you to hold you tonight?"
"Yes Chris, please hold me. I would love that." I rubbed his head and wiped his eyes and held his hand. "Let's go upstairs and lay down for a while for now, okay?"
I was drained. I could barely speak the words, and it was even harder to walk so I crawled up the two flights of stairs and flopped on the bed.
Chris took off my shoes. He took off his sweater and shoes and lay down behind me. He held me tight with his warm comforting arms, sniffling in my ear.

God, why are you letting these two walls slam me? With Chris leaving me, now my son's death? I am down on my knees in spirit praying! Please don't let these walls kill me! I wanted to run! I want to run into another mans arms for comfort and pay back, I want to run to a drink and a drug, I want to run off the planet. I wiped my tears, breathing hard. I sat up and got some water to take some sleeping pills and pain pills. This had to be a dream. I will wake up again and this will not be true!
I snatched the phone out of the wall. I didn't want any more phone calls; there was always some damn pain on that line.
I wanted a cigarette and a joint but I didn't. I wanted a drink but I really didn't. I just laid back down enjoying in the midst of this pain the pleasure of Chris' temporary comfort.

My mind was racing. Cyris wouldn't do this to me! He wouldn't say fuck my feelings! What more could I have said or done? What would have helped you Cyris? The tears just flooded. I kept wiping my eyes hoping

the pills kicked in because I was hurting and trembling. Chris grabbed me tighter. I couldn't comfort him much more than this!
Chris' arms felt so comforting and warm; I missed him so much but I knew this was just temporary.

I was sitting in a park in New York City alone, drunk, cold, and homeless, looking for somewhere to sleep for the night. I approached a man.
"Excuse me sir, can I clean your house and wash and iron your clothes for something to eat, and a bath, and a nap?"
"No miss! I'm sorry, I can't help you!"
I asked two more men but I was refused.
Then a handsome tall man came by. He appeared to have money with all the gold and diamonds he was wearing. He had on a black tailor-fitted suit and shiny black expensive shoes. He smelled sweet like honey and he spoke so gently and compelling.
"Baby, you don't have to do a thing for me!" he said to me. "Let me help you! Come with me!" He offered out his hand.
Mesmerized, I grabbed it lady-like with my fingertips.

He took me to a beautiful palace; it was all white with gold trim and statues and shiny floors made of marble and bright chandeliers and mink furs thrown on the floor. He sent me to a beautiful bedroom with everything I needed to wash and groom myself. There were clothes everywhere and I was suppose to pick an outfit. I chose a red leather jumper and red leather pocketbook that matched my shoes, with a white and red scarf tied around my locks. I was beautiful for my "might-be-knight."
My stomach was growling; I needed a grub and quick. I opened up the gold doors and there it was, a banquet table full of good-smelling food. He stood there smiling with pleasure at my appearance and choice of attire. I turned around and said, "Damn, I'm on time for something! Are you having a party?"
He stood there with his hands folded in front of himself looking edible himself! "No," he said, "this is all for you!"
Surprised I said, "For me? But you didn't know you would meet me! Or did you go out looking for homeless people?"
He handed me a beautiful gold robe. "Put this on," he instructed.
I put on my new robe as fast as I could. I felt like a princess, beautiful and priceless. He held out his arm for me to grab on to and I was escorted to the low table. I was told to sit down on the floor and to bend by the knees but not to touch the floor with them.
There sat all of my favorite foods: fried chicken (extra crispy); smoking hot macaroni and cheese; barbeque pork ribs with sweet sauce; collard greens; sweet potatoes; corn on the cob; corn bread; waffles bacon,

French toast, large hot pizza with extra cheese, Stakes with A1 sauce, baked potatoes, apple and blueberry pie; strawberry, cherry vanilla ice cream, a bowl of big rosy red cherries; giant pomegranates; and ice cold Pepsi. Everything that I loved was before me as if my knight had been expecting me.
He said you have your choice; breakfast, lunch or dinner?
I ate until I couldn't taste it anymore. It began to be just substance with out taste.
"Thank you so much!" I said with my mouth full of thirds.

I couldn't stop smiling. "Can I take a nap now, please?"
"Sure you can, right after you come into this room and meet my son!"
"That's nice, you have a son," I said. I hoped that he didn't have a wife though!
He took me into a dark gray room with no windows, no furniture, nothing only two chairs and a movie screen.
"Sit down, he'll be right up!"
"Okay," I replied. I sat in the iron cold chair wanting to just lie down but I knew I had to do what he wanted. I hoped this kid didn't talk much!
I looked up and there stood a handsome young man… 'my son, Cyris!'
"That's my son!" I yelled.
He laughed. "Not anymore! He is my son now! He GAVE his LIFE to ME!"

And then right before my eyes this handsome man, my "knight," began to transform into an ugly dark figure of a shadow that moved with the wind and as fast as a blink.
With an echoing deep voice and sinister giggle he said; "He is mine! He always has been and always will be, so say your goodbyes and get out of my house!" He disappeared for a minute as I sat in shock but then he reappeared, and came floating around in my face and all I saw was a dark shadow and felt a trembling evil force of tension around me and thru me and I shook in fear as he came face to face with me with red piercing eyes and yellow sharp teeth and a cloud of black smoke for a body and a smell of death decaying filled the room from his breath as he was saying; "He prepared your meal and you did eat. You always ate from my table, don't you Angel?" He laughed harder and more sinister. "You like what I offer, don't you? You want some drugs, a joint maybe or a drink?" And he laughed out loud and the room shook, then he disappeared again.
Something so beautiful had turned so ugly and evil.

"Oh Cyris, is that you baby?" I hugged him and he held me. I lay in his chest like I used to and wished that I could stay there forever.
"Mom," he said, "It's so good to see you! Are you okay? I'm so sorry, Mom!"

"Cyris are you okay?"
"Not really mom!"
"Cyris where are we baby?"
"Mom, this is Satan's house! We are in Purgatory like you told me about but there are so many departments here. I'm in a holding cell for crimes I committed but didn't pay the price for on Earth. Like the attempted murders, plus something's you didn't know about. Mom, I shot five other people when I was robbing them but no one died."
"What? Damn baby, I had no idea! Wow!" I paused to soak that in.

"Cyris what's a cell? Like prison?"
"Yes, but it's worse! I can't do anything there but watch my family on tape. I see their life and my son's life and it's just like you said: everything looks good now that I don't have it! Everything is more appreciated now that I want it! And I understand more about what my purpose was on earth, and I realize that I didn't do anything with my body or mind or spirit or my talents. I have to account for that; it would have been on the scale to help weigh out some of the bad things I've done. I don't have many good deeds to give me balance, Mom! I can't even get the people I hurt forgiveness because instead of taking my life I was suppose to ask them to forgive me then I wouldn't be punished for it now. The soul never dies mom we all are here waiting and a lot of us are suffering tremendously. I never repented for my sins so now I have to pay for them so when I am judged than all my sins won't count if I get punished for them now than I can still hope some living people will forgive me and I have to start forgiving people so I might still be able to get into heaven, For some sins God forgave me so those sins don't count but If I hurt people and I didn't forgive people then I will not be forgiven. That stuff really does count, and since I committed suicide I get no pleasures; some people who is dead get to mingle with stars or historical figures. Others get to kick it with people they knew that passed away; they have people to pray with and have conversations with. They can see other people's lives; not just their family's but also their friends.'

" I stay in a cell and watch you eat and everything looks so good! I remember how it tasted. I actually get hungry but I can't eat and I can't sleep when I'm tired. I watched as you slept and cried many nights because of me, and when I saw my son getting beat by a grown man who is not his father, I hurt so much! I can't stop the pain I caused you and my family! I didn't think or care enough. I can't hug you or talk to my dad and sisters or help my son! I can't get any sex and I'm really horny – I can't even beat my meat! I am so hungry mom, when I see you eat a cheese steak! I remember what it taste like and I want a bite I get so angry that I can't help my sisters and warn them of people and things I see that are going to harm them.

"It's tormenting to look and be so powerless that you can't even help your loved ones. It's more punishing knowing that jail would be a paradise compared to here! I cry but without tears, and the time is long and on-going since we never sleep. Life is twice as long for us here then it is for you. I can't read or write my raps – there's no one to rap to anyway! The part that hurts the most is that because I committed suicide, I can't come to you in spirit like the other spirits came to say goodbye to you! I couldn't come to you Mom! I couldn't say goodbye to no one! I couldn't even go to my own funeral! I had to see it on tape! I was told that I didn't deserve to go and see anyone or be there. They weren't allowed to feel my presence because of all the pain I caused.

"You're the only one I've been allowed to talk to other than my angels, and yeah, Mom, there really are angels! I have to tell you the truth – I really thought it was the weed talking half the time you told us things! I really wish I'd listened to you then. I would have if the stories had been believable but I guess I'm too hardheaded and didn't listen. I had to do things my way because I thought it was the easy way out. I've learned, Mom – you must tell others that this is a real place and it's miserable! Pray for me mom, so I too can have a chance to enter Heaven. I can only enter it now if you forgive me for everything that I did that was hurtful or harmful. It's true, Mom – forgiveness and prayers do help the dead! Mom, you really do have juice.

"You were right about everything you said you saw in your dreams; all of it is true mom! I'm so sorry I didn't listen to you. I know now that it's too late. After I leave you I have to go into the torment room and suffer for my sins that don't constitute death, even little stuff like stealing a candy bar and making someone cry, some sins that I thought were forgiven because I asked! But I wasn't forgiven because I didn't forgive others who done the same thing to me, as I wanted to be forgiven! Since I didn't ask God to deliver me from the evil and since I chose to hang out with evil, I must now do my time with evil. Then I go back to my cell.

"It's harder for me in this prison than a man for example who was saved, who is now doing time for attempted murder or murder even. He forgave others and was killed; he's still doing a bid but his cell is in a much less evil place. His place is like a mobster's jail cell; when a member of the Mob is in jail, anything or anybody they want is brought to them and they are never alone in there. They can't get out and visit with others in another part of Purgatory or on earth to visit family or friends for a good reward. Now, the person who is working on his character and changing in his cleansing stages and forgiveness levels, he gets rewarded. The person that died and was saved before he died is helping others to be saved. The person that died normally and wasn't saved, he had to do certain things to change his heart before Judgment time, and possible be punished for his sins that didn't constitute death. When I say that doesn't constitute death I mean the everlasting death in the hell fire for there sins. The people that have done good deeds have something to put on their scale. If you die with crimes under your belt, whether you got caught or not you pay for it, either here in the cell with no pleasures or in the torment room! There are no rewards for me.

I wish I could tell suicidal people that being dead is not better than being alive!"

He looked at me with his big sad eyes. "Goodbye mom. Stay strong!" He backed away from me.
"NO! NO!" I screamed. "Don't go! Don't leave me Cyris! Please come back! I need you!"
He disappeared. I walked out the room and everything went dark.
I heard a voice say, "Get out! Leave me to my son!"

I opened my eyes from my dream.
Chris had gone to work and the reality hit me hard. Cyris was really dead! At least I was able to hold him and see him one more time, thank you God so all that the angel has showed me was true. Death is not better.
I put the cover back over my face and let out a loud painful scream until I felt someone pull the covers off my face. I saw and heard my angel.
"GET UP!" he yelled. "And don't go back to sleep either! You have been sleeping all of your life! Wake up! God has heard your cries and He will bring you peace and give you direction. Angel, you will never be alone. I will always be with you. I always have been since the beginning. You have asked why you have suffered so much. Well, you couldn't understand it then but you had to experience it. You had to suffer so much pain to die! Now that the old you is dead, the new you can live! We needed your painful experience to help you obtain the knowledge and wisdom and understanding you prayed for and to help others who think death is a option. Angel understand your son had to die to tell you the truth about the death you crave so much!"
As he spoke all of my pain left my body, I finally felt that peace I prayed for, I had renewed strength and I knew there was nothing I couldn't go thru now because I had God and my angels with me. I felt the Love of God and I felt special, and now I understand my purpose in life, to help some one decide to live and to teach them how and why!
I was not a bastared child. I was a blessed child, Gods child and angels came and talked to me and touched me.

I suffered so much because to know knowledge is to know pain

"Now GET UP!" he yelled.
I sat up and smiled!

The TV was on and the movie "City of Angels" was playing. There was a song in the movie, "Angel," by Sarah McLachlan that I loved. The words were comforting: "You're in the arms of an angel, where you'll find some comfort there." I felt my angel's wings hug me from behind. I folded my arms and felt his wing tips touch my fingers.
With a happy tear in my eye, I was in the arms of an angel.

"For mine Angel shall be with you and shall care for your soul."

BARUCH CH 6V.6

THE LORD'S PRAYER

Don't just say it – be about it! Do you really know what you were saying at church? Yes, Jesus said that this is how you pray! But did you ever really try to understand the prayer? This is what I understand it to say. Check it out!

Our Father, which art in heaven…

Before we begin our prayers, we must first acknowledge who are we praying to. There are many fathers and gods; Father the priest; your natural father; Satan, the father of lies. Who do you serve? Who do you praise? Who do you worship? Who is your God? Identify where you find your God!

Holy be thy name…

God's name is HOLY! Always keep his name holy! Don't use bad words with it!

Thy Kingdom come…

The kingdom is coming to Earth as it is in Heaven. Be ready; think about what Jesus said. He is going away to prepare a place for us, a mansion. The kingdom is God and His splendor is coming for His people.

God's will be done…

We always want to do things our own way. But are you praying for God's will to be done? Will you will accept what His will is in your daily decisions and responses? No matter what happens today, surrender. Can and will you accept it?

On earth as it is in heaven…

God's will is that we, His children, live on Earth as it is in Heaven, with song and praise, worship and patience, happiness and humility, gratitude and peaceful spirits. Keep your mind on spiritual thoughts. Do not give Satan a place in your heart; do not seek out material and fleshly wants. Be mindful of your words; watch your tongue. Do not be self-centered – be God centered.

Give us this day our daily bread…

Give us the word and understanding of it today, as we read it. Take it into your heart and don't be like the sower who let the seeds fall on the bad ground. Once you hear the word, you let Satan come and take it away. The word is our food – we need it to live.

Forgive us for our trespasses as we forgive those who trespass against us…

When you pray and you ask God to forgive you for what you have done or what you owe to others, you must also be willing to forgive those who have hurt and betrayed you. You must forgive even those who took what was yours or trespassed on your life and space or who owe you money – you must forgive them! Jesus forgave those who did painful things to Him; for all we know, they could have done a lot more to Him to degrade Him. There were a lot of kings in those days with soldiers that practiced immorality and they killed Him. Who are we to not forgive? We all want forgiveness for our dirt. We know that Jesus understands everything we've been through because He was here on Earth, too! Don't just say, "forgive me" in your mind; say, "forgive me for…" and "for whom…." Ask for the humility of Christ to do it. Understand that they really don't know what they did to you or the penalty they will suffer for the harm they caused you. Remember that everyone can change and do their time and repent. God forgave them, so who are you not to? You cannot be forgiven if you do not forgive!

Lead us not into temptation…

God does not tempt anyone, but He will lead you to the one who does for correction and punishment. It's a test of faith and a test of your allegiance. He gave us free will. We are free to choose under different situations.

Deliver us from Evil…

This says that only God can deliver us from evil. We are to ask Him and no one else! Evil is too strong and wise for us to fight or escape. If you really want to get out of an evil situation, you have to ask God to deliver you and be specific!

For thine is the kingdom, the power, and the glory…

God is the Kingdom; all the power we need comes from Him. Don't look to yourself or to other people's gods and idols for power. Don't believe that you did powerful things or said powerful words – God did it! The power is all His so stop trying to take away His glory. You pray for Him to place some of His power in you to edify your life and to help others. Ask for the power to forgive and to love in God's way of loving. That's where we go wrong; we take the glory and praise and feel like a god, a savior to people, and we expect to be rewarded!

For ever and ever…

By ending your prayers, you are acknowledging that God is forever. His word is forever, His love, His kingdom, His power… all is forever and ever.

Amen

To all men and woman say, "Thank you. Thank you for hearing and answering my prayers."

When you pray, use not vain repetitions as the heathen do; they think they will be heard for their much speaking.

MATT 6v7:

We say this prayer in every group meeting. With no meaning or understanding or heart, you're not thinking about what is really being said. It's just a repetition of words. Try saying this prayer again, but this time, think about what you are asking. What do you want to work on and forgive? Who are you praying to?
Jesus said, "Don't get on your knees and pray to me! Pray to my Father which art in heaven," as He did. He said He is God's word.

ABOUT THE AUTHOR

Rashida Denise Ali Myers is a proud mother of six beautiful children. She is a wife for 25 years, a poet, and a counselor. She lives in Philadelphia, PA, but was born and raised in New York City. She suffers from bipolar depression, Fibromyalgia (a painful muscle disorder) and Osteoarthritis but she doesn't let these conditions stop her from being productive.

Rashida's a suicide survivor and by sharing her heart in this emotional novel, she hopes to learn and to let go of the pain.

She would like other survivors of suicide or abuse and anyone with a tear in their eye to know that she understands their pain. She wants those people to know that there are options other than death.

She wrote this book because an angel told her too. She hopes that it will be a deterrent to violence, drug abuse, and any idea of escape through death. She hopes it will bring comfort to the reader to let them know that they too have an angel who cares.

Whether you are a spiritual person or not, God counts your tears. Be blessed.

This is Rashida's first novel, If the public enjoys this one, look forward to more.